Nicholas Rinaldi

D0067962

The
JUKEBOX
QUEEN
of MALTA

SCRIBNER PAPERBACK FICTION
PUBLISHED BY SIMON & SCHUSTER
NEW YORK   LONDON   TORONTO   SYDNEY   SINGAPORE

SCRIBNER PAPERBACK FICTION
Simon & Schuster, Inc.
Rockefeller Center
1230 Avenue of the Americas
New York, NY 10020

First Scribner Paperback Fiction edition 2000

SCRIBNER PAPERBACK FICTION and design are trademarks of Macmillan Library Reference USA, Inc., used under license by Simon & Schuster, the publisher of this work.

Designed by Karolina Harris

Manufactured in the United States of America

1 2 3 4 5 6 7 8 9 10

The Library of Congress has catalogued the Simon & Schuster edition as follows:
Rinaldi, Nicholas, date.
The jukebox queen of Malta / Nicholas Rinaldi.
p. cm.
1. World War, 1939–1945—Malta—Fiction. I. Title
PS3568.I47J85   1999
813'.54—dc21   99-13322
CIP

ISBN 0-684-85612-3
0-684-86742-7 (Pbk)

Acknowledgments

With special thanks to Nat Sobel and Judith Weber for their insight and refreshing good sense, and Marysue Rucci and Bill Scott-Kerr for their patience, intelligence, and sound advice. And deep appreciation to Tom Cuddihy, Len Engel, Dennis Hodgson, Nick Montemarano, and Leo O'Connor for endlessly reading and encouraging, and Orin Grossman and Robert Wall, of Fairfield University, for their thoughtfulness and earnest support. Also to David Rosenthal, for his enduring fascination with jukeboxes. And especially Jackie, who lived with the carob trees, the heat, and the clumps of cactus, and kept the car on the road during the long journey.

For David, Fabiana, Sherine, and Carolyn

Contents

8 CONTENTS

Malta is most particularly a country where history has had to be reinvented continuously. . . . Each generation makes its spasmodic attacks on the subterranean mysteries, and each emerges with its own story; but with each discovery the mysteries take on another aspect and require the story to be retold.

—NIGEL DENNIS, *An Essay on Malta*

"Malta of gold, Malta of silver, Malta of precious metal,
We shall never take you!
No, not even if you were as soft as a gourd,
Not even if you were only protected by an onion skin!"
And from her ramparts a voice replied:
"I am she who has decimated the galleys of the Turk
And all the warriors of Constantinople and Galata!"

—ANONYMOUS, SIXTEENTH CENTURY

Under repeated fire from the skies, Malta stood alone . . . in the center of the sea, one tiny bright flame in the darkness, a beacon of hope for the clearer days which have come.

—FRANKLIN D. ROOSEVELT

MAP OF MALTA & GOZO

SCALE OF ENGLISH MILES

Miles 0 ½ 1 2 3 4 5 6 Miles

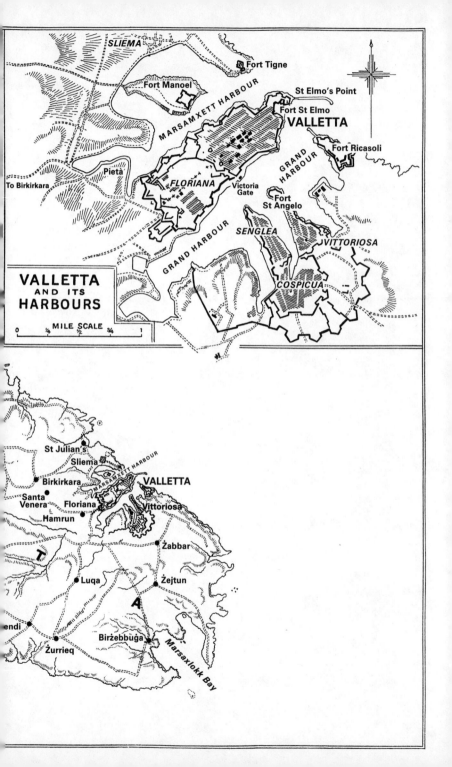

VALLETTA
AND ITS
HARBOURS

0   ¼   MILE SCALE   ¾   1

SLIEMA
Fort Tigne
Fort Manoel
St Elmo's Point
Fort St Elmo
VALLETTA
MARSAMXETT HARBOUR
Fort Ricasoli
Pietà
GRAND HARBOUR
To Birkirkara
FLORIANA
Victoria Gate
Fort St Angelo
SENGLEA
VITTORIOSA
GRAND HARBOUR
COSPICUA

St Julian's
Sliema
Birkirkara
VALLETTA
MARSAMXETT HARBOUR
Santa Venera
Floriana
Vittoriosa
Hamrun
Żabbar
Luqa
Żejtun
...endi
Birżebbuġa
Żurrieq
Marsaxlokk Bay

Part I

ROCCO AND MELITA

April Blitz, 1942

I have never been to a place before or since that had such a visible atmosphere of doom, violence, and toughness about it.

—RAF PILOT LEO NOMIS

One

BUY LACE—SAVE MALTA

They had names for the wind, for the different gusts and breezes that blew across the island. There was a wind that brought rain in October, and that was good, relief from the heat and the dust and the merciless sun that beat down through the long, torrid summer. But there were other winds, less welcome. The worst was the xlokk, which began in the Sahara and blew across the sea, picking up moisture and bringing hot, humid weather that sucked the breath from your lungs and brought on lethargy, inertia, frayed nerves.

When Rocco was told he was being sent to Malta, he recognized the name, Malta, but had only the fuzziest notion where it was—somewhere out there, far off, north or south, in a hazy distance, as dark and mysterious as the name itself, which he repeated over and over, hearing the strangeness, almost tasting it: *Malta, Malta, Malta.*

It was, they told him, in the middle of the Mediterranean, just below Sicily. It belonged to the British, and—the thing he didn't want to hear—it was being bombed day and night by the Germans and the Italians.

He knew nothing about the winds, the majjistral and the tramuntana, the grigal and the scirocco, blowing through the green clumps of cactus and the sun-scorched carob trees, nor did he know about the rows of houses and tenements made from blocks of limestone that were quarried on the island. The limestone was soft enough to cut with a saw, but in the open air, baked by the sun, it hardened, shading to a rich golden brown.

It was early April when they told him to gather his gear for Malta. There was an American team over there, a major and a few lieutenants, who needed a radioman. They were doing liaison work, talking with the British, who were having a hard time of it with the bombing, hanging on by their fingernails. They'd already moved their ships and submarines out of the harbor, to safer waters, off to Egypt and Gibraltar.

"Why me?" Rocco said to the sergeant who handed him his orders.

"Because you have such frantic brown eyes," the sergeant said, with no trace of a smile.

They put him aboard a Liberator and flew him to Gibraltar, where they gave him cheese and Spam in a sandwich, and a beer, then shipped him out on a British bomber, a Wellington, loaded with sacks of mail, and ammunition for the Bofors antiaircraft guns.

Rocco rode in the nose, with the front gunner, catching a view of the sea through the Plexiglas—a thousand miles of water passing beneath them, from Gibraltar all the way to Malta. The crew was exhausted, making the long run daily, back and forth, sometimes twice in a day. The gunner slept the whole way, undisturbed by the roar of the big Pegasus engines. From ten thousand feet, Rocco watched the wakes of freighters and warships, white scars on the water.

The plane entered a long cloud, and when they emerged, back into clear sky, Malta lay far to the left, a dark pancake on the sea, the electric blue of the water turning to a clear vivid green where it rimmed the island. The Wellington seemed to hang, unmoving, as if the distance to the island was too great to overcome.

As the pilot banked, correcting for drift, they were hammered by turbulence, the wind toying with them, bouncing them around. Then, abruptly, they hit a downdraft and the plane plunged, dropping in a long, slanting dive toward the island, a chaotic downward slide, as on some desperate magic carpet hopelessly out of control. The gunner, asleep in his harness, never knew a thing, but Rocco, unbelted, was hoisted in the air and pinned to the top of the cabin, unable to move—unable to think, even, it was that sudden—staring straight ahead through the Plexiglas as the island rose to meet him: streets, roads, church domes, dense clusters of stone buildings, small green fields crossed by stone walls, and smoke, plenty of smoke.

Then, as suddenly as it had begun, it was over. The propellers bit air again, and as the plane pulled up out of its long fall, Rocco was thrown to the floor, grabbing for something to hold on to, but there was nothing.

They put down at Luqa aerodrome, the largest of the three airfields, and it was a rough landing, the plane bouncing and swerving on the runway. Only a half hour earlier, the field had been raided by a flight of Stukas. On the ground, planes and trucks were burning, coils of black smoke rising thickly from the wreckage.

Carrying his duffel bag over his shoulder, Rocco trudged along toward a stone hut, the smell of the fires catching in his throat. Before he was halfway there, a siren sounded, and when the crew from the Wellington broke into a run, Rocco ran too, but he stumbled and went down hard. When he pulled himself up, back on his feet, the crew was gone, and he was alone on the tarmac.

In the weeds at the edge of the field, a tall figure in slacks and a Florida sportshirt, lanky, with thick dark hair, was urging him on, waving with both arms. Rocco scrambled, and leaving the duffel where it was, ran like hell, the roar of an attacking Messerschmitt loud in his ears. As he neared the edge of the tarmac, again he went down, tripped this time by a pothole, and the Florida shirt bent over him and, half-dragging, half-lifting, pulled him into the safety of a slit trench.

Rocco was breathing hard. "Close," he said, feeling a weird mix of fright and exhilaration, a wild alertness brought on by the proximity of death. It was his first time in a war zone, under attack, and what he felt, besides the fear and the terror, was personal resentment and a flash of anger, because if somebody was trying to kill him, actively and deliberately trying to do him in, what else was it but personal?

The Messerschmitt turned, a quick loop and a roll, and when it came back across the field now, its guns ripped into the parked Wellington, and Rocco watched, amazed, as the plane split open and blew sky-high, the cargo of anti-aircraft shells spewing light and color and a riot of noise in the gathering dusk. It wasn't just one Messerschmitt up there, but three, coming and going, strafing at will.

"I'm Fingerly, Jack Fingerly," the Florida shirt said. "You're Kallitsky, right?" The voice was American, a smooth baritone raised almost to a shout while the 109s swept back and forth across the field.

"No—I'm Raven," Rocco answered, noticing the lieutenant's bar pinned to the collar of Fingerly's shirt.

"They were supposed to send Kallitsky. What happened?"

"I don't know a Kallitsky."

"You're reporting to Major Webb?"

"Right. But if you're expecting Kallitsky, I guess I'm the wrong man." He was thinking—hoping—they would put him on a plane and fly him right back to Fort Benning.

"No, no," Fingerly said, soft and easy, with the barest hint of a drawl, "if you're here, you're the right man. Welcome to I-3, you're replacing Ambrosio."

"What's I-3?"

Fingerly arched an eyebrow. "Don't you know?"

Rocco had no idea.

"Intelligence," Fingerly said. "I-3 is Intelligence."

"I thought Intelligence was G-2."

"It is, but even Intelligence needs somebody to tell them which end is up. I-3 is the intelligence inside Intelligence. Didn't they tell you anything back there in Georgia?"

"They said Major Webb would fill me in."

"Major Webb is dead."

"When did that happen?"

"A bomb got him, yesterday. He was having a pink gin at his favorite bistro, in Floriana. I kept telling him, the gin in St. Julian's has more zing to it, more sass, but he wasn't a man to listen. He'd be alive today. Anyway, we've got a lot of work ahead of us, Kallitsky, I hope you're up to it."

"Raven," Rocco said, clinging to his name.

The 109s were gone now, and he glanced about, scanning the devastation—the bomb craters, wrecked planes, the stone huts fractured and smashed, and the burning remnants of the Wellington, its big wings crumpled, in disarray, the ruptured fuselage hot with a bright orange glow, like an enormous bird that had, in its death throes, simply gone mad, twisting its wings wildly. There was a line in Nietzsche that he only half-remembered, something about an abyss, about looking into the darkness and horror of a murky abyss. That's what it was, all around him, a gloomy chaos, and the one thing he was sure of was that he had to get out of there, away from the airfield and out of Malta, off the island, by boat or by plane to Gibraltar, and from there, one way or another, back to the 9th Infantry and the people he knew.

"So this is it?" he said. "This is Malta? I belong here? You don't think this is all just a big mistake?"

When he looked at Fingerly, it wasn't Fingerly he saw but a cloud of smoke, shaping and reshaping itself in the fading light of the day. His eyes were smoke and his mouth was smoke, his tall, lean body dissolving, vaporous and gray. It was Malta, Malta was doing this—everything shifting, turning, uncertain.

When Rocco looked again, Fingerly's face was still full of shadows, but mostly, now, the smoke was just the smoke from his cigarette. "Those Messerschmitt 109s," he said, "you grow attached to them, you'll miss them when they take a day off." He passed a cigarette to Rocco, and Rocco lit up, and he too, for a while, was nothing but smoke, drifting and vague.

He was a corporal. When he enlisted, a few days after Pearl Harbor, what he knew about, more than anything else, was secondhand cars. He'd been working at a used-car lot on New Utrecht Avenue, in Brooklyn, under the el, where the BMT trains rattled by on their way to Manhattan, and he liked it so much he figured that's what he'd do for a living: work with cars. Tune the engines, polish the chrome, apply the Simoniz with a big floppy rag, and smell out the customers, sell to the ones in need, real need, of secondhand. He knew a little, too, not much, about Melville, Nietzsche, and Edgar Allan Poe, because he'd taken some night courses at Brooklyn College, thinking he might go on for a degree, but it was nothing he was sure about, just something he was considering. And now, anyway, there was the war.

"Cars," he said to the recruiting officer. "That's what I know."

But the 9th Infantry, Second Corps, to which he'd been assigned, was overloaded with men in the motor pool, so they put him instead into radios and gave him a crash course in wireless communication, teaching him, among other things, about wavelengths, kilocycles, grid circuits, magnetic storms, cosmic dust, and the aurora borealis. It didn't seem to matter that he had no real aptitude for any of this, as long as he knew which switches to throw and how to deploy his antenna.

Cars were good, he really liked them, and he liked Melville and Poe too. But Malta, the idea of Malta, was not appealing. He didn't like it that he'd been pulled out of his unit and shipped off to strangers, half around the world, and he liked it even less that he was a target for the 109s. They were supposed to send Kallitsky, but they'd sent him instead, and he wondered how they could do that to him. How could they make a monstrous, life-threatening mistake like that?

"Don't fret about it," Fingerly said, casual, with friendly indifference. "The entire planet is a mistake, didn't you know? You'll get used to that too."

Fingerly's car was an old Austin Seven, pale yellow, the fenders dented and the upholstery held together by strips of black tape. The sun was down, slipping away behind the long rows of stone tenements, and in the semidark they drove toward Valletta, first through Paola, then past Marsa and up through Hamrun and Floriana. The marks of the bombing were everywhere. In town after town, houses and buildings were down, massive heaps of rubble. Every few hundred yards, there were gangs of men clearing the mess and keeping the roads open. Women too were out there, bending and lifting.

"Nothing gets them down," Fingerly said. "They've had bombs falling on their heads almost two years now, and just look at them, they're cleaning up."

"Where are the trees?" Rocco said.

"What trees?"

"The forest. They told me there was a dead volcano covered with trees."

"Who told you that?"

"The pilot, Brangle. On the Wellington."

"It's the war," Fingerly said jauntily. "Everybody lies. See how debased life has become? You can't trust anyone anymore."

Not only were there no mountains on Malta, but the highest point was only about eight hundred feet. Here and there a grove of olive trees, but no woods, no forest. A lot of prickly-pear cactus, and low stone walls surrounding small fields where vegetables grew in a shallow layer of soil. The nearest volcano was Mount Etna, in Sicily, a hundred miles away, not dead but very much alive, giving off wisps of smoke that could, on a clear day, be seen from Malta.

"Raven, Raven," Fingerly said. "What kind of a name is that—Lithuanian?"

It was Italian. Rocco's grandfather had been Ravenelli, from Verona. A tailor. He thought it would be easier in the cutting rooms on Seventh Avenue if he went as Raven instead of Ravenelli.

"Was it? Easier?"

"He was mostly out of work."

"Chica boom," Fingerly said.

"Chica who?"

"A song, Raven, a song."

Rocco remembered, yes, "Chica Chica Boom Chic," fast and bouncy, a Carmen Miranda bauble.

"Life is a tease," Fingerly said, "you never know what next. Nevertheless, I think, Rocco Raven, we are going to get along very well together, you and I."

"You think so?" Rocco said, sounding not at all convinced. Already there was something about Fingerly that made him uneasy, the velvet manner, something glib in the tone, and he was beginning to wish it had been somebody else who had pulled him into the trench, back there at Luqa, when the Messerschmitt attacked.

"We're a team," Fingerly said, "that's all that matters here. You, Maroon, Nigg, and myself. I hope you know how to use that wireless."

Maroon was away, on the neighboring island of Gozo—scouting the territory, Fingerly said vaguely. And Nigg was in the Green Room at Dominic's, gambling and smoking cigars. Rocco thought it would be good luck if, somehow, he could make his escape and find his way home to Brooklyn. His father, with whom he had a muddled relationship, had sold the house in Flatbush and moved on to another neighborhood. But still, back there, it was Brooklyn, with trees and backyards, and baseball at Ebbets Field, and all those other good things—egg creams, peacocks in the zoo, beer in the bowling alleys, and cars whose motors he could tinker with, making them purr. In a park one night, in lush grass on the side of a hill, he made love to a girl he'd been dating, Theresa Flum, and he thought she was the one, his forever. But she had a different idea and went off with somebody else, leaving him in a state of despair from which he still wasn't fully recovered.

"Here," Fingerly said, taking a lieutenant's bar out of his pocket, "you better wear this. The Brits are very class-conscious—unless you're an officer you can't walk into the better clubs. Remember, though, it's just make-believe, like the rest of your life. After Malta, you're a corporal again."

When they reached Valletta, Fingerly parked outside the city gate, and they walked the rest of the way, through streets lit by a half moon. Here there was so much rubble it would have been near impossible to drive. From Kingsway they crossed over on South and turned down Strait, a long narrow street, less damaged than some of the others, cobblestoned, barely ten feet wide, descending all the way down to the fortified area at the tip of the peninsula. Only a slender ribbon of the night sky showed above the three- and four-story stone buildings. In places, the cobbles gave way to slate stairs, and at the far end, down toward Fountain Street, the neighborhood was crowded with bars.

"In the days of the Knights," Fingerly said, "they fought duels on this street. Isn't it a great place for swordplay? So narrow, and all the stairs. And down the hill there, the bars and the bordellos. The sailors call it the Gut."

They were heading for Number 79.

"It's really a brothel?"

It was. Nigg was billeted there too, on the top floor, in the room next to Rocco's. Fingerly lived somewhere else, on Merchants Street. "If you're not happy," he said, "we can put you in the Capuchin monastery around the corner, but they make lousy coffee."

"Who pays the rent?"

"You do. With pounds and shillings. I'll cover it tonight, for the balance of the month, but after that it's your lookout."

"I'm rich?"

"You're poor. Your GI salary is being banked for you at Fort Benning, you'll find it waiting if you live to claim it. Here on Malta we're free-floating and pay our own way, so you get, from me, a subsistence wage to keep you in business. I-3 keeps an account in the Banca di Roma on Kingsway. If they get bombed, we'll all have to start working for a living."

"Banca di Roma?"

"You know them?"

"I thought Rome was the enemy."

"It is, but the Maltese think it's smart to keep them around, on the theory the Italians won't drop a bomb on one of their own. It's the safest bank in town."

From his shirt pocket Fingerly took an envelope with BANCA DI ROMA printed on it in embossed lettering and passed it over. "There's your first Malta pay, plus a bonus for getting here alive. The last replacement we had was killed by flak on the way in, he was an awful mess. I'll get you some ration cards too, you can't buy matches or soap on this island without a card. Not to mention bread."

The house belonged to Hannibal Serduq, who lived on the second floor with his wife and family. He also owned the bar across the street, the Oasis.

The entrance had three low steps and a door with ornamental grille-work. Inside, in the blue light of the foyer, sat the doorman, Nardu Camilleri, Hannibal's father-in-law, a shrunken old man in a dark suit, bald except for some white fuzz above his ears. On a small table beside him stood a glass bowl for tips, containing coins and crumpled bills from all around the Mediterranean.

As they passed the parlor, Rocco saw the women, three of them, waiting for their clients. The room was stuffed with furniture. Against one wall was a pianola, and above the mantel, a painting of the Madonna in a gold frame. One of the women, older than the others, was busy over a newspaper. She wore a red slip with black ruffles, and had a black eye. The other two were on the couch, playing cards. One had streaks of gold in her hair, and a wooden leg strapped to her thigh. The other, the youngest of the three, was plump and lovely, in a blue silk negligée windowed with lace. Her eyes locked onto Rocco's and she smiled.

"Later," Fingerly said, nudging Rocco along. As they started up the stairs, there was a clatter from above and two children came rushing down, a boy and a girl, on their way to the shelter, where they slept at night. The boy wore a Boy Scout uniform.

"Hey, hey," Fingerly called, blocking their way. "Going to run right through me?"

The boy stared.

"Joseph, Joseph, it's me, Fingerly. Aren't we friends?"

"You give me some chocolate? Ambrosio gives me chocolate."

"Ambrosio is gone," Fingerly said. "He's never coming back."

The boy lowered his head. "I know, he is gone. He was my friend."

"Well, this is Rocco, Rocco Raven. He's going to be in Ambrosio's room. His real name is Kallitsky, but we'll forgive him for that."

"Hello, Kallitsky," the boy said.

"Hello, Joseph," Rocco said.

"You give me chocolate?"

Rocco turned his pockets inside out. He was thinking of Brangle, the pilot on the Wellington, who'd had no sleep for twenty hours, keeping himself awake by munching on chocolate.

"Rocco is your new friend," Fingerly said.

"We don't like him," the boy said, turning to the girl. "Do we like him?"

The girl shook her head dubiously.

"Well, you'll get to like him," Fingerly said. "He's from Brooklyn and he knows all about cars. He specializes in secondhand Chevrolets."

"I'm Marie," the girl said, a few years younger than the boy. Around her neck, on a silver chain, was a medal bearing an image of the Blessed Mother. There were soldiers in Rocco's outfit who wore the same medal.

"Here," Fingerly said, taking a chocolate bar from his shirt pocket. "I paid two packs of cigarettes for this. You'll have to split it."

"You bought this for me?" the boy said.

"I bought it for both of you."

"I'll take it," the boy said, reaching.

"Not till I break it in half."

But before he could, the boy, in a swift, easy move, grabbed it from his hands and lunged past him, down the stairs and out the front door, into the dark. The girl hurried after, shouting, "It's mine, Joseph, half is mine, give it back!"

"Sweet kids," Fingerly said.

"They live here?"

"Hannibal's brood. There was a third, died a year ago. Undulant fever."

One flight up, Fingerly knocked at Hannibal's flat, and Hannibal came to the door, a burly, square-shouldered man, holding a chunk of bread. There was a long scar across his cheek.

"Rocco may be here for a while," Fingerly said, peeling some notes from a roll he took from his pocket. It was British currency. "This will cover him till the end of the month."

Hannibal looked at the money. "It's not enough," he said.

"It's what we agreed on when Ambrosio was here."

"I know, I know," Hannibal said, rolling his head, "but it's the war, everything is more expensive."

"How much do you need?"

"Three more, by the month."

"That's more than what I'm paying for my two rooms on Merchants Street."

"Yours will go up too. You will see. And I am giving him board as well."

"One," Fingerly suggested.

"Two and a half," Hannibal said.

"One and a half."

Hannibal nodded grudgingly, and Fingerly gave it to him in coins.

Rocco looked past Hannibal, into the apartment, and saw the wife, Beatrice, clearing dishes from the dining-room table. She was plain-looking, her hair in a net. She paused, eyeing Rocco, looking him over, then she turned, carrying off a stack of dishes.

Hannibal shook Rocco's hand. "We don't usually take house guests," he said. "But the war, it makes everything different. We change the sheets once a week and give you a fresh towel. If you use the women, that's extra."

His front teeth were ground down to little more than stumps. There was a wart on his upper lip and his jaw was crooked, as if it had been broken more than once. Rocco was impressed by the hands—the grip seemed strong enough to bend iron.

Rocco's room was upstairs, on the top floor, in the rear. On a table by the bed was the radio Ambrosio had left behind, and a stack of French picture magazines. Ambrosio had gone AWOL to Majorca, dropping out of the war, slipping away on a fishing boat. He had relatives there, among the olive trees, and was not expected back.

"He used to pick up everywhere on this," Fingerly said, as Rocco inspected the radio components. "He pulled in Billie Holiday from the Lincoln Hotel."

Rocco threw switches and turned dials, fiddling with the frequencies.

"You can handle it? How's your touch on the key?"

"As in dot-dot-dash, good old Morse Code? I sometimes don't spell right."

"Well, try to get it straight," Fingerly said, taking a folded paper from his pocket.

Rocco read the message: *The monkey is in the box. The Fat Lady has no head.* "This is coded, right?"

"Can you do it, or do we need Kallitsky?"

Rocco stared hard at the glowing tubes in the transmitter. "I'm better than Kallitsky. You know it. Or they wouldn't have sent me." He made some adjustments, moving the dials, then rubbed his hands together and, putting his finger on the key, established contact and sent the message. A moment later it was acknowledged.

"You did it right?"

"If I didn't, we'll never know."

"Send it again."

"They got it," Rocco said, resisting. "It was received."

"Do it again."

"This is why you hauled me out here all the way from Benning? To send a message about a monkey in a box?"

"Don't push your luck, Raven."

Rocco hung back, giving Fingerly a long, stony look. Then, relenting, he sent the message a second time.

"Good," Fingerly said. "We'll eat at Dominic's, but first let's go talk to the whores, they get lonely down there."

On their way down they ran into Nigg, just in from Dominic's and looking petered out. When Fingerly introduced Rocco, Nigg stared long at his face. "You're not I-3," he said.

"It shows?" Rocco said resentfully.

"You have the wrong eyes for I-3. Wrong everything. Are you lucky?"

"I used to be, but now I'm not so sure."

"If you're not lucky," Nigg said, "I don't want to know you." He was shorter than Fingerly, with dark eyebrows, a bony forehead, and slack wide lips, an odd loneliness about the mouth and jaw. His shoulders were narrow, and his chest concave. Physically, he seemed fragile, yet there was a hardness in his voice, a darkness, that set Rocco's teeth on edge.

Without taking his eyes from Rocco, Nigg said to Fingerly: "You told him about the Major?"

Fingerly nodded.

"Well," Nigg said to Rocco, "too bad you never met him. He knew a lot about French wines and pagan religions. You know anything about pagan religions?"

"I read some Nietzsche," Rocco said. "He wasn't very big on God."

"Nietzsche had a cigar up his ass."

He started up the stairs, and Fingerly called after him. "You heading back to Dominic's, or are you through for the night?"

"Who knows," Nigg shrugged. "I'll be picking up Vivian, then we'll see."

"We'll catch up later," Fingerly said, certain that Nigg would return to Dominic's, because there was nothing he liked better than to gamble late into the night. And the food at Dominic's was the best on Malta.

He brought Rocco into the parlor and introduced him to the whores.

Rocco lived there, in the brothel, three days. He ate the bean stew and the fried rice that Beatrice made, slept on the cot Ambrosio had slept on, and had frantic, unfriendly dreams that were interrupted by air-raid sirens and bombing raids. He shaved and washed in a bathroom cluttered with douche bags and hoses, and various other arcane paraphernalia, some of which he recognized and some he did not. In his room, at the wireless, he sent the messages Fingerly gave him to send, and downstairs, in Hannibal's apartment, he had coffee with the women.

The oldest, Simone, kept mostly to herself, doing crossword puzzles in *Il Berqa*, the Maltese-language paper. She was world-weary, over the hill, yet Rocco knew, from the barracks talk at Dix, and then at Benning, there were GIs who liked their women on the stale side, slightly jaded. Even the black eye could be a turn-on. The other two, Aida and Julietta, played cards, double solitaire, and when Rocco joined in, it was triple solitaire. Julietta, the youngest, had a canary in a cage, which she carried around with her from room to room. The skinny one, Aida, took off her wooden leg and insisted on showing Rocco the stump where her left leg had been cut off above the knee.

"I don't want to see it," he said, and really didn't. Amputations made him queasy. There had been a boy in grammar school, in the first grade, with a missing hand, he'd lost it in a car accident, nothing there but a knot of skin at the end of his forearm. He used to wave it in front of Rocco's face, meanly, as if Rocco were somehow to blame.

"But you must," Aida said, lifting the faded housedress she wore during the day, to reveal what looked like a big pink sausage. "You must. There. I *want* you to see it."

They played another round of triple solitaire, and Julietta won.

"She's cheating," Aida said. "She always cheats."

Julietta made no effort to conceal the cheating, taking cards from any part of the deck and playing them with no regard for the rules. Her cotton housedress was loose and boxy, a row of buttons down the front. Without makeup, she was still attractive, but less enticing than at night, when she waited for her clients in the parlor.

"Take me to America," she said to Rocco. "You don't have to marry me, just take me to America, and I'll never cheat again."

Every now and then, Rocco knew, from Fingerly, a soldier or a sailor would latch onto a girl in one of the houses and there would be a wedding, but it hadn't happened on Strait Street for a long time.

"Just take me," Julietta said impishly, "I'll do everything for you, anything at all. I'll be your slave!"

They were in the dining room in Hannibal's apartment, at a table covered by a checkered oilcloth. It was shortly after noon. Beatrice was in the kitchen, preparing a stew, and Simone, with cold cream on her face and a blue towel around her head, was eating a sandwich, watching the card game with undisguised boredom.

The old man, Nardu Camilleri, sat at the head of the table. For a long time he said nothing, simply sat there, lost in thought. Then, with a fiery glance, he launched into a rambling monologue about the future of Malta. He was small and withered, but his voice, though raspy, was full of passionate conviction. He envisioned, after the war, a Malta that would emerge as the major power in the Mediterranean.

"A new Malta," he said, thumping the table with his thumb. "After the bombing, a phoenix from the ashes!" He paused to clear his throat, then he went on forcefully, "Mark my words! As soon as the war is over, we declare our independence and we throw out the English. Then we annex Italy. Sicily we don't want, it's too full of thugs and mafiosi. Rome we give to the pope, but the rest of Italy is ours. We will call it Greater Malta!"

Rocco liked him: the bony dome of his head, the intensity of his gaze, and the sureness in his tone, as if every word were a religious affirmation. He was balmy and old, and wonderfully gnarled, his skin coarse and rugged like the bark of a tree. His feet, as he sat there at the table, had roots growing into the floor, spreading out, grabbing onto the beams and the floorboards.

"Believe me, this will happen—Malta will rule the Mediterranean. Even the Turks will come under our thumb. We defeated them when Dragut fought against us, in the Great Siege, and we shall tame them again. The Greeks and the Egyptians will send ambassadors. Tunis and Tripoli will be on their knees!" He glared truculently. "You think this will not come to pass? Even the French will show respect. The whole world will honor us, because if it weren't for us, all of Africa would belong to Hitler, and Europe too. We saved Europe once—from the Turks, four centuries ago—and now we are saving it again, from the Fascists. Without Malta, Europe would be a garbage pit!" He gestured vigorously with his small hands, as if addressing a lecture hall, his dry voice rising and sifting with a wistful urgency.

It was, for Rocco, a dizzying notion: tiny Malta a world power. He dropped a card, and didn't bother to pick it up.

"Our houses are bombed," Nardu Camilleri acknowledged, rocking his head from side to side, "and our airfields are pummeled. But the more we lose, the closer we are to winning. Victory is around the corner, I can taste it, it's within our grasp. Any day now the bombers will start falling out of the sky. We will not even have to shoot them down. They will fall from sheer exhaustion, of their own dead weight. Europe is in the palm of our hands. I hope we have statesmen big enough to understand our destiny. First we beat back the Germans and the Italians, then we throw out the British and come into our own. The British are through, isn't it obvious? They are finished as a nation. If it weren't for us, holding out here as we have done, they would already have caved in."

Beatrice called anxiously from the kitchen. "*Papà*, don't talk like that. If you talk like that, they'll put you in jail."

People had been put in jail. Some had even been sent into exile, off to Uganda. They were people involved with the pro-Italy movement, people who, before the war, had wanted to dump the British in favor of the Italians.

"Don't mix me up with those fumbling idiots," the old man retorted. "Those traitors, wanting to unify with Italy. I will never be one of them. I say to hell with Italy and England too. To hell with Napoleon, and the Greeks, the Romans, the Arabs, the Phoenicians, and all the other Fascist oppressors who put Malta under the yoke. And the British, especially the British, who have been here too long, a hundred and fifty years. After our revolution, when we gain our independence, we will not speak English anymore. We shall speak only Maltese. Especially you women, when the men come to make love to you—you will make love in Maltese, and it will be better love than when you did it in English."

Beatrice waved a hand, scoffing. "And you? You've spoken English so long, you don't even remember any Maltese."

He eyed her fiercely. *"Kull ħmar iħobb jisma' lilu nnifsu jinħaq,"* he said unfalteringly, quoting a proverb he'd learned as a child, and then, for Rocco's sake, served it up in English: "Every ass enjoys the sound of its own braying."

Beatrice came right back at him, answering him in kind. *"Kulħadd ibati b'tal-ħmar*—There is something of an ass in everyone!"

But it was as if the old man, her father, had never heard. His eyes danced exultantly. "After the war," he said to Rocco, "there will be a new world order and a new economy. And do you know what will drive the new economy? Have you any idea?"

Rocco waited.

"Maltese lace," the old man said. "Yes, lace," leaning toward Rocco in a mild ferment. "The famous lace made by the hands of the women of Malta. More precious than oil," he said, gloating, "more valuable than Asian ivory. Demand will drive the price sky-high. Our women will have to work night and day, harder than ever—and we shall have to breed more of them, more females to work the lace, because men are no good at this, no good at all, as you may have noticed."

Simone was eating another sandwich, chewing methodically because she had bad teeth. Her chewing had a vaguely aggressive quality, something menacing in the grinding of her jaws. Her robe had fallen open and one of her breasts was exposed, a large, sagging thing, only a short distance from the old man's face. He stared boldly at it, as if preparing to take a bite out of it.

"After we annex Italy," he said with unabated zest, "and after we punish the Turks for what they did four hundred years ago, we will form alliances to solidify our position. Lace will do it all, lace is the key that will unlock every door."

The bombers were up again, going after the docks. They could hear the bombs slamming down into Senglea, Cospicua, Vittoriosa.

Nardu Camilleri lifted both hands toward Rocco, warmly. "When you go home, tell your friends. Perhaps, in America, you will become our agent. I could set you up with the better makers and you will be among the first to profit from the postwar boom." He spoke of lace doilies, lace tablecloths, lace bedspreads, lace wedding gowns. He talked of lace shirts for the men, lace ties and lace waistcoats, lace scarves, lace berets, lace costumes for the dancers of ballet.

Aida, the thin one, lifted her housedress and applied olive oil to her one leg, massaging it into her skin. The oil was from a cruet on the table, next to the vinegar. She lifted her leg high in the air, her bare foot beautifully arched, her toes coming to within inches of the old man's face. And still he talked, about lace and about Malta, as if the bare foot and the leg were not there, as if Simone's breast were not there, as if the sirens were not wailing and the bombs were not falling on the docks across the harbor.

Rocco was exhausted. Ever since he left Fort Benning, he'd hardly slept, and he felt now an immense fatigue, his body weighed down and disintegrating, sifting away. Nardu Camilleri rambled on about Malta, Julietta cheated with the cards, and the canary sang, a tuneful chirping. Aida complained about her wooden leg, and, as Rocco laid a red nine under a black ten, he wasn't at all sure if he was asleep or awake. He'd entered a soupy zone in which he seemed to be moving, precariously, in a lopsided dream, seeing doors that looked like faces, and faces that looked like trees. Nardu Camilleri was a brown cloud. And Julietta was a smudge of sunlight barely visible through that cloud. And more than ever he knew he had to get away, or the island would seduce him, charm him, break him, and in the end, sooner or later, it would kill him. With a struggle, he got himself up to his room and flung himself on the bed, not bothering to pull off his uniform, so worn down he wasn't even aware he was closing his eyes. But even the letting go was not easy, because nothing was easy any more. Even sleep was an effort, moving from here to there, awake to not-awake, abandoning consciousness.

There was a smell of roses, he didn't know why. He opened a door and went through, entering a room where a woman was lying on a table, in repose. Her body was opened. The opening ran from her chest straight down across her abdomen, and there were things inside her: green leaves, flowers, old theater tickets, strings of pearls. The opening was a neat, clean line, as if a zipper had been unzipped, the two sides drawn back, allowing the gems and flowers to overflow.

He put his hand inside her, into the flowers and sapphires, and felt a strange coldness there. Both of his hands were inside her, into her silence, and, far down, he found red roses, and they glowed.

He was walking. It seemed he had always been walking, and as he turned a corner, he came upon Nardu Camilleri, in a heavy overcoat. He was selling lace. "Buy lace," he was saying, "buy lace and win the war. Save Malta!"

Rocco dug into his pockets, wanting to buy some lace so he could save Malta, but he had nothing on him. He couldn't believe the emptiness of his pockets.

"Don't you want to help?" Nardu Camilleri asked.

"I lost my wallet," Rocco said.

"You lack substance? You don't have the wherewithal?"

Again Rocco searched his pockets, but came up empty.

Nardu Camilleri's eyes were full of disappointment. "You are the only one who can help us," he said. "The only one."

Rocco walked slowly down the street, thinking he really didn't give a damn about lace. If he had known that Malta was famous for lace, he would have ignored his orders and gone somewhere else.

The street was empty, a light rain falling. Then the rain stopped and he was in the room again, where the woman was on a table. It was Julietta. "I wouldn't come to America with you even if you dragged me," she said.

"Why not?"

"Because you don't care about me. Isn't it true?"

It was true, he was not wild about her. He hadn't slept with her and wasn't eager to, though there was something warm and generous in her eyes. He turned his pockets inside out, but his pockets were empty.

Then, going closer, he saw that the woman was not Julietta but someone else, someone from his future, waiting for him. He looked inside her, into the opening in her body, and now, when he looked, it wasn't roses that he saw but a lake, right there inside her, a blue expanse of water, rippled by a breeze. He stood there pondering the water, and then, in a moment of abandon, he dove in and swam, the water washing over him. He felt alive and vigorous, better than he'd felt in days. This was the answer, yes, the blue of the water, and the blue of the sky.

But as he swam, in his dream, he heard a bomb whistling down, coming right for him, as if it knew exactly where to find him. The bomb was not part of his dream, but inside the dream he could hear it, and he knew it was real. It hit the house and exploded, and he was in it, fully inside it: the bright, shivering blast, immense roar, soul-searing, white and vivid, all around him.

THE KESSELRING MEMORANDUM

December 1941

To guarantee safe passage of supplies from Italy to North Africa and to maintain air supremacy in the area, it is critical that Malta be neutralized.

The aim of this assault will be to destroy the island's aircraft and demolish the antiaircraft gun positions. Attacks must be made both day and night, with a constant variation in tactics.

The enemy is to be kept off balance by the use of different bombs for different actions. Apart from the usual low-level SD 2 bombs, use of even the smallest antipersonnel bombs is to be considered.

The island must be completely cut off from its supply lines of materiel and personnel. Sea convoys are to be reported as early as possible by long-range reconnaissance and attacked.

Most of all, it is essential to destroy Malta's value as a naval base by bombing its docks and all shipping in its harbors.

—Field Marshal Albert Kesselring
Commander in Chief South

Three

A NIGHT ON THE GUT

In the glare of the explosion, when the bomb hit, Rocco felt lifted, spread out, separated from his body, and, in a rush, everything around him fell away. Then a concussed feeling, as if he'd been dropped flat onto hard rock. An enormous groan heaved through the house, a great wrenching and moaning of beams, plaster flying, mortar crumbling, a fierce wind gusting through the timbers. Slowly, the dust cleared, and he saw the ceiling was gone and the roof had been torn off, and the whole back wall of the house had been ripped open. It was the simmering end of the day, the sun still up but on its way down, small rust-colored clouds drifting overhead.

All that was left of the whole top floor was the small shelf of flooring his bed was on, jutting out from a wall. The radio was gone. Where Nigg's room had been, and all the other top-floor rooms, there was only empty space, and he wondered if Nigg had been there, upstairs, when the bomb went off.

Below, in the wreckage, he saw a flicker of movement, then nothing. Then a flash of yellow—it was the bird, Julietta's canary, on the splintered remains of a bed. It made a few chirping sounds, then it was up, flying, right out of the house, up through the hole in the roof.

Cautiously, he got himself down, hanging on to the sheared-off edge of the flooring, lowering himself onto a heap of mounded rubble. It shifted under his weight, and he fell, sliding down a slope of debris. He got to his feet, wincing, and as he glanced about, a bitter taste rose from his stomach. The pianola lay in pieces, the black and white keys loose and scrambled among fragments of crystal from the chandelier. He thought he saw an arm, and went closer, but it was only a rolling pin from the kitchen. A rat scrambled out from under some plaster, paused, nose twitching, then scampered off into a pile of laths.

He began pulling away at things, in a kind of frenzy, digging into the pile. Planks, broken chairs, chunks of plaster. If they were there, he had to find them, had to dig down and get to them. He called to them: *Julietta! Beatrice! Aida! Simone!* He was thinking of the kids, Joseph and Marie, and the old man, Nardu Camilleri. And Nigg—especially Nigg—angry at him for being dead, angry at all of them, but Nigg more than the others, because he and Nigg were, after all, in the same army. He pulled a heavy door from the pile and threw it aside. He found eyeglasses, cushions, a wig, pieces of clothing, a toilet seat. He picked up lamps and bureau drawers, hurling them wildly, with a strength he didn't know he had.

Then, out of breath, sweating, he saw how hopeless it was. His left hand was bleeding. If they were there, under all that pile, they were dead anyway, had to be. It was crazy to stay here.

He moved to the rear of the house, where the back wall had blown out, and, climbing over a heap of broken limestone, found his way into a long alley that brought him over to Old Bakery Street. The bombers were gone, and an eerie silence hugged the cobblestones. He hurried around the corner and back onto Strait Street, and saw the blast had left the front wall of the house completely intact. Windows all along the street were blown out, but the front of the house was solid, yielding no sign of the destruction within. Far up the street, a dog was barking; Rocco could barely see it, a noisy spot of brown.

He set off downhill, toward St. Elmo's, past a string of bars, then turned and went a couple of blocks over to Merchants Street, where Fingerly had his digs above a tailor shop. Merchants had been badly hit, several buildings gutted. It was wider than Strait Street, full of stores, with apartments above, and the rescue units were already at work, taking away the injured.

Two soldiers carried a stretcher from the remains of the tailor shop. It was a woman, gray hair badly singed, one arm hanging down from the stretcher, her wrist swinging back and forth, rhythmically, as if she were telling herself a nursery rhyme.

"Are there others in there?" Rocco asked, as they got the woman into a Red Cross ambulance that had somehow found a path through the rubble.

"If there are," said one of the soldiers, a corporal, "we won't find them tonight."

"You didn't take out an American, did you? A tall American?"

"When they're dead, it's the same if they're American or Albanian. Tall, you say?"

"Dark hair."

"We had a tall chap, yes. Why don't you check with HQ tomorrow, they should have it all sorted out by then. This bloke wasn't wearing no uniform, though."

Rocco wandered off, feeling a need to keep moving. He went up Merchants and turned a corner, walking aimlessly. The streets of Valletta were laid out on a grid, less than a mile long. It was hard to get lost there, yet when he turned off Merchants, he was uncertain of his way, and didn't much care.

Eventually, he came upon the Barracca Gardens, overlooking Grand Harbour. Across the water were the dock areas and stone fortifications jutting out into the harbor. Smoke rose from a fuel depot hit earlier in the day, and the soursick smell of burn came to him from across the water. The sun was down but the sky was still lit with color, high clouds fanning out like russet veils. The harbor was littered with the hulks of bombed ships, dead in the water, on their sides or deep under with only a bow or a funnel sticking up. If Fingerly was dead, and if Nigg was dead, then he was on his own, alone on Malta, no radio and nobody to report to, in a British war zone that was getting bombed to hell. It scared him, being alone. Somehow, and fast, he would have to figure it out and get off the island. But how? *How?*

The water, in shadow, was black, and he gazed at it hard and long, feeling an enormous loneliness out there. The loneliness drifted from the water and crept inside him, making him feel vulnerable and small.

He was walking again, on Old Mint, then across on South, and when he reached Kingsway he knew where he was again, and at the lower end he crossed over to Strait Street, down into the Gut. The sun was gone but the moon was up, spilling light into the limestone streets. He went from pub to pub, beer-smelling seedy places dark with heavy coats of varnish, lit by candles and lanterns because the electricity was down after the last raid—noisy, beer-swilling dives with names like Oyster, Inferno, Harem, Big Peter, and never enough tables, moiling crowds of soldiers and sailors, mostly British and Maltese, but Canadians too, and New Zealanders, a few Australians, and tarts who lolled around waiting to be picked up.

In his American uniform, he was an oddity. " 'Ere, it's a Yank, look at the Yank, won't you? Thought y' was all sunk at Pearl 'Arbor. A pint for the Yank 'ere, a pint for the Yank."

Someone put a mug in his hand and he drank. Someone slapped him on the back. Someone whistled in his ear. He drank another, then pushed his way out and stood in the dark, on the cobbles, smoking a cigarette from a pack Fingerly had given him.

He moved along, to the Oyster, where a blue-haired waitress in a short dress served mugs and sandwiches from a battered metal tray. As she came out from behind the bar, hands reached from all over, wanting a touch of her, going for her legs, thighs, shoulders, a quick feel of her as she pushed past, magical, delivering the ale, the rum, the whisky neat, the jam on toast. She loved it, her eyes glittered. They wanted her to stand on a table and take off her clothes, but all she did was laugh, a throaty, sexy, glad-to-know-you giggle.

Three Lancashire Fusiliers sang "Lili Marlene," making a bad job of it, and a burly sergeant from the Royal Artillery shouted them down. Plenty of smoke from the cigarettes, a great gray cloud, like the smokescreen they put up over the docks to shield the ships from the bombers. They were fast-talking and fast-drinking, from Devon, Dorset, Cheshire, and West Kent, a noisy, raucous mob, yakking and muttering, cursing, wheezing, groaning, moaning. Body heat and sweating armpits. Great cloudbursts of laughter, dispelling the nervous tension. Names like Stale, Barm, Scone, and Copperwheat, names unlike the names he was used to, bantered back and forth in jest or in anger, as a taunt, or a challenge, or even a caress. There was a Pebbles and a Lake, a Hillock and a Bone, a Kettle and a Marsh. Not men, kids. Young. Like himself, and younger. Too young to die, and still not believing it could actually happen—not to them, and especially, he thought, not to him. He was twenty-one, and had just survived a 500-pound bomb.

He met an American, a pilot flying for the British, Tony Zebra, from New Jersey, slumped in a booth and working on bourbon. His brown hair was longer than regulation, and his uniform was a hodgepodge—blue RAF jacket, brown army pants, and a purple shirt from a rummage sale. He'd had orders for India and had been on his way from Montrose, in Scotland, but when he reached Gibraltar they detoured him into Malta, and now there was no getting out. He'd been really looking forward to India. He'd spent a lot of time thinking about it, and was still bent on getting there: the Taj Mahal, the Ganges, the Himalayas, and the sacred cows, and the women in saris, with the red dot on their forehead. He read books about India. He had dreams in which he walked barefoot through heavy grass, looking for a tiger.

"New Jersey?" Rocco said.

"Hoboken." He'd been working his way through college, selling vacuum cleaners, but when he met up with an RAF recruiter, instead of finishing his senior year he went to England to learn how to fly. That was a few weeks before

Pearl Harbor. A lot of Americans had done that, signed up with the RAF before America was in the war, and though America was now in it, many continued flying for the British because they knew the British planes.

His first week on Malta, Tony Zebra was shot down three times. The following week, he crashed head-on into a Stuka, and on impact, as both planes disintegrated, he was thrown free and parachuted into the sea. They gave him credit for destroying the Stuka even though he wrecked his own plane in the process, and he was promoted from sergeant pilot to pilot officer. A few days later he went after a Ju-88, firing from only fifty yards, but missed, hitting instead a Hurricane that showed up out of nowhere, flying right into his line of fire.

"I keep telling them how much better off they'd be without me," he told Rocco, "but they won't listen. Not even a month on this godforsaken rock, and already I'm a lieutenant. Before you know it, they'll be giving me medals." He swallowed more bourbon, and, glassy-eyed, looked at Rocco as if he knew him from long ago but couldn't remember when or where. "Come over to Takali, I'll show you around," he said. Takali was where he was based, by Mdina. The other airfields were at Luqa and Hal Far. "We'll do some flying and shoot down a few Stukas. You ever fly?"

"Only in the Catskills."

"Nobody flies in the Catskills."

"I did."

"That's because you're crazy."

"I'm crazy? You're crazy."

"God is crazy."

Rocco really had flown in the Catskills, before the war, but very little. He'd been up a few hours, in a Piper Cub. Flying was good, he liked it—but cars, for him, were better because that's what he knew. Down on the ground, on the road, that's where he was comfortable, where he belonged.

"Takali," Tony Zebra said.

"Sure," Rocco said.

"You do that. You come visit."

"I will."

"You bet."

He went out into the night again, into the blackout, the only light coming from the moon and from the doorways when the soldiers passed in or out of the bars. He thought of Fingerly, and the flames curling up out of the blown-out windows above the tailor shop. Maybe he was dead, yes, and if that was the case it would be, possibly, good luck and good riddance, because in the short time that he'd known him he didn't like him, didn't like him at all. But it was bad luck too, because without Fingerly, how was he going to find a way off the island?

He went into the Mermaid, where a girl at a piano was banging out a patriotic song, singing with a hard, brassy voice about the white cliffs of Dover. A knot of sailors hovered around the piano, glazed, in a dreamy stage of inebriation, and Rocco, looking on, felt disconnected, he didn't belong. He didn't sail, didn't fly, he wasn't a gunner. He did dot-dot-dash for Fingerly, but the radio was gone, and for all he knew Fingerly too was gone, cashed in his chips. But then he thought that couldn't be, it wasn't likely, because Fingerly was too complicated, or at least too clever, to be dead. In any case, the white cliffs of Dover were far away, and though the girl with the brassy voice made them sound worth dying for, they meant nothing to him. They weren't Brooklyn, not the Bronx, not Manhattan, and Rocco, wobbly on his feet, felt more isolated than before, a stranger in somebody else's war.

Four

THE SHELTER

He was on the street again when the sirens began to wail, not at all sure where he was. He'd been on the Gut, roving from bar to bar, but then he'd turned off, wandering. It was dark but not late, not deep in the night, and the cool air and the walking cleared his head. The sirens riveted his attention.

A stream of people came down out of the houses, out of the rows of three- and four-story tenements, not running, not in a panic, but with quiet haste, on their way to an underground shelter, and Rocco fell in with them. After turning a corner, he got his bearings and saw they were leading him back to Strait Street: mothers with babies, old women in black dresses, men in sweaters, a boy with a harmonica. A kid wearing a frog mask rushed past him, chased by a kid with a Pinocchio nose. A girl had a fit of sneezing. A white-haired man, mumbling to himself, carried a ledger under his arm and had a pencil lodged over his ear, his shirttail hanging down out of his pants like a white flag flying at half-mast.

The entrance to the shelter was in the rear of a bar, the Inner Sanctum, by a billiards table. A trapdoor in the floor opened onto a spiral stairwell cut into stone, sinking some forty or fifty feet into a cavern. It was like that all over Valletta, tunnels and caverns chiseled deep in the underground limestone—some of them new, cut with pneumatic drills, but many, like this one, old, dating back to the time of the Knights. From Nardu Camilleri, Rocco had heard more about the Knights than he really wanted to know. When they lost Jerusalem, they went to Acre, and when they lost Acre, they went to Cyprus, and then to Rhodes. When they lost Rhodes, the emperor gave them Malta, though they didn't want it. It was barren rock, undeveloped, and vulnerable to attack. Yet they took it, because there was nothing else. And now Rocco felt the same way, that he too had nothing else, he was stuck here for the duration. Nothing to shield him from the bombs but the hard rock of Malta, which even the Knights had never wanted.

The stone steps, wedge-shaped, were narrow and steep, turning round and round, and dimly lit. Halfway down, there were maybe a dozen steps with no light at all. The old ladies managed well, they were experts at this; but Rocco, groping, had to brace himself, putting his hands against the curved stone walls on either side of him, like descending into another one of his bad dreams.

Below ground, it was dry and cool. At the far end was another entrance, coming from Old Bakery Street. Tiers of bunkbeds, three beds high, ran along one wall, and the children scrambled for the top bunks, hugging dolls and small wooden toys. The boy with the harmonica played tunelessly, random notes, pointless and annoying.

At the far entrance, women were reciting the rosary, some in housedresses, some in black faldettas. They stood before a picture of the Blessed Mother that hung in a high niche. The monotonous droning echoed off the walls—the same words, in Maltese, over and over again, "Sliema għalik, Marija, bil-graz-zja mimlija . . ."

On the stone floor, next to one of the bunks, three soldiers were shooting craps. One, a handkerchief tied around his head, called out to Rocco. "What's a Yank like you doin' 'ere in the middle of Malta?"

"I wish I knew," Rocco said.

" 'E wishes 'e knew. I wish I knew why I was 'ere. You know why you's 'ere, Tommy?"

Tommy, the one with the dice, shaking them, ready to roll, flashed a wicked grin. "I'm 'ere to rob you buggers blind. Hot seven coming up." He rolled and the blue dice came up seven, and with a quick gliding motion of his hand he swept up his winnings.

The one with red hair had his boots off and was massaging his feet. " 'E's a bastard, in't he? A ballbuster, that's what 'e is."

Two bombs hit in rapid succession. The ground trembled and white dust shook from the limestone walls, filling the air like mist. A baby cried. An old man coughed violently, gagging and choking. The women continued with the rosary, their voices swelling with audible anxiety.

The black-haired soldier with the handkerchief around his head drew a pint of whisky from under his shirt, took a swig, and passed it to Rocco. Rocco took a mouthful, letting the liquid lave over his tongue, burning, and felt it warming its way into his stomach.

Moments later the all-clear sounded, and the soldiers went back up. The children too, and most of the old ladies and men. But some, Rocco saw, stayed down. They were living there, with suitcases, and clothes tied in bundles.

He stretched out on one of the bunks, on a thin, straw-stuffed mattress, and closed his eyes. He thought of his mother, who had died long ago, and his father, who was living now with another woman, in Bensonhurst. The last few years, he'd seen his father less and less. There was too much on which they didn't see eye-to-eye, and when he left Brooklyn and went into the service, he simply said good-bye over the phone. His father had been blaming him, criticizing him for making wrong choices. He wanted him to get into construction, where there was good money, but Rocco liked it better on the used-car lot. And when Rocco started the night courses at Brooklyn College, his father thought he should take management and accounting instead of the Poe and the Melville. And he never really took to Theresa Flum, either. He thought Rocco was wasting his time with her. Well, he'd been right about that, and Rocco understood now that he would have been better off if he had listened. Things fall apart, it seemed a law of nature. Two long years she had twisted him around. She'd meant so much to him, and then she went off and got involved with somebody else. It made him so mad he drove off one night, speeding, turning fast, down by Ebbets Field, and crashed the car into a telephone pole.

He still carried her picture in his wallet, a black-and-white taken in a booth at Coney Island, after they'd been swimming. Her hair was wet and clung to her head, making her look solemn, like a nun. She hated that picture, but Rocco held on to it because he found it hard to let go of the past, even the bad times. The car was an old Plymouth, with a big chrome radiator grille. He used to pick her up on Sundays and drive her around. They would park at a spot by Gravesend Bay, and, holding her in his arms, it had seemed to him that life was a blissful neon dream that would never end. He had really liked that car, and felt terrible when he wrecked it. But what he also felt, strangely, was a sense of release, a kind of elation, as if he had really wanted to crash it, and, now that it was done, he was washed clean.

In his mind, as he lay there in the shelter, close to sleep, he wrote to his father. No paper and no pen, just the thoughts, like so many other letters to his father, nothing he would ever put in the mail. "Please send, when you can, cigarettes, coffee, chewing gum, some Mounds Bars, and a can of shoe polish. I liked it when we went to those Dodger games, the few times we went, but why did they always lose? Also, if you can, a fresh change of underwear, I lost everything when they bombed the bordello."

When he woke, he was still there, on the straw-stuffed mattress. Somebody had thrown a blanket over him. His watch showed one, but he didn't know if it was morning or afternoon, and didn't care to ask. Another raid was in progress and the shelter was crowded again, and again the old women gathered at the far end, praying the rosary.

He looked at his watch and still it showed one. It had stopped. He didn't bother to wind it. It was better that way, out of time, outside of it, not knowing if it was day or night. He was pulled back toward sleep and closed his eyes, but it was a strange sleep he had, in and out, hearing the women, then not, then hearing them again, and always the smells, sweat and urine, cologne, clothes slept in night after night, crotch smell and armpit smell, diaper smell, aftershave, Palmolive soap, witch hazel.

Another bomb went off, and he was wrenched awake, thinking, with a sinking sensation, that he was still in the house on Strait Street and the others were all dead in there, under the debris, and the knowledge that he was alive while they were dead filled him with a sense of guilt, as if he'd been in some way responsible. If he had never been there, in the room on the top floor, then, somehow, the bomb might never have hit, and, for better or worse, they might all still be alive. It was illogical, a kind of sorcery, yet he couldn't shake it off, the sense that there was some sort of equation here, an obscure connectedness, which he couldn't solve.

Then a darker thought came slanting in. What if Fingerly wasn't who he said he was? And what if Major Webb was not dead but alive somewhere, waiting for him to report in? But how? Why? How could it be? It was too complicated, and for the moment he was, restlessly, a tangle of what-ifs, doubting, racked by suspicion, yet he saw it for what it was, paranoia plain and simple, wrong thinking, and he didn't want to go that way. But still it haunted: *what if?*

A woman came by, passing out hard biscuits. Later, the same woman, with a man, stood near the spiral stairwell with a cauldron of warm soup, ladling it into aluminum bowls. Rocco thought it must have been hell getting that big pot down all those stairs.

A woman on the bunk beside his was nursing her infant.

"How old?" he asked.

"Four months." She had no stockings on, bare feet in a pair of scuffed black shoes.

Behind a screen was a chair with a hole in it and a bucket underneath. It was that, or you could use the toilet upstairs, in the bar. Rocco let his urine spill out, a steady yellow stream, mingling with the urine of the others who had been there before him. It amused him, how we are, in our waste, all the same. Even German piss was no different. Even the piss of Mussolini. Even the piss of the pilots of the Stukas and the Ju-88s and the Savoia Marchetti 79s. There was an extra bucket off to the side, for when the first bucket got full.

He went back to the bunk and slept, and now he dreamed about Nigg, and Aida with her one leg. She was hitting Nigg over the head with her wooden leg, beating him hard. Fingerly was there too, pumping away at the player piano, and what came out of the piano was not music but smoke.

A boy stood close to him, staring. He thought the boy too was part of the dream, but realized, slowly, that he was real. The boy's face was round and smooth, his eyes large, brown, full of a quiet curiosity. Then, for no apparent reason, he stuck out his tongue, meanly, and ran off toward the far end, where the women were praying. He went partly up the stairs, at the Old Bakery exit, and sat perched on one of the steps, chin in his hands, gazing vacantly.

Rocco studied him through the distance, and then, slowly, recognized him, and went over to talk to him. "You're Joseph, right? You're the boy from the house. You remember me?"

"I remember you," the boy said, not moving from the step.

"Where's your sister?"

"She's . . . somewhere."

"Have you been back to the house?"

"The house was bombed."

"Yes, I know. I was there when it happened."

The boy said nothing, he seemed in a daze.

"Are you all right? Where are you staying now?"

"With my aunt."

"Where's that?"

"Not far."

He was still on the step, sitting, toying with one of his shoelaces, flipping the end of it back and forth.

Rocco put his hand on the boy's knee. "What about your mother, your father? Are they all right?"

The boy looked away, emptily.

"The girls—Julietta and Aida? And Simone?"

Still he said nothing. He seemed to have something important on his mind, which he didn't want to share. Rocco wondered if the bombing of the house had been too much for him and he might simply have lost his senses.

Then he remembered a chocolate bar he'd picked up at Dominic's, still in his shirt pocket. Inside the wrapper it had broken into several pieces.

"Here, I got this for you. You want it?"

The boy looked at it, indifferent, then took it and held it.

"You want to eat it now? Or do you want to save it?"

The boy hesitated. "I think I'll save it."

"That's a good idea," Rocco said.

"They bombed the house. It's all gone, nothing's left."

"I know," Rocco said.

The boy was quiet again, then he stood up. "It's time for me to go," he said, and with a fairly brisk step made his way up the stairs.

Rocco went over to the bucket and passed more urine, then he returned to the bunk. He dreamed of a door he couldn't open, and a car that wouldn't start, and a wilted flower. He dreamed of a goldfish out of its bowl, squirming on the tiled floor of a windowless bathroom.

Five

THE HOUSE
ON WINDMILL STREET

When he woke, he was clammy and cold. In the bunk to his left a woman held a child in her arms, but she was not the same woman who had been there before. "What day is it?" he asked.

It was Sunday.

"Are you sure?"

"Yes, yes. Sunday."

"Afternoon?"

"Morning. But it's almost afternoon."

It took some time for him to absorb this. He tried to remember when he first came down, thinking back to the night when he hit the bars, after the bomb struck the house and the house fell down all around him. He'd been napping, late afternoon, stretched out on the bed—and then the bomb. That was Friday, and now it was Sunday. Saturday he had lost completely, in and out of sleep.

He watched as an old woman wet a handkerchief with water from a jar. She wrung it out, then wiped her face with it. A boy in brown shorts ran a toy truck back and forth, the same boy who'd had the harmonica. Now he had the truck, making truck noises deep in his throat.

Rocco was thinking of Fingerly, wondering if he was alive or dead, and Nigg too, but mostly Fingerly, because Fingerly was in charge, and without him it was not going to be easy. A bomb struck and more white dust shook loose from the limestone, forming a fine mist that settled slowly. Rocco was up, now, on his feet, groping through the crowd, heading for the stone staircase, feeling a need to get out of there, up into the open air. He'd been too long underground. Another bomb struck, and more dust sifted through the air.

He moved quickly up the spiral steps, round and round, ascending the narrow shaft, and with the constant turning and the lack of air he felt dizzy, claustrophobic. Halfway up he paused, listening to the pounding of the guns. Then he pushed on, moving toward the faint light above, and, breathing hard, reached the top and was in the bar again. A few soldiers were slumped in a booth, shirts open, perspiring, with mugs of ale. The air was warm, much warmer than down below, and when he stepped outside onto the street it was warmer still, a wild hot blast of the midday sun. Only then, in the sun, did he realize how cold and dank it had been in the shelter. When he looked up, he saw a Stuka buzzing by, very low.

He turned off Strait Street, onto Nicholas, then up along Old Bakery, littered with blocks of limestone from the collapsed buildings. The air stank with the powderburn smell of spent explosive. He climbed up a hill of rubble, and went down the other side. For some distance the street was clear, and he moved along briskly. Bombs slammed into the dockyards across the harbor, and the pom-pom guns sent up their fierce barrage.

Ahead, he faced more wreckage and another high mound to cross. He thought of turning back and cutting over to Kingsway, but continued on, making his way up over the rubble. And then, as he came down on the other side, he saw, up ahead, a girl walking, casual, giving no attention to the raid, making her way, like himself, through the clogged, debris-laden street.

There was a freedom in the way she moved, a confidence and self-assurance. She paused to look up as yet another Stuka swept by, this one trailing a plume of black smoke from its fuselage. Then she looked back, over her shoulder, and saw him coming along half a block behind her. She lingered, gazing steadily, then turned and continued on, her long black hair, clasped by a silver barrette, falling loose and wanton over her shoulders, all the way down to her waist. Her skirt flowed lazily, folding over her calves and thighs. It made his blood jump. He supposed that she too had come up out of some dark hole, craving sunlight, wanting to move and be alive, and he slowed his gait, not wanting to catch up too soon. The air shook with the roar of the antiaircraft barrage, but he no longer heard it: it was background, out of focus, an untuned annoyance at the margin of his senses.

He lagged behind, watching as she struggled up a hill of fractured limestone, and when she reached the top, she paused and looked back again. Rocco came to a stop, and the two of them stood motionless, gazing through the distance. Then she went on and disappeared down the farther side of the mound.

He hurried on, feeling a vague anxiety, thinking he might lose her: out of sight, she might turn off into a doorway and he'd never find her. He went quickly up the pile of wreckage, and, reaching the top, was relieved to see her still there, ahead of him. She slowed to look at a bureau that lay broken, on its side, studying it as she passed. And then, in a soundless moment, the air weirdly quiet, something happened. As she walked along, she was suddenly on fire, her body a long tongue of flame.

He froze, thinking, in a kind of panic, that a shell had struck, an incendiary. Then he thought it must be the sun, the bright glare reflecting off broken glass in the debris. Her hair was ablaze. Her arms, her legs, walking and on fire. And then, as he stood there, rooted, the flame died away and, mysteriously, she was herself again, moving ahead through the rubble.

It was Malta, Malta again was doing this to him, making him see things that weren't there. He had a feeling he'd passed through some sort of gate, an invisible portal, and his life would never be the same.

She walked at a quicker pace now, and he followed, not rushing, making no effort to catch up, simply following, watching: her arms, legs, the hair long and black, the movement of her hips as she made her way through the debris, weaving left, then right, lithe and agile.

All around them the air thundered with the attack, bombs pounding into the docks, and he saw now what the pattern was. The planes went into their dive over the dockyard area, on the other side of the harbor, by Senglea and Vittoriosa. They screamed down and released their bombs, then, pulling out of the dive, crossed the harbor and flew over the Valletta peninsula. If the guns at St. Michael's and St. Angelo didn't get them, the guns at Valletta had a go, and if the Valletta guns missed, there were still the guns at Fort Manoel and Fort Tigné. Coming out of the power dive, the Stukas were slow and vulnerable, quite a few got shot up and they ditched in the water.

Another Stuka passed over, low, and Rocco looked up. It was damaged, he saw holes in the wings. But it was still up there, turning north, heading back to Sicily.

When he started walking again, she was far ahead but moving slowly, giving him time to catch up. At the top of Old Bakery, by St. John's Cavalier, she paused and looked back, then crossed over to Old Mint, and again, on the corner, she looked back, careful not to lose him, and made her way onto Windmill, a short street, only a couple of blocks long, leading toward the bastions overlooking Marsamxett Harbour. Windmill had been bombed, but nothing as bad as Old Bakery.

As he came around the corner, he saw she had stopped in front of a building damaged in a previous raid. Part of the roof was gone. She seemed to know the house, seemed to know where she was. She glanced back at him, and when she saw he was still following, she turned and went inside.

When he reached the place, he hesitated, looking it over. Multiple cracks ran across the front wall and several of the stone blocks had been dislodged.

Inside, she stood waiting by a staircase, a short distance from him. It was the closest they had been, and he saw how lovely she was: her dark eyebrows, and large blue eyes, the long slope of the jaw, and full, sensual lips. There was no furniture in the house, only a few smashed chairs. Some of the walls were down, but most of the debris had already been cleared out.

She stood there at the foot of the stairs looking at him, then she turned and went slowly up. He watched her go, the hem of her skirt dancing lightly off her legs. She was almost at the next floor before he started up.

After the first flight, there was another, and when she reached the top, she turned and looked down, waiting for him. Her face bore a quiet seriousness, her eyes suffused with a soft intensity.

He followed her down a hallway and through a door, into a room where there was no ceiling and no roof, just the four walls, badly cracked, and above, the blue sky. There was a bare mattress on the floor, and against a wall a table with only three legs, and near it, on the floor, a broken lamp. Sunlight reached in, touching an edge of the mattress. A closet door stood open, nothing inside, just chunks of broken plaster.

She turned to him, her eyes sultry, lips parted, an oily film of perspiration covering her face and arms.

They stood a moment, not talking, just looking. Then, feverishly, they were at each other, embracing and kissing hungrily, in a kind of delirium. He caught a wild, reckless scent from her, seaweed and thyme, lilac and mint.

They went down on the mattress, and she bit at his ears. He was thinking ocean, sky, wild grass, and for a moment, a blind, dazzling duration, it was as if he were in freefall, hurtling down through different zones of fragrance and smell, through lilac, leather, sweat, descending through layers of time.

It was not until they had worn themselves out and were lying side by side, exhausted, that he realized the guns had stopped and the raid was over. The sun had slanted away from the mattress and formed an oddly shaped geometrical pattern on the wall, by the three-legged table. Above, the sky was hazy from the oil fires at the docks.

"There's no roof," he said.

She looked at the sky. "It's better without a roof."

A few wispy clouds drifted by.

"You've been here before?"

"I had a friend who lived here," she said. "Before the bombing." She spoke with an accent, a shade too precise in the way she shaped her words, yet softly musical.

"Is your friend all right?"

"She wasn't hurt."

"But the others? Not so lucky?"

"No."

"So why do you come back?"

"We used to play in this room. When we were young."

"Right here?"

"There was a radio. We listened to the American songs. We talked about what we wanted for ourselves when we grew up."

"What did you want for yourself?"

"Oh, we used to dream. I wanted to meet a foreigner and go away to another country. I thought it would be clever to be married to a banker and live in Switzerland, in the mountains."

"I'm not a banker," he said.

She laughed. "Bankers have a boring life. I'm glad I outgrew that."

A bird flew past. Then another. She nestled close to him, and made a low humming sound.

A whole flock of pigeons circled above. Disappeared, and then returned. They circled again, then descended through the open roof, settling down all around them—on the broken bureau, on the three-legged table, on the chunks of broken plaster. They filled the closet.

"I want to be one of them," she said. "Wouldn't it be wonderful? To fly?"

Two Hurricanes passed over, low, and the roar of the engines scared the pigeons off through the shattered roof, a burst of wings, but one stayed behind, dark, with orange eyes in a somber gray head. It walked full circle around the mattress, then settled down by the three-legged table.

"Silly bird," Rocco said. "Crazy, brain-damaged pigeon."

"Never talk to a bird that way," she said.

"You know this bird? This bird is a personal friend?"

"I just think it's better to be polite."

"Am I not polite?"

"Did I say you weren't?"

"Yes, something like that."

She was roughly the same age as he, maybe younger, yet there was something about her that made her seem older, something in her eyes, her manner. He was taller than she was, though not by much, and her skin was lighter. She ran her fingers across his chest, touching the crop of dark hair there. She touched his eyebrows, and his nose. He had good strong hands, worker's hands, but gentle. His face grubby, in need of a shave.

She'd grown up speaking Maltese and learned English at school, she said, from nuns who had learned English from other nuns who got their way of talking from the British wives of the British businessmen who had settled in Sliema and St. Julian's.

"Nuns?" he said. "You had nuns? I had nuns."

He'd had them in grammar school. One, with a ruddy face like raw meat, threw chalk at him, with good aim, hitting him more than once on the head, and another, with a long nose like a pen, stood him in the corner. But one— the pretty one with long lashes—had liked him, she made him the flag boy and he ran the flag up the flagpole every morning in the small ragged garden in front of the three-story wooden schoolhouse, and took it down when school let out in the afternoon.

"They were good to you? The nuns?"

He shrugged, and for a while they just looked at each other, gazing, his dark brown eyes into her blue eyes. Then they were touching again, she touching him and he touching her, a slowsweet arousal, like awakening out of sleep, and again, eagerly, they were at each other. But this time it was different, more relaxed, less frenzied, and yet, oddly, more intense, more focused and precise, as if they were musicians, playing the same music over again but doing it now with a special verve, a tightened brilliance in the phrasing and modulation, a sweetly heightened tonality that comes, now and then, as a welcome surprise.

She noticed the pigeon was gone. "Do you think we embarrassed him?"

"I think we gave him something to tell his friends about."

She was up, off the mattress, climbing into her clothes. "I hate the bombing," she said, "I hate the war."

"Does anyone love it?"

"Yes, some do, they love the shooting and the killing." She looked at her watch. "I'm going to be late," she said fretfully.

"For what?"

"I have a life, you know. There are things I must do."

"Tell me your name," he said, reaching for his clothes.

"Does it matter?"

"I think so. Yes."

"It does? Then tell me your name first."

He told her his name.

She considered it, as if thinking it over, as if his name were a hat she was try- ing on, to see if it fit. "It's a nice name," she said, "I like that name. Rocco Raven."

"What do you like about it?"

"It reminds me, somehow, of a place where there are rocks and trees, and birds, and a waterfall."

"My name isn't a waterfall."

"No, but it flows."

"Are there waterfalls on Malta?"

"We don't even have a river."

"Tell me your name."

"I don't think so," she said. "Maybe tomorrow."

"Where?"

"Here," she said, and she started to walk away, out of the room and down the stairs, moving quickly. "But only if you are very lucky," she said, glancing back.

He slipped into his pants and followed her down, pulling his shirt on as he went. "If I'm lucky? You mean if you're lucky. Do you come here often?"

"I told you, I had a friend. We listened to the radio."

She was all the way down now, onto the street, and he caught up to her, tucking in his shirt.

"Hey," he said, "you can't just go away like this. Tell me where you live."

"You mustn't follow. If you follow me, I won't come back."

"That isn't fair," he said.

"I know, I know. Life is unfair. But maybe tomorrow."

He stopped following her. "Maybe not," he called out. "Did you think of that? Maybe I'm the one who won't be here."

"Then we shall see," she said, tossing a smile over her shoulder as she walked away, and he thought maybe that was how it was on Malta, the girls were easy but they liked to tease, they liked to keep you guessing. And the other thought he had was that girls everywhere, perhaps, were like that, they knew how to tantalize, it was in the blood, the thing inside them that made them what they were. With a body like hers, he thought, so supple, so well put to- gether, she could go ahead and tease all she wanted.

He was learning the differences among the planes. The dive-bombers with one engine were the Stukas, the Ju-87s. The ones with two engines were the Ju-88s. The bombers that bombed from high up, with three engines and rotten aim, were the Italian Savoia Marchetti 79s. And the fighters that strafed with machine guns and cannons were the Messerschmitt 109s. One had nearly killed him when he came in at Luqa, on Tuesday, and he knew he would never forget that.

He wondered, and continued to wonder. Life was so short. Did he like her? Really like her? Did he want to see her again? A shave, he needed a shave. And a bath. He walked down Old Bakery, whistling softly, some old tune that came back to him, he couldn't remember the words.

The Times of Malta—April 12, 1942

HEAVY RAIDS ON NAZI WAR FACTORIES
Day Sweeps Over Northern France

HITLER AND HIS STAFF AT LOGGERHEADS

BURMA: MAJOR JAPANESE OFFENSIVE AGAINST CHINESE FLANK

U.S. BOMBERS RAID PHILIPPINES
First Blow Struck in MacArthur's "Liberation" Pledge

THE MALTA FRONT: RAF FIGHTERS ATTACK RAIDERS
2 ME109s destroyed
1 JU87 probably destroyed
3 JU88s damaged

SALE OF POULTRY
The Director of Agriculture notifies that the Government Farm has the following purebred mature stud cocks for sale:
3 purebred Black Minorca Cocks at £1 each
3 purebred Rhode Island Red Cocks at £1 each
1 American Mammoth Bronze Turkey at £3

HOCK'S EAGLE BAR & RESTAURANT, Old Mint, Valletta, reopening today. The public invited.

LOST between Sliema and Rabat, hubcap of a Rolls-Royce Phantom II. Finder will be handsomely rewarded.

PERSONS having articles in the Auction Stores of the late FRANK A. COHEN are requested to notify the wife of the deceased at 11 Windmill Street, Valletta, not later than April 30th, 1942, after which date Mrs. Cohen shall dispose of all articles irrespective of any previous arrangements with her husband.

IN MEMORIAM. In loving memory of Joseph Tonna who lost his life one year ago, April 9, 1941, at the early age of 17 years. Gone but remembered forever by his mother and father.

Six

A JUKEBOX
FOR ZARB ADAMI

After wandering about for a while, Rocco stopped off at a police station to check the casualty lists, looking for information on Fingerly and Nigg. There was nothing. He went over to Royal Army Headquarters and was bounced from desk to desk, but finally found a Maltese woman, a civilian, middle-aged, who had census files on the non-Commonwealth people on the island. She had never heard of I-3, but was determined to be helpful.

"Fingerly? On Merchants Street? Bombed Friday last, and you want to know if he's dead or in hospital?"

She put down the apple she'd been eating and scanned with dazzling speed through a folder she took from a file drawer. She found a Fuggerman, a Funnly, a Zwingerman, a Dingerly, a Fingerson, a Fangly, and a Fudge. But no Fingerly.

"Webb," Rocco said. "Major Webb. Could you look him up?"

"Who's he?"

"He was the one in charge, the one I was supposed to report to. He was killed before I got here."

There was no Webb.

"Try Nigg. Try Maroon."

But nothing, they were all unknown.

"I guess even I'm an unknown," Rocco said.

"You are," she said pleasantly, with an inquiring look. "I have no idea who you are."

He asked about getting transport off the island, but she wasn't encouraging. He could go out on a Wellington, to Gibraltar, but the waiting list was so long, the war would probably be over before his turn came up. A week ago they'd sent someone out on a submarine, an American reporter, but it went down and all hands were lost.

"Is there a place I can get coffee?"

"Two flights up and off to your right," she said. "It's only tea and no sugar, but they have terrific scones."

When he left the building, he went out to the City Gate, and after some asking around, he found out which of the buses would take him to Dominic's, in St. Julian's, where Fingerly had brought him, his first night on Malta. The bus was crowded and slow, all of its windows blown out, and there was some walking to do when he got off. He spoke to the bartender and the maître d', and a few waiters, asking about Fingerly and Nigg. One of the waiters thought he'd seen Nigg a day or two earlier, though he wasn't sure. The bartender was certain he'd seen Fingerly. "The American officer," he said, remembering. Yet when he described him, he mentioned gray eyes, pale gray, but Fingerly's were brown, dark brown, and Rocco went away disappointed.

He slept that night in the shelter under the Gut, and the next morning, toward ten, after a slice of stale bread and a can of juice, he headed over to the bombed-out house on Windmill Street, up to the room on the top floor, and found everything as it had been: the mattress, the broken lamp, the broken bureau, the table with three legs. She'd said she would be back, but he had his doubts. He thought he might never see her again.

Through the hole in the roof he looked at the sky and saw nothing, no planes, no clouds. Not even any pigeons. He went back down onto the street and walked to the corner of Old Bakery. Here the damage wasn't too terrible, but at the far end, where the street descended toward St. Elmo's, it was all rubble. He smoked a cigarette, then went back up, disappointed, thinking she wouldn't come. And why should she? It was a war, a siege, easy come and easy go.

He stretched out on the mattress, shaded from the sun, but the sun was edging over and would soon be on him. He thought about Fingerly, wondering if he was really dead. And the others, on Strait Street. Strange, the way the boy Joseph had reacted in the shelter, not talking. Nothing about his parents, nothing about anyone in the house. A few planes flew over, low. Hurricanes. They were the old workhorses, sturdy but out of date. A 109 could knock down a Hurricane, and a Spitfire could knock down a 109. Rocco knew that, he'd heard the talk. There weren't enough Spitfires on Malta, that was the problem, and without them, the island would go under. How lunatic it all was. Not so long ago he was home, working at the used-car lot, taking everything for granted. Buses, trolleys, taxis, stores full of anything you needed. But here there were bombers, day and night, and he wondered if he could handle it, the noise, the stink of oil burning, the sirens, the wreckage. And now, too, there was this girl, with the elusive smile and the silver barrette in her hair, who wouldn't tell him her name, and she was part of it, part of the confusion and uncertainty. He could handle the bombers, maybe, if he put his mind to it, but was he ready, really ready, for her?

A tugboat moaned in the harbor. Then, from nearby, on the street, a tinkling sound, a bell on a goat. Laughter. A baby cried. A dog barked. A woman called to her children. And then, improbably, as in some sort of dream, she was there, coming up the stairs. "I'm late, I know," she said. "Did you think I would never come?" She stood over him, blocking the sun, her shadow falling across his face, her hair radiant, streaks of black fire.

"That's what I thought," he said.

"Well, here I am," she said, letting herself down onto the mattress. "Are you angry with me?"

He didn't say he was not.

She had a hand on him, inside his shirt. "Rocco Raven," she said, musing on his name as if it were a polished stone she'd picked up on the beach. She tilted her head with a wry smile. "You want me to go away? Is that what you want?"

He studied her eyes, the soft angles of her face, trying to figure what it was that was different about her. It was the lipstick. Yesterday there hadn't been any, but today the deep luscious red. And the dress, smooth and silken, clinging to her body in the right places, pink roses on a field of black.

"You like it?" She got up and showed it off, running her hands down her sides, across her hips.

"Come back," he said.

"No, no, not today. I can't."

"Yes, you can."

"I can't, really. I have to make a delivery, and then some other things."

"What other things?"

"Come with me," she said. "I have a car."

"Where?"

"Up the street, by the gate. I have to go to Marsaxlokk. We'll stop on the way and get you some clothes. You're a mess."

His only clothes were the clothes he'd been wearing when the brothel was bombed, as he lay napping, dreaming of roses, lace, and luminous pearls. The jacket was torn, the crease long gone from the pants, buttons missing from the shirt, and plaster dust so imbedded that the khaki seemed a dingy shade of white.

"You don't have a car," he said.

Almost nobody on Malta drove any more, unless you were a doctor, or in the government, or with the military. Horses were back on the street again, wagons, and the horse-drawn *karrozzins*. A lot of bicycles.

"Yes, yes, a car," she said, "it's my cousin Zammit's."

He was up and following her, down the stairs and out of the house, over to Kingsway, heading for the City Gate. Some of the shops were still open, a chemist, a florist, but most were closed and boarded up, out of stock, nothing to sell, many of them wrecked by the bombs. On the corner of Strait and Ordnance, people were lined up for kerosene, getting it from the same vendor Rocco had seen before, on Merchants.

The car was outside the City Gate. "This?" Rocco said, giving a low whistle. "This is yours?"

It wasn't a car, it was a hearse, and not just a hearse, but a pink hearse, an old Studebaker dating from the early 1930s.

"It's not mine," she said.

"I know, your cousin Zammit's. What's that inside? A coffin?"

She laughed. "Does it look like a coffin?"

He took a closer look.

"It's a jukebox," she said. "Zammit makes them. I'm bringing it to a bar in Marsaxlokk. Come, you'll enjoy the ride."

Rocco studied the jukebox through the window. "He made this? Your cousin?"

"That's what he does, he makes jukeboxes."

"He has a factory?"

"Oh, no, no, there's no jukebox factory on Malta. It's just Zammit, he works in the house. He used to be a repairman, he could fix anything. But he loves jukeboxes, so now, with the war, with nothing coming in, no jukeboxes from America, he makes jukeboxes of his own. He's very clever, Zammit is."

"Where is Marsaxlokk?"

"Not far, you will see."

Rocco had never traveled in a hearse before. It was solid, comfortable, with good springs, in good shape for its age. The speedometer showed a hundred and twenty thousand miles. The engine hummed—a smooth, steady ride, you could hardly feel the road.

"It belonged to Silvio Sforza," she said. "They were undertakers for three generations. In Malta, the horse-drawn hearse is still preferred, but Sforza was very progressive. When he died, there was no son to inherit the business, so the widow sold everything. The hearse was old. Zammit fixed it up and had it blessed by a priest, to ward off the evil spirits. And just to be sure, he painted it pink. Isn't it wonderful? All hearses should be pink."

"Where do you get the gas?"

"From the Hampshire Regiment. Zammit made a jukebox for them, for their barracks, so they give us petrol. That's how life is on Malta."

They drove out through Floriana, past the arcades of St. Anne Street and the arch of the Portes des Bombes, then down through Ħamrun, through densely populated areas, past churches and rows of three- and four-story housing built from honey-colored blocks of limestone, the globigerina stone of Malta.

Her name was Melita, Melita Azzard.

"I saw a street named Melita—somewhere. Yes?"

"Oh, many streets. When the Romans were here, their name for the island was *Melita*. It means honey, the honey of the honey bee."

"And *Malta* comes from a Phoenician word that means woman."

"Who told you that?"

"An old man I ran into. Nardu Camilleri."

"It doesn't mean woman. It means a harbor, a safe haven."

"That's what he said too. And he said a harbor is a woman."

"He was crazy."

"Hey," he said breezily, "life is crazy. Love is crazy."

"No, love is not crazy, but it's always, you know, a mistake." There was a loneliness in her tone, as if, in the past, she'd been disappointed.

From Ħamrun they moved out through Paola and on to Tarxien, and there she brought him to a tailor, a distant cousin of a distant cousin. "He does very fine work and he has good fabric from before the war. It's impossible to get cloth anymore. The shops in Valletta, most of them are out of business."

The tailor was a quiet man, sixtyish. He measured Rocco for a new uniform, holding pins in his mouth as he worked with the tape measure. The color of the cloth was a shade off the official khaki, but who on Malta would notice—or care?

In a back room he had some double-breasted suits, and Melita insisted

Rocco get one, because the new uniform wouldn't be ready for a while and the one he was wearing needed a cleaning. Rocco resisted the suits; they were baggy and made him look like a down-at-the-heels native.

"Does he have any slacks?"

"He does, but on Malta you need a suit."

"I think I should try some slacks."

"But first the suit. Do you want the gray or the blue?"

"Are we having a quarrel?"

"A disagreement maybe."

In cardboard boxes, there were socks, handkerchiefs, underwear. "He's giving good prices," Melita whispered in Rocco's ear. "These are wonderful buys. It's not like shopping on the Strada Reale, where they don't even have anything to sell anymore."

Still, the bill was hefty. Melita bargained the tailor down in Maltese, and Rocco, paying with the money Fingerly had given him, realized he had better find Fingerly fast, because in no time at all he would be broke. He wore the slacks and the blue sportshirt, and carried the suit, the gray that Melita chose, which he'd agreed to but only after a struggle, and left his uniform to be cleaned.

Below Tarxien, on both sides of the road were open fields crossed by low fieldstone walls, the fields green with vegetables. Amid the furrows, antiaircraft batteries were in place, surrounded by sandbags. The roadside was ragged with clover and wild roses, and large clumps of cactus.

"It's prickly pear," she said, pointing to the cactus. "See the red fruit growing from the lobes? It's good, good to eat."

There were soldiers everywhere, British and Maltese—on the road, walking, and on bikes, in trucks, moving from one town to the next. They sat in doorways, eating from tin cans.

"There's talk of an invasion," Melita said, "maybe this month, maybe next. I don't think so, though. I think they are just going to bomb and bomb."

They were halfway along to Marsaxlokk. The road ran straight for a while, and up ahead a truck rumbled along, full of soldiers, laughing, having a good time, waving at the hearse, no shirts on, just helmets and pants. After a brief commotion, they hung someone down off the back of the truck, dangling him by his ankles, his head barely a foot off the road.

Melita tooted angrily. "They can't wait for the Germans to kill them, they have to hurry and kill each other."

They pulled the soldier back in, and he squatted there at the rear of the truck, laughing, gesturing at the hearse, mocking. It had been a joke, letting himself be hung out that way, horsing around, scaring the traffic. Melita put her arm out the window and, tooting again, held her hand high, giving him the fig.

"Is that what they taught you in school?"

"That and some other things."

"It must have been some school you went to."

"They taught us the history of Malta in Maltese, and British history in English. We read Dickens, Jane Austen, and Ernest Hemingway, though the nuns worried about Hemingway, too much sex and drinking."

"And they made you go to church every Sunday."

"I still do. Don't you? Oh, you should go, you should, it's no good not to go."

Before the war she had taken courses in Renaissance art and had hoped to do more studying in Florence, but money was short and it hadn't worked out for her, so she took a job at the law courts, and at nights she picked up stenography. Then the courts were bombed and there was no job for her, so she worked with her cousin Zammit, helping with the jukeboxes. She got to be so good at it she could go out to the bars and dance halls and make minor repairs, when their jukeboxes broke down. She was still interested in art, though, and was hoping to find work after the war at one of the museums.

"Say something in Maltese."

She became self-conscious, shy. She spoke a few sentences.

"Again," he asked. "More."

And again she spoke, a rhythmic combination of hard and soft sounds, weirdly musical.

She looked at him pertly. "Now tell me what I said."

"It was poetry. Right? You thought I wouldn't know?"

She rocked her head from side to side, coyly. "What I said is a secret, a secret wish. And I will never tell."

She took the turnoff for Marsaxlokk and headed down toward the bay. "If there is an invasion, they think it will come here. This is where the Turks came ashore, in the Great Siege, right here. It's the same spot where Napoleon landed."

She made some quick turns, descending through a village of stone houses down to the harbor and the promenade lined with palm trees and oleander. Then she cut in, away from the water, onto a side street, and after a few more turns pulled up in front of a bar, a small, shabby place between a butchershop (closed—no meat) and a pharmacy, which was open, because there was still a plentiful supply of Mercurochrome, though aspirins and foot plasters were hard to come by. Above the narrow doorway hung a red-and-white sign, THE JAVELIN, with an old javelin suspended below.

The bar was dim and uninviting, owned by Zarb Adami, a short, dour man with small dark eyes cloudy with disappointment. On a wall, a picture of King George, and a despondent-looking Madonna. The name, "The Javelin," was in honor of one of the destroyers in the fleet. The theory was that if you named your bar after a ship in the garrison, you could expect the ship's sailors to come to your bar when the ship was in port. But it hadn't worked out that way for Zarb Adami. Whether *Javelin* was in port or not, his only customers were a handful of dingy locals—broom pushers and shabby old men—grumbling over their beer. That's why he was investing in the jukebox: to bring in more business.

He went out to the hearse with his son, a boy of fifteen, and with Rocco's help they carried in the jukebox, and Rocco couldn't help but feel he was handling a coffin. There was a difficult maneuver at the door and Melita agonized, telling them to move left, move right, and hold, hold—fearful they might drop it and smash it to pieces. They set it against the wall where the Madonna hung in a blue frame, and Zarb Adami had to get up on a chair to raise the Madonna so the jukebox could fit underneath.

The box was impressive. Zammit had made it, ingeniously, from scraps of broken furniture and secondhand mechanical parts. Melita plugged it in and the colored lights came on. There was a glass window near the top so you could watch the records as they played. The sides of the box and the lower portion of the front were ornamented with stained glass, lit from within. The inner lights could be set to differing levels of intensity and could be made to blink on and off. The wooden parts were of bird's-eye maple. Melita herself had salvaged the wood from a dumpsite where they put the rubble when they cleaned up after the bombings. She went from dumpsite to dumpsite, picking up splintered doors, smashed bureaus, broken chests, and she brought these home to Zammit, who cut them into usable pieces and fitted them together into sturdy panels. The stained glass, too, she picked up at the dumps, from the bombed-out churches, small sections that Zammit pieced together cleverly—fragments of red and blue glass, yellow or green, with, sometimes, the eye of a saint showing, or a hand, or a toe.

"Isn't it wonderful?" she said excitedly to Zarb Adami. "Don't you love it? Look how it changes everything, how it brightens the room. You should be very proud. It's going to bring you many, many customers. Wait and see!"

"I hate it," Zarb Adami said bitterly.

Melita was stunned. "No, you don't hate it," she said, unable to believe what she heard. "You can't. How could you say such a thing?"

"I never wanted it. It's too big, too noisy. And it costs, it costs!"

"But if you never wanted it, why on earth did you order it?"

He ran his fingers through his hair, desperately. "It's because of that *idjota* across the street, up at the corner, at the Jackal. When he bought new bar stools, I had to buy new bar stools. When he bought a radio, I bought a radio. When he changed the price for beer, I had to change my price. Now I stand by my door and all day I see them going up to his place because he put in a jukebox, such a crowd he has."

"You don't like it?" Melita asked. "You really don't want it?"

"In my heart," Zarb Adami said, "I despise it."

"Then I'll take it back," she said. "Zammit will sell it to someone else."

Zarb Adami, hands in his pockets, stood facing the jukebox in a state of crisis. She had released him, he was free. But it was not a freedom he wanted, because he had no desire once again to go through the agony of having to make a decision.

"No," he blurted, after a long silence, "I bought it, I'll keep it. It's delivered and done."

Melita put her hand on his arm. "Believe me," she said, "you will not be unhappy. Zammit's jukeboxes are the best. I know what he has, at the Jackal, he has an old Seeburg from a secondhand dealer in Valletta, who got it from somebody in Palermo. When the sailors see Zammit's box, they will all want to be here. Even you will get to like it, it will be like an old friend. When you come in and open up for the day, it will be as if you have someone from your own family here with you, to keep you company. And when the music plays—ah, that's the best. It will give you a lift. Believe me, you are doing the right thing. It will change your life."

Zarb Adami was subdued. "Yes, yes," he said without conviction, "you are right, in my head I know you are right."

She showed him how to adjust the sound, and how to empty the coin box. She showed him how to change the needle when it needed changing, and how to put new records in, if he wanted new records. The recordings were mostly American. There were a few old Maltese favorites, and some patriotic British pieces by Gracie Fields, but mainly it was the American big bands and American vocalists. Nobody wanted German or Italian recordings, because of the war. People who owned them threw them away. They were pulled out of the jukeboxes, in anger, and tossed into the trash.

Zarb Adami plugged in a coin, made a selection, and the platter swung into position. As the music came on, Melita made some adjustments, increasing the bass and lowering the volume, making the sound right for the room, not too loud, not too soft. This dim, depressing, beer-smelling room, with the dark, sticky varnish on the bar and on the wainscotting, and the same dark, sticky varnish on the three small round tables and the four stools at the bar—the place was too small for a jukebox, no room at all to move around. Even the sound of Harry James on the trumpet, "I Don't Want to Walk Without You," was not enough to banish the gloom and the claustrophobia. Put in brighter lights, she thought. Paint it white and fill it with flowers, let in fresh air, get rid of the smell. But how could she tell him any of this when even she, if she were a sailor, would never risk a malt here because no matter what was done to liven the place up it would still be dark and dismal because the darkness flowed from Zarb Adami himself. It oozed out of him, he bequeathed it to the walls and the floor and everything around him.

He kept feeding coins into the jukebox, wanting to hear every record, wanting to be sure everything was working properly before he signed the invoice, acknowledging receipt.

Melita grabbed hold of the boy, Zarb Adami's son, and danced with him, a slow rocking movement. The boy had wooden feet. Drawn in close, feeling her breasts against his chest, he blushed, his cheeks and ears flamed scarlet.

"Dance," she said. "It's easy, see? You mean the girls haven't grabbed you yet, you never danced?"

"Leave him alone," Zarb Adami said. "Can't you see the boy is too young?"

Glenn Miller came on, "I've Got a Gal in Kalamazoo," and she grabbed hold of Rocco for a quick, lively jitterbug. There was no room at all, like dancing in a closet, yet somehow they carved a space for themselves. Rocco, into the rhythm, knocked over a chair behind him, and Zarb Adami was not pleased at all.

They danced through "Moonlight Becomes You" and "Yesterday's Roses," and Woody Herman's cut of "Blues in the Night." Zarb Adami, looking on, had a bewildered, tortured look in his tired eyes. There was nothing happy in his gaze, no sense that life, for him, would ever be anything but worse than it was.

And suddenly, then, the awareness was upon him that the boy, his son, was gone. Rocco and Melita saw it too, felt it, like a news flash: the boy had run off, up and out of the bar, impossible to say where, never bothering to say good-bye, and even Zarb Adami understood, when he saw he was gone, that he was gone for good.

The bleakness in his eyes was pitiful. Rocco wanted to do something for him, wanted to say something, to help somehow, because he understood that look of complete aloneness. But there was nothing to be said or done, because it was clear that Zarb Adami had created his own loneliness a long time ago and was determined to share it with no one.

* * *

In the hearse, on the way back, Melita ate a pretzel that Zarb Adami had given her. "What a peculiar man," she said. "He hates jukeboxes. Despises them!" The pretzel was delicious, she hadn't had one since before the war and she wondered where Zarb Adami had got it, in which back room or underground den of which black market. "And what about you?" she said to Rocco. "Did you hate Zammit's jukebox too?"

"No, I liked it," he said, then added hesitantly, "Too much stained glass."

"You don't like the stained glass?"

"Reminds me of church."

"But this is Malta. Church is very important for us. St. Paul was ship-wrecked here, and we've been Catholic ever since. Come to Santa Venera with me and you'll meet Zammit. Do you want to meet him?"

"You live with him?"

"I live in Qormi, in a room above a pharmacy. Zammit has no space in his house for anything but jukeboxes. You will like him."

"How old is he?"

"Oh—old, over forty I think."

"Forty isn't old."

"For Zammit it is. Wait till you meet him."

"I don't want to meet him."

"Yes you do."

But he didn't. It was a sour note for him, the thought of meeting one of her relatives.

"Then some other time," she said, and for a while they drove on in silence.

"I think you're unhappy," she said. "Why are you unhappy?"

"I'm not unhappy."

"But you are. If you don't want to meet Zammit, then I think you must be unhappy."

"Does that make sense?"

"Should it? Why must everything make sense?"

She was a good dancer. He wanted to remember that and never let it go. Dancing with her in that lackluster dive—so good on her feet, the way she moved, the weave and flow of her body. Magical.

She turned off the main road and headed east, toward the sea, on a narrow dirt trail, a cloud of yellowish-red dust swirling behind them. "There's a cove I want you to see, a pretty spot, by the water."

"I thought you were in a hurry to get back."

"I am, there's too much to do. But it can wait."

They passed terraced farms, and fields purple with clover. A few palm trees. The rough, bumpy trail brought them to a spot where there was a massive growth of big-lobed cactus. She slowed, taking the car around, and what spread out before them, on the far side of the cactus, was a gentle curve of land, rock-strewn, and the glistening sea.

"You like it?"

He liked it, the low insistent waves lapping against the shore.

"Are you glad I brought you here?"

He was glad she'd brought him.

"Make love to me," she said.

It surprised him. "Here? Now?"

She leaned into him, her lips on his, and he felt her softness. Then, playful, she broke away and climbed into the back of the hearse, and he followed.

There was a blanket to lie on, it had been under the jukebox.

"Love is better in strange places," she said.

She pressed close to him again, quick and urgent, wanting him, and he followed her lead, turning where she turned, moving as she moved. He wondered how many coffins had been there, in that space—coffins of oak, pine, maple, coffins of copper and steel—how many had made the trip in this hearse, this box on wheels. Were they still here, somehow, the dead, with their memories, lingering?

She closed her eyes, and as she moved beneath him, he saw the moisture gathering at her pores, and as her fingers pressed into his back, he thought that even if the planes came and bombs fell, nothing could touch her, because, in her quiet, mysterious way, she wasn't even herself, she was all of the dead who were waiting to live again in the sun, and she was the flowers too, the flowers that had gone with them, carnations and roses, and heavenly honeysuckle. She turned, and moaned, and then, out of the long, sweet, spicy flavor, he heard her small sudden laughter, soft and nibbling, as if, after the onslaught of her passion, she saw it now for what it was—a fit, a seizure, a mere flash of madness, and yet, despite its being only that, a simple trick of the glands, she knew it was the glittering best thing that could have happened for her that day, the best she could have hoped for or imagined.

"It's such a wonderfully silly thing, making love," she said. "Are you angry, that it made me laugh?"

He wasn't angry, he was glad. He liked the dimple at the tip of her chin, the way it deepened when she smiled.

She became thoughtful, dreamy. "Do you think the dead are all around us, watching?"

"The dead are really dead," he said.

"Oh no," she said, "never think that, they are never dead. Don't you feel them, don't you sense they are always around, looking and remembering? Don't you know how jealous they are?"

They left the hearse and strolled along the cove, wading in the water, then she led him up a path, onto a knoll, where they had a far view of the shoreline, and they settled down in the grass.

An air raid developed, a small one, a few Stukas going for the airfield at Takali. They could see them in the distance. The Stukas were quickly in and out, diving, dropping the bomb load, then peeling off and heading for home. One came low across the island, on its way out, seaward. Its shadow passed over them. Then came another, and a third, the three rising over the water, turning back toward Sicily. In a matter of moments, the sky was clear and the antiaircraft guns fell silent.

"How boring," she said. "These Germans, all they know is to bomb and bomb." They were in the grass, idle, savoring the sudden quiet after the bombing run, the dreamy warmth of the sun. Amazing, the shifts of mood and tempo, because of the raids. From serene to desperate, and now, with the planes gone, it was peaceful again.

Then, behind them, at a distance, the sound of a single plane approaching. The engine groaning, then sputtering, and still they didn't look, but when it went dead, they turned and saw the plane high up, falling, a black silhouette, plunging. When they first saw it, it was behind them, but when it came down it was in front of them and to the right, crashing into the rocks along the coast, a red roar, a column of smoke making a scar in the sky.

They watched, riveted, and while the plane burned, it was Melita who saw it first, from the corner of her eye, the white thing floating down. Then Rocco saw it too, coming straight for them, the mushroom shape with the pilot dangling underneath, swinging, coming fast, boots grazing inches above them as he slid by and whipped down, and, hitting the ground, he collapsed and rolled over, snarled in the parachute.

Painfully he got to his feet, disentangling and unbuckling, and a breeze took the chute and carried it off the knoll, out to the water. He stood there, in obvious distress, massaging his backside. It was Tony Zebra. Rocco had met him in a pub, the Oyster, on the Gut, after the house on Strait Street had been bombed.

"God, do I hate Malta," he said. "This rock-hard, bone-brained, godforsaken place. I think, this time, I broke my ass. This is the third damn plane I lost this week and nobody will want to see me alive." He pulled off his leather helmet, and there was a lot of blood coming from the side of his head.

"Look, he's hurt," Melita said.

"I'm not hurt."

"Yes, you are," Rocco said.

"I'm fine, I'm fine."

"We have to take care of him," Melita said.

"I'm fine, I tell you, never felt better, except for my rear end. Must have cracked my pelvis."

"He looks terrible," Melita said.

"Damn 109 came at me out of the sun. Never even saw the bastard till he blew past."

"Here, I'll help you," Rocco said.

"Don't touch me," Tony Zebra said, taking a step back. "Don't touch me!"

Half of his left ear was falling off.

"Light me a cigarette, will you?"

Rocco lit one and handed it to him. Blood from his torn ear was all over his flight jacket.

"This is a lousy cigarette. Don't you have anything better than this?"

"It's Moroccan."

"Where'd you get Moroccan?"

"From Fingerly."

He dropped the cigarette, half burned. "That Fingerly, didn't I tell you not to trust him?"

They walked him off the knoll, slowly, helping him along, pausing along the way because he was in pain. And then, just as they got to the hearse, he passed out.

Melita helped Rocco get him into the back and she put the blanket around him. He was still breathing, but he was pale, yellowish.

"Is he going to be all right?" she wondered.

"He's okay."

"I don't think so."

"It's just his ear, they'll stitch it together."

"He looks so awful. He said he broke his pelvis."

In the back of the hearse, Tony Zebra seemed a crumpled bird that had fallen to the earth, and who could say if he would ever fly again? They brought him to the Mtarfa hospital, and when he came to, an hour later, he was talking about a girl he'd known in New Jersey, somebody who really liked him, but he hadn't liked her half as much as she liked him, so nothing ever developed between them, and now he thought that might have been a terrible mistake, not liking her more. He was not smart about women, he understood that about himself. It was something he had to work on. He could see her face, smell her perfume, could even remember her telephone number and the street she lived on, but for the life of him, hard as he tried, he couldn't remember the color of her eyes.

+ *April 13, 1942* +

THE MALTA FRONT: TWO MAJOR ATTACKS ON ISLAND

AUSTERITY BUDGET
Increased Tax on Beer, Spirits, Tobacco

JAPANESE ADVANCE THREATENS CHINESE FLANKS AND REAR

FRANCE CHANGES HER COURSE: VICHY SUCCUMBS TO GERMAN PRESSURE
Recall of U.S. Ambassador Expected

———

THE WHIZZ-BANGS
+ Malta's Front-Line Concert Party +
A Musical Revue at the ADELPHI THEATRE

———

DOUBLE THE BENEFIT
in case of death by accident
THE NORTHERN ASSURANCE CO., LTD.
15 Strait Street, Valletta

Seven

FINGERLY'S FAT LADY

The next day, before she went to Zammit's to work on the jukeboxes, Melita stopped off at the small parish church not far from Zammit's house. In a back pew, she prayed for her mother and her father, a Hail Mary for each of them. Her mother had died just before the war, of a stroke, and when it happened, Melita was overwhelmed. It was a catastrophe, impossible to understand. Then the war came, and her father was killed on the first day of the bombing, and it was too much. Even now, she couldn't understand how God could let it happen, the bombing and the killing. She prayed for her parents, and then she prayed for Rocco, whom she couldn't get out of her mind. It was all so sudden, the way they met, and she was still astonished at how quickly it had become physical.

While she prayed, saying the words mechanically, she thought of him, and saw him, his high forehead and brown hair, and his strong shoulders. He was good-looking. Not like a movie star, yet handsome, his nose straight and slender above wide, firm lips, and his cheeks slightly sunken, forming hollows under his cheekbones. But mostly it was his eyes, something she saw in them, a kind of shyness. Not fear or timidity, but a sense of caution, a thoughtfulness. There was something in his glance that suggested he was sincere, that he could be relied upon.

But yesterday, and the day before, she had simply let herself go. And she would again, she knew that. Something had sprung loose in her, and it bothered her, leaving her confused. It was the war, the war made everything sudden. It had brought them together, she from Malta and he from so far away. They would never have met had it not been for the bombing. So the war was good, even though it was bad, and she wondered about that. Could something good come from something bad? Something right from something wrong? She prayed to the Virgin, thanking her for Rocco, and even though she had sinned with him, she thought the Virgin would understand. She thought of going to confession, but decided to wait a while before doing that, because she suspected the priest would be far less understanding than the Blessed Mother.

She left the little church, and on her way to Zammit's she wondered if she should say anything about Rocco. She wanted to talk about him, wanted to tell somebody. She wanted to tell her friend Christina, but Christina was busy at the Adelphi, in Rabat, putting on a show for the troops. She was a cabaret dancer. She'd performed in Paris, Genoa, Tunis, and Barcelona, and was dancing in Valletta when the bombing began, so now she was stuck there till it was over. She was English, from Cheshire, willowy, with long blond hair, and Melita liked her. They had met in a shelter during an air-raid alert, and there was, between them, an immediate feeling of closeness. Christina danced for the soldiers, with a group called the Whizz-Bangs, and she also spent long hours working for the RAF, at the big tabletop map in the underground command center—they called it the Hole—moving the markers and tracking the course of the incoming bombers. She was busy, too busy-busy as she always said, yet she liked it that way, active and on the move.

Melita so much wanted to tell her about Rocco, but she decided, for the time being, to say nothing. It was better that way, better not to speak too soon, not even to Christina, because with things like this, it could be unlucky to say anything prematurely. Life had an unpleasant way of turning things around, happy into not happy, and this time, she thought, she really didn't want to be disappointed.

Years ago, when she was in school, there had been a boy she liked, but he never noticed her. It hurt so much. She was young, fifteen, and he was a little older. She had a terrible crush on him. He went away and studied in Rome for a while, and when he came back, six months later, it surprised her how different he was. He wore silk ties and velvet gloves, and used a cigarette holder when he smoked. She found it hard to believe she'd wanted him so much. He was a snob, always talking, talking—about Italy, about the restaurants he'd eaten in and the wealthy people he'd met. He still didn't notice her, but now she was glad. She couldn't believe what a fool she'd been.

On Old Mint, in Valletta, Rocco had a sandwich at Hock's—corned beef from a tin, more gristle than beef—then he set off walking, crisscrossing through Valletta's broken streets. People still lived there, coming and going, despite the wreckage—about six thousand, he'd read in the paper, of the twenty thousand who'd been there before the war.

He lingered briefly by the ruins of the Opera House, observing the slabs of marble and the fractured columns, and then, as if there were something he'd forgotten and only just remembered, he set off again, moving quickly now, heading for the bombed-out house on Strait Street—because, sooner or later, he had to go back there. It was something that was tugging at him, drawing him back.

He crossed on South Street, passing a smashed military van, and when he turned onto Strait, looking far down, was amazed to see in the distance, on the narrow, sloping street, Nardu Camilleri in his brown vest and white shirt, tan cap on his head, moving stiffly with quick short steps. Rocco set off after him, but Nardu was a long way off and disappeared around a corner. Rocco ran to catch up, but when he turned the corner, the old man was gone, and Rocco thought it may not have been him after all. Valletta was full of old men in brown vests.

A man with three goats was going house to house. He milked the goats, using a pail, and the housewives at their windows handed pitchers down to him, which he filled from the pail. The nannies were dark, with long shaggy hair.

Rocco got back onto Strait and continued on down, finding Hannibal's bar, the Oasis, still closed. Across the street, the front of the house, Number 79, was unchanged, except that the door was wide open, and when he stepped inside, he saw that some of the debris had been removed, though by no means all. Standing there, looking at the ruined interior, he felt eerie, unbalanced, as if he'd died there, in that house, when the bomb went off, and had been given, somehow, a second life. In places, planks had been laid down by the rescue workers, walkways across the unstable debris. Rats scrambled through the splintered furniture, and as he stood there pondering the wreckage, something inside him sank and he felt again a powerful urge to get away, to get off the island.

There was a noise behind him, and when he turned he saw Fingerly in the doorway. The sun, flooding the street behind him, created the illusion of a nimbus, as if the light were radiating from Fingerly himself.

"I thought you were dead," Rocco said.

"What an awkward idea."

"You're not dead?"

"Why should I be?"

"Is Major Webb dead?"

"Of course he's dead. Dead as a doornail."

"If he's dead, how can you be alive?"

"I work harder than he does."

The same Fingerly, tall and angular, same Florida shirt hanging loose over his khaki pants, and the same vague hint of a drawl, as if he might have been from Texas but was doing his best to keep it a secret. The only difference was that he was now a captain, silver bars pinned to the collar of his shirt, just back from an I-3 briefing in Alexandria. He held a pint of Four Roses in his left hand, casually, down at his side.

"Is that for real," Rocco asked, pointing to the captain's bars, "or did you find them in a rummage shop?"

Fingerly floated a lazy, self-conscious grin. "Stick with me, Raven, I'll be a colonel before you know it." He unscrewed the cap on the Four Roses.

Rocco nodded toward what was left of the top floor, the small ledge with the bed on it. "I was up there," he said, "sleeping right up there when it happened."

Fingerly lifted the bottle, about to drink, but didn't. "The young one, Julietta. You had a thing for her."

"Well, I wouldn't call it a thing."

"You were smitten."

"Me? Smitten?"

"You took notice."

"She had . . . good eyes."

"In that case," Fingerly said, "you'll be happy to know I saw her yesterday in Rabat. She lives, Raven. She's working out of a house on San Nikola." He took a swig and passed the bottle to Rocco, who simply held it, didn't drink, too busy absorbing what Fingerly had just said.

"You thought they were dead? I told you, Rocco, whores have a charmed life." There was a rumble in his tone, a lazy resonance. "The wooden leg too—Aida—working out of the same house as Julietta. But Simone has retired from the trade and has decided to spend the rest of her life making lace. After the war she's going to open a shop."

"They're okay? All of them?"

Even Hannibal and Beatrice were all right. For Beatrice, it had been close—the kids, on their way out to the shelter, had forgotten their snacks and Beatrice ran down after them only moments before the bomb hit.

"Life is a wet dream, Rocco. It's a comic opera."

Rocco felt dumb, as if a trick had been played on him. If life was a comic opera, then he was a clown. He took a sip of the whisky, and passed the bottle back to Fingerly.

"You wish they were dead, right? Because now you feel like a jerk." A fly was buzzing around, between them.

"Nigg too?" Rocco asked.

"Nigg too, alive and kicking. Nothing can kill Nigg. The sonofabitch was at Dominic's, with Vivian, gambling in the Green Room. She's some number, that Vivian."

Rocco remembered his first night on Malta, when Fingerly brought him to Dominic's and Nigg turned up with Vivian. Nigg hung out in the Green Room, betting on the bombs, whether they would hit a movie house or a bar, or a convent, and he was losing. Vivian was so bored she was flirting with everyone, flaunting herself, to annoy Nigg. She flirted with Rocco, and he enjoyed it, but he had the good sense not to offer any encouragement.

"If you're still interested in Julietta," Fingerly said, "here's her address." He scribbled a number on the back of a book of matches and stuck it into Rocco's shirt pocket. "Too bad about the radio, though. A total loss, huh? That was a damn good piece of equipment." The way he said it, it sounded as if it would have been better if Rocco, rather than the radio, had been lost.

The fly, circling lazily, landed briefly on Rocco's nose, then took to the air again.

"I was thinking," Rocco said, "since there's no radio, I guess I'm not needed anymore."

The fly settled on Fingerly's shoulder, where it seemed to be at home.

"Oh, you're needed, Raven, you're needed, don't ever feel useless. I'll scout up a new wireless and you'll be busy before you know it. Anyway, the good news is that Maroon is coming back from Gozo. Come along, I'm on my way to pick him up, we'll be one big happy family." He ran his long fingers through his hair, which was combed back off his forehead, and the fly on his shoulder took off, circling, then came down again exactly where it had been.

"By the way," he added, "nice duds, where'd you pick them up? Could be a bit sharper, though. The pants look like 1929."

In the Austin Seven, they drove out through Floriana and branched off to the right, going through Pietà and Msida, heading northwest toward Marfa Point on the far end of Malta. End to end, the island was only about seventeen miles, but the roads were slow, twisting through small towns crowded with jeeps and trucks. It seemed much of a sameness, the densely clustered rows of houses a few stories high, flat-roofed, in towns that merged one into the other, with the shops and the vegetable stalls and the long queues of women and old men waiting for bread, and always, wherever you looked, the churches.

"It's a terrific island, Raven, you're going to love it. Home of the Maltese dog, the Maltese cat, the Maltese Cross. And Maltese fever, which comes from the milk of the Maltese goats. But now they pasteurize the milk—most of it— so it's not such a threat anymore. Do you know there are fifteen different species of orchid on this island?"

He swerved to avoid a chicken, barely missed a stalled truck, and went off the road, rumbling wildly in the weed-choked gravel.

"Malta fungus," he said, angling back onto the road. "It grows on Filfla and was used, in the old days, to heal wounds inflicted by rapiers and stilettos. And best of all, yes, the number one label—the Knights of Malta. How could we forget the Knights?"

At a bend in the road they hit a hole and bounced fiercely, nearly flipping over. Fingerly wrestled with the wheel, veering left, then right. In the end, the car came to a dead stop in a ditch.

He got out of the car and looked it over skeptically. "The Knights, Rocco, I ask you, where would the world be today if the Knights hadn't stopped the Turks dead in their tracks right here on this island, 1565? The Turks would have pushed on into Europe and killed off the Renaissance. No Galileo. Think of it. No Palestrina, no Giordano Bruno." Then, glancing at the car, a little uncertain, "You think we can do this?"

Rocco shrugged, and they grabbed hold of the front bumper.

"Heave," Fingerly said.

They heaved, and moved the car sufficiently out of the ditch to get it started again. Fingerly revved the engine, and, with Rocco pushing, the Austin crawled back onto the road and they drove on into open country, farmland, small plots of terraced acreage and low stone walls, Fingerly talking the whole way, his voice drilling into Rocco's skull and Rocco wanting to break loose from it, wanting to shake his head and make all the Fingerly words drop out.

"The Knights, Rocco, the Knights," Fingerly went on, with heavy timbre. "Doesn't it make you feel you were born too late? You could have been one of them, one of the flowers of Europe, right down there at St. Elmo's, hand-to-hand against the janissaries. Were it not for the Knights, there would have been no Shakespeare, no Rabelais, no Jean-Jacques Rousseau, no Voltaire, no Enlightenment. No Benjamin Franklin, Rocco. History is a web, it traps us all."

Even Rocco could see how excessive this was. If the Turks hadn't been stopped at Malta, then surely at Sicily, or southern Italy. Fingerly had this way of pushing things to the extreme, it was part of his extravagance, part of his irony, so that when he said, grandly, that history was a web, it was hard for Rocco to know if he was serious or merely joking, or joking yet expecting to be taken seriously, if you were fool enough to do that.

"Let me drive," Rocco said.

"My driving makes you nervous?"

"I want to feel the wheel."

"This is left side of the road, you know, the Brits have it all backwards. You sure you can handle it? You don't want to get us killed, do you?"

With the steering wheel on the right, Rocco did feel peculiar, especially with the oncoming traffic. But it was good, it forced him to listen less to Fingerly and to concentrate more on the road. Fingerly was going on and on about the Knights, their whoring, their gluttony, their wealth, their loose living. After they beat off the Turks, they fell into the soft morass of decadence, and when Napoleon sailed in, they tucked their tails between their legs and abandoned the island, the glory days over.

"I thought they were the good guys," Rocco said. "Weren't they the good guys?"

"Of course they were the good guys. They saved us from the Turk. But good guys have a way of losing their grip and forgetting who they are."

"Hospitals," Rocco said. "They ran hospitals. Didn't somebody tell me that?"

"That's how they started, sure, in the Middle Ages. They ran a hospital in Jerusalem for sick pilgrims. The Knights of St. John Hospitalers. But when the Turks went after them, they learned fast how to use swords, maces, and other instruments of death—like, for example, boiling oil. They sailed in galleys rowed by slaves and raided enemy shipping. They're still around, you know. But nothing like the old swashbucklers. Most of them, now, are married men with families, pillars of the community, and you don't even have to be Catholic anymore. There are Protestant Knights wherever there are Protestants. Even in Singapore. There's an Eastern Orthodox group in Mount Vernon, New York. They raise money for hospitals. Isn't it wonderful? Nearly a thousand years these guys have been obsessed about hospitals. But now that there's a war on, maybe they'll don armor again and hone their swords. Those suits of armor, they weighed over a hundred pounds."

There was a herd of goats on the road, and Rocco, going a shade too fast, had to slam on the brakes. An old man wearing a battered felt hat prodded the herd with a big stick, trying to urge them across the road and into a field, with little success.

"You think they'll get out of the way," Rocco said to Fingerly, "or will I have to run them over?"

"You will have to edge very slowly into them. Nudge them. They'll get the point."

Rocco did that, the bumper pushing slowly into the herd, but this only confused them and made matters worse. The road was a turmoil of goats, bleating, baaing, giving their goaty calls and hopping about skittishly, a mass of swirling horns and wildly bucking hooves. The goatherd, enraged over the way Rocco was complicating things, started banging on the rear fender with his stick.

"Keep it going," Fingerly said. "Don't stop, don't stop."

Rocco leaned on the horn and poured on the gas. The goats scattered, some to the left, some to the right, and looking back in the mirror, Rocco saw the old man waving his stick, his mouth working furiously, shouting what could only have been a string of profanities—cursing Rocco, cursing the car, cursing the goats, cursing the war, cursing the Germans, cursing God, and cursing himself, cursing the unholy ground he stood on, and all of it, every word, lost in the noise and clatter of the goats and the roar of the Austin's engine.

What Rocco did hear was the sirens. They were coming from Mosta, ahead of them, and it wasn't just the sirens of Mosta but sirens from all over the island, from Hamrun and the bastions of Valletta behind them, and Luqa to the southeast, and Mdina and Rabat in the southwest, the sirens of the island surging and forlorn, a despairing chorus filled with a foreboding that made him want to curl up and hide.

"We should get off the road," he said.

"Nonsense."

"I'm pulling over."

"Don't do this," Fingerly said. "Keep going."

Rocco pulled over and stopped and got out. Fingerly sat a moment, then reluctantly climbed out. They looked skyward and saw the formations of bombers heading for Grand Harbour and the dockyards. Already the barrage was up, clouds of flak forming a protective box, shielding the dockyards, defying the planes to come near.

Fingerly took a pair of binoculars from the car.

"Germans or Italians?" Rocco asked.

"Marchetti 79s. Half of them will jettison their bombs and turn away before they get anywhere near the target. They have no stomach for the fight."

He passed the binoculars to Rocco, and Rocco watched with a kind of gluttony, caught up in the drama. Fingerly was right, a lot of the planes unloaded before they got anywhere near the flak. But some held steady, going right into the barrage, and Rocco saw the bombs dropping like clusters of eggs and heard a crumping roar when they detonated. A funnel of black smoke rose from somewhere near the docks.

One of the bombers, hit, went down, twirling lazily on its axis, into the sea. Another swung off on a long arc, trailing smoke from an engine. One had its whole tail section blown off and it plummeted like a rock.

Then it was over, barely nine or ten minutes, the sky clear, the planes gone. There had been raids that lasted hours, some that lasted whole days. This was just a quick run, a teasing reminder there was more on the way.

Fingerly took over the driving again, and ahead of them now loomed Mosta and the big dome of the rotunda church. It was huge, monumental, dominating the rows of two- and three-story housing spreading out around it.

"Third biggest dome in the world," Fingerly said, "can you believe it? Right here in nothing-Mosta."

Less than a week earlier, two days after Rocco flew in, the Mosta church had been hit by a bomb, but the bomb didn't explode. It punched a hole in the dome, plunged into the church, and skittered about wildly before coming to rest. Two other bombs fell nearby and also failed to detonate. All over Malta they were calling it the Miracle of Mosta.

The road brought them to the center of town, and Fingerly pulled up in the plaza beside the church. A procession was in progress, gray-haired men in dark suits carrying a statue of the Blessed Mother on a wooden litter, followed by a line of women in black faldettas, praying the rosary. The procession moved along slowly, the old men struggling with the weight. Halfway up the church steps, the litter tilted at too steep an angle, and the Virgin, leaning precariously, was on the verge of toppling. Hands reached up from all around to save her, and with a collective groan the men managed to straighten the litter and shouldered it into the church.

Fingerly took a carton of Chesterfields from the back seat of the car, and when Rocco saw the cigarettes, he knew Fingerly hadn't brought him there just to look at a hole in the roof.

It was an enormous church, circular in design, with a vast, open floor, nothing in the middle, and it was perfectly clear that what mattered here was the dome. The altars were set off at the periphery, as if of no consequence.

The interior of the dome was ornamented with slanting rows of rosettes, so arranged as to create an illusion of endlessly spiraling lines, vanishing upward. And now, amid the rosettes, there was this hole made by the bomb, a few yards wide, a shaft of sunlight slanting through like a spotlight in a theater.

The priest who had led the procession knelt at the main altar, in a niche in the rotunda wall, and the women, kneeling, went on with the rosary in loud, chanting voices. The painted statue of the Virgin, positioned by the altar, seemed bold and garish, the colors coarse, the cheeks plump and too red-dened, the dark eyes small and unappealing, lips turned down at the corners, as if the man who made it had deliberately added touches of ugliness because the ones who commissioned it had not been willing, perhaps, to pay enough.

Here and there, groups of people stood about, looking up at the hole. A nun, young, in a blue habit, was taking pictures, moving about, photographing the hole from every angle. She roved across the marble floor, the camera to her eye, focusing and snapping, and snapping again. Rocco heard an old man whispering to himself, "Miraklu, miraklu."

"Let's go," Fingerly said, setting off across the wide marble floor, and Rocco, after hanging back, caught up with him, following through a door that led to the sacristy.

There were several rooms back there. Fingerly turned left, through one door, then right, through another. The sacristan, a cumbersome, slow-moving man, was in the vestry, setting out the albs and chasubles for the next morning's masses. His eyes were slow and mechanical, drained of feeling.

He looked at Rocco but spoke to Fingerly. "Your friend?" he asked, not smiling.

"From America," Fingerly said.

The sacristan nodded woodenly, making Rocco feel less than welcome. Then, motioning to Fingerly, he moved off stiffly to a cabinet at the far end of the room.

"Wait here," Fingerly told Rocco.

The sacristan unlocked the cabinet, and from a lower shelf took out a small box and set it on a vestment case. Fingerly put the carton of cigarettes down beside it. Through the distance, Rocco recognized the box as a cigar box. Fingerly opened it, pulled away some protective wrapping and bent close, examining the object inside. He picked it up, turning it in his hands, then put it back and nodded his approval.

The sacristan closed the lid and handed the box to Fingerly. They shook hands and exchanged a few words, then Fingerly, signaling to Rocco, led the way out through the church, where the women were still praying and the statue of the Virgin, in a cloud of incense, seemed a gaudy department-store mannequin, preparing to fly up and make her escape through the hole in the dome.

Fingerly drove, the cigar box next to him on the seat. Not till they were well out of Mosta did he let Rocco have a look.

"Gently," he said, lifting the box and passing it over.

Rocco opened it, removed the wadded paper, and found a small statue: a woman, naked, some seven inches tall, hardened clay of a reddish-brown color, the surface highly polished. The breasts were exaggerated, voluptuously large, as were the hips and thighs. The head was disproportionately small, and the mouth and nose were gone, worn away by the roughness of time. The thick, bulging thighs tapered into small calves and tiny feet.

"A fertility goddess," Fingerly said, swinging wide to get around a horse-drawn wagon. "They found a bunch of these in the digs at the temples. There's one like this in the Abela Collection, in Valletta, but no head and no feet. They call her the Venus of Malta. This is a much finer specimen. Stacked, isn't she? The old Maltese, whoever they were, used to worship her. The archaeologists call her the Fat Lady."

"You got this for a carton of cigarettes?"

"The cigarettes were for the sacristan. He's the middleman. You have any idea how much a carton of Chesterfields goes for on the black market? *If* you can find them?"

Again he swung wide, passing another wagon.

"Take a good look, Raven. Isn't she worth adoring? Don't you want to get down on your knees? An earth mother, a million-dollar fertility mom. This is what they worshipped back there in the good old days, in the Copper Age. We're talking third millennium, Raven. Does it make you tight in the groin?"

Rocco turned the earth goddess in his hand, unimpressed. A lump of hard, polished clay, breasts and thighs grotesquely out of proportion. It was old, and old made it valuable. People had prayed to it. He wondered how that was done, kneeling or standing, or squatting. He wondered if burnt sacrifices were offered, and if the prayers were ever answered.

"This?" he said. "This is it? This is what I-3 does on Malta?"

"It's a sideline, Rocco, just a sideline. Everybody in I-3 has a hobby."

Rocco closed the box and put it back on the seat, between himself and Fingerly.

"Major Webb? Was he collecting too?"

"The only things Major Webb collected were the whores in St. Julian's and pink gins. Remember him kindly, he was a good man."

"And the others?"

"Ambrosio? Sucking toothpicks in Majorca, dropped out of the war. Nigg? Addicted, as you've seen, to games of chance. Maroon I've taken on as a ten-percent partner, he's bringing some stuff back from Gozo. I would take you on as a ten-percenter too, but frankly you might prove a liability. Besides, I already saved your life once already, and I figure one favor in a lifetime is plenty. Fair enough?"

Ahead on the road were two motorcycles, Brits in uniform, traveling slowly. Fingerly honked and went racing past.

"When peace breaks out, after the war, Raven, the cats who fattened on the war are going to be buying up like crazy. Art will be a new form of currency. And prehistoric art—like this sexy little lady—will be at the apex, out of sight."

Not only did he have the sacristan in Mosta, but he had sacristans all over Malta, in Mellieħa, and Żejtun, and Sliema, and Birżebbuġa. It was hard times, people needed cash for food on the black market. After Malta, he was heading back into Egypt and expected to move out from there into Palestine. "A relic from the Crucifixion, Rocco—one of the nails, just one. You know how much that would bring on the international market? The Archbishop of Cincinnati would pony up a hefty chunk for that. Or a panel from the original Ark of the Covenant. You think the Lubavitchers are going to pass that up?"

Off to the left, in a field, lay the wreckage of a Marchetti 79, a tangled heap, recently downed, wisps of black smoke still curling from one of the engines. Rocco leaned back, dangling an arm out of the car. "What kind of a proposition did you offer the Count?"

"Which Count?"

"At Dominic's. The one who plays the piano."

"What did he say?"

"That you offered him a proposition."

"He said that? I offered a proposition?"

"That's what he said."

"Strange he should say that to you."

"I guess he was just making conversation."

"It's the war, Raven, the war, it creates such confusion. We were just having an amiable chat at the bar and he thought I was setting up a deal?"

He drove with only one finger on the wheel, casually guiding the Austin through the bumps and potholes. Then, as he pulled out a cigarette and lit up, not even the one finger was on the wheel. He took his time, inhaling deeply, and as he exhaled, sending jets of smoke through his nostrils, the finger wandered back to the wheel.

"I'm out of cash," Rocco said.

"I know, you need your wampum. Hang on for a few days."

"How do I buy lunch?"

"You're that hard up? Didn't I tell you not to squander? You overpaid for the clothes."

"I should go naked?"

"Well, they might like you better for it."

Rocco didn't tell him anything about Melita. He didn't tell him about the mattress in the wrecked house on Windmill Street, or about the birds that flew in through the open roof, or about the lamp and the three-legged table. He didn't tell him about the jukebox full of American records, and the pink hearse, because if he told any of this to Fingerly, somehow, in the telling, it would get lost or damaged, and Fingerly, in his way, would nibble around the edges, making it seem as meaningless and trivial as the goddess in the cigar box. Which was something else Rocco found hard to understand. This misshapen lady, with her noseless face and shrunken feet and fat bulging body: who could worship her? Who could find anything here to admire? And yet, strangely, she continued to haunt, a muffled hymn out of the past, stone temples, cycles of the moon, blood rituals, human sacrifice, her distant power echoing from long ago.

Marfa Point was up at the northeast corner of the island, the shortest crossing point to Gozo. When they arrived, the sun was going down. Maroon had planned on a late crossing, with enough light for him to find his way, but difficult light for the 109s, if any happened to be hanging around.

Fingerly parked on a low rise where they had a clear view of the water. Before them, across the three-mile channel, lay Gozo, less than half the size of Malta. Between Malta and Gozo, inside the channel, sat the tiny island of Comino, barely a square mile of rocky land, famous for the cumin that grew there. In the fading light, Comino and Gozo were indistinguishable, blending, appearing as a single landmass.

They sat in the open car, watching for Maroon. Fingerly used binoculars.

"He'll be alone, in a powerboat."

Fingerly had urged him to use the ferry, but Maroon had his mind set on the powerboat. If there was an alert, the ferry wouldn't run. And even if there wasn't an alert, if the captain had a hunch about enemy planes, he wouldn't venture out. He had frequent hunches, two or three a day, and these, combined with the alerts, made a hash of the ferry's schedule.

Gozo, mostly farmland, was virtually untouched by the war, receiving little of the bombing and strafing. "The Germans don't get much of a thrill out of bombing fig trees," Fingerly said, still scanning with the binoculars. "More fun bombing churches and hospitals. It's the German mind, very quota-conscious in the matter of death."

"If Gozo is so safe," Rocco wondered, "why doesn't everybody over here pick up and go over there?"

"Ah, but what kind of a war would it be? When the Stukas come, who would be here to shoot back?"

At the start of the war, quite a few had moved across to Gozo, about three thousand. But uprooting, leaving everything behind, wasn't easy, and most chose to stay where they were, even though it meant bombs, shelters, curfew, out-of-date movies, and greasy soup at the Victory Kitchens. The surprising thing was that the bombing seemed good for mental health. As the war progressed, the number of patients in the mental wards on Malta declined, while those on Gozo increased.

"It's a fact, Raven, check it out. War is a cure for all sorts of mental disorders."

Then, with an audible tightening in his voice: "There he is." He watched for a long moment, then passed the binoculars to Rocco.

The boat knifed through the water, bouncing, leaving a wake. Rocco saw Maroon's hair whipping in the wind. He was alone, in a blue shirt and wearing a beard, with a large box secured to the back of the boat.

Rocco passed the binoculars back to Fingerly. They were both out of the car now, standing, peering eagerly.

The sun was sinking, a big red ball, half of it already gone. It did crazy things with the sky, igniting the clouds into a blaze of color. It did things to the water too, casting a rosy sheen that faded to violet and black.

"He should have taken the ferry," Fingerly said anxiously. "I told him to take the ferry."

"What's in the box?" Rocco asked.

"Bones."

"Whose bones?"

"An elephant, Raven. A pigmy elephant."

Rocco thought about it, then said, "There is no such thing as a pigmy elephant."

"Not now, no. But there was. In the Pleistocene, and they were right here, in this neck of the woods." He worked at the binoculars, adjusting the focus. "That's what's in the box, a mini-elephant. Not a baby elephant but a full-grown beast the size of a St. Bernard. They have one in the Smithsonian—ever see it?"

"I was never so lucky."

"That's what Nigg says about you, he thinks you're unlucky."

Then they saw it, and it was Rocco who saw it first—a 109 rising in the sky, coming up from behind Gozo. High up, it caught the sun and the sun painted it red. It rose, then it was diving, descending toward the channel.

Fingerly dropped his hands to his sides. "Oh shit!"

The 109 pulled out of the dive and swept right over the powerboat, guns chattering. Then it pulled up in a wide slow turn, coming right over the spot where Rocco and Fingerly were parked, and went back for another try at Maroon. Again the pilot missed, and again he turned and swung back for another run.

It kept on that way, on and on, Maroon weaving left, then right, and the 109 sweeping back and forth, firing and missing—the pilot inept, too young, a bad shot, maybe himself too frightened to remember how to aim, sending dozens of rounds into the water. And the whole time Fingerly was talking to Maroon as if Maroon could actually hear him. "Hard left, Maroon, hard left. Watch it, watch it—the sonofabitch is right behind you!" And when Maroon went right instead of left, from Fingerly came a low, grieving moan, lonesome and unforgiving, aching, a depth of feeling Rocco hadn't imagined him capable of.

Then, as the plane closed yet another time, Fingerly was no longer talking and calling but was leaning over into the Austin and honking the horn, as if, magically, the horn might distract the pilot and throw off his aim. It was the only time Rocco ever saw Fingerly lose control that way, and in the wildness of the moment, he liked him. He was over the edge, all smoothness gone, hammering on the horn as if convinced it could make a difference. Then, beaten, he stopped honking, and just stood there and watched.

"I don't believe this is happening. I fucking don't believe!"

Maroon had already traveled a long part of the three-mile run, with less than a mile to go, and Rocco was beginning to think he might make it. But now Maroon did a strange thing. He slowed the boat, and took it into his head to shoot back at the plane with the only weapon he had: a flare gun.

The plane came low over the water and Maroon sat there, in the boat, one hand on the wheel, the other with the gun, and when the plane got close enough, he launched a flare that blazed purple, and missed. He reloaded and fired again. And again.

Fingerly was in despair. Again he was talking to Maroon, shouting, urging him on, telling him to throw away the gun and put the boat into high. But Maroon held the boat steady and slow, firing one flare after another, as if he'd snapped, as if it had all been too much for him and he'd regressed to infantile playfulness, in love with the phosphorous hiss of the flares, never knowing what color would flame out next—red, azure, raging yellow.

Rocco felt, for a moment, weirdly detached, seeing the boat and the plane as if in a snapshot, Maroon sitting there, one hand on the wheel, the other holding the flare gun high in the air, firing, but no motion, everything suddenly frozen, locked in a frame: Maroon, the plane, and Maroon's right hand lifted, the flare from the gun rising but unmoving, a blaze of azure light in the silent stony air. He saw Maroon's blue shirt and his full, black beard, and behind him an incongruous seagull that had somehow wandered in, hovering, immobile in the shimmering day's-end wreckage of the sky.

Then it was all moving again, unfrozen, the boat tossing and Maroon's flare rising to meet the oncoming plane. The 109 came in low, raking the water with its machine guns, and then, crazily, against all the odds, the flare somehow got sucked up into the Messerschmitt's manifold and did enough damage to send a stream of black smoke pouring out the back. Maroon hurled the gun into the air, figuring he was home free.

But the 109, trailing smoke, turned and came right back at him. And now Rocco too was talking to Maroon, not shouting like Fingerly but silently, in his head, telling Maroon to move it, get it going, because he was so close, and if he hadn't slowed, wasting time with the flares, he would already have been ashore. *Move it, move it,* saying it not just in his head now but aloud, *Gun it, give it the gas, go,* shouting so hard his throat felt stripped and torn, and something inside him wanted to weep.

Maroon had the boat in high gear now, swinging left, and right, moving fast but not fast enough, because this time, as the 109 swept past, the bullets slammed into Maroon so hard they hurled him out of the boat, into the water, and when he came back up he was flotsam, adrift, face-down. He was less than a quarter of a mile away. They could see the blood, the widening pool of red in the murky water, lit by the last glimmers of daylight as night came on.

Eight

THE GREEN ROOM

On the drive back, in the dark, Fingerly was quiet, concentrating on the road. He didn't even light a cigarette. They passed through Mellieha, and St. Paul's Bay, and Naxxar, and when they reached St. Julian's, he turned off, and pulled up at Dominic's. "Let's go find Nigg," he said, "before he loses everything in there and slashes his wrists."

They went in through the bar, passed through the dining room, and went to the Green Room, which had been, before the war, a stylish haunt for roulette and vingt-et-un, but now, with the siege on, the playing tables had been moved aside and a bald clerk sat at a mahogany desk, taking bets on the bombing. Dominic offered odds on just about anything. You could bet on whether the bombs would hit the Cathedral, the Palace, the flagpole at St. Elmo's, or the toilets in the Floriana bus depot. You could wager on the statue of Queen Victoria in front of the National Library, whether she would lose a few fingers or get smashed to bits completely.

Nigg was by a blackboard, studying the numbers, a near-empty tumbler of whisky in his hand. His eyes had a hot, vaporous intensity, like steam coming off a roof after a quick summer rain.

When Fingerly told him about Maroon, Nigg never shifted his gaze from the blackboard. "The boat went down?"

"Blown to pieces," Fingerly said.

"It's the luck of the draw," Nigg said flatly. He was with Vivian, but she was in the dining room, having dessert with a navy captain.

A few men in blue serge stood by the mahogany table, placing bets with the bald clerk. In a far corner, at a table with setups, a bartender poured drinks for some naval officers. Only one woman was in the room, a middle-aged Norwegian with long legs and upswept hair, in an easy chair by the fireplace. She had a standing high-odds bet that the archbishop's residence would be bombed on a Sunday, while the archbishop was out to tea. Smoke from the cigars caressed the green velvet draperies and hung lazily in undulating layers.

A radio report came in from Hal Far, assessing the damage at the aerodrome, which had been bombed an hour earlier. A few Stukas had torn up the landing strip, but no planes had been lost, and none of the Stukas had been knocked down. There were no winners in the room on this one.

"I need to replenish," Nigg said, moving toward the bartender at the white table.

"Did you lose a fortune on Hal Far?" Fingerly asked.

"I never bet on the airfields. The Jerries hit them every day, so the best you can get is even money, and that's dumb."

Fingerly asked for some Irish, neat, and Rocco took a beer. Nigg was on Seagram's. The bartender nodded toward the hors d'oeuvres, and Rocco took one, a fluffy, buttery thing with a piece of shrimp on it. Fingerly stepped away, crossing the room to talk to an admiral.

"When they blew up Strait Street," Rocco said to Nigg, "you know, I thought you were still inside. It was a hell of a thing, everything just sort of fell away."

"Right," Nigg said, turning his glass, "that's the way it happens." His eyes were fastened on the blackboard across the room.

"What's the shrewd bet these days?"

"The shrewd bet," Nigg said, "is buses."

"Buses pay off?"

"When I was betting on churches, I was always in a hole."

He had bet on the Number 34 to Kirkop, and it was hit. The 40 to Lija, and it too was blown apart. The 54 to Naxxar, and it was smashed beyond recognition, nothing left but a few blackened pieces of tin.

"I hope you won't ever bet on me," Rocco said.

"Dominic doesn't take bets on people. But if he did, you're somebody I would bet on. You have that look, like any minute a bomb is going to fall on your head."

"One already did."

"Maybe you'll catch another."

"If that happens," Rocco said, "I hope you'll be standing right next to me."

The plan for Nigg, after the war, was that he was to go back to Harvard and finish his undergraduate work, then on to medical school, and eventually move into his father's practice. His father was a specialist in pathologies of the rectum and lower colon, with a high-class clientele on the Upper West Side. "Hemorrhoids are pure gold," he was fond of saying. But Nigg had none of his father's enthusiasm for the nether regions of the human anatomy, and would have been content to spend the rest of his life in the Mediterranean, gambling. In Cairo he won, and in Alexandria he lost. In Palestine, he broke even. When he got to Malta, in three straight nights at Dominic's he wagered and lost almost everything he had. A week later he won it back, and celebrated by buying on the black market a pound of Siberian caviar, a case of Moët & Chandon 1939, and a box of Tutankhamen lambskins imported from New Jersey via Portugal, all of it (the caviar, the champagne, and the condoms) put to good use in a room in the Phoenicia Hotel during a forty-eight-hour sex binge with Vivian, who offered to marry him if he would give up gambling and drink less, but he was not in a promising mood. Two days after the lambskins ran out, he went back to Dominic's and lost everything he'd won. So now, having lost his initial amount, and having regained it, doubled it, and lost it again, he was attempting to recover his equilibrium and get back in the game, and what was doing it for him was buses. With buses, he was winning big.

The Norwegian woman with the long legs leaned back and yawned, touching her hand lethargically to her mouth. A log burned in the fireplace, and at the mahogany table the bald clerk was slow and deliberate, like a priest at mass. The deep pile of the Persian rug was easy underfoot, a lavish design of vines and leaves curling and unfurling with maze-like intricacy. Rocco could see why Nigg liked it here. There was a mood, a tone, a fatalism that glowed darkly. If you had to gamble and lose, this was the place.

Fingerly, returning from his tête-à-tête with the admiral, tried to persuade Nigg to join them in the dining room, but Nigg merely shrugged, showing no interest. He had business with the bald clerk, setting up his bets for the next day. How could he do that, Rocco wondered, betting against the buses when he knew they were loaded with people?

He liked the idea of betting on Queen Victoria, though, that she might, in the next raid, lose one of her fingers, or her nose. He looked toward the mahogany table, half-inclined to place the bet, but Fingerly, at that moment, had his ear, telling him about the high-class whores he knew in St. Julian's, fancy suede-shoe women who read books and went to museums. "They listen to

Mozart," he was saying, "they know about Gauguin and Van Gogh, they read Thomas Mann, Raven, they'll charm the pants off of you"—and then, from the corner of his eye, Rocco glimpsed the Norwegian woman by the fireplace, not sitting now but standing, light from the burning log flickering on her black satin dress and on the small shiny thing in her hand. Hard to tell, from the corner of his eye, just what it was, the thing in her hand, some sort of ornament, toy, a small odd shape, her hand rising with the gleaming thing in it—then, turning, looking straight on, he saw it was a gun, raised and pointing, and their eyes met, and for a long moment that drew itself out interminably, all he could think was what beautiful eyes she had, hazel and softly desperate, movie star eyes, eyes filled with loneliness and longing, and the word that wandered through his mind was languor, because that's what it was: her eyes possessed languor, they expressed it, they were languor itself, the embodiment and source of it, and it was not until it was altogether too late, the long slow moment twisting and bending idly, that he realized she was about to shoot.

Nine

MISS SICILY SINGS
FOR MALTA

The gun went off with a tiny popping sound, puny and insignificant. She fired three times, *pop, pop, pop,* the small dry sounds like timid punctuation marks amid the rippling sotto voce conversation and the sounds of money changing hands. Before she fired, she had stood there, by the fireplace, looking Rocco straight in the eye. Then, slowly, her arm moved, and detaching her eyes from his, she fired at an admiral in a white uniform, some six or seven feet from where Rocco stood. It was the same admiral Fingerly had been talking with only moments earlier.

When Rocco heard the first shot, he thought, that instant, with a sense of relief, that the gun was after all merely a toy. But when she fired again, he knew it wasn't a toy, and as she fired the third time he leaped, grabbing for the gun but catching her wrist instead, and they both went down on the rug and the gun tumbled away. The woman fell heavily, Rocco on top of her, and he was aware, as they went down, that she was larger and sturdier than he'd thought, big-boned and strong.

He hadn't meant to knock her down.

"Are you all right?" he asked, feeling, strangely, a need to apologize.

She said nothing and didn't look at him, stared right past him with her large hazel eyes.

The admiral, astonished, stood where he was. "Crazy woman," he said, with a raised voice. "I don't even know her, never saw her in my life. What's she shooting at me for?"

The first bullet had ripped his sleeve above the elbow and grazed his arm, but the second had lodged in his chest, by the shoulder, a small stain of blood spreading slowly across the front of his white jacket. The third bullet vanished into the woodwork.

A group of navy men helped the admiral out to a car and took him to the military hospital. They had wanted to wait for a stretcher, but he insisted on walking out on his own.

The woman was made to sit on a chair, to await the police, a few ensigns keeping watch over her.

"Did you have to hit her so hard?" Fingerly said to Rocco, as they made their way to the dining room.

"Too hard? You think?"

"Like a ton of bricks."

Rocco was still thinking of her eyes, dreamy and quietly reckless, that long moment before she pulled the trigger, and still couldn't imagine what kind of lucky turbulence in her brain had made her turn and shoot the admiral instead.

In the dining room, the lights were low and the windows were covered with heavy draperies, in observance of the blackout. At the piano, Count Otto von Kreisen, a lean, elderly man known to his friends as Freddy, was playing a medley of Viennese waltzes. Rocco had met him, his last time at Dominic's, and had spoken with him at the bar. He was in international trade. He bought limestone in Malta, which he sold in Luxembourg, where he bought gumdrops and sulphuric acid that he sold in Albania. In Albania he bought prunes and sold them in Egypt, and in Egypt he bought marble that he shipped to Malta because Malta, rich in limestone, had no marble of its own. He went round and round on his trading tour, always returning to Malta, but now the circle was broken and he was stuck there, unable to get safe transport off the island. Rather than run the gauntlet of the Stukas and the U-boats, he'd decided to sit it out until the siege was over, little imagining he'd be hung up for over two years. He was German, from Bavaria, tall but slight, with narrow shoulders, a large nose, long tapered fingers, and remarkably small ears. He despised Hitler, hated him for the mess he was making in Europe, and favored a restoration of the monarchy. He had mentioned to Rocco, whimsically, that he fancied Malta was being bombed so mercilessly because the Führer knew exactly where he was.

He played waltzes, only waltzes, pleasantly nostalgic. The "Acceleration Waltz," the "Roses-from-the-South Waltz," the "Lemon Blossoms Waltz," the "Bewitchment Waltz," the "You-Only-Live-Once Waltz." There was a sadness in the way he played, but also a liveliness, a playful good humor, even at times a sauntering optimism. Once, after losing heavily in the Green Room, he went to the piano in the dining hall and played the "An der schönen blauen Donau." People who were there said it was the most beautiful rendering of "The Blue Danube" they'd ever heard. Even people who were not there were saying that. They'd heard so much about it that it became part of their collective memory, as if they had actually been there, humming along as the Count played.

The dining room was crowded with officers and government people, and a sprinkling of foreigners who, like the Count, had been stranded on Malta when the bombing began—an Algerian banker, a Greek herpetologist, a countess from Poland, a few sheiks from Tunisia and Bahrein. There was a bevy of reporters who couldn't wait to get off the island because there was nothing more to write about here, except that the bombs were still falling and the houses were being blown to pieces. At a table near the piano, Nigg's girl, Vivian, sat with a blond navy captain. When she saw Rocco, she opened her mouth, smiling, mockingly seductive, and curled her tongue.

"How's your appetite?" Fingerly asked, opening the menu.

Rocco had no appetite at all.

Fingerly ordered lampuki for himself, and for Rocco he recommended the *pulpetti tal-moch*. "You've got a rare treat ahead, Raven. *Pulpetti tal-moch* is a specialty of the house."

Food, on Malta, had been rationed for over a year, but despite the shortages, Dominic was still able to offer a menu, thanks to his black-market connections in Sicily. Once a week, on his boat, at night, he made the sixty-mile run into enemy waters, to a dock at Pozzallo, where he picked up whatever he needed: pork, veal, sacks of rice, bushels of mushrooms, barrels of olives, vintage wines from Marsala and Castellammare. The Luftwaffe knew the boat—it was orange and red—and they let it alone, the requisite payoffs having been made, through the Pozzallo contact, to the appropriate staffelkapitäns at the various airfields in Sicily. Occasionally, Dominic brought back with him a staffelkapitän or an oberstleutnant, in mufti, passing as a businessman, for a bit of entertainment, and while the staffelkapitän or the oberstleutnant was under his roof, Dominic could relax, confident that all of St. Julian's would be untouched by the bombs. Trafficking with the enemy was not just good business—it was good sense and patriotic too, a way of keeping the neighborhood safe.

The dining-room walls were hung with paintings in gilt frames, depicting scenes from the siege of Malta in the sixteenth century, when the Turks, led by Dragut and Mustapha Pasha, fought against the heavily outnumbered Knights. One painting showed the death of Dragut, in his tent, dying of a shrapnel wound. Another depicted the armies clashing at St. Elmo, which the Turks took at a cost of eight thousand men. Fingerly knew it all, reeling off the names and dates, the battle sites, the numbers of the dead.

Even before he got into the *pulpetti tal-moch*, Rocco knew something was wrong. He was cold, dizzy, and when he looked at the far wall, behind the piano, the wall seemed to move ever so slightly, like a bedsheet on a clothesline.

The waiter, Vittorio, brought a bottle of Bordeaux, an Haut Brion, which Fingerly tasted and approved. Dark rich red in the glass, almost black.

"After the Turks took St. Elmo's," Fingerly said, "they beheaded five Knights, tied the torsos to wooden crosses, and floated them across the harbor toward Fort St. Michael. What a fabulous scene for a movie—the headless bodies on the floating crosses, drifting in the fog. Can't you just see it?"

Rocco ran his finger along the stem of his wineglass, and, vividly, he saw the fog and the mutilated corpses.

"And La Valette? How does he retaliate? He beheads all of his Turk prisoners and uses their heads as cannonballs. Fires them one by one at the Turkish lines. Chica boom, Raven. Don't you love it?"

The wine warmed Rocco and took away some of the dizziness. The walls were steady again, but the paintings were out of focus, a hazy blur.

Nigg came out of the Green Room, in a surly mood.

"It's terrific wine," Fingerly said, urging him to sit. "I'll have Vittorio set a place for you."

Nigg glanced about, looking for Vivian. "I hate this place," he said gruffly, but whether it was because of bad luck in the Green Room or because of Vivian was hard to tell.

They watched as he crossed the room to Vivian's table. She was still with the captain, but as Nigg approached, she got up and met him by a pot of ferns. Nigg seemed agitated, and Vivian in turn showed a flash of temper, and for a moment they fell to arguing, quietly but with passion. Then, in a huff, she returned to the table, picked up her purse, murmured something in the captain's ear, and rushed off with Nigg.

Rocco stared across the room at the captain, who seemed, in his abandonment, completely baffled.

"Is she a whore," he asked, "or does she just like to fool around?"

Fingerly lifted his glass. "What do you think?"

"I think she's a tease."

"Oh, she's that all right. She's the daughter of one of the muckamucks in the local government. She wants to be an actress, but her papa won't let her, so she's embarrassing the hell out of him by slumming with the military riffraff. It's delayed adolescence. She's twenty-three going on thirteen."

Rocco felt strange again. The whole room seemed to be moving, like a ship in heavy waters. When he looked at the painting of Dragut, it was not Dragut he saw but himself, his own face and body, wounded, stretched out on a litter, dying in a wretched tent, far from home.

"What am I eating?"

"You don't know? Not a clue?"

It was a large, fried patty, like a fishcake, but it wasn't fish.

"Brains, Raven. You're eating brains."

"Whose brains?"

"Pig's brains. But these days, maybe it's goat. Or cat. Or dog."

Rocco looked across the room, toward the wide, white wall behind the piano. The Count was still playing, roaming through another waltz, and the wall behind him was covered by a web of red veins. There was blood on the wall, thick rivulets branching and flowing crookedly, and blood on the piano as well, and on the Count, on his white jacket, on his hands, on his sparse black hair combed flat against his scalp, on his forehead, on his face.

"Are you going to be okay?"

"Sure, no problem," Rocco said.

He picked up his fork, but when he looked again at the food on his plate, he knew he was in trouble. A tide rose all around him. He could still hear the rhythm of a waltz, but it was muted, faint, from far away.

He was up from the table, moving swiftly toward the men's room. The sounds of clattering plates and cutlery magnified in his ears and seemed the clanging of swords, as if he'd stepped into one of the paintings, into the rage of ancient battle. The cries, the calls, the sound of cannonballs crashing home. In the bathroom, he leaned over the sink, retching. It was a violent spasm, from deep inside him, as if death were nested there in the pit of his stomach, and he was vomiting it out.

He rinsed his mouth, washing away the foul taste. And still he lingered, leaning over the sink. The room was black tile rimmed with gold. There was a marble trough for a urinal, and two stalls. Above the sink hung a mirror in a gilded frame, throwing back at him his frayed image, eyes sunken and bloodshot from lack of sleep.

When he returned to the dining room, there was tea on the table, in a pink and white teapot, and Fingerly was talking with Dominic, recently back from his weekly run to Sicily. He was making a tour of the tables, sporting a maroon cummerbund and a matching bow tie. He was short but broad in the shoulders, and rotund, almost as wide as he was tall, with a rugged, gravel-toned voice and an overpowering smile.

"We are so glad to see the Americans," he said, when Fingerly introduced Rocco. "With the Americans in the war, it will be over quickly, very fast. We like the Americans."

"And we like the Maltese," Fingerly said. "Right, Rocco?"

"Yes," Rocco said, "it's a great country."

"We are a small country," Dominic said.

"True," Fingerly said, "small, but great in spirit."

"We welcome the Americans," Dominic repeated. "Tell me, when will they send their big army?"

"Not soon enough for me," Fingerly said.

"Ah yes, not soon enough. I understand, I understand."

Rocco wondered exactly what it was that Dominic understood.

"Rocco keeps a stable of thoroughbreds, back in Texas," Fingerly said. Then, to Rocco: "After the war, Dominic is setting up a stable of his own. He loves racing. Maybe the two of you can do business."

Rocco was dumbfounded.

"I shall look forward," Dominic said. "Where do you race? At Santa Anita? The Kentucky Derby?"

Rocco shrugged. "Anywhere," he said, feeling strangled by Fingerly's silly lie.

"I shall come to America to see your horses. We will exchange ideas about breeding."

"Nice." Fingerly grinned. "How wonderful for both of you."

Dominic left them and made his way across the dining room, smiling, nodding, shaking hands, and, reaching the piano, mounted the low platform. The Count greeted him with a vibrant glissando.

"Texas?" Rocco said. "I'm from Texas?"

"Rocco, Rocco, you're a stranger in a strange uniform, on an island that's getting bombed into the sea. Would you prefer I told him you deal in second-hand Chevrolets?"

Rocco was about to ask what was wrong with secondhand Chevrolets, but Dominic, with his booming voice, hands raised high above his head, giving the V-for-victory sign, announced glowingly that his weekly trip to Pozzallo had been a greater success than ever before. Not only had he brought back an abundance of food and wine, but this time, to his own amazement and delight, and for the joy of everyone, he had returned with a special and extraordinary guest. "Not General Kesselring," he said drolly, "who deserves to be roasted on a spit for bombing us day and night, and not *Il Duce*, who should be hung in a smokehouse like the Fascist pig that he is—no, no, the person I bring you is one of the angels, beautiful beyond words. Ladies and gentlemen, I present to you: Angelina Labbra, Miss Sicily of 1941!"

The Count played a lively flourish, and Miss Sicily appeared, emerging from the massive ferns in the foyer, dark-complexioned, with lively green eyes, a delicately arched nose, and a fierce, toothy smile. A heavy application of rouge gave her cheeks a neon glow. Her hair was platinum, and her silver lamé dress clung to her body as if grafted to her skin. As she crossed the room, making her way toward the piano, she rolled her hips voluptuously, throwing kisses with both hands. It was easy to imagine what she would have looked like in a bathing suit, or even without one. She was greeted with vigorous applause—a few whistles, and plenty of foot-stamping from the younger lieutenants.

"A tart from Palermo if ever I saw one," Fingerly said in Rocco's ear. "But she has a great dentist. Ever see a Sicilian with straight teeth like that? Dominic must have been all over her in the boat, all the way home."

When she sang, she surprised everyone, singing not a torch song, but a hymn, the "Panis Angelicus." Hymns were her specialty. Her voice rose and fell with celestial smoothness, rich with feeling, her sensuous lips opening and closing over her magnificent teeth, and it was a marvel, a paradox, that such an earthy body could produce such a heavenly sound.

After she sang, Dominic auctioned her off. She was going to be on Malta for a week, and a chaperone would be needed to drive her around and show her the sights, the privilege going to the highest bidder. The proceeds from the auction were earmarked for the Orphans' Fund.

Fingerly lit a cigarette. "You know who's in charge of the Orphans' Fund, don't you? Dominic's brother-in-law."

The bidding was fast and furious, the captains, majors, and colonels vying hotly, but one by one they dropped out, leaving the field to a brigadier and a navy man, a vice admiral who spent most of his time in an underground room beneath the Upper Barracca Gardens. The brigadier, holding a cigar, and the vice admiral, holding a sherry, nudged each other up toward three hundred. But before they got there, the Algerian banker, a portly, middle-aged man, gray at the temples, brought an end to it with a resounding bid of five hundred pounds, leaving the brigadier and the vice admiral, and just about everyone else in the room, agape.

Miss Sicily seemed grander, more dazzling, than when she first appeared, the neon glow of her rouge even brighter than before. "I love Malta," she said in English, with a heavy accent. "I love all of you. I love God, and I love the world. Is not the world a wonderful, divine, and happy place?"

A bomb, a big one, struck nearby, shaking the building and making the tableware rattle. The lights blinked off, then on, then off again with finality, and the busboys, as if waiting for just this moment, rushed about from table to table distributing candles, and as they were lit, the Count, in the semidark, struck up another waltz, playing with his usual ease, never missing a beat.

It was out of the ordinary for a bomb to fall so close to Dominic's, and there were some in the room who wondered if the presence of Miss Sicily might not have ushered in an era of bad luck. There was disgruntlement too because a foreigner, the Algerian, had won in the bidding. It dampened morale, and the noise level in the room descended to a disappointed hubbub.

The mood brightened, though, when the chef, Lorenzo Pazzi, in white garb, head covered by a puffy chef's hat, entered the dining room, wheeling in a seven-tiered layer cake lit with dozens of magnesium sparklers, all ablaze, sending off cascading showers of white and blue sparks. It was the Miss Sicily memorial gâteau, covered with icing and scoops of whipped cream, and adorned with delicately sculpted sugar-paste roses. Dominic announced, grinning, that the cake had seven layers in honor of the seven sacraments. Then added, deadpan, that the cake was, in fact, a celebration of the seven deadly sins.

More bombs went off, but not nearby.

"Isn't it delicious," Fingerly said, "living in a war zone?"

Rocco stared at the floor, thinking he might be sick again, feeling weird, unbalanced, adrift. Like being on a movie set, part of the action, the camera moving in for a close-up—but he doesn't know his lines, and no idea what next.

Fingerly looked at him as if he were slowly dissolving. "You're not in the throes of an identity crisis, are you?"

"Is that what this is? I'm losing my mind?"

"Only if you want to. But don't worry, it's not that terrible, you'll get used to it. Give it time, you'll adjust."

"Adjust to what?"

"To everything, if you relax and let it happen."

Just then, what Rocco noticed, what caught his eye, was that all of the gilt-framed pictures on the walls were lopsided, knocked crooked by the bomb that had put out the lights. Somehow they looked better that way, less ponderous, amusingly off center, and when he looked again at Fingerly, Fingerly too was tilted, like the paintings, and seemed, like them, more interesting that way: slanted, teetering, about to slide off and float away. He was eating a slice of the Miss Sicily cake and had a feathery smudge of whipped cream on the tip of his nose. Rocco wondered: Should he trust him, or should he hate him? Should he adore him? Sometimes he seemed a medium-grade genius, grabbing names and facts out of the wind, but other times he seemed merely glib and clever, faking it, making it up as he went along. Rocco knew virtually nothing about him. Nothing about where he was from, or about his family, or his past—his boyhood ambitions, his hobbies, the girls he dated in high school, the games he played or didn't play. It was as if he'd been born whole, dumped fully formed onto the planet, and even the planet didn't know if he was safe or truly dangerous.

+ *April 14, 1942* +

COMPULSORY LABOR SERVICE
All males between 16 and 60 to register for
war work repairing aerodromes
WORK HOURS: 7:30 to 4:30
One Hour for Lunch
Time lost during raids to be made up later
Skilled: 7 shillings
Unskilled: 6 shillings

———

FARSONS MILK STOUT
An Ideal Beverage for Rheumatic Invalids and All Workers
Brewed and Bottled by Simonds-Farsons, Ltd.

———

WRIGHT'S COAL TAR SOAP
The protective properties of Wright's are contained in no other toilet soap. Yet its antiseptic lather is kind to the tenderest skin—whether of baby or adult. Because it is the only toilet soap that contains Liquor Carbonis Detergens, it discourages infection and keeps the skin clear of sores and blemishes.
AWARDED THE BLUE SEAL OF MERIT

Ten

ZAMMIT

As it turned out, the Norwegian woman who shot the admiral was not a stranger, as the admiral had protested, but had been, for some time, his mistress. He had broken off with her after becoming involved with a younger woman, a circus performer from Belgium, from Liège, a Jewish girl who had come to Malta to get away from the Germans, but now the Germans might take Malta and she worried about where to go next. In the circus she had been a bareback rider, performing somersaults on the back of a white Arabian with a braided tail. Now she spent most of her time knitting. The Norwegian woman, whose disdain for circus performers was exceeded only by her contempt for men who took her favors lightly, never spoke a word after she shot the admiral. She was put into a hospital, in a mental ward, for observation, as there was some serious concern that she might attempt suicide.

Rocco learned all of this from Melita, who found out about it from Christina, who had picked it up while working in the RAF Ops Room, deep down in the Lascaris bastion, so deep, and the air so foul, they called it the Hole. There was an almost giddy buzz in the underground corridors, about how the admiral had nearly got himself killed from fooling around with two women—he, an admiral, who should have known better. Not just an admiral but a married man, in his fifties, with a wife and three grown children in Surrey.

"Isn't it a shame?" Christina said gleefully, when she told Melita the story. "Isn't it a delicious, wonderful shame?"

She'd been having an affair of her own, for over a year, with an English reconnaissance pilot, Adrian Warburton. Everyone called him Warby, and she did too. He came and went, flying all over the Mediterranean. He took aerial photographs of the entire two hundred and fifty miles of the Via Balbia, from Benghazi to Tripoli, and of the Calitri viaduct in Italy, slated for demolition by commandos. He had blue eyes, blond hair, and was almost never in proper uniform, favoring gray flannel trousers, a cravat instead of a tie, and desert boots. A little reckless too, taking any kind of a risk to get a picture. At the Gulf of Taranto, he flew so low he tore an aerial off an enemy battleship.

Christina lived in a flat on Vilhena Terrace, in Floriana, and Warby spent more time there than at the officers' mess. She sewed his cap for him, and did some knitting. She sewed his buttons. He was not very demanding sexually, she confided to Melita, and, to her amusement and dismay, he wasn't much of a dancer either. The only time he would venture onto a dance floor was when the band played "Jealousy," and then, in his stiff, clumsy shuffle, he would step all over her toes.

"Wooden feet," she said despairingly to Melita. "In the sky he's an acrobat, there's nothing he can't do. They give him medals. But on the ground he has wooden feet!"

It was exciting for her that he was an ace, famous at reconnaissance—but this, the very thing that appealed to her, his wizardry in the sky, put him at risk, and she worried, whenever he went up, that he might not return. Was she bad for him, the wrong person? He pushed the odds, and she did nothing to restrain him, nothing to rein in his impulse for danger and adventure, because she was herself a part of it, caught up in the stir and frenzy of the war. Would she be for him, she wondered, a jinx?

As she poured out her doubts and uncertainties, Melita listened, and they drank coffee. The war was hard. To be a soldier was hard, but to fall in love with one was worse. They were at Christina's place, in Floriana, roses and cabbages growing in boxes by the windows. The coffee was made from grinds that had been used three times over, pale and watery, no kick, and when Melita looked at Christina, she thought Christina was like the coffee, tired and worn out. Her long hours as a plotter for the RAF were taking their toll, and the dancing too. And this thing with Warby, it was wearing her down.

Christina offered more coffee, but Melita wanted no more.

"It's awful, I know," Christina apologized. "I told Warby to bring coffee his last time in Cairo, but he forgot. How could he forget? He brought stockings, fudge, and Egyptian wine, but he forgets the coffee. And he can't dance, so what good is he?"

The rest of that week, and on into the next, while Fingerly searched for a wireless for Rocco—and did whatever else that he was doing—Rocco traveled with Melita in the hearse, from town to town. Not so easy on the dusty, winding roads, but they were good days, in the car together. They talked, they bantered. He teased, and she teased back. He teased her about her hair, so long that it caught in the car door when she pulled it closed, and she teased him because he couldn't sing, couldn't carry a tune, could only whistle, and not very well. Sometimes, after a long silence, he would reach back in memory and pull up some lines from Edgar Allan Poe, remembering them from the night course he'd been taking just before he enlisted, poems of loneliness and darkness, of loss and nevermore. The instructor had made them memorize passages that they liked, of their own choosing, and Rocco, who had a difficult time with memory, used to run through the lines while working at the used-car lot, repeating them over and over until he had them right.

> A green isle in the sea, love,
>   A fountain and a shrine,
> All wreathed with fruits and flowers,
>   And all the flowers were mine.
> Ah, dream too bright to last!

Melita liked it that he knew poetry. He knew about cars, and he knew poetry too, and that pleased her. Poetry was good, as music was good, and painting also, the paintings of Caravaggio and Mattia Preti, which were in the Cathedral, though she preferred Raphael and Botticelli, whose work she had seen only in books. She wasn't so sure about Edgar Allan Poe. She liked the lines that Rocco recited, but she thought they were sad.

In the hearse, driving, every day they were into a different town, and wherever they went, there were people who knew her. They knew her name and were glad to see her. She carried a screwdriver, a wrench, and other tools, and made minor repairs on the jukeboxes. Some were boxes Zammit had made, but there were others, from before the war, Wurlitzers and Seeburgs, and the boxes from Rock-Ola. If a wire was loose, she could reconnect it. If the coin mechanism was jammed, she knew how to fix it, and she could open the machine and change the records. If the light bulbs were burned out, she changed them, and if the sockets themselves were damaged and needed replacing, as sometimes happened, she could change those too.

In Żebbuġ there was a bartender who greeted her, grandly, as the Jukebox Queen. That's what she was, queen of the jukeboxes, delivering the music. It was music you could drink to, and music you could dance to, if you were in the mood: the big bands and the big songs, songs that bite and songs that swoon, songs that drop you off the edge of a cliff and you fall, but you never hit bottom.

"Where do you get the records?" Rocco asked, as they fox-trotted to Glenn Miller, in a bar in Attard.

"Which records?"

"All of them. You have an uncle in Tin Pan Alley?"

"A British flyer brings them in."

"Just like that? Flies them in?"

"They come from somewhere in America—Tennessee, I think—and go to Caracas. From Caracas they go to Gibraltar. In Gibraltar, the British flyer picks them up and takes them in on a Wellington."

The songs, always the songs.

"What happens if he gets shot down?"

"Then Malta will have no more music."

"You pay him?"

"We pay for the records and he flies them in free."

The pilot's family ran a fish-and-chips shop in Liverpool. After the war, Zammit was going to ship them a jukebox, gratis, to compensate for the delivery of the records. The pilot had already picked one out; it had blue lights that blinked on and off.

"You know what I think?" Rocco said. "I think there is no Zammit. I think you make these things by yourself."

"If that's what you think, then it must be time for you to meet him."

"You told him about me?"

"Well, not everything. He'd be very upset if he knew everything. This is Malta, there's no fooling around here until after the priest blesses you and you are married. Zammit is only a cousin, but since he's my oldest living male relative, he feels responsible, as if he were my uncle, or my father. The men in Malta can be very difficult about these things."

"I think we'll skip Zammit."

She shrugged.

"That's all right with you?"

"If that's what you want," she said cheerfully.

She installed four new records in Sliema, changed a light bulb in Gzira, connected a loose wire in Ta' Xbiex, and replaced a cracked piece of glass in Pietà. A half hour later, after they delivered some recordings to a bar in Paola, Rocco took over the driving and put the car on the road to Santa Venera.

"You changed your mind? Now you want to meet him?"

"No, I don't want to meet him, but you said he has good French brandy from before the war. I won't like him if he doesn't."

"Now I'm not so sure," she said, hesitating, "maybe it's not brandy but rum."

"I hate rum. Which way do I turn here?"

"Left. Then to the right."

They moved slowly through Msida, where there was a long queue of people waiting for milk. The milk was being dispensed from an aluminum truck with a big sign on it:

-PASTEURIZED-

DRINK SAFE MILK

& SAFEGUARD YOUR HEALTH

"I should get some for Zammit, he hasn't had milk for a long time."

"You want to wait on that line?"

She didn't. "It's all we do anymore, we wait for milk, bread, water, for rice when they have rice, and the kerosene. Sometimes we wait for nothing at all—people queue up, it's half a mile long, they think it's for bread, or cheese, but up front there's nothing. You know how it starts? A few old men stop to talk to each other and people think the old men know something, and word gets around: this is the queue for milk. The queue gets longer and longer, it winds around the block, and who comes three hours later is not the man with the milk but an old lady selling pencils, and she only has seven left, and they're used, the erasers are worn, but she sells for a terrific price because on Malta, right now, where can you get a pencil? Then she gets on line herself, at the back of the queue, thinking the milk is yet to come."

As Rocco drove, listening, he thought he would lose her. He thought she would be lifted somehow out of the car and carried off into the sky. He was dreaming while he drove. Any minute now it would happen: he would stop the car and jump out and watch her go, rising up, with flowers in her hair, thighs roped with grass, her pretty mouth still complaining about the lady selling pencils and the man who came later, selling marigolds, which nobody wanted, they only wanted milk, and the only place to get it was from Melita's breasts. She was in the sky, like the Madonna, being assumed into heaven.

She told him to turn right. "And you must believe in God," she was saying, "you must have faith. You must not lose your faith and your hope. You must go to confession and confess your sins, and go to communion."

He slammed on the brakes to avoid hitting a sheep that had wandered out onto the road. "I thought all the sheep had been slaughtered for food."

"Oh, there are still a few. We keep them as a reminder of the good times we used to have. That's Paulo's sheep, I recognize the scar on its nose. I hit him one day with the hearse. That sheep is so dumb, he doesn't know to get out of the way." Then, crisply, "Look, we're there, it's Zammit's house, just up the road."

Even though she had told him about Zammit's clubfoot, it still came as a surprise when he saw the large shoe with its thick sole and the awkward way Zammit walked, with a limp, swinging the left leg hard, as if the big shoe were weighted down with lead. And the other thing about him was that he was short, remarkably short—his head reaching only to Melita's shoulders. He had a small, silly mustache that was wrong for his face, like a patch of black wool pasted on his lip, and large brown eyes, eyes so intense that Rocco felt, when Zammit looked at him, that he was seeing right through him, into his bones.

He was napping when they came in, and Melita called up to him, letting him know they were there, but he was slow to come down. He washed and put on fresh clothes. He shaved and put on his best pair of shoes. But over his clothes he still wore his carpenter's apron, with nails and screws in the pouches, because without the apron he never felt quite himself and would have been, presumably, somebody else. He'd been up all night, working on a juke-box for the Zulu Bar in Safi. He was hesitant, slow with words, not from sleepiness but because that's how he was, abstracted, like a mathematician pondering a difficult equation.

"So you are the American soldier," he said, cautious, vaguely defensive. "Welcome, welcome to my house." His hair was like a black cloud. He shook Rocco's hand, and turned to Melita. "Melita, fix something. There's bread, and whatever you find. Bring the tomatoes." Then, to Rocco, "I have brandy, vermouth, and sherry. Whisky I don't have, it's so difficult with the war."

"Brandy," Rocco said, and Zammit, nodding, limped to an oak cabinet and took out a bottle of cognac and three glasses.

"She loves brandy," he said of Melita, who had vanished into the kitchen. "It gives her ideas for the jukeboxes. Perhaps you too will have some ideas?"

He cleared the dining-room table, removing tools, screws, pieces of freshly cut wood, saucers loaded with peach pits and grape seeds. The small house was no longer a home: it was a workshop, littered with hammers, saws, spools of wire, pots of glue, cans of varnish, old phonographs (Garriolas, Edisons, Victors, which he cannibalized for parts), and the broken furniture Melita brought in from the dumps. A chaos everywhere, in all the rooms, on the sofa and chairs, even in the bathroom, in the tub, and in the rooms upstairs. Not just the tools and materials, but the jukeboxes themselves, in various stages of incompletion. He worked on several at a time, and when he grew tired of one, he would work on another. Sometimes there was an impasse, an inability to go on, and he would abandon the piece altogether. Behind the house, by the garden, stood boxes he had never finished, half-formed and misshapen things, parked there like old cripples.

"I am not a dwarf," he said to Rocco, as if it were something he'd been waiting to say. "I am short, yes, but dwarfs, real dwarfs, are shorter. The bad foot is a mystery, we don't know from where. None of the old ones had this. The parish priest says it's a blessing from God."

Rocco knew why he was saying all of this. Zammit was trying to assure him that if he married Melita and had children, the chances of dwarfism or clubfoot were negligible. He was rushing things, already imagining them a married couple.

Rocco offered him a cigarette, but he didn't smoke.

"Melita said you work with cars," Zammit said.

"I worked at a used-car lot. I tinkered with the engines, fixed them up. Before the war."

"I work on jukeboxes. Do you like jukeboxes?"

"I like the music."

"Ah, the music, yes."

Zammit had been making jukeboxes for well over a year, ever since the war made it impossible for the bars and dance halls to buy jukeboxes from abroad. He hated the business side of it, dealing with the customers. He was only happy when he had a tool in his hands. So when Melita joined him, after the law courts were blown up, it was a blessing. She spoke on the phone and talked to the customers, discussing their needs. She calmed the impatient ones, she was good at that. And she worked on the boxes, learning from Zammit. She soldered wires, installed the speakers, arranged the records and the colored lights. She enjoyed it, it was better than typing up legal documents about car accidents, theft, and assault and battery.

In the late 1930s, jukeboxes were transformed by the introduction of translucent plastic, with fancy lighting that shone through, and overnight the old jukeboxes, made of ponderous wooden cabinets, were obsolete. But now, with the war on, it was impossible on Malta to get plastic, and Zammit had no choice but to revert to the old style, producing boxes made of wood. But even the wood was hard to get. Malta had no forests, no lumber of its own, and with no wood coming in because of the siege, there was only the salvage from the bombed-out houses and the dumps.

It was Melita who came up with the idea of using stained glass.

Zammit was skeptical.

"Why not?" she said. "Try it."

He tried it, and it worked. Not only did it work, but it liberated him, freeing him from the dead formalities of the old designs and affording possibilities that even plastic didn't hold.

He embarked upon what Melita spoke of as his early mannerist phase, making oversized, muscular jukeboxes vivid with colored glass. Some of these were as much as seven feet tall, while others were short, squat, and very wide. He made them full-bodied and odd-angled, in bizarre geometrical shapes, and always Melita was there, urging him on: make it bigger, make it wider, make it crazier and livelier, with more glass. Make it glow. Make it shine, make it so that it's a music all its own and you don't even have to turn on the record to hear the song.

He worked obsessively, into the night. Mornings, he'd be up at six and off to church, where he heard mass and went to communion—he was deeply religious, always with a rosary in his pocket—and then, after a small breakfast, he would be back at work again.

Melita, humming, came in from the kitchen with bread, tomatoes, and a bottle of olive oil. She took a sip of brandy, and glanced slyly at Rocco. "Is he boring you, talking about the jukeboxes? Has he shown you his scrapbook?"

"We've been talking about the weather," Rocco said, touching his glass to hers.

"Too cold for April," Zammit said. "Soon it will be May and it will still be cold. It's the war, everything mixed up and backwards."

Cold? Rocco thought it warm, a lot warmer than any April he could remember in Brooklyn. The nights cool, yes, but with the sun up, you could raise a sweat just walking.

Melita cut the bread into thick slices, then cut open a tomato and rubbed it across the bread until the bread turned pink with the pulp and juice. She drenched the bread with olive oil and added oregano and thyme. "We call it *ħobz-biż-żejt,* bread and oil."

"And that's the last of my oil," Zammit noted plaintively.

"Tomorrow we'll find more," she said. "Somewhere on this island there has to be oil."

They ate and talked, and sipped brandy, and mostly now it was Melita who spoke, telling about the jukeboxes, the ones they sold and the ones they didn't, the successes and the failures.

"Did he tell you about the Bethlehem Jukebox?"

Zammit had not.

"Did he tell you about the Fingers of St. Agatha?"

He had not spoken of that, either.

"Why do you want to tell him about those long-ago things?" Zammit said, waving his hand.

She poured herself more brandy, her eyes darting deliciously, back and forth, between Rocco and Zammit.

Not long after Zammit found his way into stained glass, his work took on a religious tone. His Counter-Reformation Baroque, Melita called it. He made jukeboxes adorned with rosaries, religious medals, madonnas, pictures of the saints. He arranged for each jukebox to be given a special blessing by the parish priest, Father Maqful, and he sold them—at discount, because of the religious aspect—to churches and religious schools. They were used for the Friday night youth dances in parishes all over the island.

Still, he wanted more, there was yet another step. What he had in mind was to make jukeboxes that were musical reliquaries, containing the relics of the saints. He prepared sketches for the St. Agatha Jukebox, which would have on display, under glass, some of St. Agatha's bones, a finger or a toe. She was an important saint for Malta, she had lived there for a while, before she was martyred in Sicily. But when Zammit approached Father Maqful, the old priest rejected the idea outright, because a relic in a jukebox was, plainly, not the sort of thing that the archbishop would approve.

For Zammit, the idea died hard. He was thinking of the incorrupt arm of St. Francis Xavier, and the dried blood of St. Januarius, which liquefied every year on his feast day, and the body of Mary Magdalene, yielding a sweet odor in a church in Vézelay. There was the finger of St. John the Baptist in Maurienne, and the body of St. Nicholas stolen from Myra and carried off to Bari, where pieces of the body were pilfered and brought to the village of Porta. Perhaps, for one of the jukeboxes, he might have a knuckle, or a few locks of hair.

One day, after Father Maqful had again turned a deaf ear, he took all of his sketches and diagrams, and in a fit of despair, burned them in the kitchen stove. He blamed the saints because, obviously, they had failed to rouse themselves and use their powerful influence. After the burning of the sketches, he created only one more jukebox with a religious theme. It was the Bethlehem Jukebox, containing a blue star that shed its beam on a stable containing the Holy Family, with snow, made from tiny bits of rice paper, falling on the scene. But he was never able to get the snow to work right. It got all over the records, making the needle skip, and with maddening regularity it clogged the motor that drove the turntable. Of all the jukeboxes, this one was the most disappointing, and it eventually took its place with the other fiascos in the garden behind the house.

He moved next into what Melita spoke of as his neoclassical phase, a style that he'd been laboring in for the last several months. Abandoning the excesses of his early, middle, and late baroque, he now made boxes with neat, circumspect lines, trim and unobtrusive, with fine appointments, never overdone, and never merely ornate.

It amused him, the terms that Melita used. Baroque, mannerist, Counter-Reformational. "She studied art, she knows these fancy names." When he worked, he didn't reflect on the style, it was simply something he felt, a need to make the box one way rather than another, moving it along in a certain direction. Now, in his neoclassical phase, he was plain rather than ornate because the work felt more comfortable for him that way. He still used stained glass, for want of anything else, but he avoided the more garish color tones and opted, overall, for a general simplicity of design. Still, in recent weeks, despite the success of his latest boxes, his work was undergoing yet another change, and he was aware that, day by day, he was on his way into something different.

"Come," he said, "I will show you my newest piece, what I am working on right now."

He brought them upstairs, to his bedroom, which was as much of a workroom as any of the other rooms, cluttered with awls, screwdrivers, and finishing saws. By the bed stood the jukebox he was working on for the Zulu Bar in Safi, all but finished. It was slender, warm, engaging, a blend of birch and chestnut, with a modest amount of stained glass and, the new accent, a considerable quantity of glass tubing—spirals, loops, straight runs—through which there flowed colored liquids of a pastel hue, pink in some tubes, lavender in others, bubbles effervescing through the liquids, so that the whole effect was one of freshness and vivaciousness. It was, clearly, a transitional piece, the genial beginnings of an exuberant romanticism.

He pressed a lever, and a record swung down onto the turntable. It was Gene Autry, singing "Have I Told You Lately That I Love You?" Zammit had a growing passion for cowboy songs, especially when they were lonely and forlorn, songs of the heart. In the jukebox for the Zulu Bar there were songs by Jimmie Rodgers, Hank Snow, Tex Ritter, four or five others.

Rocco was fascinated by the percolating liquids.

"How'd you do that?" he asked, curious about the technology. "How'd you make the bubbles?"

"He's a genius," Melita said, not fawningly but with simple admiration for Zammit's talent.

"God is good," Zammit said. "Sometimes I hardly know what I am doing, but my hands know. God is in my hands. In my fingers."

Gene Autry was still singing, and Melita swayed lightly to the rhythm. Rocco peered into the jukebox, puzzling, unable to understand how Zammit had created the bubbles, and Zammit, by the window, was looking out at the garden, gazing at a fig tree.

"Gene Autry?" Rocco said.

Zammit smiled. "You like him?"

Rocco looked at Zammit, short and slight, the big shoe on his clubfoot, and much as he tried, couldn't imagine him out on the range with the prairie dogs and the hoot owls, and the everlasting tumbleweed.

Zammit's scrapbook, which he'd kept for years, was stuffed with pictures of jukeboxes, some in color, some black-and-white, which he'd cut out of magazines. There was a 1927 AMI, and a Seeburg Audiophone from 1928. A 1929 Dance Master. The first Wurlitzer (1933) and the first Rock-Ola (1935). Then, after 1938, the gleaming, booming, light-up models made of multicolored translucent plastic—the Gem, the Regal, the Throne of Music, the Rock-Ola Master Rockolite. Mingled among these were pictures of some of the early machines that were the forerunners of the jukebox—the Edison Automatic Phonograph, from the 1890s, containing one song, which you could play for a nickel, and the turn-of-the-century Multiphone, which offered a choice of twenty-four songs. The Hexaphone, the Graphophone, the Automatic Entertainer.

Zammit's favorite picture was from a magazine that had come out the year before he was born. It showed Peter Bacigalupi's *Kinetoscope, Phonograph, and Graphophone Arcade* in San Francisco, in the year 1900. The arcade was a long high-ceilinged room with rows of music machines in elegant wooden cabinets. Above the machines were paintings in frames, creating a museumlike atmosphere. On each machine was a linen napkin to clean the earphones before and after use. The room was lighted by two chandeliers, each fitted with clusters of pressed glass lampshades. Zammit had always felt he would have been happy living in such a place, in such a time. He would repair the machines when they needed fixing, and the rest of the time he would sit around, watching the people who came in to enjoy the music. He would sit in an easy chair, and he would see the smiles, the eyes, the feet tapping to the rhythm, heads and shoulders swaying. Nobody would go away disappointed, he would make sure of that. He would always have the best music, and machines with the best possible sound. But that was 1900, in San Francisco, before he was born, and now it was 1942, Malta, and the world sinking fast in a lunatic war that everyone knew would be crazier yet before it ever went away.

Eleven

THE WORD FOR SNOW

Rocco had been sleeping at night in the shelter, but now he moved into the house on Windmill Street, which he had all to himself. There was the mattress upstairs, on the floor, and downstairs, in the kitchen, a stove that ran on kerosene and a sink that sometimes had running water.

When Fingerly found him, he was in a long queue on Zachary Street, a few blocks from Windmill.

"I promised you a wireless," Fingerly said.

"You did?"

"It's on a farm down by Maqluba."

"I'm on line here, I've been waiting an hour."

"What's this for—milk?"

"Kerosene, I think."

"Come, I'll get you all you need." He was already on the move, heading for the car, by the City Gate.

From Valletta they drove south, on bad dirt roads, kicking up a lot of dust, down past Luqa airfield, through a region that had been heavily quarried, to a small farm between Żurrieq and Qrendi, and the whole way Fingerly was complaining about Maroon, still couldn't forgive him for getting himself killed while crossing over from Gozo.

"I told him to take the ferry, three times I told him. If he'd've listened, he'd be here today, strutting like the turkey he was. He was almost in, damn him, but he slows and shoots with that dumb flare gun."

"He's dead," Rocco said.

"You bet he is," Fingerly answered, as if he deserved to be.

He had three divers working in the channel off Marfa Point, trying to recover what they could of the pigmy elephant. The divers were fishermen who couldn't fish any more because their boats had been shot to pieces by the Luftwaffe.

It was hard to imagine the bones were anything more than splinters, after the boat blew. "What are you going to do? Glue them together?"

Fingerly rocked his head from side to side. "What you suffer from, Rocco Raven, is a lack of faith. No hope, no vision of the future, no confidence the future will really be there when you need it. What you need is more ambition."

Maybe so, Rocco thought, maybe so. But he was beginning to suspect that what Fingerly suffered from was a deficiency in the area of common sense. He really did believe his divers were going to find those bones.

The farm was a farm of only a few acres, terraced slopes planted with cabbage. The house was squat and cube-shaped, made of yellowish blocks of limestone, angled into the side of a hill and looking as if it were sinking into the earth. At a distance from the house, and away from the cabbages, a radio mast rose beside a small stone hut surrounded by a riot of weeds and vines.

The farmer was among the cabbages, working with a hoe. Fingerly waved, and the farmer waved back. He was short and old, olive-dark, no teeth in his mouth, a black vest over a white shirt, sleeves rolled up to his elbows. He said nothing, just waved, and Fingerly, with a leisurely stride, brought Rocco over to the hut.

The wireless was on an old workbench—a transmitter and a Hammerlund receiver, an HRO50, in a workspace crowded with tools. Hanging from pegs were scythes, sickles, pruning hooks, an old plow with a harness for a mule. In front of the workbench was a stool, and by the receiver, an ashtray with some butts in it.

Rocco switched the units on, the tubes lighting up, the dials glowing eerily. "What's a farmer doing with a setup like this?"

Fingerly lifted his long arms and clasped his hands behind his head. "Because he's a farmer he shouldn't have a wireless?"

"Jesus, just look at him—his shoes are coming apart, his pants are falling down, he probably uses magic incantations to grow the cabbages. And he has this world-class equipment that he can't possibly know how to operate? He doesn't even have any teeth in his head."

"You disparage the man because he's too poor to have dentures? What kind of a perspective is that?" Fingerly looked at Rocco with the barest hint of a smile, his end-of-discussion smile, his let's-forget-it smile, his chica-chica-boom-chic smile.

"You want me to send?"

"I want you to listen." He opened a drawer on the workbench and took out a yellow pad and two pencils, the pad almost as astonishing as the wireless, because paper, on Malta, blank paper, was practically nonexistent. Pencils too. He wrote down three frequencies he wanted Rocco to try. "Put it all on the pad," he said. "Whatever comes through."

He left the hut, and Rocco, perched on the stool, looked through the doorway, watching as Fingerly went off into the cabbages and talked to the old man. Fingerly talked, then the old man talked, then neither of them said anything for a while.

Rocco worked the dials, locating one of the frequencies, but there was nothing. On the second, a message was coming through in dots and dashes. He listened, getting the hang of it, then grabbed a pencil and started writing. It was an open code, a jargon code, words standing for other words, in sentences that would make sense if you had the key.

> SUMMER BEATS SNOW
>
> ANYHOW BLESSES THE GREAT EMPTINESS
>
> LOST IS LOST, DUMB IS DUMB
>
> WEAR YOUR OVERCOAT

There was nothing for a while, then the transmission began again, the same message over and over.

He tuned to the third frequency, and something was coming through there too, in dots and dashes, but different, in cipher—no words, just groups of letters, five in a group:

> GEIFK USMOL WYWQA ECXPZ QPFHM VNBYU
>
> OLIKU JYHTG TFRDE WSAQX MLKJN BGVFC

There were other lines, then a pause, then the same message was repeated. When Fingerly came back, he took a look at the pad and nodded vaguely.

"Who've I been spying on?" Rocco asked.

"Does it matter?"

"I want to know who's going to be pulling the trigger when they catch up with me."

"These are permissive days, Raven. Radio spies don't get shot, they just rot in jail. Give that first frequency another try."

Rocco tuned the frequency, but still there was nothing.

"You need kerosene? Right in there." Fingerly pointed to a door, and, opening it, Rocco found a roomful of supplies: tins of corned beef, sacks of potatoes, cases of wine, jars of preserves and pickled vegetables, wheels of cheese, strings of dried figs.

"Where'd he get it all? He works for Dominic?"

"He hoards. He's been hoarding ever since World War I. He knows about hard times, he remembers. There, the kerosene's behind the potatoes. Take a can. Take two."

"You paid?"

"Uncle Sam paid. Paid through the nose. I should take it out of your salary."

"Uncle Sam is a skinflint?"

"He just likes to keep his accounts in order."

They put the kerosene in the car, then, walking, Fingerly took Rocco over to see Maqluba, a quarter of a mile beyond the farmhouse, just outside the village of Qrendi.

Maqluba was an ancient sinkhole, a hundred feet deep and over three hundred wide. A small village had stood there, long ago, over a subterranean cavern, and when the cavern collapsed, the village sank into the hole. Now, down at the bottom, there was nothing, just a tangled mass of grass and old trees. A church at the edge, overlooking the hole, had been left standing, but only fragments remained, worn away by wind and weather. The legend was that God destroyed the village because the people had lost their faith and were living in sin.

Fingerly liked the spot. He was fascinated by the lingering sense of catastrophe. "You know what *Maqluba* means? It means topsy-turvy. When the town sank, the people who came to look at it gave it this smart new name. Topsy-Turvy Village."

A good name not just for the sinkhole but for the whole island, Rocco thought, a capsized, upside-down nightmare, nothing straight, nothing neat, nothing orderly, bombs falling day and night, people in the shelters barely surviving on watery cloacal stew and rotting green meat peeled from the bones of anemic, underfed goats. The hospital for the insane had been bombed. The leprosy hospital had been bombed. The Cini maternity hospital had been bombed. The baking of cake was banned because of the shortages—and yet at Dominic's, if you had the cash, you could still get pastries made with *rikotta*, and twenty-year-old whisky from Scotland. Up was down, left was right, yes was no, and no was maybe.

Fingerly, at the rim of the sinkhole, unzipped his pants and released a long stream of urine that fell golden and swift into the foliage below. Rocco joined him, unzipping and peeing. "It's history down there," Fingerly said, "you have to take good care of it, you have to water the past and keep it alive. It's the mother, the source of all the good things we know."

Wildflowers grew in profusion, tiny irises and narcissi, marigolds, pimpernels—pink and blue petals, yellow and red. Rocco wondered what kind of a hell it must have been for the ones who were there that day, in the small village, hundreds of years ago, when the ground broke underneath them and their world came to an end.

"I want you to monitor those frequencies," Fingerly said as they headed back to the car. "Every morning, seven to nine. We'll switch the times around after a week or two."

"How do I get here? You're giving me the Austin?"

"Take the bus to Qrendi," he said, nodding toward the box-shaped limestone houses less than a mile away.

"What if they bomb Qrendi?"

"Then take the thirty-two to Żurrieq."

"What if they bomb the thirty-two?"

"If they bomb the thirty-two and you're on it, then it won't really matter, will it?"

The following morning, when Rocco went to the Portes des Bombes for the bus to Qrendi, he found it was no longer running, because of the petrol shortage. He got on the 32 to Żurrieq, an old bus, badly dented and scratched. Most of the windows had been knocked out, and the few that remained had strips of tape across them to prevent shattering. It was a vehicle that had seen better days. On all the buses, there were ornaments and various good-luck charms up front, by the driver's seat, and pictures of the driver's favorite saints. On this bus, on the visor, the driver kept only one saint, the Little Flower, St. Theresa, with a few sprigs of lily-of-the-valley fastened to the picture by a paperclip.

Before the bus was halfway along to Żurrieq, before it even reached Kirkop, it was bombed.

The bomb hit the road a short distance up ahead. It was a dirt road, packed earth and gravel on top of the limestone substratum, and the bomb opened a huge crater, tossing up dirt and chunks of limestone that landed all over the bus. The driver, a thin, ascetic-looking man with a large black mustache, remained uncommonly calm. He seemed in his late thirties, with a deadpan face and dark eyes that were remote, expressionless. First he went from seat to seat, making sure no one was injured, then he made everyone get out because he was going to have to drive off the road, over a rugged field, to get around the bomb crater. But then, when everyone was off, before he moved the bus, he announced he would have to remove every piece of gravel and rock that had fallen onto the roof.

It seemed unreasonable. "If you just start up and drive," Rocco said, "the stuff will fall away on its own."

But the driver would not be swayed. He answered, with maddening sangfroid, that the debris, falling off, would scratch the paint, and when Rocco pointed out that the bus was already horribly scratched and dented, the driver looked at him as if he were an infidel.

While the passengers stood by and watched, the driver climbed onto the roof and, one by one, lifted the pebbles and chunks of limestone with extreme care and tossed them off to the side of the road. A woman, and some of the men, tried to reason with him, but he was no longer listening.

With a shrug, Rocco took off his jacket, climbed up onto the roof, and lent a hand.

"Take off your shoes," the bus driver said.

"What?"

"Your shoes. They'll scratch the paint."

Rocco took off his shoes, and noticed the driver had removed not only his shoes but his socks as well, and it was suddenly clear to Rocco that the man was mad. He was living in some tender dream of the bus's nativity, when his bus was new and untouched, as sleek and precious as a beautiful woman, responsive to his touch, steering left, steering right, the brakes released, cruising with sweet acceleration—not just any woman but the Little Flower herself, his special patron, whom he wooed morning and night with impassioned prayers, she with the face of an angel, the face of a woman he had met in his dreams, the nose, the eyelashes, the molded chin, the sweetly contoured corners of her lips.

The sirens sounded again, another air raid on its way, and the passengers, still at the edge of the road, shouted at the driver, urging him to get back in the bus and move on. There was a priest with a beard, a woman with three children, another with a baby, an old nun with a shopping bag full of knitting, and a bald man with most of his teeth gone. The old nun was vociferous, shouting in Maltese, brandishing the big crucifix on her black rosary beads. The driver would not be hurried. After the debris had all been lifted away, he took a towel from under his seat and wiped the dust off the windows, the few that the bus still had. He never smiled.

On a Monday, Melita moved out of the room above the pharmacy on Triq Dun Mario, in Qormi, and moved in with Rocco, into the bomb-damaged house on Windmill Street, in Valletta.

The walls and ceilings had lost much of their plaster, but compared to some of the neighboring buildings, this one was in good shape. Rocco had brought down the mattress from the roofless room upstairs, putting it in the living room, and had salvaged a bedstead from the ruins next door. He'd also found a table and a few chairs for the dining room. The lights worked when there was electricity, and the toilet flushed when there was water—but water was a chancy thing, some days merely a trickle, most days nothing at all. For both of them, it was an adventure, Rocco thinking of it, with full awareness, as something new and different, some sort of turning point. He'd made love before, but had never actually lived with anyone, in the same house, same rooms, as if married.

She brought with her a frying pan, a small espresso pot but no coffee to put in it, a peacock feather, a suitcase full of clothes, a box of books, a small radio, and, to power the radio when the electricity was down, a hand-operated generator. She also brought a cat, Byron, named for the poet, who'd had a flaming affair with a married woman, an Austrian, when he visited Malta over a century ago. He was, at the time, twenty-one, living in rooms on Old Bakery Street, around the corner from Windmill, in a building that now housed the Telephone Exchange. He hated Malta, deriding it as a barren isle "Where panting Nature droops the head . . ." He disliked the heat, the sun, the sultry scirocco, the parched landscape, the hilly streets where he dragged along with his deformed right foot.

> Adieu, ye cursed streets of stairs!
> (How surely he who mounts you swears!)
> Adieu . . .

The affair with the married woman was passionate but short-lived. She was willowy and sylphlike, the daughter of a baron, and clearly adventurous, but Byron's interest quickly waned, and when she sought to renew the affair a year later, he found reasons to avoid seeing her.

"Byron?" Rocco said, putting his finger on the cat's nose. "Is he going to seduce the neighborhood?"

"This is a lucky cat," Melita said, holding him in her arms and stroking his head. He was red, tiger-striped. "He doesn't know how really lucky he is."

In the bombed areas, the cats and dogs were orphans, left behind when their owners rushed off to safer parts of the island. In the first year of the bombing, the Malta Boy Scouts put out food for them, but now, with the shortages, there was little left for the animals. There were butchers who would skin a cat and pass it off as a rabbit, and who but the most astute would notice? On the black market, a rabbit could fetch as much as twenty-five shillings, even if it was a cat.

"Very lucky," Melita said, pinching one of its ears, and the cat darted from her lap.

In the suitcase were dresses, undergarments, stockings, skirts, and the sweet scent of sachet. She had three pairs of shoes, all badly scuffed. On one pair the soles were worn through and she had put cardboard inside to protect her feet. When the cardboard wore out, she replaced it with linoleum that she took from a bombed-out building. Her few pieces of jewelry were in a coffee tin: earrings, a silver necklace, bracelets of wood and silver. She had bobby pins, half a tube of toothpaste, a nearly empty bottle of cologne, two bars of soap, one pencil, a fountain pen, and half a bottle of ink but no paper to write on. She had books, lots of books: an incomplete set of George Sand, much of the Brontë sisters, some of Jane Austen, pieces of Ann Radcliffe, chunks of Fanny Burney, a smattering of Virginia Woolf, a sizable amount of George Eliot, a few bits of Gertrude Stein, some choice small morsels of Mary Wollstonecraft, and a Douay version of the Bible. Also a copy of King James's *Daemonologie,* a discourse against satanism and witchcraft. Page by page, the books were being used for toilet paper, because there hadn't been any paper in Malta for a very long time.

Rocco scanned the titles. "You've read them all?"

"Some, yes, in school, with the nuns, but some I bought when paper became scarce. My precious books, how I hate to lose them. It's books and newspaper, that's all we have left now, and the newspapers these days have very few pages."

When the toilet paper ran out, the classics became instantly popular and, in a rush, the bookstores sold titles that had languished on the shelves for years. Her copy of *Jane Eyre* was more than half gone, and of *The Mill on the Floss* only the binding remained. *A Room of One's Own* was shut down for good, its thick, fibrous pages all used up, right to the bitter end.

On the radio, news reports came in from foreign stations, and from Italy they picked up Radio Roma's version of Tokyo Rose, a husky-voiced woman who claimed to be Maltese, passing along the latest Axis propaganda. She called herself Marlena Malta. She cajoled, she wooed, speaking in tones that were alternately motherly and seductive, urging the Maltese to stop supporting the British. She teased and taunted, making bad jokes, and always she offered personal messages for persons she claimed to know.

Ah, yes, my darling Rita Chetcuti—how well I remember those days in the playground, in Tarxien, where we grew up together. How sorry I feel for you that you will not be able to sleep tonight when the bombers come. And my other dear sweet friends, Rosa Vella and Cissy Guedalla—how I am in pain for you! See how the British make you suffer? Is it worth it, all this trouble and agony?

Rocco, perspiring, turned the handle on the generator. "She really knows these people?"

Melita smirked. "She isn't even Maltese, how could she be? A Maltese woman would never say such things—not over the radio. She took the names from a telephone book."

After the propaganda, there was opera. That was why, if you had a radio, you tuned in to Radio Roma: for the Puccini, the Verdi, the Rossini. They applaud the Germans when they blow up your opera house, then they turn right around and send you opera over the radio. It was part of the craziness, the topsy-turvy. Didn't they know it was illegal in Malta to listen to Italian opera over Italian radio? Ever since the start of the war, it was a punishable crime, you had to listen in secret. *Didn't they know?*

Rocco went on cranking the generator. He wasn't an opera buff, but he liked the music, the heightened feeling, the sonorous tones of passion and tragic love. In Brooklyn, when he went for a haircut, the Italian barber always had the radio tuned to a station that carried opera, with commercials for *Il Progresso* and Ronzoni spaghetti. They were reassuring sounds: the violins, the singers, and the announcers talking in Italian, words he couldn't understand. For a dreamy moment, as he turned the generator, he was still in Brooklyn, ten years old, in the barber's chair, the voices of the singers rising tempestuously above the full-throated orchestra, Melita's small radio on the floor making the same tinny sound as the radio in the barbershop.

This time, it was Puccini's *Tosca*. Rocco sat on a chair by the foot of the bed and cranked deep into the first act, to the point where the *Te Deum* begins and Baron Scarpia, head of the Roman police, looks lustfully at Tosca, wanting her, and decides that her lover, Mario, must die. The reception was poor, a lot of static, and moments when no sound came through at all. It was Melita's favorite opera. She liked the pathos, the darkness, the rifts and folds of tragic emotion, and whenever she listened she could not suppress the hope that this time, perhaps, through some miraculous twist of fate, it would turn out happily for the lovers. But always, painfully, the same dismal end: Mario shot by the firing squad, and Tosca, bereft, leaping from the battlements and plunging to her death.

The cat, frisky, attacked the wire linking the radio to the generator, and Melita shooshed him away. He retreated, then jumped onto the radio and perched there, as if taking possession of it as his own private domain. Melita cranked the generator through part of the second act, then Rocco took over again, but another bombing raid developed, far off at the airfields, then closer, and the antiaircraft barrage was deafening.

Rocco quit cranking, and there was nothing, only the crack and roar of the guns and the bombs—as if the noise were a place, and they were trapped inside that place and couldn't get out. The noise possessed them: it owned them, folding over them, holding them, and it seemed it would never let go. Melita sat on the edge of the bed, hands over her ears, and there was something in her face, a darkness, a fatalism, that made Rocco feel cut off from her and alone, as if she were a stranger. The cat, at the first crash of the guns, had disappeared, scampering off to another part of the house.

Then, suddenly, it was over, the planes gone. Fliegerkorps II was smart that way, always changing the pattern, sometimes bombing for hours, other times only for minutes. Keeping the defense off balance.

Melita hadn't moved from the bed. "Where are we going to get some olive oil for Zammit?" she said heavily. "He'll be so disappointed." Rocco, shirtless, was still on the chair, gazing at a large hole in the wall where the plaster had fallen away. Melita picked up the peacock feather, and, through the distance, touched the tip of the feather to the tip of Rocco's nose. "There's not an olive anywhere."

"Tell me the word for snow," Rocco said.

"Silly, we don't have snow on Malta. You think this is Sweden?" She swung the peacock feather slowly, back and forth.

"But there is a word for it, isn't there? It really never snows?"

"Sometimes a winter squall, we see a few flakes, sometimes hail. But snow, real snow, white all over, maybe once in twenty years. The Christmas before last, 1940, there was snow, but only up by Mdina. Before that, it was before I was born."

"What's the word for rabbit?"

"*Fenek.*"

"The word for rain?"

"*Xita.*" She grazed the peacock feather across his shoulders.

"The word for artichoke?"

"*Qaqoċċ.*"

That one was hard. He stumbled over it and she laughed.

"Do you eat artichokes?"

"I love artichokes."

"I'll make them for you, when they ripen. They're growing in Zammit's garden, near the squash."

"What's at the movies?"

In Sliema they had *The Maltese Falcon.* Rocco had seen it at Fort Benning, but was willing to go again, though he thought it corny, seeing *The Maltese Falcon* on Malta.

"You won't be bored?"

"I like the way Bogart lights his cigarettes. Are you hungry?"

She was starved.

"We'll eat early, then we'll catch the last show." Because of the curfew, the last show was at six.

"If we're lucky," Melita said. Meaning, if the movie house was open and running. The electricity might be down, or a bomb might have fallen and torn the place apart. Quite a few of the movie houses had been hit. Worst was the Regent on Kingsway, in Valletta, back in February, five in the afternoon, a packed house, during a showing of *Northwest Mounted Police.* The official report listed twenty-five dead, but Melita knew someone who said it was over a hundred, mostly servicemen.

"We'll eat at Dominic's," Rocco said.

She knew about Dominic's, but had never been there. "Really? You want to spend?"

"It beats the Victory Kitchens."

"I hate the Victory Kitchens," she said with a dead stare.

She dug into the suitcase and pulled out a dark red dress with lacework at the collar and sleeves.

"This?" she said, holding it up to her.

"Nice, nice."

Rocco put on his uniform, the one the tailor in Tarxien had made for him, and Melita was a long time fussing with her makeup. "Soon there will be no more lipstick," she said. "What will happen then?"

"You don't need lipstick."

"I do, I do. This dress is too wrinkled."

"Everyone is wrinkled. Nobody irons anymore."

She fretted, turning left and right, studying herself in the broken mirror on the back of a closet door.

"Wear it," he said, coming up behind her, "you look terrific." He drew her hair aside and kissed her shoulder.

"Where's the cat?" she wondered.

"How should I know? You're always pinching his nose."

"He better not get lost."

"He won't get lost."

"He's strange here, it's all new to him. You know how it is, somebody will pick him up and cook him in a stew."

"Not him," Rocco said, looking under the bed and not finding him. "He's too smart to let that happen."

"He's not smart, he's dumb."

"Is that why you pinch his nose?"

"I don't know, I don't know," she said, still fretting over the dress. "If he gets lost, I'll never forgive him."

He felt good about her. There were times when they talked and times they didn't talk, when they were just quiet, and that was good too, sitting on the rocks by the water, or in the car, good just to be with her and not have to use any words. Is she the one? he wondered. Really the one? There was a time when he'd thought Theresa Flum was the one, then it all turned sour and went bad. But here, now, on Windmill Street, the feeling was different. All of it. A different tone, different mood, and he was wondering: Is she? Maybe? Yes? Could be?

Twelve

THE MALTESE FALCON

At Dominic's, Tony Zebra was at a table with a crowd of pilots from the 249th, toasting Junior Smoots, a South African who'd knocked down his fifth plane that morning. He'd only been on the island two weeks and already he was an ace. His name was John but everyone called him Junior because he was short, young, and looked like a kid. The others seemed not much older, except for Tony Zebra, who at twenty-two was the old man in the group.

They were at a round table toward the center of the dining room, noisy and laughing, and slightly drunk. It was champagne on the house for them; Dominic was generous with the pilots. Tony Zebra's pelvis wasn't broken, and his severed earlobe had been sewn back in place with a few dozen stitches. He was using his hands as if they were planes, making wide, swooping gestures, showing the angle of attack when he last tangled with the bombers. At the piano, the Count was rippling through another Strauss waltz.

Rocco came up behind Tony Zebra and tapped him on the shoulder. "Still alive?"

"I'm in one piece," he grinned, "my bones are still connected. You met the new ace? Eyes like an X-ray machine, best eyes in the squadron. Killed two 88s, a 109, a Savoia Marchetti 79, and a Reggiane 2000."

From the far side of the table, Junior Smoots lofted a smile. He was floating in the trees. So was Tony Zebra, high as a kite.

"I've gotta make a toast," Tony said, "gotta make a toast." He stood on his chair, and, addressing the whole dining room, lifted his glass toward Junior Smoots, saluting him for the two 88s, the 109, the Savoia Marchetti, and the Reggiane 2000, attributing it all to his X-ray eyes. It was the third time he'd made the same toast, but nobody seemed to mind. *Here, here.* Still on the chair, Tony Zebra drained his champagne, and then, oddly, leaned off to one side, at a steep angle, Tower of Pisa, and Rocco had to grab him to keep him from falling on his head.

The maître d' sat Rocco and Melita at a table toward the far end of the room, by the large painting depicting the death of Dragut. On the table, between them, was a yellow rose in a blue vase. Melita drank a Malta fizz. "They're so young to be flying and fighting," she said, gazing across at the pilots.

"We're all too young," Rocco said.

"Not that young. Look at them. Eighteen, nineteen?"

"Tony Zebra is forty-nine," Rocco said, because, bruised and stitched, Tony Zebra looked old, aging fast.

She didn't laugh. "And that's what you want? You want to fly?"

"I flew," he said. "Didn't you know? A guy took me up, in the Catskills, in a Piper Cub, six or seven times. A year ago. He let me take off but wouldn't let me land, always did that himself."

"They're all getting killed," she said, "the pilots, all of them."

The pilots were brave, and they were dying. The Maltese idolized them. Rocco had seen it on the street: when a pilot passed by, people nodded, a man would tip his hat. A father would lean over to his son, pointing the pilot out. But they were dying, especially the ones in the Hurricanes, which were easy targets for the 109s.

The waiter was the same one who'd served Rocco before, when he was there with Fingerly. Vittorio.

"You remember me?" Rocco asked.

"I remember," he said fuzzily, studying Rocco's face, and then he really did remember. "You were with the lieutenant, the American lieutenant. For sure, I remember."

"He's a captain now."

"Yes? He has good luck, the war is good for him." He seemed genuinely pleased to hear of Fingerly's promotion.

Melita ordered the poached grouper, and Rocco, remembering the bad time he'd had with the *pulpetti tal-moch,* settled for pasta.

"He remembers you, but he doesn't remember me," Melita said, when Vittorio was gone. "We grew up in the same parish, in Cospicua."

"Why didn't you tell him?"

"I like it that he doesn't remember. While he carries the dishes, I can think of him when he was a brat, fighting in the streets, and he has no idea, no idea at all. Shame on him for forgetting me!"

Rocco spotted Nigg coming out of the Green Room. He seemed in a daze. He hesitated, then, head down, hurried through the dining room on his way to the bar.

Rocco put his drink down and got up to follow. He hadn't seen Nigg since that last night at Dominic's, after Maroon was killed. Hadn't seen Fingerly for some time either, and was beginning to feel abandoned.

"Been a while," he said, joining Nigg at the bar.

"Has it?" Nigg answered, with an edge. The bartender served him a double bourbon.

"You with Vivian? She inside?"

"Women are nothing but trouble. Don't you know that yet?"

Rocco brushed a fly away from his ear. "She went back to Mdina?"

"Off to never-never land, with the fairies and the will-o'-the-wisps." He looked away, and it was clear he didn't want to talk about it.

Rocco nodded in the direction of the Green Room. "You lost big in there?"

Nigg took a long drag on his cigarette. "I'll get it back," he said, flat and distant.

"What are you betting on?"

"Hospitals. I should have stuck with buses. Who's the broad?"

"Which broad?"

"At your table. She looks like hot stuff."

"Want to meet her?"

"Some other time," Nigg said, his eyes cloudy and vague. "Where are you living these days?"

"In a bombed-out place in Valletta. On good days there's enough water to cook with."

"What's the number?"

"Windmill Street. Number Nine."

Nigg wrote it on a napkin, then cocked his thumb. "I'll bet on that tonight."

"Don't."

"You're superstitious?"

"Hell, it's just not a friendly thing to do. The place was hit once already."

"Good, that'll make for better odds."

Rocco felt a flash of temper, but it passed. Fingerly had been right about Nigg: he was over the edge, living only for the odds. I-3 was bad for him. He would have been better off in the field, with a rifle, humble infantry, using all of his wits just to keep himself alive.

"I'm relying on you," Nigg said cheekily as Rocco left the bar. "You're my good-luck charm—you hear?"

In the dining room, Rocco noticed Angelina Labbra at a corner table, Miss Sicily, with the Algerian banker who'd won her in the auction. She was still on Malta, longer than expected.

As he moved along from the bar, back to his table, by a potted palm he barely missed colliding with someone coming from the powder room. It was Julietta. Her face lit up with a smile. The last time he'd seen her, in the house on Strait Street, she was in a housedress, no makeup, a rag on her head, but now she was transformed, with pearls around her throat, in a blue dress, her breasts swelling, straining against the silk.

"I thought you were in Rabat," he said.

"I am, we have a lovely new place. I thought you were in Gibraltar."

"Who told you that?"

"Your friend Fingerly."

"Fingerly is the father of lies. Are you alone?"

"I'm never alone." She nodded toward the Count, who was still at the piano, looking toward them as he bridged his way from the "Bewitchment Waltz" to the "Electro-Magnetic Polka." "He likes me," she said. "When the bombing stops and it's safe to sail, he wants me to go to Alexandria with him."

"Will you?"

"I'm thinking about it. Just thinking."

"I guess that bomb brought you good luck."

"When I saw the house," she said, "such a wreck, after the bomb, I thought you were still in there. It's good to be alive, isn't it?"

She went up on her toes and kissed him on the mouth, then turned and made her way back to her table, close to the piano. The Count, nodding toward her, touched the keys with a particular lightness.

Under the painting that portrayed the death of Dragut, Melita sat with her chin in her hand. She had torn most of the petals off the rose and dropped them into Rocco's martini.

"Who was that?" she asked with a penetrating stare.

"That? That was Julietta."

"Ah, I see, someone you know. And where is Nigg? I thought you were going to bring him back with you."

"He's drinking himself into a stupor."

"How unfortunate," she said pettishly. "He doesn't want to meet me?"

"He lost his shirt in the Green Room."

"Tell me about Julietta. You know her for long?"

"Actually, I thought she'd been killed, in the bombing."

"But she wasn't," she said, sounding disappointed. "Did you make love to her?"

"No." He smiled. "But almost."

"Really? You like her?"

He pointed a finger. "Now you're the one who's jealous."

"Jealous? Of her? That's what you think?" She leaned forward slowly, deliberately. "If you touch her," she said, without a hint of a smile, "believe me, I will get a gun and I'll shoot you."

"You would? You would really do that?" It stirred him to think she could have such a ferocious thought. Actually get a gun.

"And look at her," she said, "she's so—plump. How could you be interested in a person like that?"

He laughed. "She's just somebody I met, my first day on the island."

"On Strait Street? The Gut? She was one of the women in that house?" Her eyes slanted away sardonically.

"The Count has taken a fancy to her."

"The old man at the piano?"

"He plays well, doesn't he?"

"Waltzes, yes," she said, "he plays waltzes. Well, that's very nice. Good for her, I wish her good luck."

Rocco picked one of the rose petals out of his martini and put it in his mouth.

"No, no," she winced, "you're going to give yourself horrible cramps!"

Vittorio came with their meal, and moments later, Dominic passed by, big and fleshy, in a pink dinner jacket. He kissed Melita's hand. "Lovely, lovely, *charmante*," he said, taking her all in, his eyes hesitating over the wrinkles in her dress.

"After the war," he said to Rocco, "I shall visit America, I am going to buy up all of your horses. Nothing but the best. Give me horses that breathe fire— yes?" Then, abruptly, he sauntered off with a lightness that belied his girth, making his way among the tables, nodding and smiling, buoyed by an ocean of good feeling.

Melita clasped her hands under her chin. "Horses?"

"It's too complicated," Rocco said, rolling his eyes.

Before dessert, he spoke to Vittorio, asking if a bottle of olive oil would be possible, and Vittorio went off to the kitchen. When he returned, he whispered the price in Rocco's ear and Rocco agreed.

"For Zammit," he said to Melita.

On their way out, they stopped in the bar and looked at the jukebox, glowing plastic, all lit up, but broken and not playable.

It was big, a Wurlitzer 850, the famous Peacock model, which Dominic had smuggled in one night, on his boat, from Sicily. But it had broken down, and Dominic's electrician, after giving it his best, was unable to fix it. The inner lights glowed, but the records wouldn't spin, and the only sound, when a coin was inserted, was a cranky squeal from a misaligned gear. It was still handsome to look at, though, the molded plastic beautifully lit, with the peacock and the peahen on the front panel, richly illumined with peacock-color lighting. But the turntable wouldn't turn, and the speaker, once big-toned with a rich bass and eloquent treble, was hopelessly mute.

"Zammit could fix this for him," she said. "I am sure he could."

"I don't think Dominic wants it fixed. I think he's so mad at the Sicilian who sold it to him, he'd just as soon dump it in the sea."

"Such a beautiful thing," she said. "Zammit would love to have plastic like this to work with, all these beautiful colors, with the light shining through. It's better than stained glass."

They arrived at the movie house a few minutes before the film came on. It was an ornate old picture palace, marble columns, cushioned seats, red carpet in the aisles. The place was packed. With the sinking of the convoys, few new films were coming in, and for the most part it was only the old standbys left over from the thirties. But occasionally, as now, a recent movie turned up, brought in by a submarine or a bomber—this one, *The Maltese Falcon,* only a year old, flown in aboard a Blenheim that stopped to refuel at Luqa on its way to Alexandria.

The part Rocco liked best was the moment when Sydney Greenstreet, in a dressing gown with satin lapels, tells Bogart about the falcon, a foot-high gold statue encrusted with jewels, sent by the Knights to the emperor, when he gave them Malta. His voice crinkles with upper-class British refinement. He is Gutman, the fat man, three hundred pounds. There is greed, delicious greed, in his mouth, in his teeth, and in the movements of his tongue, in his fleshy lips, jowly face, a halo of greed surrounding the thin nap of gray on his balding dome. He talks and Bogart listens, never suspecting his drink is drugged and any moment now he will be unconscious on the floor. Later a falcon does turn up, falling into Bogart's hands, but it's fake, a chunk of lead, and in the end it's impossible to know if a true falcon does exist or if it's just a figment of the imagination.

"Do you exist?" Rocco said to Melita.

She looked him in the eye coldly. "You mean you don't know?" She was disappointed the movie didn't have any scenes in Malta.

He told her about a dream he'd had when he was a kid, a dream he'd had many times. He dreamt he wasn't real, he was part of a dream that somebody else was dreaming. It went on and on, an infinite regress of dreamers.

"Was Benny Goodman in this dream?"

"Yes, Benny Goodman was there, playing his clarinet, and Tommy Dorsey on trombone. Life was a wonderful song."

"And when did life stop being a song?" Melita asked.

"For me?"

"For you."

"I don't know. When my mother died, I think. But maybe before that."

His mother had died young, of pneumonia. He still remembered her as she lay in bed in the hospital, languishing, pale and perspiring.

"It was a long time ago. My father worked for the city, he operated a back-hoe, digging the streets when they fixed the sewers. He showed me how a back-hoe works."

"Did he remarry?"

"He's living with a widow in Bensonhurst. He doesn't handle the backhoe anymore, they put him in an office."

"It's terrible to lose your family. When my mother died, I was upset a long time. And then my father, it was terrible."

The next day, she was still thinking about the movie. "Do you really think Bogart did right at the end, when he gives Mary Astor to the police? If it were you, would you have done that?"

There was that pounding moment near the end when Bogart, Sam Spade, convinced that it was Brigid—Mary Astor—who killed his partner, and he drives her into confessing. He's in love with her. Or is he? Seems to be. And she's in love with him. At least she says she is. But he's relentless, driving for the truth, hammering, pushing, and gets it: she's guilty as sin. So it's hate-love, emotion and bitterness, her sweet neck, maybe she'll hang, and for an instant he's on the razor's edge, aware of the rotten nights he'll have if he gives her up.

But the firmness holds, the moral earnestness, and all her pleading gets her nowhere. She'll take the fall. For a blind, deluded instant she thinks he's joking, this talk about turning her in. But the cops arrive and off she goes, onto the elevator, down and gone. That's what it is, this Maltese Falcon: deception, fraud, murder, illusion. Love and betrayal. The broken heart, the stiff upper lip. Light another cigarette.

"So what do you do?" Melita said. "You're Sam Spade. Do you turn her in? Does she go to jail?"

Rocco put his fingers to his jaw thoughtfully. "Hey, if she murdered my partner, how do I know, some night maybe she'll murder me. Bogart says that, doesn't he?"

"You think so? You think she would do that?"

"You tell me. You're Mary Astor. You murdered Bogart's partner. Would you murder Bogart if you had the chance?"

"First I would make him very happy in bed, and then I would consider my options."

"A-ha!"

"Yes?"

"I'm glad I'm not a private eye."

"I hate love stories that end unhappily. There is no fun in them."

"You see it as a love story? I thought it was crime, murder. Sam Spade is a detective."

"All stories are love stories, if you dig deep enough. Hitler has Eva Braun, Mussolini has Clara Petacci. I wonder who FDR has. You think he has someone? I'm sure Churchill must have someone who sits on his knee."

That night, at the house on Windmill Street, when the sirens sounded, they climbed onto what was left of the roof and watched the planes coming in to bomb the harbor. It was a redundant gesture, there was nothing left. The docks were shut down, the harbor clogged with the sunk and half-sunk hulls of the ships and tugs that had taken direct hits. But still they came, and the searchlights formed great cones of light coming to focus now on one plane, now on another. Red tracer shells from the Bofors and the Lewises wove crisscrossing patterns of lace in the sky. The heavy guns at Hompesch and Crucifix Hill cracked and pounded, lighting the night with bright orange flashes.

All over Valletta people were on the rooftops. Most stayed below, in the shelters, but many felt more confident above, watching the action, feeling they would be all right as long as they could see what was happening. Seeing was a form of safety, a shield against harm.

Melita held the cat, cradling it in her arms. It was tense and rigid, seized with fright because of the noise of the guns.

A searchbeam locked onto one of the bombers, following it, and then another beam found it too. It was naked up there, an easy target for the guns. The plane banked, angling left, then right, in an agony to escape the lights, but before it could get away, flak tore into it and pieces of burning wreckage fell beyond the harbor, into the sea.

A rolling cheer went up from the rooftops, echoing across Valletta. Rocco, too, felt the exhilaration: *you're alive!* The one who was trying to kill you is dead. You breathe, your heart races, blood courses through your arteries. But it was awful too, this good feeling, coming as it did from the knowledge that someone was dead. You watched it happen.

Melita screamed. The cat, springing from her arms, had clawed her, and with a swift, furry leap vanished through the hole in the roof, into the darkness of the unlit rooms below. "Damn cat," she cried, arms stinging and bleeding, "run, run, never come back! See if I care!"

The bombers were gone and the all-clear sounded, a single, piercing note, like a sharp knife drawn across the taut skin of the night sky, making it bleed.

April 20, 1942

LUFTWAFFE LAUNCHES ITS HEAVIEST RAID

NAZI RUTHLESSNESS

FIVE RAIDERS SHOT DOWN IN FIERCE DUSK BARRAGE

HITLER'S BLUSTER

RUSSIAN BID TO FREE LENINGRAD BEFORE THAW

FINNS FIGHTING DESPERATE BATTLE

———

FOR SALE. Three pairs **ROLLER SKATES** practically new. Also one very good large, light, strong wicker basket, suitable for baby shelter cot. Can be seen at 32 South Street, Valletta.

CONVENT OF THE SACRED HEART, St. Julian's. School will remain closed until further notice.

Thirteen

THE NEOLITHIC CAVE

The next morning, Rocco put in his time at the radio, listening to the dot-dot-dash, getting it all down on the yellow pad. When he was done, he walked to Qrendi, to a bar on St. Agatha Street, where Melita was working on a jukebox. She changed the needle, replaced a dead light bulb and a piece of glass smashed by a drunken sailor, and performed a complicated procedure with a bundle of wires. When she was finished, they drove off in the hearse, heading for St. Paul's Bay.

She drove. They cut across to Rabat, then turned north, skirting Mosta and Naxxar. "So tell me," she said friskily, passing a motorcycle, "tell me all, I want to know all about you. All of the secrets."

"What's to tell?" he said, feeling dreary and lethargic after his long session with the dot-dot-dash. He'd already told her, at length, so much—about his dead mother, his cranky father, the used-car lot under the el, and Edgar Allan Poe, whose tales of premature entombment and death seemed a right preparation for the gloom and doom of Malta.

"No, no, no," she said, "don't tell me Edgar Allan Poe. Tell me your lovers, I want to hear about all of your lovers."

"There were nine," he said.

"Don't be silly. Why must men exaggerate? Always a big ego and bravado about making love."

"Well, how about you," he said, holding on as she swung the hearse past a slow-moving jeep. "I wasn't your first, was I?"

"Weren't you?" she said, with a gleam, and a hint of shyness.

"I don't think so."

"True, true," she admitted, "but before you it was only one, and long ago."

"What happened?"

"When I went to confession, the priest scolded me so horribly, I was intimidated. He said I was a bad girl. He scared me, and I decided to be good."

"And now?"

"Now I don't know, am I good or bad?"

"Do you still confess?"

"I did, last week. I went to an old priest in Santa Venera, I thought he would be understanding. But he made me say a rosary. I was so embarrassed, kneeling in the front pew and a whole rosary for my penance. People must have thought I did something completely terrible."

"You told him about us?"

"Of course I did."

"Why?"

"That's what confession is for. Isn't it? You go to confession and you confess."

"But *us*?" It bothered him. It seemed somehow unnecessary. Almost, in a way, a form of betrayal.

"Don't you confess?" she said. "In America, you don't? Oh, you should confess. If you die without confessing, you could go to hell, that's what they say."

She swerved to avoid an old man who was pushing a cart. Swirls of white dust rose from the unpaved road.

"I don't believe in hell," she said, "but who knows for sure? Who can really say about these things?"

The road swung down, and she took a turn, and then they were there, on the road that ran along the coast. Before the war, the bay had been a resort area, but now there were coils of barbed wire on the beaches, and tank traps. Here and there, cement pillboxes guarding against invasion.

The bay spread out peacefully, the water calm, gulls wheeling lazily. Were it not for the barbed wire, it would be hard to imagine there was a war. Melita drove on, following the curve of the bay, then she turned up a steep hill. They got out and she led him up a footpath, still higher, to the top of the ridge, and when they looked back there was the whole broad expanse of the bay beneath them, the long arm of the sea coming in from their left, and inland, to the right, the squared-off farms of the valley, neat rows of crops forming long green lines in the red soil.

"Come," she said, taking his hand, and brought him to a place where there was an outcrop of rock with a small cave and a thick growth of grass at the mouth.

"It's old," she said, approaching the cave. "From long ago. Part of a Neolithic temple, they think. People say different things."

He lifted her hair and kissed the back of her neck.

"You like that?"

"I like it."

She turned, and put her mouth on his. But then she broke away, playful. He pulled her back, and, still frolicsome, she was into his pockets, turning them inside out. She found chewing gum, a handkerchief, a book of matches. And then the wallet, waving it devilishly. "Ah, now I have it," she said. "The secrets, the secrets."

They were down in the grass, and she went through the wallet. It was stuffed with cards, addresses, receipts, and what was left of his last subsistence pay from Fingerly. She found a picture of his mother, taken before he was born, and a picture of his father standing by a backhoe. And the picture of Theresa Flum, snapped in a photo booth at Coney Island, wet hair clinging slick and black to the contours of her head. Melita waved it in front of Rocco's nose.

"Nothing to worry about," he said, tugging at a clump of grass. "She's gone. She's yesterday." Then, dispassionately, he told her how it had all gone wrong.

"You write to her?"

"No."

"She writes to you?"

"Are you kidding?"

There was something at the corners of her lips. A loneliness, a disappointment, a hint of jealousy. He knew those feelings, had felt them terribly when he lost Theresa.

He knew what she was thinking. She wanted to tear up the picture and throw it away.

"Go ahead," he said.

But she merely held it, looking at it, then put it back in the wallet, leaving him to do what he wanted with it.

"Who did she go off with?"

That was the hard part: she'd gone off with a friend of his, someone he'd considered a friend. "Charlie Loop, a guy I grew up with. From the neighborhood."

"Where is he now? In the army?"

"He's 4-F. He has a hole in his heart."

It was something she'd never heard of, a hole in the heart. It sounded like a bad joke.

"It's a medical thing, he was born with it."

Then he was up, off the grass, looking at the cave. "A Neolithic temple? That's what they think this is?"

He bent to look inside, but didn't bend far enough and struck his forehead against the hard rock. He saw stars.

She held him. "Let me kiss it, I'll kiss it, I'll make it better."

But he wouldn't let her near it, it hurt too much.

"See?" she said. "God punishes."

"For what?"

"For everything. You keep secrets, you have secret lovers. And you hate your father."

"I don't hate my father."

"You don't write."

"I wrote," he said.

"When?"

"Last week. Didn't I write last week?"

He hadn't.

"See?" she said. "If I had a father, every day I would write. Shame on you for not writing."

She pressed close to him, but avoided his forehead, which was bruised and beginning to swell.

In the hearse, at the wheel, before they drove off, she sat quietly. She was somber, the playfulness gone.

"Do you think this is wrong, what we do?" she asked.

"How do you mean?"

"I don't know, sometimes I'm not so sure. Living together, being together. Maybe it isn't right?"

He said nothing for a moment. Then, pulling a strand of grass from her hair, "What we have," he said, "I think it's good. Isn't it good? Don't you feel it's good?"

"Yes, yes," she said, reassuring him, "I didn't mean it that way. I'm happy, very happy. That's not what I mean."

Again he waited.

"It's what the priests say, you know? They say it's wrong, and I don't like it, feeling that way."

"It isn't wrong."

"I know, you say it isn't."

He thought then that what she was saying, trying to say, without putting it into words, was that they should get married. They could go to a priest, in her cousin's parish, and in a few minutes they would be husband and wife, and she would no longer have this feeling that she had, that what they did together was somehow wrong. With the war on, no fanfare, no ceremony, just the two of them in church and the priest saying the words.

It wasn't something he wanted to do, or even think about. He felt right about her, good about her, but here, now, with all the bombing, getting married made no sense. Soon, he imagined, he'd be pulled out of Malta and reattached to his unit, taken out as abruptly as he'd been sent in.

"Why are you looking sad?" she said.

"I'm not sad. I'm very happy."

"I want you to be happy," she said.

"Then I am," he said. "But I want you to be happy too."

"Why do you think I am not happy?"

"You seem—troubled."

"I'm tired," she said. "I'm so tired of this war. Will it never end?"

"Soon," he said doubtfully.

"Promise me one thing," she said. "While you're on Malta, promise you will make love to no one but me."

"Is that important?"

"To me it is. Very important."

"Cross my heart," he said, running his thumb over his heart, making a cross.

"What does that mean, cross your heart?"

"It means a very heavy-duty promise."

"Is it like crossing your fingers?"

"We cross our fingers for good luck."

"On Malta, we make the horns."

She showed him, extending the pinky and index finger of her left hand, but keeping the other fingers folded over her palm. "We make the horns to save us from the evil eye."

Several days later, when she saw her friend Christina, she told her about the picture in the wallet, and Christina thought it was not a good sign. They talked about it, whether it was good or bad, or simply nothing at all. It was bad, yes, because it meant he was still thinking of this other girl, feeling the hurt—but it was good too, because, as Rocco himself had said, it was a reminder of what a fool he'd been.

Melita vacillated, back and forth, and in the end she wanted to believe it was more good than bad, because if he kept the picture, it meant he was thoughtful and caring, he didn't run through women as if they were water. This girl, even if she was the wrong one, she had been a part of his life, and even though it was over for them, he respected her enough to want to remember her. Those were good qualities—remembering, respecting, having a care for the past.

Still, she didn't know. In some ways, emotionally, he seemed so young, too eager and impetuous. She was thinking ahead to the end of the war, what it would be like when it was over. Would he still want her, after the war? And would she want him? Would she?

"It's a seesaw," Christina said. "Yes?"

That's what it was.

And for Christina too it had been a seesaw. When she came to Malta in 1940, it was to be a brief stop for a dancing stint in Valletta, then on to Tunis, where there was a young judge, a Frenchman, with whom she'd been involved. They had talked about marriage, and she was on her way back to Tunis to see what might develop. But before she left Malta the bombing began, and like so many others, she was stranded. Then, months later, she met up with Warby and fell for him in a big way. People thought they were meant for each other, she the pretty cabaret dancer and he the daring flying ace. But it was hard for her, because he was always flying off, doing reconnaissance over Sicily, Naples, Benghazi. When he was home, they put brandy in their ginger ale and had a good time, but when he was away, flying over enemy territory, she was never sure she would see him again.

"Yes, a seesaw," Melita said vaguely, nodding slowly, thinking not so much of Warby and the risks he took but of the picture of Theresa Flum in Rocco's wallet. She was sorry she hadn't torn it up when she had the chance.

On Sunday, the 26th, Old Bakery was hit again. At the top of the street, around the corner from Windmill, a bomb struck the old building that housed the Valletta Telephone Exchange, the same place where Byron had stayed during his first visit to Malta, long before there were telephones.

When the bomb fell, Rocco and Melita were playing cards on the floor beside the bed. The explosion shook the house and sent plaster sifting from the cracked walls. They waited till the planes were gone, then hurried out to see the damage. The telephone operators were stumbling out of the ruins, disoriented, coughing from the dust, a cloud hanging over the neighborhood like a sour mist: one woman with her hair burned away, another with her face and arms blackened from the blast.

There was a woman with a hand blown off—in a daze, stunned, no idea where she was or what had happened, no awareness that her hand was gone. Rocco put his belt around her arm, tightening it, stanching the flow of blood. Melita brought her over to a block of limestone and sat her down.

"Is there anybody else in there?" Rocco asked a gray-haired woman who hovered nearby.

The woman glanced uncertainly at the ones who had come out. "I don't know, I don't know."

"I'm going in," he said, moving toward the wreckage.

"Don't," Melita said, "it's not safe."

But he went, and she hurried after him, stepping smartly. "If you're going, then I'm going too."

"No," he said, at the big hole where the front door had been.

"Why not?"

"Wait here," he said.

She waved a hand petulantly. "Oh, go," she said. "Go, go."

He went in, into the dust and smoke. By one of the switchboards he found a girl on the floor, amid the broken plaster and tangled wires, earphones still on her head. She moved an arm and moaned, and he picked her up and, climbing through the debris, brought her out. The rescue workers had arrived, and they took her from him and put her on a stretcher.

Rocco turned to go back in, but a man in a helmet stopped him. "We'll take it from here," he said.

The rescue crew brought a few others out—one unconscious, one with a broken leg. The lucky thing was that everybody was alive, nobody had been killed in there. A telephone crew was already at work, setting up emergency lines.

It was after five when they got back to the house, and Melita was on edge. She'd been fidgety all day, even before the bomb. It was a mood she was in, testy and irritable, and it was unlike her.

"Must have woke up on the wrong side of the bed," Rocco said, making light of it, but she wasn't amused.

By suppertime she was miserable. They ate at a Victory Kitchen, and afterward, at the house, as night fell, she was even more despondent. Rocco, tired, sleepy, was talking about the latest Tommy Dorsey record that had come through, "Last Call for Love," with "Poor You" on the other side, but Melita didn't want to hear about it, couldn't care less about Tommy Dorsey and his trombone, the best trombone ever, smarter, wiser, truer, smoother than any other trombone, simply wasn't interested.

"I hate music," she said.

"No you don't," he answered, baffled by her mood. All day he'd been confused, wondering what was bothering her, and now it was night and he was sagging toward sleep.

"Yes, yes, I hate it, I do, music and everything else, I hate it all. I hate everything."

He stared at her, amazed to hear her talk like that, yet he was so sleepy he could barely keep his eyes open.

"I hate Malta," she said. "There is nothing to love anymore, nothing to cherish. I hate the dust, the bombs, the heat. The flies. Everybody hungry and afraid."

She was warm, perspiring, in a chemise, barefoot, pacing back and forth. Rocco thought she might be in a fever and tried to get her to lie down, but she wouldn't. She pulled off the chemise and used it to wipe the sweat from her body. And still she paced, back and forth, restless, unburdening herself in a seething monologue.

Rocco slumped in a chair.

"I hate my body," she said. "I hate it. I hate making love. I hate your body and you and your big thing you stick inside me, and all the sweating when our bodies are together."

He was so tired, so close to sleep, he wondered if it was really Melita talking or some crazy dream.

"Don't you understand how nothing means anything to me anymore? I hate the world, all of it. I hate the jukeboxes."

"No," Rocco said, protesting drowsily, "you don't hate the jukeboxes."

"I do, I do."

"How could you hate them? You love them."

"I'm so tired."

"Let's go to bed," he said, not moving from the chair.

"I can't sleep," she said.

"I'll make tea, tea with milk in it, the way you like."

They still had some tea. It was rationed, and they didn't have much left, but enough. He could throw the leaves into a pot of hot water on the kerosene stove. And they had a can of condensed milk he could open.

"I hate tea with milk in it," she said with abandon. "I hate life, I hate death. I hate the movies!"

He thought they might go for a walk, they could go to Hock's for a brandy. But she disliked Hock's, and was annoyed with Rocco for suggesting it.

"We'll go somewhere else," he said.

"I don't want somewhere else."

She walked through the house, upstairs and down. He massaged her shoulders, but still she was restless.

He was exhausted. He threw himself on the bed and fell asleep.

She woke him. "Sing," she said, knowing he couldn't. "Anything. Don't you have a national anthem?"

He tried, but it was hopeless. She went upstairs, onto the roof, and came back down.

"You don't know anything," she said.

"I guess not," he said.

"Do you hate me?"

"Try to sleep," he said, stretching out again on the bed.

But still she resisted. She went from window to window, pulling open the blackout curtains. Then, as the first glimmer of dawn lit the east, first light, she collapsed onto the bed, beside him, and passed out.

Fourteen

POKER AT
THE POINT DE VUE

They slept late the following morning, and when they got up, she was still out of sorts.

"Stay and sleep," he said. "Take the day off, get a rest."

But she wouldn't. She made tea for herself—without milk—and ate a piece of bread, then she was off to Santa Venera, on her way to Zammit's to work on the jukeboxes, driving off in the pink hearse.

Rocco hitched a ride with a Red Cross truck and headed for Maqluba, the truck taking him part of the way, down into Tarxien. A jeep and a baker's van took him the rest, and when he finally got there, it was long past the hour when he was supposed to listen at the wireless. He tuned in anyway, briefly, roving through the airwaves, and took down some coded messages that came in on the frequencies Fingerly had told him to monitor: *Mud speaks louder than birds. The soup is cold. Cancel dinner.*

It was close to noon, a bright, hard sun beating down. He switched off the wireless and walked to Qrendi, where he hitched a ride to Takali, thinking he'd look up Tony Zebra and see what was doing.

The airfield at Takali was a dirt runway, unpaved, nothing but rocky earth and worn patches of grass, heavily cratered from raids the previous day. Crews were out with shovels, shirtless in the sun, working furiously to fill the holes. The planes were parked in roofless pens made of sandbags and blocks of limestone, protecting the planes from shrapnel and flying debris when the bombs fell. Only a direct hit could get them—and, of late, the direct hits had been growing in number.

The officers' mess was a mile off, at Mdina, on a hill overlooking the airfield, in the Point de Vue hotel. Rocco walked the mile up a steep grade, raising a sweat, and found Tony Zebra on the roof of the big two-story building, on the open veranda overlooking the plain. To the north lay Mosta, with its big-domed church, and far to the right, the densely clustered stone houses of Valletta and the neighboring towns. Black smoke floated up from petrol fires all around the harbor.

On the rooftop veranda, a few pilots from the 249th and 603rd were lounging around, reading magazines and writing letters. One was in a wheelchair, recovering from a crash landing. He wore dark glasses and held an unlit pipe in his hand, on his lap, just sat there in the wheelchair, didn't move and never said a thing.

At a small table a poker game was in progress, four in the game. A windup phonograph played a Glenn Miller tune, the bright, smooth, distinctive sound coming crisp and haunting from the spinning black disk. They played it over and over, the same record. Saxophones blending with a sultry clarinet.

" 'In the Mood,' " Rocco said, locking onto the lush, jaunty rhythm.

"Hell, we're all in the mood," Tony Zebra said, lighting a cigarette. "Even Bull Turner's in the mood. Right, Bull?"

Bull Turner, poring over his poker hand, didn't look up. He was short and hefty, a Canadian, older than the rest. He'd been the squadron leader of the 249th, and had just been promoted up to wing commander at Takali. "Time to change the needle," he said testily, then swallowed down a glass of orange juice.

There was a peevishness in the air, an irritability, a sense of anger and frustration, because the previous afternoon, directly over the airfield, Junior Smoots had been shot down by a Messerschmitt. The Spitfire went out of control, into a pancake spin, and when Junior Smoots finally managed to get out of the cockpit, the parachute streamed and never opened. He was less than a thousand feet up when he jumped, the failed parachute flapping and waving above him like a long white scarf. The plane wandered off on its own and smashed into a quarry.

"Have some bourbon," Tony Zebra said, pouring liberally into a tumbler.

Rocco wasn't keen about bourbon so early in the day, but on Malta, if you found bourbon, you weren't fussy about when or where. "Junior Smoots? The one I met at Dominic's?"

He had knocked down five planes, an ace, and now he was out of it. They didn't say he got killed, or crashed, or died. They said he went west. That's how they spoke of the ones who didn't come back. They went west.

At the poker table it was Harry Kelly, from Texas, Daddy Longlegs, Bull Turner, and Zulu Swales. They were playing for cigarettes, a haphazard pile of Woodbines, Flags, and Caporals in the pot. Even the pilots were on short rations, forty a week, and if they wanted more they had to hit the black market, or get lucky at poker. It was a high-stakes game. Tony Zebra, a dedicated chain-smoker, nervous about losing, figured it was smarter just to watch. He kept the phonograph going.

Daddy Longlegs was Raoul Daddo-Langlois, but whenever they said his name it always came out Daddy Longlegs. He was British, a Channel Islander, and had walked away from quite a few crashes. Only a few days earlier, he'd had a head-on with a 109. The 109 lost a whole wing, ripped off at the root, but Daddo-Langlois, lucky, lost only a wingtip and managed to limp back to Takali. "He knocks them down," Tony Zebra said, "but he does it the hard way."

The fighter squadrons rotated readiness. Today it was 126 and 229 from Takali, and 185 from Hal Far. At Takali, 249 and 603 had the day off. Nothing was going up from Luqa.

In the poker game, Kelly and Daddy Longlegs folded, and now it was only Turner and Zulu Swales. Zulu Swales raised, throwing in two cigarettes, and Bull Turner called. Swales had two pairs, nines and sevens, but Turner had a straight and he raked in the cigarettes, adding them to the pile he'd already won. Harry Kelly dealt the next hand.

"Rocco Raven is from Brooklyn, land of the Brooklyn Dodgers," Tony Zebra said, "—not that it means anything to you creeps from the far-flung provinces of the Commonwealth." He was cranking up the phonograph, preparing for another run of "In the Mood." "He works a wireless for Uncle Sam but would really rather fly a Spitfire. You think we can lend him one?"

It was meant as a joke, but it came across lame because at that moment, on that day, there were almost no Spitfires left on the island, and very few Hurricanes.

"Doesn't a raven have wings of his own?" Zulu Swales said, gazing fixedly at his cards.

"Maybe he wants the machine I bailed out of two weeks ago," Harry Kelly said. After damaging a 109, he was shot down and had to bail out over the water. The chute opened only partially and he hit the water hard. His bones didn't break, but he was badly bruised and one side of his face was still discolored, purple fading to yellow.

Daddy Longlegs looked at Rocco through narrowed lids. "Are you the Rocco Raven that's been running around with a dynamite blue-eyed Maltese beauty queen?"

Rocco glanced sourly at Tony Zebra, who'd obviously been talking.

"There are no blue-eyed women on Malta," said Zulu Swales, who'd been there only a week and was an almanac of misinformation.

"This one has blue eyes like you've never seen," said Harry Kelly, who had never seen them.

"Does she have a cousin?" Zulu Swales asked.

"She does, she does," said Bull Turner, "but he's hogging them both for himself."

Harry Kelly, lifting his head, howled like a hound in heat and laid down his cards, four queens and a jack, his lusty wail sounding vaguely like an air-raid siren. So far, that day, there had been two big raids, one early in the morning, the other at ten.

"They shot up the ferry," Daddy Longlegs said, diverting attention from Harry Kelly's winning hand.

"Who shot up the ferry?"

"The seven-thirty raid. Up at Marfa Point. I got it from the scullery maid."

"That's not all he gets from the scullery maid," said Harry Kelly.

"Casualties?"

"Five or six wounded."

"It's the Hun," said Zulu Swales. "The Hun has a mean streak. They listen to Mozart, but they're depraved."

They rambled on, for a while, about the differences between the Germans and the Italians, the Italians living by an old-fashioned code of chivalry, as if still flying in World War I. The first year of the bombing, in 1940, they dropped Christmas cards over the airfield at Takali. And just last November, in '41, when a wing commander went down over Sicily in a Hurricane, they flew over Takali and dropped a message saying he'd been buried with full military honors. The Germans never did anything like that. They strafed civilians and blew up the fishing boats. They'd already dropped more tonnage on Malta than they'd dropped on all of Greater London during the 1940 Blitz.

It was Tony Zebra who mentioned the Christmas cards, and Bull Turner laid into him.

"That's the whole muddy trouble with you, Zebra—you're in the middle of a shooting war, piss and shit rising around your ears, and you want somebody to send you a goddamn Christmas card!"

It was said of Bull Turner that with his mouth alone he could stop a herd of stampeding elephants. In the bistros in France, before Dunkirk, he would drink up a storm, then he'd pull out his pistol and shoot the glasses off the bar. After Dunkirk, stranded in France, he went on fighting, stealing fuel in hit-and-run raids and blasting away with machine guns. He had a reputation. Now, here on Malta, he was a wing commander playing uncle to a bunch of kids, beating them at poker, and drinking orange juice.

"*I'll* send you a Christmas card," Harry Kelly said to Tony Zebra. "Next Christmas, just see if I don't."

But it was a clumsy thing to say, because nobody knew if any of them would even be alive next Christmas.

"It's the Hun," Zulu Swales said again. "They're a different breed."

"The Hun, sure, the Hun is vicious," Bull Turner said, "but the fact is, it's everybody. People kill because people kill, it's part of the rot and fever of the human brain."

He set his cards face-down on the table and told them about a café he'd been to in Mdina, his first week on Malta. There were three clay pots on a shelf behind the bar. When he asked what was in them, the bartender lifted one of the lids and showed him the severed head of a German pilot who had parachuted down and was butchered by a crowd of angry Maltese farmers.

Tony Zebra had heard the story before. "These Maltese," he said, "they have wild imaginations, especially the bartenders."

"I saw the head," Turner said grittily.

"Sure you did, but it was all shriveled up. How do you know it was even human?"

"You're saying I didn't see what I saw?"

"You saw what you saw, but how do you know it's what you think you saw?"

"He saw the head," Zulu Swales said.

"I saw it," Turner said, glaring at Tony Zebra, "and if I had it here, this minute, I'd stuff it up your arse."

"Hey," Tony Zebra answered breezily, "up yours!"

They exchanged a long, dead stare and there was, for a moment, a breathlessness, as if the air and everything around had drawn in, and for the barest instant it seemed Bull Turner might boil over. But then, with a surly twist of his head, he pulled his eyes away and got back to the game. "Let's finish this stinking hand before I have a bowel movement," he said. "Anybody holding a royal flush?"

Despite his temper and his sometimes rapturous profanity, they were all aware he had a complicated mind, a hidden intricacy of intention that made him deadly in the sky and even deadlier with a deck of cards. He knew, for example, that in the game of poker, there were 2,598,960 possible hands you could be dealt. Of these, 40 were straight flushes, 624 were fours-of-a-kind, and 3,744 were full houses. He kept numbers like that in his head, and had an uncanny knack for calculating the odds.

"We're playing for cigarettes," he said to Rocco. "You have any weeds?"

"I have Luckies."

"Should we let him in with his Luckies?" Turner growled cheerfully.

Rocco pulled up a chair and was dealt in. He lost, and lost, and lost. Then he won, and then again he lost. Daddy Longlegs and Harry Kelly were sharp, and Bull Turner was even sharper. He was eating bully beef from a can of Maconochie's Bully Beef. That's what they ate, Maconochie's, morning, noon, and night.

"Too bad he's in dot-dot-dash," Bull Turner said of Rocco, who had just folded again. "Would have made a damn good pilot. Got the right look of desperation in his eyes."

Daddy Longlegs opened a black-market chocolate bar and passed it around, and by the time it got back to him, there was nothing but the empty wrapper. He put a match to it and let it burn.

The sirens at the airfield sounded, another raid on its way in.

Kelly and Daddy Longlegs went to the balustrade, searching the sky. It would be nine or ten minutes before the planes reached Malta, but they were up and looking, Zulu Swales and Tony Zebra too, peering into the distance, each wanting to be the first to spot them. Down on the field, the work crews disappeared into shelters and slit trenches.

Two Hurricanes went up from Takali, rushing to gain altitude so they could attack the incoming bombers from above. Two, that was all. Then they saw another, from Hal Far.

On a good clear day, from the rooftop veranda, you could see Mount Etna. This was a clear day, but not a good one, and all there was out there, beyond St. Paul's Bay, was dreamy haze.

"Ju-88s," said Harry Kelly. He spotted thirty-two.

"Twenty-nine," Tony Zebra said.

They argued for a while, twenty-nine or thirty-two.

Zulu Swales thought it was thirty-one.

The 109s, smaller, were harder to count.

"Twenty Messerschmitts," Daddy Longlegs said, and nobody disputed him, because he had keen eyes, the keenest in the squadron now that Junior Smoots was gone.

The main body of the bombers headed for Grand Harbour, and the rest fanned out, coming for the airfields. Only one of the three Hurricanes was in view, tangling with the Messerschmitts.

"Who's that up there in the Hurricane? Is that Slim Yarra?"

"No, that's not Yarra."

"It's Tweedale, right? Tweedale with his violin."

Gordon Tweedale, an Australian, played the violin and wrote poetry. And he had a good eye. In the air, in dogfights, he'd already knocked down six and damaged a few others.

"That's not Tweedale," Harry Kelly said, "that's Bull Turner up there."

"Bull Turner is right here, men, never fear," said Bull Turner, still at the table, holding his cards. He and the pilot in the wheelchair were the only ones not standing. They were also the only ones not wearing a tin hat. Even Rocco had put one on, from the pile in the box by the stairs.

"Bull Turner, huh? He's really losing it," said Harry Kelly.

"That 109 is going to clip his ass."

"Wow!"

"Geez!"

"Hell, that was close. Come on, Turner, pull out of there."

"Turner is right here, lads, holding a dynamite hand. Come back and play this one out."

"Jesus, he's bloody losing it."

"It's off to the farm for old Bull. Time to put him to pasture."

"Isn't that the sloppiest roll you've ever seen? Decrepit. He's losing his touch."

"Bull Turner is not losing his touch, you dumbdick whistle-suckers. Bull Turner is sitting right here and he's holding three bloody aces." He was still at the table. Really holding three aces.

"Look at that," said Daddy Longlegs, "he had that 88 dead in his sights. Missed him. Did you see that? Let him slip away."

"That's not the Bull Turner I used to know."

"Lost his edge."

"Gone to seed."

"Is that the kind of flying got him his DFC?"

"Eating too much bully beef, that's the problem. Too much canned Spam cooked in engine grease, too much moldy bread, too much maggoty black-market chocolate."

Several of the 88s moved into position for a bombing run over Takali. The first descended in a shallow dive, slanting down and coming through the flak. As it passed over the field, releasing its bombs, it was low, almost level with the

Point de Vue, which was perched high on the hill, overlooking the valley. They could see the pilot in the cockpit and the bombardier in the windowed nose, and the rear gunner behind the pilot.

All of the guns were going, the pom-poms and the Lewis machine guns, and the big ack-ack guns barking and banging, hurling flak high and wide. The flak burst in black cloudpuffs, and splinters of shrapnel fell back to the ground, pattering down, a few pieces chattering onto the open veranda. Tracer shells from the Bofors formed long, willowy lines of fire sweeping across the sky. It was a rumbling, thunderous music, the guns and the roar of the bombers, and the whistle and crash of the bombs crumping down with a rough *woomph,* cratering the field, plowing up huge quantities of dirt and limestone, enormous clouds of yellow dust hanging and swirling, sifting lazily.

Then the second 88 began its run and Bull Turner now was out of his chair, sudden, making a rush for the balustrade, his service pistol high over his head. He was not tall, but at that moment he seemed the biggest man there, a swarming immensity, his body pressing against the railing, feet spread apart, right hand forward with the pistol, left hand bracing his right forearm, and as the Ju-88 came on in its shallow dive, passing low over the field and dropping its bombs, Bull Turner fired round after round, even though, with just a pistol, he knew, and they all knew, there was no chance of doing any damage whatsoever. Kept firing, again and again, until the gun clicked empty, and then, as the plane pulled away, gaining altitude, he hurled the gun itself and it sailed birdlike toward the plane, on a long arc, falling among the carob trees and the cactus down below.

The next plane began its approach, and, glancing about wildly, Bull Turner grabbed a chair and hurled it with great force. Rocco was amazed it flew as far as it did, tumbling in the air, end over end, a long parabola, sinking finally into the carob trees. Then another chair, aimed at the next plane, and another, heaving them with grunts and great puffs of breath, amid the roar of the bombs and the banging of the ack-ack guns.

Then he just stood there, breathing hard, heart pumping, hands hanging down at his side, and they knew he was all right. They'd heard the stories about how he went berserk in the bistros in France, and now they had seen it for themselves, the anger, the passion, and they felt good about it, because when you didn't have enough planes to fly against the Hun, what you felt, what you couldn't help but feel, was rage, and Bull Turner had rage enough, and fire enough, for all of them.

"Shit, Bull, now we don't have any damn chairs left to sit on," said Daddy Longlegs.

Bull Turner didn't seem to hear.

Tony Zebra's face was full of blood. A splinter of shrapnel from the spent ack-ack, falling from the sky, had slashed his nose, and blood was pumping out all over him.

Bull Turner took a look at him, then he turned and went to the pilot in the wheelchair, who was still there, hadn't moved, with the dark glasses and his mouth hanging open, and the unlit pipe in his hand, on his lap.

"This man is dead," he said. "Can't you all see he's dead? Been dead a long time. Somebody wheel him out of here and get him where he belongs."

The pilot in the wheelchair was not breathing. Rocco saw it, and wondered why he hadn't seen it before. None of them had seen it. He'd just been sitting there all that time, with the dark glasses, locked in his strange silence, gone, mouth open, bereft of words or meaning.

Bull Turner lifted a hand and pointed to Tony Zebra, who was still bleeding, looking as if he might faint away. "Take care of him," he said, "pour some whisky into him and fix him up, he has to fly tomorrow. Find somebody to repair that nose."

Then, with surprising agility, he hoisted himself over the railing and, getting himself down off the roof and onto the long slope of the hill, made his way into the carob trees and the clumps of cactus, looking for his gun.

Three aces, he'd said, almost voluptuously. The question was, did he have a pair to go with the aces, giving him a full house, or did he just have the three aces and nothing else? If he'd had only the aces, they would not have beaten a flush, which is what Rocco was holding when the bombers showed up, five hearts off the queen, and he really could have used some of those extra cigarettes.

Below them, in the valley, the airfield was badly cratered, and the work crews were already busy. A few hawks circled high above the dust. Only one of the two Hurricanes from Takali had returned, which meant that one was gone, knocked down, into the sea or into the hard rocky ground of Malta.

Later that day, when Rocco got back to the house on Windmill Street, Melita wasn't there.

She had planned on spending the day at Zammit's, in Santa Venera, working on a jukebox, and had said she'd be back by three or four. Rocco thought they might catch another movie, at the Majestic in Sliema, but here it was already past five, the movie due to come on at six, and they hadn't eaten yet. He went out to a pay phone, in a coffee shop on Kingsway, and called Zammit, to see if she might still be there.

She wasn't. She'd left over an hour ago, yet Zammit expressed no alarm. He suspected she was probably on a queue for bread somewhere, or off shopping for vegetables.

Rocco went back to the house and fed the cat, giving him milk from a tin and some scraps of goat's meat. By five-thirty, it was clear they weren't going to get to the movie, and he went out to the City Gate, looking for the pink hearse.

He bought a newspaper and browsed through the headlines—Burma, Leningrad, the new Vichy government. Three Wellingtons had raided the Comiso airfield in Sicily, during the night. The paper reported light damage to military targets on Malta from the previous day's raids. Military targets meant the docks and the airfields, and as everyone well knew, the raids had been nothing if not heavy, and if the damage was light, it could only have been because there was so little left to destroy.

At seven, he returned to the house. Maybe a flat tire, he was thinking. Or the carburetor. It was old, the hearse. But even if it had broken down, she should have been back by now. There had been plenty of time to grab a bus, or hitch a ride.

She had an aunt, and he thought maybe she had stopped off on the way. He went again to the coffee shop, to call Zammit for the aunt's number. But the line, now, was out. That's how it was with the phones, working one minute, dead the next.

He reassured himself, thinking she had to be at the aunt's. Where else would she be? Must have stopped there, expecting to stay a minute or two, and then, somehow, was delayed.

Then he thought she might be doing this on purpose, punishing him for something he'd done or not done, said or failed to say, something of which he wasn't even aware.

Could that be it?

But why, how?

He remembered how vexed she'd been at Dominic's, about Julietta, when Julietta kissed him. Is that what it was? Was she still mad at him for that?

As darkness came on, he was sure something was seriously wrong. She must have been hurt, he figured, in one of the raids, while driving from Zammit's. He had shut that thought out, but now it was full upon him, irresistible.

He had an awful night, listening for every sound, hoping it might be her. He went to the City Gate again, looking for the hearse. Not till after midnight did he fall asleep, and then he was awakened by the sirens. Another false alarm, not a raid. Often a few planes would start out for Malta but would turn back before reaching the coast—it was a way of getting the sirens going, so nobody could sleep.

In the morning, he returned to the coffee shop, and now, luckily, the phone was in service again. He called the hospitals, the ones between Santa Venera and Valletta, to see if she'd been admitted anywhere. There was always a long wait, and a few times the line went dead and he had to ring back. In the end, he had nothing.

He left a note for her at the house, on the kitchen table, then hurried off to the farm near Maqluba, where he put in his time at the wireless. He listened, writing down the coded messages that came through, and, as soon as he was done, set off to see Zammit.

Zammit called the aunt, but Melita wasn't there.

"She'll be back," he said reassuringly. He didn't seem worried or concerned.

"Did she call you? Talk to you?"

Zammit shook his head. "I feel it," he said. "I know it. Everything will be all right."

"She does this? She goes off without saying? Has she done it before?"

Zammit shrugged. It was as if he knew something, and yet, when pressed, he had nothing to say. He had an extra bicycle at the house, which Rocco borrowed, preferring to pedal back to Valletta rather than suffer the long wait for the bus.

When he got back to the house, the note he'd written lay untouched on the kitchen table.

It was a horrible day. There were moments when he was sure she was dead, and other moments when he thought she had simply gone off, having tired of him. He felt abandoned. It had been such a rush, the emotional intensity, the suddenness, the dark brilliance of their nights and days, and now, just as suddenly, it seemed over. He was baffled, didn't know what to think or imagine.

It was a problem in time. He used to think time was a straight line, running forward without interruption, but he knew now that it wasn't, it was more like a storm, a tempest, a whole ocean pounding and heaving, ebb and flow, whitecaps and troughs, and what you had to watch for, close to shore, was the rocks. The rocks would tear you apart.

He didn't want to think she was dead. It was too awful. And he didn't want to think she had left him, because that seemed, in a way, almost worse.

If she had simply gone, walked out on him, then why had she left all of her things? The suitcase of clothes, the radio, the peacock feather, the cat? Her box of books. Maybe, in a few days, she would send Zammit for them, or a friend.

But then, again, he was sure the worst had happened. He thought of her lying injured somewhere, in a hospital bed, or in a pile of rubble by a house that had come down. Or dazed, wandering about, not knowing where she was.

He got on the bike and pedaled, thinking he would find her. He went again through Valletta and Floriana, then out, away, all the way off to St. Paul's Bay, to a spot overlooking the beach where, one day, they'd had a picnic lunch. He circled back through Mosta, keeping his eyes peeled for the pink hearse. He stopped at police stations in the various towns, consulting the casualty lists. Then returned to the house exhausted.

It had been a day of heavy raids. Tuesday, the 28th. In the morning, the Church of St. Publius in Floriana, just outside Valletta, was bombed. The attack had been deliberate, the dive-bombers clearly going for the big dome. They hit the church with three bombs, one piercing the dome and penetrating to the underground crypt, which was being used as a shelter. About a dozen people were killed, including a parish priest. In the air, two Canadian pilots were killed, flying Hurricanes.

That night, he didn't want to sleep, resisted, but sleep overcame him, sneaking up on him, rolling over him like a fog. He had wild, turbulent dreams.

He was aboard the Wellington again, the plane that flew him in to Malta, but this time it was Tony Zebra, not Brangle, in the pilot's seat. The bomb bay was full of chocolate bars and they all belonged to Fingerly. They were on their way to bomb Benghazi. The Wellington belonged to Fingerly, as the chocolate belonged to Fingerly, and the sky belonged to Fingerly. Even Tony Zebra belonged to Fingerly. Even Rocco and Rocco's shoes belonged to Fingerly, though it was unclear if Fingerly belonged to himself or somebody else. Over Benghazi they dropped the chocolate bars, and the Germans on the ground were surprised out of their skulls: a rage of exploding chocolate, making huge craters, dimpling the earth. When Rocco looked back, there was nothing down there but chocolate flames licking skyward, a roiling mess, and he had done it, he himself, Rocco Raven, caused all that damage, because he was the bombardier.

The next day, he was on the bike again. All the way to the farm near Maqluba, where he sat a while at the shortwave. Then a meandering ride back, going through the small towns and villages, stopping again at the police stations. She hates me, he thought, that's why she's doing this. She wants to make me suffer. But then the opposite thought, that she was dead somewhere, and, pedaling up the long hills, he was in a state of confusion, tears mingling with the perspiration streaming down his face.

After five, he was back in Valletta, biking through the City Gate, along a narrow lane cleared of rubble. He crossed on South, and, as he turned a corner, onto Windmill, he looked down the block and there she was, sitting on the stone steps outside the house, in a blue dress, waiting.

"I made you worry," she said guiltily.

It was strange to see her, all his anger and anxiety gone, washed away, and he felt timid toward her, as if meeting her for the first time, and sensed that she felt the same toward him. They were shy of each other.

"You could have left a note," he said, not with ill humor but softly, as an observation, a statement of fact. "Three days," he said. "I looked all over Malta. I thought you were gone."

"That's what you thought? I was dead?"

"That's what I thought."

"I had to go away so I could think," she said. "I had to be alone."

"What did you think about?"

"Everything," she said.

"About us?"

"About us, yes. It was all moving too fast, I had to stop and give myself time to think. Life is too complicated. I'm sorry I hurt you."

"Did you figure it out?"

"Figure what out?"

"What you went away to think about."

"I made you some Jerusalem artichoke soup," she said, leading him into the kitchen. "I couldn't get any Jerusalem artichokes, so I used potatoes instead."

"Doesn't that make it potato soup?"

"It does, if you want to think of it that way, but I think of it as Jerusalem artichoke because that's what I set out to make in the first place. In potato soup you use fat instead of butter, and I had planned on using butter, but there was no butter so I decided on margarine. It was hard to get the margarine, really hard. I had an awful fight with the storekeeper. If you think of it as Jerusalem artichoke instead of potato, it will make it taste better. But maybe you don't feel like eating."

"You're home," he said.

"Yes," she said.

"Are you sure you want to be here?"

"I think so, yes."

"Maybe you want to stay away for good?"

"Then I wouldn't have come back. But maybe you don't want me now. Maybe you want me to go away again?"

"You gave me a scare. You know?"

"I just needed to be alone. It's the bombs and the guns, so many years of the bombs and the guns. After a while it drives you crazy and nothing is right anymore. What about you? Do you want to go away?"

"I'd rather be in Brooklyn," he said.

"Alone?"

"Sometimes I feel like that," he said. "It really has been moving too fast, hasn't it."

"You don't want to be with me."

"I didn't say that."

"You'd rather I go away?"

There was still the awkwardness, the hesitancy, as if they were strangers. And yet there was a sense of connection, an old belonging, as if they had known each other for years, and now, here, they were together again, in the same room.

He looked at her, and there were depths in her he didn't understand, layers and dimensions, dark places that made him uneasy. It flashed through his mind that the most sensible thing would be to get on a plane, if he could get aboard, and get out of all this, quickly, back to his unit. Because it was beyond him, too much for him. Something about her made him feel inadequate, as if he lacked something and would never know what it was. Easier, he thought, to live with the old familiarity of cars, on the used-car lot, among the second- and third-hand Fords and Chevrolets, which he tinkered with, making them sound if not new at least good enough to pay money for, good enough to drive off into the hum and buzz of traffic. But that was before the war and the bombing, when there was a kind of devil-may-care innocence and the ground you walked on was solid, you knew it was there, under your shoes. Back home in Brooklyn.

He ate the Jerusalem artichoke soup, thinking it was that even though it wasn't.

"I couldn't get any meat," she said, "I tried and tried. I thought maybe a little pork, but nothing, so I did the soup instead. Do you like it?"

He liked it. But he wasn't hungry. He was tired. And she was tired too.

"Did you do your dot-dot-dash while I was gone?"

"I did my dot-dot-dash."

"Did you miss me?"

"Yes, I missed you."

As they sat there in the kitchen, sipping soup, he sipping, she sipping, the cat looking on from the top of the wooden icebox in which there was no ice, there was, suddenly, a kind of normality, an ordinariness, as if nothing had happened, as if she hadn't just come back after having disappeared for three days.

"I'm bad, I know," she said, "I did wrong. I should have told you. But if I had told you, there would have been all this long talking and explaining, and I never would have gone. But I had to go, because how else could I do the thinking I had to do? So you see? I'm not bad, I'm good, I'm trying to be good for you, but maybe you don't think so. Do you still love me?"

He liked her, wanted her, was obsessed with her, the sound of her voice, the music of her arms, the sweep and glide of her eyes as she scanned the room looking for the cat.

"Did you take care of my Byron while I was gone? Did you feed him?"

"I pulled his tail."

"I bet you did!"

"I hung him on the clothesline by his ears."

"I know it, I know it. Yes, you would do that, I knew you would. Poor pussycat!"

The cat was still on the icebox, next to a vase containing dried flowers. Melita took a coin from her purse and threw it at him, missing but coming close. The cat looked sourly at her. She threw again, closer, and this time he roused himself, half-rising, but not quite. The third toss hit him in the haunches and brought him to his feet. With a slow, surly arrogance, he moved down from the icebox and onto the sink, furry and lithe, hovering there by a stack of dishes. But then, when Melita clapped her hands, he was quickly gone, a leap, a red blur, through the door and off to some other part of the house.

"So where did you go?" Rocco asked.

"You really want to know?"

He waited as she took more soup.

"I stayed with a friend, in Floriana."

"Which friend?"

"Christina."

"The English girl?"

"I told you about her. Didn't you meet her? The dancer?"

Rocco had met her, and had seen her perform once, when she did her Spanish dance, black top, bare midriff, arms covered with black lace, castanets in hand, the long, silk paisley skirt flaring from her hips as she turned, beaming a steamy, hungry smile.

"She's thick with Warburton, isn't she? The reconnaissance pilot."

Melita sighed, nodding. "Well, God knows what will come of it. They're having a hard time."

"They quarrel?"

"Doesn't everybody?"

He shrugged, tilting back in the chair. "So you talked? With Christina?"

"We talked."

"You told her mean and ugly things?"

"I told her ugly and terrible things."

"About me?"

"About both of us."

"I thought you ran off with one of your old boyfriends," he said.

"You had horrible thoughts, I know. I deserve everything you imagined."

So that was it, that's all it was. She'd been with Christina. How easy and uncomplicated. She'd moved in with him, but it was too sudden, too quick for her, and there was a recoil, she felt a need to pull away. But she was back now, and that was good, the frantic part was over. Time was not a storm, it was only the wind, an easy wind, and if you listened hard, what you heard in the wind was music, turning and twisting, lifting and falling. That was what she did for him, that's how she made him feel: like a song. If he didn't marry her and bring her to America, he was crazy.

Was this right, he wondered. Am I getting it right?

He watched as she moved about the house, going from room to room. He followed her. She didn't go through the doorways, she floated right through the walls. Right through the furniture she went, as if it weren't there.

"How did you do that?"

"Do what?"

"You walked right through that wall."

She smiled. "I do it all the time. You've only just noticed?"

"But how? How did you do it?"

"You want to know all of my secrets?"

"Yes, everything."

"There are some secrets a woman must keep to herself," she said. "Especially on Malta, and especially during the war."

She did it again, stepping toward the living-room wall as if it didn't exist, then right through, vaporous, ghostly, blissfully mysterious. He wasn't sure. Was it Melita who had come back to him, or was it the ghost of Melita? She had died and come back. Or was it someone else?

He saw what she meant, how easy it was to lose your mind if you lived on Malta. The bombs and the guns, the infernal noise, day and night. He tried to walk through the wall, following her, but bumped his nose, hard, and it hurt.

"What's the word for snow?" he asked.

"Go away with your word for snow."

"What's the word for broken heart?"

"I don't know such a word."

"What's the word for ghost?"

"There are good ghosts and bad ghosts, which do you want?"

"What's the word for floating and drifting and never being sure?"

"There is no such word, not in a single word."

"What's the word for welcome home?"

"Come," she said, "I'll show you."

She walked again through another wall, and he had to go through the doorway to find her, and she went through many walls, one after another, and he pursued her, doorway after doorway, and when he found her she was upstairs, in the room under the broken roof, with night coming on, and it seemed to him, when he caught up to her, that she was on fire, small flames curling lazily from her skin, blue fire from the blueness of her eyes. Even her breath was blue and burning, and he was afraid to undress her for fear of the conflagration he would find.

Part II

HEAT, SUN, DUST OVER EVERYTHING

All nature is merely a cipher and a secret writing. The great name and essence of God and his wonders, the very deeds, projects, words, actions, and demeanor of mankind—what are they for the most part but a cipher?
—BLAISE DE VIGENÈRE, *TRAICTÉ DES CHIFFRES*

When the difference between a cannon shell over your head and a cannon shell in the cockpit represented an immeasurably short space on a German reflector-sight, or an immeasurably short time in a German head, it was beginning to be terrifying to believe that your fate depended on your own vigilance, and yet terrible to think of it in the blind capricious hands of chance.
—RAF PILOT JOHNNY JOHNSTON,
TATTERED BATTLEMENTS

Sixteen

ZAMMIT DISCOURSES ON THE INTRICACIES OF THE SOUL NARDU CAMILLERI GETS A HAIRCUT TONY ZEBRA GOES FOR THE BIG ESCAPE

"No invasion," Melita said. "I feel it, I know it in my bones. Not today, anyway." It was a hope, a wish.

In April, over 6,700 tons of bombs had hit the island, more than three times the tonnage dropped in March. And now it was May, the first of May, and who could say if it would be easier or worse than April had been?

That morning, early, before the first raid, she went with Rocco to Maqluba, in the pink hearse, wanting to see him working at the wireless.

"So now you're a spy? You listen to other people's conversations? You're a peeping Tom?"

"If I knew what they were saying, it might be more fun."

He tuned to Fingerly's three frequencies and wrote down the coded messages, then he let Melita take over. She was captivated by the glowing tubes, the orange and purple luminosity. She played with the dials, ranging from one frequency to another, picking up a lot of dot-dot-dash.

Then she got bored. "This is what you do for a living?"

"How about cars?" he said.

"Cars?"

"Cars."

She waited.

"For the jukeboxes. Zammit could build the jukeboxes out of old car parts."

She thought about it, skeptically, but the more she thought, the more she liked it.

When they told Zammit about it, he liked it too. It was the best new idea since Melita had come up with stained glass.

Wrecked cars and trucks littered the island. They were pushed to the side of the road, to keep the way clear for military traffic. Eventually they were towed to the junkyards, but even the junkyards were bombed, and cars and trucks that had been bombed once already were bombed again, hammered and twisted into weird, phantasmagorical shapes.

"Yes, yes," Zammit nodded, "cars, broken cars. A new kind of jukebox, like nothing ever before."

The idea flamed.

Melita went with Rocco to the junkheaps, with pliers and hacksaws, scavenging for usable parts. They climbed among smashed Austins, crushed Healeys, burnt-out Fords, and accordion-folded Rolls-Royces, moving from wreck to wreck like insects among flowers. The yards were surreal gardens filled with nightmarish metal blossoms, and the astonishing thing was that, in the midst of so much ruin, they found, with some searching, fancy chrome hubcaps as good as new, hood ornaments that gleamed, headlamps and taillights that blinked on, and window wipers that still wiped.

Zammit loved it. "More," he said. "Bring me more. Bring me everything!" He was eager and busy, as excited as a child, working feverishly, day and night, with little sleep, his eyes suffused with an otherworldly glow.

He made jukeboxes with radiator grilles. He made them with spark plugs and red taillights that flashed on and off, with horns that honked and windows that cranked up and down. It was, for him, a wildly new direction. After his early mannerist period, then his Counter-Reformation Baroque, and his neo-classical chic, and his brief flirtation with introspective romantic rapture, he was now, in Melita's phrase, into a meta-modern mode, and he was having the time of his life. Where to put the headlights? How to use the carburetor? What to do with the speedometer, the glove compartment, the muffler? Should he attach a steering wheel? Did he dare insert a clutch?

He was working on seven jukeboxes at once, and in each of them were the hit songs of 1941 and 1942. "In the Blue of the Evening," "Jersey Bounce," "Moonlight Cocktail," "Tangerine" . . . In one he had "Be Careful, It's My Heart" and "Take the 'A' Train," and in another, "Bewitched." The jukebox in his bedroom had "Don't Sit Under the Apple Tree with Anyone Else But Me."

In the universe of jukeboxes, some were cool, icy, serene, while others were hot, red, vampy, and mean. Even Rocco knew that. A jukebox had personality. Zammit's theory was that a jukebox not only had personality but it also had a soul. It had a soul made up of the souls of all the singers whose recordings it played.

"When a singer makes a record," Zammit said, warming to the idea, "his soul is right there, in the grooves, vibrating in the needle. When Sinatra sings, it's his soul you are listening to."

With his heavy eyebrows and small black mustache he looked a little like Charlie Chaplin, and it was hard for Rocco to take him seriously. They were at the dining-room table, eating a tossed salad Melita had made, fresh lettuce with slices of cucumber from Zammit's garden, with olives, chopped peppers, small chunks of cheese, a generous sprinkling of oregano. Melita had bartered for the cheese and the olives, trading a brand-new Benny Goodman for the olives, and a 1938 Billie Holiday for the cheese.

"If Sinatra's soul is in the record," Rocco said, exploring Zammit's idea, "then his soul is in every record he ever made? In every copy?"

"Why not? You imagine the soul is locked in the body? When I shout and my voice echoes off a mountain, it is my soul rebounding off the mountain— my very soul. Echo, echo, echo. The soul itself, repeating itself."

Rocco thought it odd that Zammit should mention a mountain, there being no mountains on Malta. The only mountains Zammit had ever seen were in the movies.

"Good enough," Rocco said, still probing, testing. "So Sinatra's soul is in every record he ever made. As is Bing Crosby's? And Dinah Shore's? And Lena Horne's?"

"Exactly. Isn't it so?"

"And this jukebox," Rocco said, turning and looking through the archway into the living room, pointing at a jukebox to which Zammit had just put the finishing touches, an imposing thing with a radiator grille and two blinking headlights, and a window wiper that squeaked annoyingly, so it was better to keep the window wiper switched off, "this jukebox—any jukebox—it has a soul of its own?"

"Yes. A soul of its own."

"But it has twenty-four records in it. Doesn't it therefore have twenty-four souls?"

"Of course it does. And they are all part of the one soul that is the soul of the jukebox. In the same way that all of us, each of us, has a soul, but all of our souls are part of the one big soul that is the human race. Isn't this what is meant by the communion of saints? The souls of all the living and all the dead, joined together in a single, wonderful song."

Rocco leaned across the table and moved in for the kill. "Even Hitler is part of this one soul? Yes? Yes?"

"Even Hitler."

"And Mussolini?"

"Him too, much as I regret it," Zammit said, shaking his head sadly, "part of our painfully evolving human life."

Rocco didn't mind being part of one big soul with Sinatra and Lena Horne, but Hitler and Mussolini were something else. Nothing Zammit said seemed at all plausible or realistic, and much of it, in fact, sounded vaguely heretical. If the bishops of Malta caught wind of Zammit's jukebox theology, Rocco figured they would be hauling Zammit into the square in front of the Cathedral, with hooded monks beating on drums, and if the Germans didn't drop a bomb on him first, the monks would be burning him at the stake.

"To you, Zammit," he said warmly, with feeling, lifting his glass, "to your gigantic, jukebox soul." Zammit worked on jukeboxes, and Rocco liked to work on cars—it was a bond between them, they were comfortable around mechanical things. And Rocco also liked it that Zammit had a silly little mustache, and an eccentric mind full of soaring, heretical fantasies.

While Melita was in the kitchen, boiling water for a pot of tea, Zammit put his hand on Rocco's arm. "She's a good girl," he said. "Be sure you do right by her."

Rocco was struck by his directness. "I will," he answered. "Don't worry, I'll do right by her."

He meant he would treat her well, be good to her, not hurt her, he would take care of her. He did not mean that after the war he would come back for her and bring her home with him to New York, because all of that, the future, was too filled with shadows and uncertainty. While the bombs fell and people were dying, it was better not to think too far ahead.

The brandy was low, so they drank vermouth. On Zammit's newest jukebox, Bing Crosby sang "Be Careful, It's My Heart," and while it played, Melita sang along.

"Isn't she beautiful?" Zammit said. "Doesn't she have the prettiest voice?"

She had a pretty voice, and a pretty body. Rocco wished he had a camera so he could take her picture. But where, on Malta, in all the bombing, do you find a camera and a roll of film?

Zammit poured more vermouth, and he was talking again about the jukeboxes. He had made some good ones and some not so good. He thought the jukeboxes he was making now were better, on the whole, than the jukeboxes he'd made in the past, but still there was more to accomplish, another stage that had to be reached. The hubcaps and headlamps were interesting, they would occupy him for a while, but there had to be something beyond all of this, something larger and more mysterious that had not yet crystallized, and he wondered if it ever would. He felt an urge, a need to create, but where the urge was taking him he had no idea. It was like a promise inside him, something he couldn't quite visualize, yet he knew it was there, baking inside him, and he had to be faithful to it, had to go on working, and must never stop.

During the March and April raids, it had been the Germans who did most of the damage, yet the Italians were also there, dropping bombs. Nobody on Malta forgot it was the Italians, in 1940, who had flown the first raids. Even though the Germans were more destructive, it was the Italians who evoked a special bitterness, because it was felt they had stabbed Malta in the back.

All over Malta, now, families with Italian names were denying their Italian past and identifying themselves as pure-blooded Maltese. They hated Mussolini, with his Savoia Marchetti bombers and his Macchi and Reggiane fighter planes and his three-engined Cant Z 1007 medium bombers made of wood and capable of carrying a dozen bombs. They hated his fat Fascist jowls and his Fascist lips and his big Fascist teeth and his Fascist whore Clara Petacci. In fact, some of them felt he was such a gargoyle that he, Mussolini, *Il Duce,* could not possibly be Italian but was a bastard of mixed blood and criminal ancestry, from Africa no doubt, descended from some monstrous mongrel warlord, and when they thought of him that way, as not authentically Italian, it seemed to them that being Italian was not so terrible after all, and the ones with relatives in Ragusa, Catania, Cosenza, and Reggio entertained again kindly thoughts toward the towns their ancestors had come from.

"But we are all Maltese," the old man, Nardu Camilleri, insisted. "We have nothing to do with Italia! Nothing!" He was in a barber's chair, in a damaged shop on Kingsway, getting a haircut, between a furniture store that had been demolished and a haberdashery that was blown to rags. "There is no Italian blood in my veins. None! If there were, I would open my wrists this minute, here, now, with a razor, and let it all flow away. I piss on Italy! I step on it! I throw it away in the garbage!"

It was a voice that Rocco, coming along Kingsway after picking up a newspaper, recognized instantly. When he peered into the partly wrecked barbershop, he saw Nardu Camilleri in the first chair, close to where the big window had been before it was blown out in the bombing. The top of his head was bald and only a few wisps of barely visible gray grew above his ears, nevertheless, once a month, religiously, he went for a trim. While the barber snipped away at the empty air above his baldness, Nardu ranted on against Italy and the Italians. He decried the Italian planes (junk compared to the German machines), the Italian pilots (cowards), Italian ships (slow, cumbersome, no radar, and their gunners had bad aim), and the puny Italian bombs (they went *pop*, like firecrackers, instead of *boom*, and never fell where they were supposed to). He found unpleasant things to say about Italian art, Italian architecture, Italian opera, and the Italian pope, as well as Italian cars and cooking. Only a fragment of the big wall mirror remained, and from where Rocco stood on the sidewalk, the jagged edge of the mirror ran crookedly through Nardu Camilleri's reflection, making him seem a man who'd had half of his face torn away. Propaganda posters hung in the shop, caricatures of Hitler and Mussolini, and outside, on the street, in chalk: BOMB ROME.

"In any case," Nardu Camilleri said, "Italy, by bombing Malta, has besmirched herself and dishonored her name forever. Is Camilleri Italian? Never! Before the English came, before the French, before the Arabs, the Romans, the Greeks, and the Carthaginians, we were Maltese. Before the Phoenicians, we were Maltese and nothing else! The name Camilleri was Camilleru. It was a whim of my great-grandfather, in the last century, to change the *u* to an *i* because he thought it would make it easier, that way, to transact business in Sicily and Naples. If your name sounded Italian, you were in a better position to deal with the Italians. So all these names that you hear, these names that sound Italian—they are not Italian, not a one of them, and anyone who thinks they are is ignorant of history."

Rocco waved his hand in front of the old man's face, catching his attention.

"Nardu? Nardu? Do you remember me?"

The old man studied him, and then remembered. "Ah, yes, you are the American. I remember you well. I thought you were among the lost."

He signaled the barber, and the barber applied some rose water and drew away the sheet. Stiffly, Nardu got out of the chair, paid the barber, and, stepping through the empty space where the door had been, joined Rocco on the broken sidewalk.

"Where are you living?" Rocco asked. "You didn't go to Rabat with the women?"

"This is where I live," the old man said, gesturing with both hands and looking up and down the street. "Could I leave Valletta? Valletta is the jewel. We have everything here. The Cathedral, the Opera, the Palace of the Grand

Master, the Market, the Auberge de Castille, the Casino Maltese. I shall never leave. I have lived here all my life. This is my soul, it is my existence."

He spoke as if it were all still there, but there was nothing. The Opera and the Auberge de France were in ruins. The Auberge de Castille was a mere shell. The Market had been hit, and the Palace too. Even the Co-Cathedral of St. John was damaged, though it was only the German chapel that had been hit, built long ago with funds from the German Langue of the Knights.

Nardu Camilleri seized upon the irony. "See? They bomb us, but they cannot touch us, they only destroy themselves. The German chapel," he said gleefully. "Isn't it wonderful? There is a God! Don't you see? There is a plan in the universe, justice will be done!" Then, with a renewed sense of Rocco's presence, he looked him up and down, studying him from head to foot as if seeing him for the first time. "You? A soldier? Where is your gun?" He pointed skyward. "Why aren't you up there, fighting against the bombers? What good are the Americans if they don't fight?"

Amused by the old man's spirited rebuke, Rocco explained, halfheartedly, that he was a different kind of soldier, working a wireless.

"You listen? You send? What good is that?"

"Frankly," Rocco said, "I don't really know."

"Get a gun. When the Boches come, you can shoot back. When the Mussolini macaronies arrive, shoot the cowards between the eyes. Look at you, you are helpless."

His gaze wandered idly, the whole long length of the street, shops and office buildings in ruins, a powdery yellowish dust covering everything.

"In Malta, we have a proverb," he said. "*Id-dinja mxattra, il-għajnejn tibri, din l-art ħamra u l-firien tiġri.* You understand Maltese, don't you?"

Rocco grinned, helpless.

"It means the world is a mess and badly jumbled. That's what it says. 'The world is disheveled, eyes search and stare, the earth is red, rats are everywhere.' We say this when everything is falling apart and we have lost hope. But we also have another saying: *Il-qattus għandu sebat irwieħ*—'A cat has seven lives.' In America, you say nine lives, but in Malta we say seven, which is closer, I think, to the truth. Nevertheless, the meaning is the same: 'No matter how bad things get, you must never despair.' Especially if you are a cat. Tell me, have you considered the proposition I offered you about Maltese lace? You will be our agent in America?"

"I'm thinking it over," Rocco said doubtfully, with a smile. "I'm giving it some serious thought."

"Don't think it over too long. I'm an old man, before you go again to the toilet I could be dead in my grave." As he spoke, he glanced about. The afternoon sun glinted off the rubble, acres of broken bone-bright stones casting stark shadows that seemed holes in reality, into which you could fall and disappear.

Then he was moving, walking off, a cracked, riven expression on his face, as if aware, suddenly, of the ruin and catastrophe all around him. "I must go now," he said brusquely, his faded gray eyes slanting into the shadows. "You—you stay alive, if you can."

Rocco watched as he walked off with quick short steps, like an old mechanical toy whose spring was shot, but there was still some action in him, even though he was running down.

———

MESSRS. V. MARICH & CO. advise that their premises at the Palace Square, Valletta, have been damaged through enemy action and they are now at VICTORIA GARDENS, Sliema.

———

MESSRS. E. MAISTRE & SON, Printers, Stationers & Rubber Stamp Manufacturers, of 138 Britannia Street, Valletta, would like to inform their clients that owing that their premises at the above address have been demolished through enemy action they have transferred their business to 14 SAQQAJJA HILL, RABAT.

———

Owing to enemy action, WALTER BONDIN have transferred their office to No. 29 Milner Street, Sliema. Tel. No. Sliema 558.

———

At Takali, Tony Zebra was thinking about the American, Sergeant Walcott, who flew off the *Wasp* back in April, but instead of flying on to Malta with the rest of his RAF squadron, Walcott took a right turn and put down south of the Atlas Mountains, in Algeria. He got rid of his uniform, made his way to the American consulate, told them he was a civilian who had crashed in the mountains, and asked for repatriation to the United States. Or so, at any rate, the story went.

"Smartest man in the RAF," Tony Zebra told Rocco. "Why didn't I think of doing that? Malta is finished. No food, no ammo, no fuel, and damn near down to no planes. What's left? Hang around and wait to become a freaking POW when the white flag goes up?"

On a Wednesday morning, May 6, he was on readiness with three other Spitfires. At nine forty-five, radar picked up incoming bombers, and they got the signal to intercept. Tony Zebra was last off, and in the air they formed up, line abreast, climbing, going for altitude so they could attack from above.

Still climbing, they entered a cloud that hung like a thick shelf above the island, and it was while inside the cloud that Tony Zebra knew this was his moment to quit Malta forever. He'd been thinking it, planning it, and now it was upon him, the decision to go, like a struck match. Follow Walcott, off to Algeria.

The odds were dicey, the Spitfire carrying just enough fuel to get him there, so if he ran into strong headwinds, or strayed off course, bad news. He'd fly due west, crossing into Tunisia somewhere between Bizerte to the north and Sfax to the south, both loaded with Germans and Italians. Then on to Algeria. The trick was to slip through unnoticed by the 109s.

Crazy.

Yes. For sure.

But why not?

He was that desperate.

He kept thinking of Walcott. If Walcott could do it, he could do it too. He had his St. Jude medal with him, always did.

When he came out of the cloud he was alone, heading not in the direction of the bombers but across the sea, for Africa, toward Tunisia and beyond. He felt calm and free, confident, nothing but clear, open sky ahead.

Before he was halfway along to the African coast, he spotted, below, a quartet of Ju-88s in a tight box formation, a diamond-shaped pattern. He scanned the sky, looking for 109s, but the 88s were alone, unescorted, crossing underneath him, probably from Bizerte.

Then he saw what they were after—far down, on the water, off to his left, a small ship the size of a destroyer, and from the way it was churning the water, it was moving along at a hefty speed. He knew the ship, it was the *Welshman*, he'd seen it before, fast and cocky, scooting back and forth between Alexandria and Malta, Malta and Gibraltar, bringing in ammunition, fuel, canned milk. It traveled solo, without escort, making forty knots, one of the fastest in the Mediterranean, doing the thousand-mile run from Gibraltar in a day and a half. Churchill called it his greyhound of the sea. The Germans knew of it, and there was a rivalry among the squadrons as to which would have the honor of sinking it.

Tony Zebra kept to his course, wondering if the 88s had spotted him, and wondering, too, if the *Welshman* had spotted the 88s. The 88s flew on steadily, wings and bodies gray and green, for camouflage. It was just himself, the bombers, and the ship, distant from each other, separate but connected, caught in the weirdness of the moment. The sky, blue and lazy, seemed indifferent—a sky that had seen ships sailing for Troy, and it couldn't care less, if it even remembered. He studied the fuel gauge. When he looked down at the bombers again, they were still humming along, on course toward the *Welshman*.

Then, as if the decision were not his but the plane's, as if the plane were choosing and he was merely following, the stick moved forward, with his hand on it, and the plane went into a dive, straight for the bombers.

The steep line of his descent gave him a searing speed, and, swooping down, he pulled up under the bombers, attacking from below and astern. The gunners never saw him. He blew in, blazing away at the rear bomber in the diamond, and saw pieces flying off the wings, but nothing fatal. He pulled past, swinging on a wide arc, and came around again, from underneath, going again for the same plane. All four of the bombers were aware of him now and they broke formation, splitting away and turning, weaving wildly in a kind of mayhem. He kept after the one he had picked out, turning with it, bending, the G-forces yanking at his body, pulling at him, his body stressing against the harness, and the sweat poured off of him, as it always did when he flew in combat. As he closed on the 88, he got it in his sights and was about to fire, but off to his left, and above, a sunburst flashed in the sky, and a rage of debris scattered far and wide. Two of the 88s had collided, their bomb loads exploding in a fireball.

He pulled sharply to the right, avoiding the blast, and saw that the bomber he'd been pursuing wobbled, in trouble, then it went limp, lost altitude, and pancaked into the sea. He hadn't shot it down, he knew that. It must have caught some shrapnel from the collision. The fourth bomber was racing back to Bizerte.

He got back on course for Africa, aiming for the distant coastline, but when he checked the fuel gauge, he saw it was hopeless. Still he flew on, determined to make it, pushing the engine with sheer willpower, urging it on, as if simple thought could keep it going. Then, painfully, realism broke in, and drenched in sweat, the harness hugging him firm, he banked the plane and swung back for Malta.

When he arrived, he didn't have fuel enough to make it to Takali, so he went in at Hal Far. The *Welshman* had already sent a signal to the Y Corps on Malta, reporting a lone Spitfire had knocked down three attacking 88s. They sent the call numbers of the plane and asked for the pilot's name because they wanted to give him a case of champagne on their return trip.

When Tony Zebra got from Hal Far back to Takali, his squadron leader gave him a stiff dressing down for splitting away from the flight and flying off on his own—because going it alone was a recipe for disaster, not only for yourself but for the ones you left behind. In response, Tony Zebra told him to eat shit, expecting that his insolence would earn him a ticket out of Malta, but the squadron leader, after recommending to Tony Zebra that he swallow a pint of goat piss, informed him that, against his better judgment, he was putting him up for a decoration, because what else do you do with a hotshot cowboy who storms around on his own and disposes of three bombers in one day?

Tony Zebra didn't want the medal. He explained—tried to explain—that two of the bombers had simply collided, and the third had somehow gone down on its own, but the squadron leader wasn't listening, and nobody else was either. There was a growing sense that despite his obviously mediocre flying skills, he was an intuitive genius, with a nose better than radar and an uncanny knack for knocking planes down. The people who flew with him were nervous about getting too close because anything near him, friend or foe, tended to fall out of the sky, even when he didn't shoot.

They gave him the DFM.

Seventeen

THE PIGMY ELEPHANT

On the farm near Maqluba, some days, as Rocco sat out the hours monitoring the three frequencies, there was nothing, but most days there was a lot of dot-dot-dash that he got down in pencil as accurately as he could, spelling out the words and the non-words that made up the codes and ciphers filtering through the air.

Ciphers, codes, dot-dot-dash, there was a rhythm to it, and when you got tired you could move off to another frequency and catch, with luck, a song. One day he caught Glenn Miller doing "Chattanooga Choo-Choo." Another day it was "Lili Marlene." But mostly it was dot-dot-dash, everybody talking in code, the British, the Germans, the Italians, the Greeks, even the Turks and Tunisians, the air laden with waves and signals: a weave, an embroidery, threads on a loom, London to Cairo, Gibraltar to Malta, Greece to Alexandria, Berlin to Benghazi. If you could see it, if the signals could be rendered visible in the air, it would be lace, an interweaving of delicate strands, each going its own way, with its own throb, its own energy, its own secret, its own evolving, intertwining pattern. The submarines used code and the diplomats used code. The generals and admirals used code. Even the pilots had a code, talking on R/T, G for George, D for Dick, L for Lydia, telling each other where they were, in what position over the island and at what altitude, but when the battle was on, it was all in the open, *en clair*, nothing but raw immediacy: bitten-off words, frightened chatter, groans, terse warnings, *dive, dive, pull out, break left, watch your rear, he's on you! on you!* The Germans and Italians too, voices crackling in the high frequencies: *fertig, ja, avanti, subito, beständig, südlich, sofort, schnell.* And one day, when a shot-up Hurricane went down in flames, plunging from more than a mile high, Rocco picked up the blood-curdling scream of the pilot burning alive in the cockpit, a piercing wire-thin cry, shrill and unearthly, all the way down. Then nothing. Blank. The sky empty. It stayed with him. Later, browsing through the frequencies, he caught a few static-interrupted phrases from Red Barber doing a Brooklyn Dodgers game, relayed on shortwave by some compulsive Flatbush fan who knew there were other fans out there, across the ocean, wanting to listen. Somebody hit a home run, but the name was lost in the static. Then Billy Herman singled to left, and Pee Wee Reese bunted him over to second. Then Arky Vaughan was up, but the reception fell apart and the game disappeared in the ether.

Friday morning, while Rocco was monitoring the frequencies, Fingerly drove up in the Austin Seven, in a new sportshirt, yellow and blue, covered with flowers and hummingbirds. When he came in, what he put on the table, in front of Rocco, was a quart-size aluminum thermos with a red plastic top.

"My divers found it at the bottom of the channel, at Marfa Point," he said with a swagger, gloating. "Take a look, Raven. Unscrew the cap."

It looked like one of the antipersonnel bombs the 109s were dropping on the villages. Thermos bombs, they were called. Kids, picking them up in the street, had their hands and faces blown off.

"This is safe? I won't blow up?"

"You scoffed, didn't you? I remember. You thought it a big joke, sending divers into the channel."

"The pigmy elephant? It's in here?"

"No, Raven, the pigmy elephant is not in there."

"Then I really can't imagine. This is just like Christmas."

He opened the thermos, and inside were several sheets of paper rolled into a scroll. He took them out and flattened them, looking them over. They were covered with cipher.

"Send it," Fingerly said.

"What is it?"

"It's Maroon's Gozo Report."

"Is that what he was doing? Writing a report?"

"What did you think he was doing, harvesting honey?"

"Shacking up, I thought. Isn't that what you said? What's in the report—descriptions of his one-night stands?"

"Babalu," Fingerly tossed off jauntily.

"I know, I know. Chica boom."

"Hell, Raven, if we're ever going to invade Sicily, we've got to put a force out there on Gozo and use it as a jumping-off point. If we don't know about Gozo, how can we use it? Where to put the ammo dumps, where to set up HQ, where to lay out the airfields the engineers will have to build."

"I thought the Brits had all of that figured out by now."

"They do, they do. We have their report. But if we're putting American troops and American equipment there, we need an American report, don't we?"

"Do we?"

"As it turns out, Gozo is a backwater, nothing but farms and churches. Inadequate sewage disposal, inadequate roads. Inadequate harbor for this size operation. And no whores. No whores, Raven—can you imagine an entire island of twenty-six square miles with no whores? The invasion of Sicily will have to be put off indefinitely." He took a pack of Camels out of his shirt pocket and lit up. "Send it."

"All eight pages?"

"Seven."

"I have eight."

Fingerly grabbed the pages and glanced through.

"Here," he said, holding one back, "send these." He put a match to the one page, and let it burn in the ashtray.

At the transmitter, Rocco established contact and sent the report. It took a while, his finger rusty, slow on the key, and as he tapped out the long message he felt vaguely uneasy about sending in cipher and not knowing a word of what he was putting into the air. For all he knew, he might have been broadcasting a hit list for the Palermo Mafia.

Fingerly drove him back to Valletta, but instead of going up through Hamrun, they detoured into Paola, at the inmost point of Grand Harbour. "You think that pigmy elephant doesn't exist? Is that what you think? I'm going to make a believer out of you, Raven. I'm going to show you that faith has its rewards and it pays to put trust in humble fishermen who know how to do their job. I'm going to show you something you'll never forget."

"Speaking of faith," Rocco said, "I'm sort of overdue. You know that, don't you?"

"Overdue?"

"For my pay. The subsistence wages."

Fingerly put on an innocent face. "I forgot? Again I forgot?"

"I just thought I should mention it," Rocco said, not wanting to appear pushy but feeling he had to say something. He was low on cash.

"Patience, patience," Fingerly said. "I'm low myself right now. In a couple of days you'll have it. Don't give it another thought."

Rocco had noticed how Fingerly had a way of being late, always, with the pay. It was a kind of power game, a not too subtle way of asserting control.

"In a couple of days," Fingerly repeated, tapping the steering wheel with his forefinger.

He pulled up in front of an old warehouse, and taking a flashlight from the car, led the way down a steep flight of stairs to an underground level. The electricity was down. Using the flash, they walked through a long stone corridor, past padlocked doors, their footfalls echoing off the dank, mildewed walls. Rocco was thinking again of Edgar Allan Poe. At the final door, Fingerly took out a key, opened the padlock, and, inside, located a few candles.

Rocco's eyes adjusted slowly. He was aware of a great jumble of things crowded together.

"There," Fingerly said, pointing, and Rocco saw it, on a table, the bones all wired together, a four-legged skeleton the size of a large dog.

"That's an elephant?"

"A pigmy elephant. *Elephas falconeri.*"

"How do you know it's not just a baby elephant that never grew up?"

"Science, Rocco," Fingerly said with laidback enthusiasm. "Science knows about these things. My divers did a great job, didn't they? These bones were scattered all over the bottom of the channel, they found every damn one of them. There's a taxidermist here in Paola got them wired together. From the Pleistocene, isn't it amazing?"

Rocco touched the bones, they were smooth, coated with varnish, so old it depressed him to think something had lived and died that long ago. An entire epoch of time, hundreds of thousands of years, gone in a blink.

There were other things. A lance, a suit of armor, a painting in a gold frame. A shield, a crucifix. A sword. A gold goblet. A stone tablet with a Roman inscription, and another tablet with writing he didn't recognize at all. The Fat Lady was there, the small statue Fingerly had got from the sacristan in Mosta. It was with two others—one, like the first, in a standing position, naked, but with no head, and the other wearing a skirt and lying down, asleep. All three with exaggerated breasts and hips.

Rocco's eyes roved from object to object. It was a hoard. He picked up the figurine from Mosta, and then the other one, the one just like it except for the missing head, and saw that the one from Mosta was better. The legs on the other one somehow didn't seem right.

"Don't get the wrong impression," Fingerly said. "I've paid for all this, cash or barter. I'm not here raping the land, the way Göring and his mob are doing in Europe, sacking the museums and the private collections. This is good, clean American capitalism, a free exchange among free men, value for value."

The lance had cost him three cartons of Philip Morris. The suit of armor had cost two hundred American dollars. The stone tablet with the Roman inscription had cost three loaves of bread and a dozen eggs. "Bombs are falling everywhere, so think of it as a salvage operation," he said, his tone resonating with sincerity. "I'm rescuing the past so it can survive into the future. Somebody has to do it. History, romance, precious antiquity—tell me, Rocco, what does America know about the Knights of Malta?"

There was a mace, a dagger, an old Bible. "It's a lot of stuff," Rocco said. "How will you get it off the island?"

"There are ways. I'll figure something."

Rocco picked up the dagger, feeling the heft, tossing it from hand to hand.

"The dealer I got it from said it belonged to that old pirate, Dragut. He was some hell-raiser, you know. He attacked Naples, then he raided Corsica and carried off seven thousand into slavery. That's seven thousand, Rocco. When he took Reggio, he enslaved the entire population. Well, the Knights took captives too, and turned them into slaves. For a long time, Malta was the biggest slave market in Europe."

"He's the one who died, right? He was killed in the siege."

"Dragut? When he sailed against Malta, he was eighty years old. Isn't it incredible? He was still spry and feisty. He pitched his tent by the trenches, close to the action, and ate with his men. The Knights sent all of their prostitutes off to Sicily, for safekeeping, and when Dragut heard of it, he laughed. 'At my age,' he said, 'what could I possibly do with them anyway?' "

Rocco still held the dagger, feeling the weight of it, the subtle balance. "And this? It's his?"

Fingerly shrugged. "Well, the dealer said so. But in desperate times, Rocco, desperate people will say anything. It's of the period, though, so it has some value, and maybe Dragut really did slit a throat or two with it."

Rocco had a sense of a huge underground network out there, New York, Rio, Paris, Madrid, agents and dealers grabbing deliriously, a great web of buy and sell, the hush and fever of under-the-table action, Oran, Alexandria, the private collectors and even the museums grabbing what they could while the war was on and the getting was good. And Fingerly was right there at the hot center, a prince of contraband, who couldn't wait till the war moved up into Italy so he could scavenge through the ruins of the bombed-out monasteries for the gilt-edged psalters, the reliquaries, the lapis lazuli, maybe a fire-singed Donatello, and who knows, maybe a piece of a Leonardo, damaged, yes, but still a Leonardo.

"Here, take a look at this." Fingerly lifted a sheet, revealing a heavily orna-mented coffin on the floor. It was Egyptian. He removed the lid and played the flashlight on the mummy within. The wrappings, brownish-gray, seemed to have merged with the flesh itself, but at the mouth and lower portion of the face, below the eyes, they had been drawn away, revealing teeth, gums, tongue, part of the upper lip, and part of one cheek. The nose was gone. The skin at the lip and cheek had the appearance of hard old leather, dark brown. Rocco wanted to reach out and touch it, but something inside him recoiled and he simply stood there, motionless, looking. Surrounding the mummy, in the cof-fin, were amber beads and amulets, and odd-looking artifacts Rocco didn't recognize.

"You didn't pick this up in Malta."

"No."

Fingerly had got it in a village between Cairo and Luxor, from a papyrus dealer who served as a middleman for a band of grave robbers. The mummy was Zed Mir Min, a scribe from the time of Akhenaton, the pharaoh who had turned his back on the old Egyptian gods and risked everything on the one god, Aton, who lasted for a while, but then the old gods came back. Zed Mir Min wasn't a pharaoh, but he would fetch a price.

"It used to take them about seventy days to mummify a corpse."

"That long?"

"They soaked them in brine. Then they dried them out and applied resin and red ochre." He held the flash on the mummy's face, and seemed weirdly captivated. "Been dead more than three thousand years," he said, gazing steadily. "This is what we are, Raven, this is what it's all about. Maroon just got there a little before the rest of us." There was a seriousness in his tone, a quiet vulnerability, that Rocco hadn't heard from him before, and would never hear again.

"How did you get it here?"

"Aboard a destroyer, a tin can. Ever been on one? Like riding a bucking bronco. From Alexandria to here, a thousand miles, and they detoured, chas-ing a U-boat."

"Did they get it?"

"The U-boat? Hell, it got us. Put a big hole amidship with a torpedo. We barely made it, came limping in to Grand Harbour with water washing over the bows. Nigg was with me, he puked the whole way."

"I feel dizzy," Rocco said.

"It's the air, no ventilation this far down. But it's bomb-proof. It better be. Unless they hit it with a Panther bomb."

They went back up. In the car, Fingerly put the key in the ignition, but before he started up he took a folded sheet of paper from his shirt and handed it to Rocco. "What do you make of this?"

Rocco scanned it. It was a list of the island's supplies—wheat, flour, ammunition, white oils, black oils, how long they would last. Wheat and flour till early June, fodder till July, meat already exhausted, coal till only the end of May.

"What does it mean?"

"What do you think it means?"

Rocco hesitated. "It looks to me like the white flag."

"On the button. Smart, Raven, smart."

"The Brits are quitting? You think so?"

"It sure looks that way. Here it is, already May, with no hope of a convoy till June, if even then. If these numbers are right, they won't be able to make bread, and you know how the Maltese feel about their bread."

"Where'd you get this?"

"From you. It's one of the ciphers you caught."

"Mine? One of mine?"

Only then did Rocco realize he'd been listening all these weeks not to the Germans or the Italians, but to the British, and it threw him for a loop. Spying on your enemies made sense, but spying on your friends seemed pushy, if not downright antisocial.

"Why?" he asked.

"Because we have to. How else can we know what they're going to do? They don't always come right out and tell us, you realize. As we don't always tell them. So they listen to us, as we listen to them, and if they pull out of Malta unexpectedly, then all bets are off, aren't they? It changes everything."

Everyone knew what surrender meant. It meant the Italians and the Germans would move in and take over. It meant the British and Maltese servicemen—probably the entire garrison of thirty-five thousand—would become prisoners of war, because if there was no way to get food and supplies into Malta, how, in the moment of collapse, do you get the garrison out? Rocco and Fingerly too, if they didn't slip out in time, they would be part of the general roundup, behind barbed wire. Not a fancy idea, not by a long shot. It meant the Maltese politicians who supported the British presence would be out and the handful who had been Italian-sympathizers before the war would be in, and Malta would no longer be a base for attacking the convoys that brought supplies to Rommel's Afrika Korps in North Africa, and Rommel could win. He'd have a very good chance. In fact, he was doing all right as it was: he'd already retaken Benghazi, months ago, and was dancing across North Africa, preparing to attack the Gazala line. If he won in Africa and pushed the British out of Egypt, he would have a clear path to the oil fields in the Middle East.

"So?" Rocco said. "Do we get out of here before it hits the fan?"

"Don't rush things," Fingerly said, turning the key in the ignition. "We still have work to do."

"What sort of work?"

"You're catching the dot-dot-dash, aren't you?"

"I should keep listening?"

"You should keep listening."

"You're serious?"

"Of course I'm serious."

"And you? Closing in on the lost and lonely Maltese Falcon? Or just another Fat Lady?"

"Chica boom, Raven. Babalu to you."

"Look, I'm just a wireless jockey, I know, but from my humble point of view, if I'm allowed a point of view, I think we should get our asses back to Gibraltar and from there I reconnect with the Second Corps, where I belong."

"What about the blue-eyed sweetie you've been making around with?"

"What about *what about*?"

"Love 'em and leave 'em? Just like that?"

"We'll take her with us."

"You can't do that, Raven. It's not in the rules."

"Sure I can."

"You're the boss?"

"When the time comes, I'll handle it."

"Yes? You will?"

"I will," Rocco said, knowing it was impossible, but believing, for the moment, really believing he'd find a way.

Fingerly took both hands off the wheel and gave a round of applause. "I like it, I like it. He'll handle it. That's what America needs, more like you, Rocco Raven. Before you're finished here, you're going to get a medal."

"That's a prediction?"

"It's a promise."

The air-raid sirens began to sound, a long, rueful groaning and wailing, smeared across the hot afternoon air like a swathe of whipped mud.

Fingerly was buoyant. "Don't you love it? Don't you love it when they bomb? It's fireworks, Raven, fireworks. Rockets and Roman candles."

The bombs, yes, the big and the not so big. The small 50-kilogram bombs, which could do a surprising amount of damage if they fell where they were meant to, and the 1,000-kilogram bombs that always did damage no matter where they fell, and the 2,000-kilogram bombs that left craters twenty feet deep and sixty feet across. There was the Satan bomb, the Mad bomb, and the new maxi-bomb, the Panther, driven by rockets, designed to drill through forty-five feet of rock. And the mini-bombs, antipersonnel devices with delayed-action fuses: pencil bombs, thermos bombs, flashlight bombs, and small butterfly bombs fluttering on metal wings. Bombs whistling, singing with dark mezzo voices, with teeth and tongues and flaming red hair, and bombs that were horses galloping down the wind, whinnying, snorting, stampeding, and the best bombs of all, the duds—the bombs that landed and never went off, the flukes, the mistakes, the failures, the castrati.

———

SPORTS FLASH—New York: Lulu Constantino suffered his first defeat as a pro after 56 wins when he was outpointed by Chalky Wright, the world's feather-weight champion according to the New York State Commission.

JAPAN: A terrific eruption of the Asama volcano in the center of the main Japanese island is reported by the German radio. It is added that the damage is not yet known.

MACARTHUR AND THE PRESS

General MacArthur, the hero of Bataan and Commander-in-Chief of the United Forces in Australia, told war correspondents at Melbourne: "In the democracies it is essential that the people should know the truth. One cannot wage war in present conditions without the support of public opinion, which is tremendously molded by the Press and other propaganda forces."

Eighteen

THE FIRST DAY OF
THE BOMBING

The bombing had begun in June 1940, a Tuesday morning, just before seven. The usual early rush at the market stalls was over, and in Valletta people were beginning to arrive for work. At the dockyard, across the harbor, the gates were crowded with workers coming in by bus and bicycle.

Melita had already started her day at the law courts, in the old Auberge d'Auvergne, on Strada Reale, filing papers she had typed the previous afternoon. She faced a busy morning—more typing, and then some steno work for Judge Borg. When the sirens sounded, she was crouched down, working at the bottom drawer of a filing cabinet overstuffed with copies of documents relating to marriage annulments and separations. Two others were working at the files, one a slight, anemic girl, young, with thin black hair, and the other much older, full-faced and corpulent.

When the alert sounded, confusion spread throughout the building. A young attorney, on his way to a hearing, said it was nothing, nothing at all, just a drill. Then a court clerk came in, shouting it was not a drill but the real thing and everyone was to go to the shelter—but he was an unpleasant person, not well liked and known to be an alarmist, nobody ever took him seriously. Melita went to the window and saw there was confusion in the street as well, people running for the shelter, but others standing about, uncertain, studying the sky.

"What do you think?" said one of the girls, the young one with too little hair on her head. Her name was Maggie.

"I think we should go see," Melita said, leading the way upstairs onto the roof. The sky was vacant, no planes, just the clear blue of June, early morning, already warm, and by noon the heat would be blistering.

"It's nothing," the girl Maggie said.

"Nothing at all," said the other one, the heavyset woman, whose name was Cettina Amante.

But then they saw them, far up, tiny specks glinting in the sun, coming from Sicily. And after they saw them, they could hear them too, the droning of the motors. In the distance, the planes seemed almost motionless, suspended in the sky like pieces of a gigantic chandelier, ponderous, sluggish, approaching slowly, as if reluctant to arrive. It was really happening: the war was on.

They stood rooted, watching. They didn't even think of going to the shelter, just stood there on the roof, transfixed, watching the planes in a kind of mystification. There were ten bombers, tri-motors, in a V formation, escorted by a flock of fighters. When they were nearly overhead, the antiaircraft batteries opened up with a thunderous roar, painting the sky with gray-black dabs of ack-ack. Three of the bombers veered off to attack the airfield at Hal Far, the others went for the ships in Grand Harbour.

The noise was deafening, Melita clapped her hands over her ears. The heavy guns choked the sky with shells and exploding ack-ack. They hit nothing. The planes came on and the bombs fell with a ground-shaking roar, some exploding close by, in Valletta, others slamming into the dockyard across the harbor. From Valletta and the neighboring towns, huge flocks of birds rose in the sky and flew inland, away from the bombs and the guns.

There was a shivering wildness in it: the noise, the rage, the stink of cordite, the sheer savagery of all that metal being hurled about. Melita felt it: the cutting loose, the complete recklessness of the moment. Where the bombs hit, they kicked up smoky spikes of dirt and dust a hundred feet high, yellow clouds from the pulverized limestone buildings. The dust hung in the air, forming a haze that settled slowly.

"It's only bombs," the young one, Maggie, said, shouting to make herself heard above the noise of the guns. There had been a fear that, when war came, the bombers would drop canisters of poison gas. The Italians had used gas in Abyssinia, and it was all the British talked about: Get ready. You were supposed to have a room in your house, upstairs, with all the holes and cracks sealed up, with wet blankets to hang over the doors and windows. Upstairs rather than down because the gas would settle and hug the ground. Gas masks had been issued, but who knew if they would really work? The older woman, Cettina Amante, had hers with her, ready to put on, but Maggie and Melita had left theirs behind on their desks.

The bombs dropped into Marsamxett Harbour on the north side of Valletta, and into Grand Harbour on the south side, churning the water into boiling fountains. A few bombs hit Valletta itself, and many went down on the far side of Grand Harbour, into the dockyard area and the neighboring towns, Senglea, Vittoriosa, and Cospicua. Melita felt a tightening, a physical pain in her stomach, because her father was out there, in Cospicua, not feeling well, home for the day. He worked at the dockyard, but when she left that morning, he had a sore throat and was sipping hot tea, thinking he wouldn't go in.

Only minutes after the first planes were gone, more planes appeared and a second raid developed. Melita, worried for her father, was already running. Off the roof and down the stairs and into the street, as fast as she could go, across town on St. John's, then down the long hill and onto the wharf, where she found a gray-haired boatman with a *dgħajsa*.

He wouldn't take her, because of the bombs.

She offered twice the usual fee, and again he refused. Then she took five times the normal amount from her purse, and, poker-faced, with a shrug, the *barklor* accepted. He was quiet, stolid, inward, and, looking at him, she knew the kind of man he was: hardworking and simple, up at five every morning so he could go to mass, a chunk of bread for breakfast with lots of butter and hot coffee, then the rest of the day with the boat and don't bother him about anything else.

He plied the oars vigorously, doing his best to get across fast. The planes were gone, but the all-clear had not yet sounded and Melita watched the sky nervously. Two more planes, stragglers in the raid, loomed into view, and again the big guns went into action. The *barklor,* busy with his oars, never looked up.

A few bombs fell in the harbor, raising huge geysers, one exploding not far from the boat, rocking it violently. Melita held tight to the rim, but the *barklor,* after the briefest pause, holding his balance, went on with the rowing. At the dockyard, oil was burning, a dense, snaking column of black smoke.

Ashore, she was running again, then walking, catching her breath, and again running, along Strada Toro. The bombers were gone and the all-clear sounded. When she saw up close what the bombs had done, she was desolate. Whole buildings were down, stone walls blown to pieces. A horse lay dead on the street, its flank ripped open, intestines spilling out, red and raw. Further along, rescue workers took a dead person from a damaged house. The streets were littered with glass, chunks of plaster, shrapnel from the ack-ack. Outside a bar, a man bleeding from the head shook his fists, gesturing angrily toward the sky.

She hurried along, breathless, through winding uphill streets, then up a street of stairs, and when she turned a corner, onto Kanzunetta, her heart sank, because there in front of her was the house she lived in, smashed to pieces.

She approached slowly, as if sleepwalking. The front wall was down and she could see the floors had collapsed, there was nothing but ruin. Again she stopped, merely looking, unable to absorb what she saw. Then, with a kind of fury, she climbed onto the hill of broken masonry and began tearing away at the wreckage, looking for him, calling to him, shouting frantically, *Papà, Papà,* pulling at the broken limestone and splintered furniture, until her skin tore and she was bleeding.

Then people were drawing her away, strangers, people she didn't know, they took her by the arms and pulled her away, and after that, all she could remember was that she was walking. They were all walking, away from Cospicua, away from Senglea and Vittoriosa, away from the docks and the entire Three Cities area, moving inland, great throngs of people, thousands, and there was only the numbing sound of the shoes on the road, the enormous herd rumbling along.

"What I remember most," she told Rocco now, "is the dust, there was dust everywhere."

They were in the hearse, driving from Żabbar to Birżebbuġa, where there was a jukebox that needed repair. Rocco was driving.

"Malta is always dusty," she said, "especially the hot months, but this was different. The dust was from the pulverized stone, the stone walls of the houses, all smashed, dust over everything."

The few who had cars went in cars, their belongings tied to the roof—mattresses, chairs, trunks. Some had horse-drawn *karrozzins* and some had bicycles, but most of them were on foot, thousands, like cattle, stomping along, pushing carts, baby carriages, or with nothing at all, just walking, dazed.

When Melita passed the Żabbar Gate, coming out of Cospicua, she saw four dead people on the ground, covered with dust and blood and flies. Flies everywhere, she hated the flies. On a doorstep, a woman sat pulling out her hair, a few strands at a time. She pulled, then she looked at the hair, dropped it, and pulled more.

"I remember a man with a herd of goats . . . so many goats, and a whole bunch of children. There was a woman carrying all her pots, she had her whole kitchen with her. There was a man with an ice-cream cart, pushing it along, his little boy sitting on top. A woman fainted and people stepped right over her. Nobody stopped, there was a panic to keep moving before the planes came and bombed again. I passed a man sitting on the ground, at the edge of the road, blood on his forehead. He was waving away the flies."

That first day, there were eight raids, the last coming just before nightfall. Bombs fell on Palm Street in Paola, Ponsomby in Gzira, a hotel in Sliema. They hit the primary school in Żabbar and a hospital that was being built on Guardamangia Hill. In Cospicua, twenty-two were killed. Bombs intended for the dockyard fell on Strada Toro and a dozen other streets.

"I still can't believe it," Melita said. "The streets I grew up on, the streets I played on when I was a little girl, where we jumped rope and went shopping. Molino, Margherita, San Giorgio, Concezione. Bombs fell on all of them. On Nuova, and Stella, and Alexandria."

On Strada Oratorio, a seventy-year-old man was pulled alive from the wreckage of a shoemaker's shop. On the same street, two days later, in a demolished house, two children were found alive in a wooden chest, where their mother had put them to shelter them from the bombs. The mother was dead under a pile of masonry.

At the end of the first day, over two hundred houses were in ruins and thirty-six people were dead. The bombers returned the next day, and seventeen were killed. There were raids every day that week. All over Malta, people were so angry they changed the names of the streets that had Italian names. Strada Toro became Bull Street. Oratorio became Oratory. Piazza Maggiore became Churchill Square. Strada Reale, the main street in Valletta, became Kingsway.

"When I saw our house, I was sure my father was dead in there, and I just went crazy. I was pulling at broken chairs, pieces of plaster, trying to find him. Then they took me away, and we were all walking, leaving Cospicua, heading inland. I went to my cousin Zammit's house in Santa Venera."

Not till a few days later did she get the news about her father. He'd been killed, but not by the bomb that hit the house. After she left, he'd decided to go to work anyway that day, despite the sore throat, and it was a bomb that fell on the dockyard, in the second bombing run, that killed him.

"So you stayed with Zammit?"

"For a few days. Then I moved in with my aunt, but that was terrible, so I went with a girl I'd gone to school with, her father runs a pharmacy."

"Your aunt in Naxxar? You don't get along?"

She stared straight ahead through the windshield. "She blames me. She blames me because *Papà* was killed. She thinks I should have insisted he stay home and rest in bed that day, because of his sore throat. Does that make sense? Am I to blame? When I left for work, he was planning to stay home, and if he had stayed, he would have been killed anyway, by the bomb that hit the house. But she doesn't see that, she can't think it through."

"How old was he?"

"Fifty-two. He was a riveter at the yard, he worked on the ships. It was so wrong for him to die. He was too young."

A plane fell out of the sky, a bomber, a Ju-88. It broke up on the ground, in a field, and burst into flame.

Rocco pulled over and they sat in the car, watching the bomber burn. They said nothing, just sat there, watching as the flames curled languidly, almost lovingly, around the broken wings and the crushed fuselage. A Ju-88 usually carried a crew of four. Rocco wondered if any of them were still in there.

"Let me drive," Melita said.

They switched seats and she drove, a little too fast for the rugged road, thumping over the potholes, quick on the turns, willfully reckless.

Fingerly had been expecting the white flag, but instead of the white flag, Malta got a new governor. On the night of May 7, Lord Gort flew in from Gibraltar, on a Sunderland flying boat, and the man he replaced, General Dobbie, flew out on the same plane, with his wife and daughter.

A few days later, sixty new Spitfires arrived, to bolster the island's defenses. They came in off the American aircraft carrier *Wasp* and the British carrier *Eagle*, which ferried them to a point about seven hundred miles west of Malta, then turned into the wind and launched the planes. For the time being, the British were hanging in.

Rocco, delighted that Fingerly had, for once, been wrong, pointed a finger in his face: "So? White flag?"

Fingerly pointed a finger right back. "Not out of the woods yet," he said, "not by a long shot."

They stood by the wreckage of the Opera House, the broken columns and slabs of marble gleaming in the sun like an ancient Roman ruin, but angrier.

"They're not quitting," Rocco said, "they're digging in. A new governor, new planes. Spitfires."

"Ah, but you know about this new governor, don't you?"

"Gort? They say he's tough. A fighter."

"True, true. But you know what else, don't you? He presided over the evacuation at Dunkirk. The man is an expert in getting the troops out when they have to be got out. Still smells like the white flag to me."

"I don't think so," Rocco said, in a betting mood. "They wouldn't send all these planes if they were quitting."

"No? You think not? Well, try this for size. In Sicily, at Gerbini—they're installing extra landing strips and hauling in all sorts of shit and supplies. The Brits picked it up in photo recon. I got it from the Brits in those last ciphers you intercepted. They're getting ready to invade, Raven. That's what all this March and April bombing was about. They've been softening up the defenses and any day now you'll see parachutes in the sky. Just like Crete."

"Wrong," Rocco said.

"Not wrong. Right." He said it with lazy, deep-throated assurance, and with his fist, playfully, tapped Rocco on the jaw. "You really want to hang around to find out?"

Rocco quickly grasped that again Fingerly was way ahead of him. "You mean we have transport out of here?"

"You bet we do."

"When?"

"I got a berth for you on a submarine, tomorrow. They'll take you to Gibraltar and from there you can reconnect with the Second Corps, they're still in Georgia."

"I've heard bad things about submarines."

"They're tight, they stink of oil, they run underwater."

"They get sunk."

"True, it happens."

"When they sink, everybody's dead."

"Usually, yes. But if you fly and get shot down, you're dead that way too."

"I think I'll wait around for a battleship."

"Raven," Fingerly said woefully, "I went through a lot of trouble to get you a berth on this submarine. If you don't take it, I'm going to lose my credibility."

"You have credibility? With whom?"

"Don't try me." The skin under his left eye puckered.

"I wouldn't dare," Rocco said.

"Be on that sub. Tomorrow."

"What about you?"

"I have business, a few loose ends."

"You're staying?"

"A few days, then I'm out of here."

Rocco hung, uncertainly. Ever since he'd arrived on Malta he'd been itching to clear out, away from the bombing, but now, handed a ticket, a berth on a sub, leaving Melita behind, it was torture.

"You have orders?"

"As in—?"

"As in orders. For me. From Second Corps."

"For you? Orders? Who's talking about orders? You wanted out, I'm letting you go."

If there were orders, Rocco thought, that would settle it, because orders were orders. But this wasn't Second Corps telling him to go, it was just Fingerly, which meant, for practical purposes, he could do what he wanted. Freedom was a terrible thing.

"I'll think about it," he said.

"Tomorrow, 1300 hours."

Rocco lit a cigarette in a relaxed, withdrawn manner that seemed to say no.

Fingerly was distressed. "Timing, Raven, it's all in the timing. That blue-eyed enchantress really spins you around, doesn't she."

A pigeon, near Rocco's foot, was pecking in the rubble.

"Just remember," Fingerly said, oddly solemn, "life is a road full of smiles, miracles, and pretty girls—follow the gold, Raven, but watch for the trapdoors."

"Is that a threat?"

"Hell, no. It's a prescription for how to live the rest of your life with a minimum of heartburn."

He turned and walked off brusquely, as if he'd be happy never to see Rocco again.

Rocco stood there, holding the cigarette, and he really didn't know about that submarine. He looked at the pigeon, still pecking around in the rubble, searching for a seed, a crumb, anything, and not finding.

Late that afternoon, at a corner table in the Oyster, Rocco had a beer, and he was thinking about Melita. She liked it when he massaged her back. She liked it when they held hands and went walking on Kingsway, and when they sat by the water, on the rocks, watching the gulls. Was it love, he wondered. Or just a complicated form of lust—the ravenous, gluttonous desire that blossoms in a war zone? Lust it certainly was, on his part and hers, he knew that, yet it was more, he thought, more than mere appetite. Or was that just a hope that he had? Whatever it was, it was something good, not bad, something to hold on to, better than baseball, better than Edgar Allan Poe, better than cooling rain on a hot July afternoon. Better than Count von Kreisen playing, over and over again, "The Blue Danube."

He drank another beer and memory took over, his mind aswarm with raveling images. The zoo in Brooklyn, with the monkeys and the seals, and the wooden horses on the carousel. And irises, a whole field of irises, he couldn't remember where. The subway trains to Manhattan, and a candystore where he drank egg creams and chocolate malteds and played a pinball machine. And his mother, again and again his mother, in a hospital bed, dying of pneumonia. He remembered the wake, the flowers. She was laid out in her best dress. How could he cut loose from that? How could he ever forget? He was six years old.

After the cemetery, his father took him home and there were people at the house. He didn't want the people, couldn't wait for them to go. The next day, dinnertime, they skipped supper and his father brought him out for ice cream. They sat in a booth, white placemats on the table, a black ashtray, the seats covered with red leatherette. It was the loneliest time. His father's eyes filled with tears, and when Rocco saw that, he too began to cry. How were they going to live without her? His father wept, and he wept, and the people near them watched, and some of them, looking on, began to cry. Rocco remembered that. Strangers, at other tables, people they didn't know, weeping because somehow they understood.

His father paid the bill and they went out into the night, cars and trucks passing with their big headlights. Steam from the sewers. Neon signs blinking. Streetlamps. Broken glass in the street. And then, six months later, that's all it was, six months, his father took up with another woman. He was lonely, Rocco saw that. His father was lonely and he was forgetting. But Rocco had the same loneliness, and he wasn't forgetting, and when he saw that his father had stopped remembering, he felt so lost. It was around that time, he now thought, that the separation began, the emotional drift between his father and himself. There was never the same feeling between them after that.

There were times, even now, when he wanted to say all of this to his father, wanted to put it in a letter, but while the bombs fell and people died, it was easier to write about the weather, when he wrote at all, or about the shortages and the terrible food. And how, anyway, would he ever find the words?

Nineteen

THE GLORIOUS TENTH

The submarine, the *Lilith*, sailed without him.

"Am I going to regret this?" he asked Melita.

Her eyes seemed to dissolve, out of focus. "You should have gone," she said.

"Yes?"

"I think so."

But he had stayed. Because of her, mainly, yes, but also because there was a strange attachment, a reluctance to separate from the misery that was Malta. He remembered what Fingerly had said, about missing the 109s on the days when they didn't attack.

Melita was pensive. "If there is an invasion, do you really want to be here? You want to be a prisoner of war?"

"There won't be an invasion," he said, surprised at his own confidence.

"That's what I used to think. But now—now I'm not so sure."

She worried for him, fearing the worst. If the parachutes came, it would not be easy.

He looked up at the sky, the azure silence, no planes, no clouds, only the hot blazing sun. So simple, so easy and free.

What if she were made of detachable parts and he could carry pieces of her around all day, in a satchel? A leg, a hand, her avalanche of black hair. Any time of the day, there would be these parts of her for him to touch. At night he could reassemble her and she could be herself again.

He told her, and she thought they might have alternating days: One day he carries parts of her around, the next day she carries parts of him. She wasn't interested in his warts or his knees, or the calluses on his feet. She wanted his penis in her purse. Or at least his nose.

"You can't have my nose," he said.

"Yes I can."

"No you can't."

"Your nose belongs to me."

"Is that what you think? Is it?"

They both thought, fleetingly, of poor Tony Zebra, whose nose had been damaged by shrapnel when he was on the veranda of the Point de Vue—and who, on Malta or anywhere else, would ever fall in love with him now, with a nose like that?

Melita was so glad that Fingerly was gone, she sold a stack of Jack Teagarden records to raise some cash for Rocco, now that he wouldn't be getting subsistence wages from Fingerly any more. She sold to a farmer in Dingli, who had become rich selling black-market vegetables to housewives from the surrounding towns, who paid in cash when they could, and with gold rings and bracelets when desperate. The farmer was so rich he was now on a buying spree, snapping up anything that looked to be a good purchase, including Jack Teagarden records, even though he'd never heard of Jack Teagarden and only had a broken windup phonograph that didn't play. Melita got a fair price for the records, and persuaded the farmer to buy a jukebox from Zammit to play them on, even though there was no electricity on the farm and probably wouldn't be until the war was over, but at least it was something his neighbors could look at and admire.

The new Spitfires flew in to Malta on Saturday, May 9. They knocked down a dozen enemy planes that day, and the score was even higher on the following day, which got to be known, on Malta, as the Glorious Tenth.

BATTLE OF MALTA: AXIS HEAVY LOSSES
Spitfires Slaughter Stukas

BRILLIANT TEAM WORK OF A.A. GUNNERS AND RAF
63 Enemy Aircraft Destroyed or Damaged Over Malta Yesterday

SHATTERING SHOCK FOR THE HUN

SALUTARY LESSON FOR ITALIANS

MALTA GRAVEYARD OF REGIA AERONAUTICA

Some said fifty enemy planes were destroyed and some said a hundred. Tony Zebra, who had been there in the thick of it, said it was more like twenty, but still that was a lot. Only three Spitfires were lost that day, and one pilot. They were all up there, splitassing around, Zulu Swales, Johnny Plagis, Fernando Farfan from Trinidad. Pete Nash knocked down two, and Jimmy Peck, an American, knocked down one and damaged two others. But the big star that day, the dark horse who amazed no one more than himself, was Tony Zebra—knocked down four planes, and did it without firing a shot.

One, a Reggiane, went down when its engine failed, the plane tipping over and plunging into the sea as Tony Zebra pursued it. Another, a 109, simply went out of control, twirling crazily and falling somewhere near Żebbuġ. The third was a Macchi C202. It put a few holes in Tony Zebra's wings, and then, as it zoomed past, he got on its tail and followed, but before he could use his guns, it smashed into a Ju-88 that crossed into its path and both went down.

Tony Zebra was given credit for the Reggiane, the 109, and the Macchi, but not for the Ju-88, which, it was argued, had been knocked down by the Macchi. He puzzled over that, trying to make sense of it, but it was nothing he could fathom. If they were giving him credit for the Reggiane, the 109, and the Macchi, even though he hadn't fired a shot, why suddenly should they split hairs and deny him the 88?

They gave him a DFC and made him a flight leader, which meant he was now in charge of a group of four planes in the squadron. It also meant he was supposed to be discreet and proper, a model for the new kids rotating into the squadron, and that, he knew, was going to be more of a burden than he really wanted. More than ever he was eager for India, still thinking of it, still dreaming and imagining: the shrines, the temples, the statues of Shiva and Parvati, and the tigers and the elephants, the bamboo, the sandalwood, the nut palms and the cardamom, the music of the sitar and the banshri. Every week he put in for a transfer, and every week his application was denied.

There was no invasion. Not yet, anyway. Nor a white flag, though nobody knew for sure there wouldn't be. The Spitfires were good news, but the convoys were still not getting in and the food supply was dwindling. When the new governor arrived in May, Lord Gort, what he brought with him was not just the Spitfires but the George Cross. It was a medal from King George, awarded to the people of Malta for their courage during the April blitz.

BUCKINGHAM PALACE

TO HONOUR HER BRAVE PEOPLE

I AWARD THE GEORGE CROSS

TO THAT ISLAND FORTRESS OF MALTA

TO BEAR WITNESS TO A HEROISM AND

DEVOTION THAT WILL LONG BE FAMOUS

IN HISTORY.

GEORGE R.I.

The people of Malta felt good about it, rightfully proud, but it was still only a medal. It wasn't meat, or clothes, or shoes, or a good movie you could watch without fear that a bomb might blow the movie house apart before the leading man had a chance to kiss the leading lady. Here and there, graffiti began to appear: GIVE US BREAD, NOT MEDALS. CAN'T EAT GEORGE CROSS.

Tuesday night, Rocco and Melita went to a dance at the Adelphi. Some slow stuff, some fast, good drums and a moody trombone. Afterward, back on Windmill, they went up onto the roof and sat a while. There was no moon, the sky hazy, only one star visible.

"It's not a star," Melita said, "it's Venus, the planet Venus. Always the brightest."

"I thought Mars was the brightest."

"No, it's Venus. That's why they call it Venus, because it's so beautiful."

"We should have a jukebox up here," he said. "Right here on the roof."

He was thinking again of what Zammit had said, about jukeboxes having a soul. In a bar, or a diner, a jukebox was a living thing, solid and alive, the way a tree in a garden was alive. But a jukebox was better than a tree because you could go up to it, drop a coin, and presto, you have music that could break your heart.

And the thing about the soul: while Sinatra sings, it's his soul, sure, but it's your soul too, because the song is your choice, paid for with your money, which you got with your hard work. Therefore, it isn't Sinatra singing, it's you. This is the song you would sing if you had a voice like that, and everybody knows it. It's you, your moment, you own it, your coin in the box. But then, too soon, your song is over, so you drop another coin, and it's "Moonglow," and there's this girl in a corner booth eating a sandwich. You look at her and she looks at you, but it goes nowhere, and you're still alone at your table, and for a while, in the slowness of the mood, the music owns you.

"Is that, more or less, do you think, what Zammit was talking about when he said a jukebox has a soul?"

Melita nodded vaguely. "I think so, sort of, except possibly for the girl in the booth, with the sandwich."

"The sandwich doesn't belong?"

"I think the girl doesn't belong."

"Maybe not, maybe not," he said. And then, as an afterthought, "The sandwich was pastrami."

The night haze had thickened, and now even Venus seemed to be dimming out.

"He wants to quit," Melita said.

"Who?"

"Zammit. He wants to stop with the jukeboxes."

"He's tired?"

"The last few months, with so much bombing, it's been hard. The orders don't come in anymore. People are worried where to get food—who cares about a jukebox? But I told him to keep working, because someday the bombing will stop and then everybody will want a jukebox again. All the bars, all the restaurants. Did I tell him right?"

"Supply and demand," Rocco said.

"I hate supply and demand, it makes life mean and miserable. As if that's all we are. But we're more than that. Aren't we more than just that?" She yawned. It was late and she was tired from the dancing. "Do you like me?" she asked.

He liked her.

"You like my hair?"

He liked her hair.

"You like my eyes?"

He liked her eyes. She, all of her, a gift, and he knew: he didn't deserve her. The price was that he had to be there on Malta, day and night, ninety-one square miles of overpopulated rock on which the Stukas were dumping all the bombs they could carry.

She yawned again, and he yawned, and again she was talking, drowsily, about Zammit, about Venus, about the jukeboxes, about time, about memory, about the festas they used to have before the war, and, while she was talking, she leaned her head on his shoulder and mumbled her way into sleep.

* * *

For a whole week Fingerly had been gone, not to be found in any of his familiar haunts, and Rocco thought he had departed Malta for good. But then,
briskly, he was back, as if a rubber band had snapped, a week to the day since
Rocco had last seen him.

He found Rocco in Hock's, the pub on Old Mint favored by the pilots, a
long, narrow place between a haberdasher and a stationer's, gaping holes in
the walls and ceiling, the mirror behind the bar suffering from multiple frac-
tures.

"Where were you?" Rocco asked.

"I had to see my dentist."

"You were a whole week in the chair?"

"He has an old-fashioned drill, with the foot pedal."

"I thought you were finished here, with Malta."

"Malta is never finished, it goes on and on. There are layers, levels, subcel-
lars under the cellars. We're in business again, Raven," he said cheerily, handing Rocco a Banca di Roma envelope containing British pounds and shillings,
"you're on subsistence, like before, but with a little extra, think of it as a cash
reward for brushing your teeth while I was gone. You still have that radio that
can listen and send clear around the world?"

The radio couldn't go clear around the world, yet it was a fine piece of
equipment and worthy of some exaggeration. It was still at the farm.

Fingerly handed him three messages, in cipher, on foolscap, to be sent between nine and ten the next morning.

"Who's this for? Joe Stalin?"

"This? This is for Mr. Ostrich, and this is for Mr. X."

"Who's Mr. X?

"A good guy."

"One of ours?"

"With the OSS."

"And Ostrich?"

"You don't want to know."

"What about this one?"

"That? That's for Daddy. He's the one who passes out spankings if things
go wrong."

"Are your teeth okay?"

"A few cavities, no big deal. Anyway, lucky you never went off on that submarine. It was sunk off Tunisia, all hands lost."

When Rocco heard that, something fell away inside him, as if his mind, his soul, had been sitting on a shelf, and when Fingerly mentioned about the sub going down, an important part of him fell off the shelf and was still falling.

"All hands?"

"All hands."

"Sonofabitch."

"You're blaming me?"

"Damn right I'm blaming you. You put me on that sub," Rocco said angrily. "Me, on a sub that went down!"

"You weren't on it."

"But you wanted me on it."

"I'm to blame for a German bomb that hits a submarine square on the conning tower and you're not even aboard?"

"If not you, then who? You're to blame for all of it—the whole, fat, motherblitzing war."

Fingerly inclined his head, with the barest hint of a smile. "Raven, that's the most flattering thing I've ever heard you say."

When Rocco looked at Fingerly now, what he saw, where Fingerly had been, was the outline of Fingerly, as if drawn in pencil on the air, and inside the outline, nothing but grayish smoke swirling fuzzily. It wasn't the first time he'd seen him that way, but now the smoke seemed denser than usual.

"What's wrong?" Fingerly asked.

"I don't know."

"Why are you looking at me like that?"

"Like what?"

"Do I have dandruff?"

"No, it's nothing," Rocco said. "Nothing, nothing at all."

Fingerly had brought back with him a bottle of Chartreuse, intending it for Rocco as a form of apology for having slated him for a sub that went down, but since Rocco was being so surly about it, Fingerly gave the Chartreuse to Warby Warburton instead, in exchange for a bottle of aftershave that Warby had picked up in Marrakesh. Warby gave the Chartreuse to Christina, who, a few days later, gave it to Melita in exchange for a Benny Goodman recording of "Jersey Bounce," and when Rocco and Melita brought the Chartreuse to Zammit's and drank it late into the night, they had no idea it had been carried in by Fingerly, all the way from Casablanca, and had been meant for them in the first place.

Twenty
NIGG

His name was Oswald, after his father's father, but his mother called him Ozzie, which he didn't like at all, and his grade-school classmates, for no particular reason, called him Waldo, until he pushed one of them out a second-floor window and the kid got his face torn up when he hit the sidewalk. In high school his friends used just the surname, Nigg, and somehow it stuck. Even his father got to calling him that. Nigg, plain Nigg.

His father, the proctologist, was a large man, taller and heavier than Nigg would ever be, with big hands, capped teeth, wavy hair combed straight back off his forehead, eyes intensely, coldly gray. Black hairs grew from his nose, and Nigg remembered how the big man, his father, would stand before the bathroom mirror, clipping the nose hairs with a pair of cuticle scissors, and always the hairs grew back. It had never been easy for Nigg to relate to him. What to think of him, how to approach him, how to touch his hands that had been busy all day exploring the derrières of board members and aging movie stars, how to look at his eyes which had peered into the foggy bottoms of stockbrokers, Mafia bosses, rabbis, retired jockeys, old nuns.

He wore peppermint-stripe shirts, red ties, and a gold watch that told the time in cities in seven different countries around the world. He grew a mustache, shaved it off, grew it back on, and shaved it off again. His wife, Joelle, who liked her sherry dry and her martinis on the rocks, considered the comings and goings of the mustache as a symptom of his ongoing identity crisis. He had been dwelling in the nether regions so long, she would say at parties, blithely, her tongue loose with gin, that he no longer quite understood exactly who he was. "And neither do I," she would add, leaning with aplomb against any available male sturdy enough to support her thickening, middle-aged body.

They lived in Armonk, above White Plains. Weekends, grilling steaks in the garden behind the house, Nigg's father tanked up on wine, Mouton Rothschild, and in a breezy alcoholic haze declaimed on the beauties and grotesqueries he had probed with his proctoscope: the rear-end wonders, the backside secrets, the back-door revelations. "Even down there, in never-never land," he would say, with a nod and a wink, "some of us, you know, are more equal than others." The steaks dripped fat onto the coals, and, wreathed in smoke, he became a bard of the bum, a living thesaurus of things fundamental, going on and on about the rump, the buttocks, the butt, the hinterland, the rumble seat, the subway, the downtown local, the south end, the last exit to Canarsie.

After the steaks, the guests gone, he would snooze, sleep off the wine—then, brightly awake, any time in the night, he would hop onto his Harley and go roaring through the streets of Armonk, waking anyone who was foolish enough to be asleep. The Harley was his weekend obsession, he let nobody touch it. He did all the repairs himself. Once, he had the whole thing apart, in pieces, laid out on the floor of the garage, and reassembled it all perfectly. He liked the throb of it, power between the legs, the rumbling roar.

Nigg liked his father better with the mustache than without it, and he liked him better on the Harley than snoring on the couch. He liked him in the red tie, with the apron on, the goblet of wine in one hand and the long, two-pronged fork in the other, presiding over the steaks on the grill, and the great burst of flame when the fat caught fire.

What he could never accept, though, was that his father was so maddeningly tall. Once, he had wanted to catch up, wanted to be as big and powerful, jealously measuring his growth, day by day. But there came a time when he knew it was never going to happen, he would never attain that height, that robustness, and it was then, or around then, that he began to hate his father and wish he were dead.

At Harvard, Nigg did well, he was smart, but he gambled, putting money out on high-risk bets with the wrong people, and when he got in too deep and couldn't pay up, they broke one of his legs. He told his father he fell down a flight of stairs.

"At least you didn't break your ass," his father said, making light of it. "How are you going to become a famous asshole doctor like your pa if your own ass isn't working right?"

In one of his dreams, his father flew high in the air, in a green surgical gown, which was not a gown exactly but a kind of cape, billowing in the wind. Nigg tried to fly up to him, but couldn't—he was on the ground, calling, and his father, higher and higher, didn't seem to hear. It was a recurring nightmare, with variations. Once, he got off the ground and flew up toward his father, and his father waved him on, wanting him to hurry along, but Nigg wasn't fast enough—he was close, then closer, but never caught up, and finally fell far behind. His father had a proctoscope in hand, using it as if it were a telescope, looking back at Nigg and laughing: wild, lusty laughter, like the times when he loomed over the sizzling steaks in the smoke of the charcoal fire and siphoned up the Mouton Rothschild, those dreamy weekend afternoons.

"A new age is dawning," he told Nigg, when Nigg was in his third year at Harvard, wondering about medical school. "Amazing things are coming along. Instead of the proctoscope, there will be streamlined instruments sliding in and out with the greatest of ease. Into the back door, into the full moon, into the murky depths and the tail-end blues. You are going to have a wonderful life," he said, jealous of the miracles yet to come. "Poking into the haunches will be a sweet adventure like never before."

But before the year was out, the war was on, and Nigg, tired of Cambridge and in debt again to the wrong people, enlisted, and when they found out how smart he was, they put him into I-3.

"Isn't he a sonofabitch?" Fingerly said to Rocco, irked because for three days he'd been looking for Nigg but had been unable to find him. They'd had a meet arranged at the Union Club, but he didn't show.

Rocco lit a cigarette, then held the match to light Fingerly's. "Did you try his digs?"

"He's never in his digs, you know that. He sleeps around with the whores in Sliema. But he may be undergoing a religious conversion. Beatrice saw him at church last week, in a back pew. What in the world would Nigg be doing in a church?"

"Beatrice? Hannibal's wife? Where'd you see Beatrice?"

"She's still around, in Valletta. The old man wouldn't leave, so she's still here, taking care of him."

"Nardu Camilleri, yes. I ran into him in a barbershop."

Fingerly handed him an envelope for Nigg, containing some of the ciphers Rocco had taken off the shortwave. "Find him, I want him to look at these. I have to be over in Rabat for a few days."

"What's in Rabat? Another pigmy elephant?"

Fingerly let it pass. "He's been losing bad in the Green Room, it's getting out of hand. If you find him, punch him in the nose. From me."

The buses were infrequent now, and crowded, and when Rocco didn't have the hearse, he preferred, despite the heat, to travel by bicycle. It was June, warmer than any June he'd known at home, a bright glaring sun that burned away the last of the spring flowers and turned the island into a bony heap of rock. Many of Kesselring's Luftwaffe units had departed for Russia, Greece, and Africa, so the bombing was less intense, but the shortages were even more severe than they'd been in April and May. The only supplies coming in were the small amounts that could be slipped in by plane or submarine, or by the blockade-running *Welshman.*

Rocco pedaled out to St. Julian's, to Dominic's, and spoke to the bartender, and to the bald clerk who handled the bets in the Green Room—but Nigg hadn't been around that day, nor on the day before. They couldn't recall exactly when they'd seen him last.

He checked a few clubs in Sliema, then back to Valletta, where most of the places had been bombed, though there were still a few spots down on the Gut where you could get a beer. Moody's, and Mary's, and Mudd's. Beer and a girl, if you were so inclined. But no sign of Nigg, and these places weren't his style anyway.

After rummaging about for a few hours, he finally did the sensible thing and headed over to Nigg's room on Old Mint. It was around the corner from the Manoel Theatre, which was being used now as a movie house.

The ground level, at Nigg's place, was occupied by a small shop that traded in stamps and coins, the name in Gothic lettering over the door: SEVEN CONTINENTS. The display cases were empty. The owner, a round-faced man whose head seemed to float away from his body, sat at a desk on which there was nothing but a black attaché case.

Rocco asked if he'd seen Nigg, but the man didn't know the name.

"The lieutenant, he has a room upstairs."

The man gave it some thought, and then remembered—but no, he couldn't recall seeing him lately.

"Are you an American too?"

Rocco nodded.

"Are you interested in stamps? Were you a collector, before the war?"

"When I was a kid, I had some Thomas Jeffersons."

"I keep everything in an underground vault. These I carry with me, they're very valuable." Already he was opening the attaché case, laying the stamps out, and Rocco realized it was a mistake to have come in. The man was desperate for conversation. He put a stamp on a sheet of paper and offered Rocco a magnifying glass. It was a small stamp, Maltese, buff-colored, no perforations at the edges, in mint condition, showing a young Queen Victoria in profile. "From the year 1860. Before the war, with this stamp, in Malta, you could buy a vacation home by Mellieħa Bay. Not a palace but a good, solid house."

"And now?"

"Perhaps a secondhand piano, or a sewing machine. But it will change again, after the war. A stamp of this quality will have its day again."

"Does it make you nervous, carrying it around?"

"I would be nervous without it!"

Rocco wondered if he was one of Fingerly's people, like the sacristan at Mosta, brokering the big wartime bargains. He glanced about at the empty cases, wondering why the man bothered to keep the store open.

"What else is there to do?" the man said. "Now and then a few old friends drop by. Are you a pilot? Do you fly?"

"No," Rocco said, "I'm not a pilot."

"I don't know where they get the courage," the man said. Then, brightening, "I have some American stamps, some valuable misprints—would you care to see some?"

Rocco declined, and with a nod, made his exit.

Nigg's room was two flights above, up narrow wooden stairs. The door was closed but not locked, and, as Rocco turned the knob, he had a sickening sense of something wrong.

The room was dark, the window covered by a heavy blackout curtain, and in the dim light filtering from the hallway he saw Nigg on the bed, in his uniform, on his back, his head slanting off at an odd angle. He had shot himself in the temple with a small-caliber pistol, the gun still in his hand.

Rocco let out a low moan, aware now, finally, of a fear, just below consciousness, that this was what he would find.

On a small table, in the portable typewriter, was a note for Fingerly:

> Tell my father I was hit by a bomb. A big one. See you—with luck—in the dream casino in the sky.

Nigg's face and wide-open eyes were masklike, devoid of meaning. He was nothing. Where his mind had been, there was a blank space. Looking at him, Rocco felt the same dizziness as when he saw the mummy Fingerly had brought back from Egypt, and had the same awareness of heaviness and weight: as if Nigg were merging into the mattress and, if left there, gravity would pull him down through the floor, into the earth under the house. He wanted to grab him and hold him and keep him from sinking away. But what he also felt was a repugnance, a horror at the thought of touching him.

The blood on the pillow was dry, yet it didn't seem he'd been dead a very long time.

Twenty-one

THE JUKEBOX MADNESS
OF ZARB ADAMI

In mid-June, two large convoys set sail for Malta, one from Alexandria, the other from Gibraltar. The one from Alexandria was hit so hard by bombs and torpedoes it had to turn back. The one from Gibraltar was pummeled mercilessly, but it pressed on. Of the six merchantships from Gibraltar, only two got through, the *Orari* and the *Troilus.* The other four went down.

At Takali, Tony Zebra was getting Ovaltine and biscuits for breakfast, and bully beef (in small amounts) for lunch. On the black market he picked up five pounds of sugar and some oranges, which he turned over to the kitchen girl, Violetta, who made them into a jam. He sat with her in the kitchen, along with Harry Kelly and Daddy Longlegs, and ate it all, on stale bread that Willie the Kid had paid heavily for before losing it to Harry Kelly in a poker game. They would have invited Willie the Kid to join them at the jam feast, but he was on readiness at the dispersal hut, waiting to fly.

Tony Zebra regretted having spent as much as he did on the sugar for the jam. More than jam, he needed cigarettes. He smoked compulsively, unable to live without a cigarette in his hands or on his lips. He smoked while he ate and smoked while he nursed a beer and played cards. He smoked on the toilet. He smoked while waiting in the cockpit, on readiness, and he smoked in the air, climbing to meet the bombers. The only time he didn't smoke was when he was asleep or in the heat of battle, his fingers on the buttons, preparing to fire. One button fired the cannons, another fired the machine guns, and a third fired the cannons and machine guns together. If he ever got to India, maybe he would give up smoking forever, because he would be too busy with the women, the ones with the dark eyes, in the silken saris, the ones who had read the *Kama Sutra* and knew all there was to know about love and its secrets—the mysteries, the dreamy, forbidden ecstasies. He searched through trash cans for half-smoked cigarettes and butt ends from which he salvaged fragments of tobacco that he rolled in strips of newspaper, making gritty newspaper joints that he smoked with a fierce and angry and delicious joy. *O India! O forever! O midnight dream of the dark machinery of love!* After the jam that had been made by the kitchen maid, from the black-market sugar and the black-market oranges, he was sick to his stomach for three days with a vicious case of the Malta dog that he thought would kill him.

At their place on Windmill Street, Rocco cranked the hand generator that powered Melita's tabletop radio, and they tuned in again to Marlena Malta. It was a kind of masochism, listening to her taunts and jibes, yet you listened, it was hard not to, because she was a name, a voice, a sound, a living person, not just an anonymous bomb from a passing plane. It was a way of making the war personal, a spooky form of intimacy.

> *Oh, you poor people of Malta. Seventeen merchant ships from Alexandria and Gibraltar, and only two reached you! How will you get through the coming weeks and months? Why do you sacrifice yourselves this way for your stubborn British masters? Refuse to help them anymore. Don't send your husbands off to the docks and the airfields, where they get killed by the bombs. Refuse to cooperate, and you will see how quickly the British will be gone. They think your island is their island—but it is yours, my friends, it belongs to you. Refuse to help them anymore. Refuse. Refuse. Refuse.*

As always, her broadcast was followed by an opera—this time, *La Bohème*, but toward the end of the first act, while Mimi and Rodolfo were singing *Amor! Amor! Amor!*, the transmission broke down into a void of hissing static, and as far as Melita was concerned it was just as well, because this was not one of her favorites, Mimi in a cold garret, dying of consumption. Too darkly romantic, she thought. Sentimental, maudlin. A tear-jerker. Dumping the cat from her lap, she grabbed a broom and started sweeping, going from room to room, wielding the broom with serious intent, like a wand, as if sweeping her way into a fairy tale in which the swish of the broom was a kind of aria, banishing not just the dust but the noise of the guns and the drone of the returning bombers.

It was only a few days after Tony Zebra had eaten more jam than was good for him that Zarb Adami, the owner of the Javelin in Marsaxlokk, decided, once and for all, that he really did not want the jukebox Melita and Rocco had delivered in April. In a fit of rage, he took a sledgehammer to it and smashed it to pieces.

His son, Salvu, who had joined the army when he ran off from home, witnessed the scene and felt responsible, because moments before his father picked up the sledgehammer, the anger had been directed not against the jukebox but against Salvu himself, who had returned that day for the first time since his disappearance. Zarb Adami railed against his son for running off and cursed him for coming back. He reproached him for joining the army and wasting his young life at a deserted outpost in the northwest, on the Marfa Ridge, to which he would have to return at the end of the day, to spend the remainder of the war there, watching for an invasion—blamed him and disowned him because he was stupid, foolish, reckless, selfish, disrespectful of his family, lacking in religion, and, being now a soldier, likely to get himself killed. His anger mounted exponentially, and his fury came to focus, finally, on the jukebox.

He hated it. He'd bought it only because he thought it would bring in more business, but it hadn't. So what good was this abominable thing that took up so much room he had to remove two tables and was left with that much less space for the handful of mawkish, crapulous sots who came to his establishment and didn't play the jukebox anyway? He hated the songs, hated the music, hated the lights that blinked on and off and the stack of records visible behind the glass, and the deep loud sound of the thing, which was, to his ears, mere noise. All of these things he said, shouting as he swung the sledgehammer, smashing the wood and shattering the stained glass. The inner guts of the machine spilled out, the speaker, the lights, the motor that drove the turntable, the records themselves. He swung and swung, reducing the wooden parts to splinters, smashing the glass, and shattering the records. Then he went upstairs, to his bed, drank a pint of gin, and fell asleep.

The boy, Salvu, sifted through the remains of the jukebox, to see if there was anything worth salvaging. He found a few small things, bent metal that could be unbent, parts of the motor, some nails and screws, a few unbroken pieces of stained glass that could be reworked into something. He put them into a box, and on his way back to the Marfa Ridge stopped off at Zammit's house, where he found Melita working on a turntable that wasn't spinning at the right speed.

"This is all that's left," he said, handing her the box.

She looked at the pieces. "He did this?"

"He was mad that I joined the army."

"What's wrong with your father? Is he crazy?"

"Yes, it's true. He has always been crazy. He loses his temper and we never know what he will do."

"You did right to run away and join the army."

"Yes?"

"Yes."

"Sometimes I think I did wrong."

"Never think that."

"My father will need someone to take care of him. My mother is dead, you know? After the war I will have to go back."

"Don't worry about your father," she told him. "Everything will work out for the best. Go back to the Marfa Ridge and be a good soldier."

He hung there, as if there was something more, something else he wanted to talk about, but all he did was say good-bye, and he went.

Later, at the house on Windmill, when she told Rocco about it, he gave her a long, slanting look that verged on a smile. "The poor kid's in love with you."

Melita waved a hand, rejecting the idea as absurd.

"It's obvious—isn't it?"

"What is?"

"You danced with him when we delivered the jukebox, and he fell in love with you. He's been dreaming of you ever since."

"Is that what you think?"

"You're his fairy godmother. He'll never be the same."

"Poor boy."

"Why else do you think he brought you those broken pieces?"

"But they're not broken, they can be used. The motor can be fixed. He thought he was doing a favor. He felt guilty for what his father did."

"He wants you to wave the magic wand."

"You make too much of things," she said, tossing her head, her long ebony hair bouncing saucily off her shoulders.

"You like it? You like having a teenage admirer?"

She looked away, musing, then her eyes swam back to his. "You're jealous. You would like a teenager of your own, bringing you presents."

"I would," he said, making light, "I'll take anything that comes along."

"Anything?" she said. "Anything? You deserve what you get."

"What does that mean?"

"Anything you want it to." Her eyes seemed not eyes but flowers, fiercely blue and incandescent.

"What's happening here?"

"You tell me."

"Is this a showdown? Are we getting a divorce?"

"Could be, could be," she said, not sounding at all whimsical.

"Really? It's that bad?"

"I'm thinking about it, seriously thinking."

"I need a lawyer?"

"You may need a mortician."

It had started in fun, but now, he saw, there was an edge to her banter, a stridency.

"I'm going for a walk," he said.

"Then go without me."

"I will," he said, and went, eager to get away, and when he was outside, up the street, in the oncoming dark, he turned and looked back at the closed door.

What does she want? he wondered. What could she possibly, conceivably, want?

Twenty-two

PROWLING THROUGH
THE CODES

What she wanted, really wanted, was a baby.

How wonderful that would be!

But said nothing, because why should she make it harder than it already was? When the war was over, there would be plenty of time, and she couldn't wait. A baby with small hands, small mouth, tiny feet and toes. Hers, her very own. Hers and Rocco's. It was two long years now, the bombing, would it never end?

Rocco brought her some flowers that he found in a field near Maqluba, and she was glad, it pleased her. He thinks of me, she thought. He wants me to be happy. I'm happy if he's happy. Often they sat in the sun, not talking, just resting, and those, for her, were the best times, the sky empty, no bombers, just the sun and the birds.

Before the war, at one of the festas, she had met a German boy, from Heidelberg. His name was Johann. He was an art student, studying the paintings in the Cathedral. They spent a lot of time in the Oratory, looking at the *Beheading of John the Baptist*. He showed her how Caravaggio used light and shade to heighten the drama, and he pointed out the lines and angles in the composition. They had tea together and took long walks, and she thought something deep was developing. Then, on All Saints, there was a party at the

Jesuit College, and he astonished her by showing up with a transvestite. The boy was young, in a dress and high heels, his face heavily painted with rouge and mascara. The way they behaved toward each other, it was very clear they were lovers. She was crushed. So cruel of him, she thought, flaunting this boy as if to punish her, deliberately wanting to hurt her. He went back to Germany, and she heard from a friend that he became a flyer, and now, for all she knew, he was in one of the Stukas that flew over, dropping bombs.

She thought of Malta as it had been before the war, people coming from all over on the big boats, with their hats and fancy dresses. And now it was gone. Finished. And it made her angry. So angry. That Kesselring, I could kick him. The *Duce,* and Hitler too. The women were right, she thought, on the farms, waiting with pitchforks when the planes were hit and the Germans parachuted down. That's what they did, waited with pitchforks, and the British had to rush to the rescue, because if the German pilots were killed, the same might happen to the British when they were shot down over Sicily.

+ *June 18, 1942* +

TENSE SITUATION AT SEBASTOPOL

GERMANS ALL OUT TO FORCE DECISION

AFTER COLOSSAL LOSSES

Terrific Artillery Duel

Raging on Narrow Front

THE FAR EAST: U.S. SUBMARINES ACTIVE

JAPANESE WARSHIP SUNK, ANOTHER PROBABLY DESTROYED

FIGHTING NAZI PAGANISM IN HOLLAND AND GERMANY

THE LIBYAN BATTLE

Tobruk a Thorn in Rommel's Flank

WANTED URGENTLY: E-Flat Alto and B-Flat Tenor Saxophones
for Dance Orchestra. Write stating price.

WANTED: Experienced assistant Barber. Apply 74 Summat Street,
Paola after 5 p.m.

Tuesday morning, early, Fingerly found Rocco at the bookstore up at the top of Kingsway where they didn't sell books any more, just newspapers, and chewing gum when they had it.

"Come," Fingerly said.

"Where?"

"I'll show you where it happens."

"Where what happens?"

"The war, Raven. I'm going to show you where the goddamn war is going on. You think it's up there in the sky, the bombers, but that's not it, not it at all. Where it's really happening is in a godforsaken hole."

They went across Valletta on foot, through rubble, past work crews clearing the streets, loading the splintered wood and cracked blocks of limestone onto wagons drawn by horses.

"You know about Code Brown?"

Rocco knew about Code Brown, couldn't read it but knew about it. It was a diplomatic code.

"You've heard about Gray, and A-1, B-1, C-1, and M-138?"

Rocco had heard of them too, more codes, names for codes.

"You've heard of ENIGMA?"

He knew about ENIGMA—the high-level German cipher used by the German military, all branches. Not just a cipher but a machine that generated the cipher. And, knowing about it, had been told, in training, he could now forget about it, because it was not a cipher he would ever be able to read, because even the hotshots in G-2 couldn't figure it out. It was just something that was out there, autonomous, on its own, like light from a distant planet. He would meet it on the airwaves, listen to it, hear it, let it lave over him, the telegraphic sequence of dots and dashes sweeping along, dense and inscrutable, a language unto itself.

"So you know about Enigma," Fingerly said breezily, "but do you know about ULTRA? Do you? Huh?"

ULTRA he'd never heard of, couldn't have, because the only people who knew about it were people who were on the list for it, and Rocco had been aware for quite some time that he was on nobody's list for anything. They walked past a bread queue outside a bakery, and farther down, a pub where off-duty flyers were whooping it up, past closed shops, closed restaurants, closed coffeehouses, past the ruins of the Opera and the Auberge de Castille.

"Codes and ciphers," Fingerly said, "that's the whole ball of wax. If you can read the codes, you're boss, you control your own little patch of the universe."

He brought Rocco down into the tunnels in the Lascaris bastion, into the underground command center beneath the Upper Barracca Gardens, the tunnels stretching out under fifty feet of rock, carved and chiseled in the time of the Knights in preparation for the day when the Turks might return. Fingerly pinned an ID on Rocco's lapel, and, from the familiar way he greeted the guards at the checkpoints it was clear he was a frequent visitor.

There was everything down there: the Fighter Control Room, the Gun Operations Room, the Naval Operations Room, and any number of small, box-like offices, walls sweaty and damp, the air foul, blown in by ventilation fans that sucked in the hot humid air of the harbor, sooty and laden with limestone dust.

There was a long, narrow room where rows of operators, men and women, sat at receiving sets with earphones, listening intently. They were on six-hour shifts, listening to Sicily, Rome, Greece, and Tunis, to Rommel in North Africa and the Italians on Pantelleria and Lampedusa. They listened to Berlin.

Most of them suffered from tinnitus. "If all you do all day is listen," Fingerly said, "just that—listen, listen, listen—waiting to catch a signal, after a while your ears begin to hum. Didn't they tell you about it at Benning?"

"My ears hum when I take aspirin," Rocco said.

Fingerly made a clucking sound. "Try gin instead."

They moved along to a small office where a pale-complexioned blonde in a blue skirt and white blouse stood before a map of Malta, pinning tiny red flags to various locations. She was plump and plain-faced, with heavy tubular legs descending out of her boxy skirt. Still holding a few flags in one hand, she took a brown envelope from a basket and offered it to Fingerly.

"Today's," she said idly, with no enthusiasm.

He smiled, oozing charm. "Nice, nice," accepting the envelope as if it held the promise of a sexual favor. "Anything important?"

"The *Duce* has diarrhea," she said, her voice rising out of what seemed a profound boredom. "Rommel's liver is acting up, and Albert Kesselring needs a root canal on one of his molars. Malta will probably survive for another week."

Her name was Pam Palmer, from Liverpool. Fingerly introduced Rocco, and she sent a bland, perfunctory smile in his direction, then turned and had a small bout of coughing.

Fingerly glanced at the ventilator grille. "Can't they do anything about the air in here?"

"We like it this way," she said peevishly. "They dirty it up for us because they know that's how we like it."

Everybody down there was coughing. The guards at the checkpoints, the listeners at the radio receivers, the lieutenants rushing from one room to another with radar information. They all coughed. The sergeants coughed, and the generals coughed. The batboys delivering coffee coughed. The admirals in control of the harbors on both sides of Valletta coughed, and before they got out into the open air, even Fingerly and Rocco were coughing.

"She feeds you brown envelopes?" Rocco asked, curious about the contents.

"Isn't she sweet?"

"You laid her?"

"Sometimes, Raven, the promise of a favor is better than the deed itself. What's in the envelope is the latest from ULTRA. But you don't know about ULTRA, do you?"

They headed over toward Hock's, for a beer if there was beer. "The long and the short of it," Fingerly said, "is that the Brits have broken ENIGMA. They cracked it a while ago with some help from the Poles, at Bletchley Park, where they run their cryptology game. ULTRA is their network for intercepting ENIGMA. They decipher at Bletchley, then send the translated text back into the field, to those who have a need to know. They've been sharing some of it with Uncle Sam. In Malta, that's me. Before it was me, it was Major Webb. This is very hush-hush, you understand."

So hush-hush, the Brits went to absurd lengths to prevent the Germans from figuring out their code had been broken. If ULTRA told them the location of a German convoy, before bombing it they sent a spotter plane, deceiving the Germans into thinking it was the spotter that had found them.

"So you shouldn't be telling me this," Rocco said.

"I should not be telling you."

"Then why *are* you telling me?"

"I figure you deserve to know, seeing as you were sent here by mistake and you're being such a damn good sport about it. If you spread it around, you could get shot."

"I need this?"

"In fact," Fingerly said, "if you spread it around, I guess I'm the one who will have to shoot you."

Rocco looked him in the eye. "Why do I like you less and less?"

"That's all right, Raven, liking and not liking are not part of the contract. Just keep tuning to those frequencies."

"If you're getting ULTRA from her, why do you need me to spy on what she's sending to London?"

"We're not spying, just listening, in a friendly manner. It wouldn't be professional if we didn't check, would it? We check on them, they check on us, and God checks on the birds, the bees, and the weather."

"God does that? He worries about the weather?"

"Don't be a wise ass. The weather takes care of itself. God worries about the codes."

The weather was insufferable—sultry, sweltering days, gritty dust sifting through the air. In Hock's, there was no beer but there was plenty of gin, a poor label that tasted like paint stripper. Rocco drank tea. He wanted to be somewhere else, in the water, swimming, riding the waves, wanted to get away, far off, away from Fingerly, away from Valletta, away from the ships capsized in the harbor, the bombs, the guns, the box barrage, away from the wireless at Maqluba and the dot-dot-dash that he was slave to.

"But codes, Raven, the codes, they're the stuff of life. Dress codes and legal codes. Hunting codes. The codes that gangs live by. Telephone codes. Codes for wooing and mating. And, soon to come, what they're already talking about, the genetic code, a whole new science in the making. It's all around us," he said, with casual zest, "the air we breathe is a code."

Rocco caught the drift, where Fingerly's mind was going: even God, if there was a God, even God was a code, the big Codemaker in the sky. And if you crack the code, maybe you discover God isn't there, where you thought he was, but somewhere else, if anywhere at all, and maybe the code you were looking at was simply something that had invented itself. It was a shell game, codes concealing other codes, a constant disguise. Fingerly too, Rocco was thinking, Fingerly was a code, in khaki slacks and flowered sportshirt, body and soul, if he had a soul—bones, organs, body tissue, a coded message that could, with the right key, be read, a message that says, after tedious analysis, not much at all, and maybe nothing, just *chica chica boom chic.*

Toward noon, Rocco went with Melita to a spot off Għallis Point, northwest of Valletta. The coastal beaches were strung with coils of barbed wire in expectation of an invasion, but here it was nothing but broad flat rocks, rugged and irregular, impossible for an invasion force—so no barbed wire, you could swim. Melita took off her clothes and went in, and Rocco was quickly behind her. They went straight out, away from shore, long, hefty strokes into the tide. She was a strong swimmer. She went under, and for a while he couldn't see her, then she was up, laughing. Then he was under, and he came up behind her, grabbing hold of her legs. They played, splashing and chasing each other, then swam side by side parallel to the shore. When they'd had enough they turned, swimming lazily, and he was back to the rock before she was, climbing onto it, a wide slab of limestone, gently sculpted, like the palm of a hand, a cluster of other rocks shielding them from the road.

She stood a long time at the edge, knee-deep in the water, looking down, then bent and reached into the water and picked something up, and held it high for him to see. It was a crab.

"Supper," she said, climbing onto the rock and putting the crab down in the sun, by her shoes. The crab didn't seem to mind. It stayed where she put it, making a slow, lazy motion with one of its pincers, but otherwise still.

"Isn't it good," she said, stretching out on her back, abandoning herself to the sun, "so good, the sun and the water. And we're here, on this rock, with this crab. Don't let him get away!"

Rocco studied the crab, the hard carapace and the five pairs of legs, then he stretched out beside Melita, on his back, watching a flock of gulls wheeling and gliding over the water.

"Together in the sun," she said, "that's what matters."

"What matters is the planes," he said, "and the bombs."

"You see planes?"

"Not yet, but any minute."

"I hate the planes."

"I thought you liked them."

"It's all so crazy, day and night, so long now. I forget what it was like before the war. Sometimes I think life is too cynical. A joke."

"It is a joke, but who's laughing?"

"It's too cruel, nothing should exist."

"If there were nothing, then there wouldn't be us."

"I know. I know."

She contemplated that possibility and it seemed not to trouble her. The possibility that neither of them might ever have existed.

"Maybe we should go away," she said. "Do you think? On Gozo, they don't bomb the way they bomb here. It makes me numb, the guns and the bombs."

Maroon had gone to Gozo, and was killed coming back. She knew about the danger, how the 109s came in low and strafed the boats that tried to make the crossing. They even shot up the ferry. But you could cross in the night, and once there, you were away from the bombing. At the start, in 1940, when it was only the Italians raiding, before the Germans were part of it, a few thousand crossed over to Gozo, and they were still there.

"I can't go to Gozo," Rocco said.

"Why not?"

"Because I'm here."

"You mean you have your dot-dot-dash, and your Captain Fingerly."

"Yes."

And even though he'd stayed on when Fingerly offered to let him go on the submarine, she knew he would not stay if orders came through. It could happen any time. If orders came, he'd be on his way back to his unit.

"I think you don't love me," she said.

He didn't like it when she talked about love.

"It's the war," he said.

"I hate the war."

"Everyone hates the war."

"If we went to Gozo, we could live in the city, in Victoria. Or if you wanted to do farming, we could do that. It's pretty land, Gozo, you would like it."

She was asking him to quit the war, the way Ambrosio had quit.

Rocco tried to imagine a used-car lot in Victoria, or Mġarr, but somehow it didn't play.

"It's true," she said, "you don't really love me."

"Why are you talking like this?"

"I think what we are doing, living together, it's because of the war. If it weren't for the war, you wouldn't think twice about me."

"Don't say that."

"It's true, isn't it? Isn't it better, sometimes, to face the truth?"

"But it isn't true."

"What do you know?" she said.

The crab had moved to the edge of the rock and was about to get himself off the edge and back into the water.

Rocco moved to retrieve him.

"Let him go," Melita said.

In a moment the crab was gone, back where he belonged.

Melita sat and said nothing. Then she went into the water again and swam, not looking back, heading straight out. Rocco watched as she went, stroke after stroke.

Dimly, he heard the sound of a plane, barely noticing. Then, even before he saw it, he knew what it was, just from the sound, the sullen blue note of the engine. It was a 109, out on a sweep, looking to do some damage.

Rocco was up, shouting to Melita, but she didn't hear. She was still swimming out, away from shore. He called and called.

Then, whether because she was aware of the plane or simply tiring, she turned and was heading back.

But the 109 had already spotted her, arms and legs splashing in the water, and went for her, the pilot imagining, perhaps, it was a soldier from one of the pillboxes out for a swim, or a luckless fisherman—thinking, possibly, it would be good sport, a test of his marksmanship, so he swept on in, giving a short burst with his guns, and, nearing shore and spotting Rocco, a burst for him too, for the hell of it, and Rocco heard the bullets skipping off the rocks all around him.

His heart beat wildly, pounding in his chest. Yet he stood there, calling to her, waving her in.

The 109 came back for another run and Rocco crouched down, making himself small. The line of bullets ran across the water, where Melita was, and as the plane swept in, over Rocco's head, he lost sight of her.

The plane didn't return. It went inland, on the hunt for bigger targets, and Rocco stood on the flat rock scanning the water, looking for her, and she wasn't there. He saw a darkening in the water, where she'd been, and something went dead inside him.

A thick silence came to him out of the water, a silence so intense it seemed audible, something he could hear, surrounding him, pressing close, pushing against his ribs, as if he were submerged in silence, buried in it, and the painful sound of it would linger endlessly. She was gone, nowhere to be seen. He stood transfixed, barely breathing.

Then, amazingly, a long leg rose from the water, straight up, toes pointing skyward, just the one leg, wet, gleaming, like a tree rising from the water, surreal and strange. And, with a splash, she was up, rising from the water and wading in, alive, her black wet hair clinging to her head and cloaking her shoulders, shining in the sun.

He thought again about the codes, how the water was a code, and the sun, and the crab that got away, and her leg when it broke above the water, and now she, her, walking in, raven-black hair, mouth of sensuous lips and small dainty teeth, lips that he kissed, tongue that reached in and touched his tongue, flesh hanging sweetly on her bones, coming to him wet from the water, more than he'd imagined. More than he could decipher or hope to understand. He felt no anger toward the pilot who had done the shooting, just a sense of relief that he had such rotten aim. And with the relief came a kind of guilt, because only when he'd thought she was dead did he see with such clarity that he couldn't live without her.

Twenty-three

THE GENERAL GEORG VON BISMARCK MEMORIAL BASEBALL GAME

A week to the day after the Messerschmitt went after Melita, Rocco played third base in a baseball game with the pilots at Takali. The game had been organized by Tony Zebra, who'd been at work on the idea for over a month. Usually, between raids, the pilots played cricket, if anything at all, but Tony Zebra succeeded, with some difficulty, in persuading them to give baseball a try.

The RAF on Malta was a mixed bunch, from England, Canada, Australia, a few Rhodesians, and quite a few Americans, and Tony Zebra thought the game would have some extra zing in it if the Americans lined up against the citizens of the Commonwealth. The zing would come from the fact that the Americans had a clear advantage, having grown up with the game, whereas the Commonwealth was into sissy things like cricket and croquet. "When it comes to balls and strikes," Tony Zebra told Rocco with malicious glee, "they don't have the foggiest. We can cheat like crazy."

Bats and balls were hard to come by—Caruana's, in Valletta, had snooker balls, soccer balls, croquet balls, and balls for rounders, but no baseballs, they had never been in the inventory—so Tony Zebra asked Rocco to check with Fingerly, and in a matter of days Fingerly came up with three canvas bags containing bats, balls, gloves, chalk for the foul lines, and a mask and a pair of shinguards for the catcher, all captured from the Germans when the British moved into Benghazi, which the Brits held for only a few weeks before the Germans took it back again.

The bats, the balls, the gloves, the mask, and the shinguards had belonged to one of Rommel's generals, Georg von Bismarck, who had been a baseball addict ever since Babe Ruth autographed a ball for him at an exhibition game in 1934. Bismarck commanded the 21st Panzer Division, and he kept his men in shape by having them play baseball, officers against enlisted men, and invariably the officers won, because the enlisted men were carefully kept in the dark about some of the basic rules of the game, like strike zones and the infield-fly rule, which were well-guarded secrets. And there was always someone in the outfield who thought he was supposed to catch the ball on one hop rather than on a fly. Nevertheless, the enlisted men understood it was their role to be kept in the dark, so nobody complained. Even when they managed to figure out the things that hadn't been explained, they played dumb, knowing it was better to lose, because if the officers didn't win, there would be hell to pay.

At the game at Takali, as a gesture of gratitude for his success in finding the equipment—the bats, the balls, the gloves, the mask, and the shinguards—Fingerly was given the privilege of umpiring behind home plate. "This is a game General von Bismarck would love to have witnessed," he said, as he scanned the batting orders of the two teams. "It would have brought joy to his heart if he could have thrown out the first ball." He said it as if he knew Bismarck personally and would have arranged to have him flown in, had there been more lead time. But Bismarck was busy in the desert, commanding a tank division for Rommel in the Qattara Depression, where he was having his way against the British. Besides baseball, he liked Prussian marches and never sent his tanks into battle without the 5th Regiment band booming lustily, even though the brassy tunes couldn't be heard by the musicians themselves, the creaking and groaning of the tanks and the roar of their guns overwhelming everything, drowning out not just the trumpets and tubas but all else for miles around—hope, fear, desire, memory, dream, and thought itself.

The playing field was laid out between the airstrip and the old Château Bertrand, a bomb-damaged mansion known as the Mad House, where some of the sergeant-pilots were billeted. It was uneven ground, rocky, pockmarked by bomb craters that had been filled in with sand and rubble. A ball hitting the Mad House was a ground-rule double. A ball through one of the windows (the glass panes long ago shattered by the bombing) was a triple. A ball over the roof was a home run. The Mad House was mad because it was a crazy mix of architectural styles, a jumble of turrets, stone cornices, and flamboyant balustrades. But, more than that, it was mad because it was simply a mad place to live, next to the airfield, which was bombed almost every day.

The day of the game was hot and soggy, the sun like overheated marmalade, oozing and sticky. Tony Zebra had invited some of the whores from Strait Street, expecting they would make good cheerleaders, and he also got word to Julietta and Aida, who were now working out of Rabat. Melita was there with Christina, who was still heavily involved with the reconnaissance ace, Warby Warburton, who put in a cameo appearance for one inning and then had to rush off because he'd just flown in from Egypt, where he was doing high-level consultation with the big boys in Intelligence, and had to race right back before Egypt discovered he was missing. Christina stayed, she was the scorekeeper.

For the Americans, Rocco played at third, and Tony Zebra caught behind the plate. Fernando Farfan, from Trinidad, wanted to play for the American team because Trinidad was so close to America geographically, but the Commonwealthers objected, insisting that Trinidad belonged to them, and if Fernando Farfan played for the Americans, it would be tantamount to treason. Harry Kelly, in right field, hated baseball and had to be dragged away from a poker game. He stood around by the foul line, entertaining the whores with card tricks.

It had been a mistake to invite the whores. They booed the Americans and cheered for the Commonwealth. They thought Zulu Swales was hot stuff. They loved Willie the Kid. Daddy Longlegs was, for them, an inspiration, and Screwball Beurling, the blue-eyed, sandy-haired Canadian ace, evoked adoration. He was Screwball because screwball was a word he used constantly: screwball Huns, screwball 109s, screwball bully beef for breakfast, lunch, and supper, screwball cactus, screwball lizards, screwball pitch from Jimmy Peck that nearly hit him in the head and sent him corkscrewing to the ground.

When Rocco was at bat, the whores threw orange peels at him, and when Tony Zebra was up, they threw wet laundry. The only American they liked was Reade Tilley, because of his mustache, which made him look like Ronald Colman in a moody romantic movie.

Rocco dropped a line drive, and moments later, when he missed an easy pop fly, the only one there who still loved him was Melita. She was arguing with the whores, trying to stop them from throwing orange peels. The oranges had been flown in from abroad, brought in by a colonel who spent a lot of time on Strait Street.

"What's the matter with you," Melita shouted at the whores, who were in their best clothes, wearing straw hats with wide brims to protect against the sun, "are you all crazy?"

"Yes, we're crazy," Julietta answered saucily, "and it's wonderful. Are you jealous? Would you like to try it sometime?"

They threw orange peels at Melita, and she threw them back. Christina, too, got into it, she stopped keeping score and threw orange peels at Julietta.

When Tony Zebra came to bat again, they made donkey sounds, braying and heehawing. They would have made zebra sounds if they knew what zebras sounded like, but didn't, and made donkey sounds instead.

As a way of influencing the outcome of the game, Tony Zebra had given Fingerly a box of Cuban cigars, clear Havana, hand-rolled. It was a straightforward bribe, though Tony Zebra preferred not to think of it that way, because, cigars or not, he considered it Fingerly's responsibility as an American to resist impartiality and favor the American team when he called balls and strikes. That, at any rate, was Tony Zebra's expectation.

The game was lost in the very first inning, the Commonwealth racing ahead with seven runs. Middlemiss walked, then he stole second, got to third on a wild pitch, and was bunted home by Stoop in a squeeze play. Lusty knocked one up against the Mad House, then Fowlow fouled out, Zulu Swales walked, and Willie the Kid hit one up the middle. Johnny Sherlock doubled, and Screwball Beurling belted one so far nobody was able to find the ball. Not only were the Commonwealthers connecting, but they were getting special help from Fingerly, who was making all sorts of calls in their favor, and Tony Zebra quickly grasped that the box of hand-rolled Havanas hadn't been enough.

By the end of the third inning, the score was 13–1. In the fourth inning, the whores threw flowers at Screwball Beurling, who batted twice that inning and hit two home runs. They kissed him and put lipstick all over him, and Aida took off her underpants and stuffed them into his pocket. She offered him her wooden leg, but he was too much of a gentleman to accept.

The game, long and lopsided, rambled on into the seventh inning, and when Rocco came to bat, hitless for the day, a fat fastball came right over the middle of the plate, and this time, when he swung, when he heard the crack of the bat connecting with the ball, he knew it was good wood, a healthy slam. He stood there watching the ball, a long one, rising, lifting, on its way clear over the roof of the Mad House—but before it was quite gone, before it was even halfway there, what he saw, what they all saw, was a *schwarm* of Stukas filling the sky, and before he had even let go of the bat, the field emptied, everybody diving for the trenches.

One by one the Stukas peeled off and went into their dive, the sirens on their nonretractable landing gears making a weird, demonic sound, and the bombs came whistling down, crumping and tossing up jagged clouds of dirt and rock. Rocco stood there watching, and Melita, running, grabbed him and pulled him toward a trench. They jumped in none too soon, a thousand-pounder falling square on the pitcher's mound, putting a hot, simmering crater in the middle of the diamond, the bases gone, home plate gone, all of the bats, and the pail full of balls. Other bombs tore up left field, right field, and the airfield, and not a single Spitfire got off the ground.

Rocco looked toward the Mad House, cracked and damaged from previous bombings, and he knew, *knew*, the ball had cleared the roof, a home run, but because of the Stukas, nobody had seen it. Not even Melita, and not Christina, who, crouching in the slit trench, was still throwing orange peels at Aida and Julietta.

Tony Zebra had given Fingerly the box of cigars, but the Commonwealthers had come up with a 1934 Rolls-Royce Phantom II, old and not in terrific shape (dented, slow to start, one of the hubcaps missing) but still a Phantom, and Fingerly, in the spirit of free enterprise, knew a good thing when he saw one. It had beam-axle suspension, synchromesh gearing, four-wheel hydraulic brakes, and all the luxury accessories befitting a convertible coupe. It weighed over five thousand pounds, a lot more than the cigars, and for Tony Zebra it was nothing but bad luck. In the course of the game, Fingerly called him out on strikes three times, even though on all three occasions the ball soared high over his head and was never near the strike zone.

Afterward, when Tony Zebra confronted him, accusing him of bad faith and disloyalty to his countrymen, Fingerly offered him a ride in the Phantom, but Tony Zebra declined. Fingerly then offered him a job with I-3, because I-3 was in need of daredevil pilots who were desperate enough to risk their lives on suicidal missions, but Tony Zebra was already walking off with other things on his mind, on his way to tell the whores that if there ever was another base-ball game, they could go jump in a lake with their shoes on, even though he knew, unhappily, there wasn't a single worthwhile lake on Malta, and not many swimming pools either.

Twenty-four

THE FALL OF TOBRUK

On June 21, the *Times of Malta* carried a front-page story on the slackening off of action in the desert fighting in North Africa. There were reports of German tank columns on the move, but an uncertainty about what they were doing. Maybe Tobruk, maybe Sollum. Maybe nothing at all. Hard to say. But while Malta was reading the story in the morning paper, Rommel, lightning-fast, had already punched his way into Tobruk, capturing all of the stockpiles and over twenty-five thousand British troops. Rommel, foxy Rommel, doing it all with magic mirrors, feinting and dodging, bobbing and weaving, never where you expected him to be.

The British Eighth Army retreated to Mersa Matrûh, and within two weeks they were pushed all the way back to El Alamein. Rommel was seventy-five miles from Alexandria.

"But bad news," Fingerly said confidently, finding Rocco in Hock's, "bad news, this time, is good news."

At Hock's, that week, there was neither beer nor whisky, nothing but flavored water, which Hock served with a kind of elegance as if it were wine.

"Look at it this way," Fingerly said, lighting up and passing the pack to Rocco, "their only reason to invade Malta is to stop Malta from jumping all over Rommel's supply convoys. But Rommel is doing so well, they figure

Malta has been zonked by the bombing, so skip the invasion. Why risk a bloody mess? Crete was costly, Malta would be worse, and Hitler never liked the idea anyway. Lucky for Malta, right?"

Rocco was wondering: Lucky, lucky? Malta had been leveled. Where was the luck?

"And it gets better," Fingerly said. "Rommel wins in Tobruk, but victory, in the long run, is defeat, because now they're so cocky they think they can forget about Malta and plunge ahead, on into Egypt. But Malta will kill Rommel in the end, bashing his supply lines. Mark my words."

"No invasion? You know this for a fact—or are you making it up?"

"Of course I'm making it up. What good is a fact unless you make it up, Raven? Fact is fiction, and fiction is fact—didn't they teach you anything back there in Brooklyn? In any case, the invasion of Malta has been canceled. The *Duce* doesn't know it yet, though he no doubt suspects."

"If you know, why don't they know? The Governor. The muckamucks in the War Office."

"They do know."

"They're still talking invasion."

"Because they don't know for sure that they know. Maybe the Germans are feeding them bad information to screw them up."

"In which case, the invasion may be on."

"But it's off."

"If they don't know for sure, how can you know for sure?"

"Because we're better, that's how. I-3, Rocco."

Rocco drank off his flavored water and stared long into the empty glass, wondering if Fingerly was a high-flying lunatic ripe for the asylum, or merely an overconfident genius whose brain had been baking too long in the Malta sun. Rocco hated him. But he also found him irresistible, because, though he was secretive, underhand, and annoyingly mysterious, there was something oddly seductive about him, a way of appearing and disappearing that was slyly rapturous and altogether uncanny. If only he would shed the dark glasses, and those silly Palm Beach shirts that he picked up in Jerusalem and Alexandria, and wherever else.

On his way back to Windmill Street, Rocco was thinking again of Brooklyn, which seemed, now, farther and farther away. Still, he remembered, and some of the best memories were of things he'd never done and places he'd never been. Like Lundy's in Sheepshead Bay, famous for raw clams on the half shell, but for one reason or another he'd never been there and was still wondering if he'd have the courage, the sheer nerve, to confront a raw clam eyeball to eyeball. And the Cyclone at Coney Island, the wickedest, most stomach-sucking roller coaster in America. He'd been preparing himself, building up to it, riding the Devil's Gorge and the Tornado, saving the Cyclone for a later day, because after that there was nothing wilder. But now he was in Malta, which was crazy enough, and though the Cyclone no longer dominated his fantasy life, he still thought about it, wondering if he'd survive the war in one piece, alive, and ever have a chance at those steep, eerie climbs and horrific, sudden drops. He didn't imagine Fingerly had ever ridden the Cyclone, though he half-suspected he maybe owned it.

When he got back to Windmill Street, he found Melita in tears. Their place had been broken into, and things were gone.

"Can you believe it?" she wept. "I don't understand, I really don't."

They had taken the radio and the hand generator, and all their rations—the canned fish and meat, the rice, the bread, the sugar. Melita had been saving the sugar, storing it up so she could barter with the farmers for melons when they came in season. They took the tea, the matches, the kerosene. The soap was gone. Even the peacock feather.

All over Malta, people were stealing. They broke into warehouses, government depots, military mess halls, private homes. They broke into bakeries, for flour and bread. A favorite time was during the air raids, when the property owners and tenants and shopkeepers were in the shelters, and the police were busy with bomb reports and rescue.

"They left the clothes," Melita said, bewildered. "Why didn't they take the clothes and the shoes too, all of it? What good is anything anymore? There is no trust, no one can be counted on. They think only of themselves."

They had left the clothes, the shoes, and her box of books, the *Clarissa*, the *Pamela*, the Mary Shelley, the George Sand. She grabbed hold of the cat. "You are so lucky," she said, cuddling it, "so lucky, lucky, they didn't take you, you stupid, silly cat, who would want you anyway, you're so impossible."

On the black market, cats were being passed off as rabbits. Goats were sold as sheep, dogs were sold openly as dogs, and horse meat was sold as imported venison from Macedonia.

"How about it," Rocco said, picking the cat up and staring him in the eye. "How would you like to be served up with fried potatoes?"

The cat, Byron, was indeed lucky, but Zammit, poor cousin Zammit, was having a hard time. What happened, with a terrible suddenness, was that he fell in love with Miss Sicily. He saw her when she sang "Panis Angelicus" in the parish church at Santa Venera, on the feast of St. Francis Caracciolo, and he was filled with a powerful yearning. Even before she sang, he felt a quickening of desire as he saw her mounting the stairs into the choir loft, the hem of her dress lifting lightly and revealing her ankles and calves. He had not seen her at Dominic's, in the silver lamé dress that left nothing to the imagination, nor had he seen her in her red bathing suit when she swam in the waters off Sliema, but when he saw her climbing into the choir loft, it was more than enough.

He pined for her. He had never exchanged so much as a word with her, yet what he felt was a passionate longing, a sense that somehow, in the scheme of things, they were destined for each other. Whenever he thought of her—and it was now a rare moment when he was not thinking of her—he felt uplifted, quickened by an irrepressible surge of desire.

His work on the jukeboxes came to a standstill. He set his tools aside and spent whole days in romantic reverie. He took long walks, strolling through streets that had been reduced to rubble, but it wasn't rubble that he saw. What he saw was the interplay of light and shadow—limpid pastels, pink and lavender, vaporous blue, folds of light sifting down from the sky. Why should he make jukeboxes any more? What was the need? He had made them out of his loneliness, out of his misery and isolation. Some had been beautiful, yes, but what was their beauty compared to the beauty of Angelina Labbra? They were mere things, artifacts. But the ankles and calves of Angelina Labbra, when she ascended the steps to the choir loft in the church in Santa Venera, they teased and tormented, and her voice, when she sang the "Panis Angelicus," was a source of light, pulsating in the gloomy darkness of the church.

Melita thought he was simply suffering from creative block and it would pass. He needed a rest, that was all. A week or two away from his tools, and then he would be eager to resume.

One evening he took out his bicycle and pedaled to Sliema, and stood outside the hotel where Angelina Labbra lived, waiting for her to appear. It was the Imperial, on Ridolfo Street. He'd heard it mentioned in the barbershop that she was living there. Would he approach her? Say something? Tell her his name? And if he did, how would she react? If he went up to her, would she think he was there for an autograph?

He waited across the street, leaning against a stone wall, his breath tightening every time the door opened, but it was always someone else. And what if he were to go to her, when she appeared, what if he were to talk to her and open his heart, saying all of the things he felt, telling her about the days he'd spent thinking of nothing but her, times when he woke in the night imagining she was beside him, imagining he was holding her, feeling her warmth? He with his clubfoot and his short, ridiculous body—if he told her this, any of it, would she laugh?

Three nights he waited outside the hotel. On the third night, he brought a bouquet of wildflowers he'd gathered during the day. It was not the best time of year for flowers, but he managed to find some grubby little things, pink and blue, that had in his eyes a preciousness, because they'd been searched for, and found, for her.

At length, after many hours, the door opened, and he saw her. She was with the Algerian banker. Zammit watched, helplessly, as the doorman summoned a *karrozzin*, and they got in and slowly drove off, the clipclopping of the horse's shoes echoing with a loneliness that left him bereft.

He sent a letter, an ardent missive filled with anxiety and tender yearning. He addressed her in a forthright manner, expressing the emotions and feelings he experienced when he thought of her. He spoke of destiny, and the mysterious way God had of bringing people together. He mentioned the war, the bombs, and how life on Malta had become intolerable, but somehow, incredibly, her presence had changed misery into bliss and pain into light and ecstasy.

He sent many letters, unsigned, pouring out his heart and soul, thinking it was better to leave the letters unsigned because then, when the moment was ripe, he would find her and tell her he was the one who had written them, and she would look at him, and she would know they were meant for each other. She would understand that in the whole long history of the earth, in the eons in which it took oceans and volcanoes to form, their love had been written and predestined. It was meant to be!

He went back to the hotel, and again he waited, hoping for a chance to see her. Many nights he returned, and finally the door opened and there she was.

Again, like the last time, she was with the Algerian, and she was laughing, a light, hollow laughter that Zammit didn't understand. How could she be with this fat, ugly man, his mustache foppishly waxed, his fingernails daintily manicured, his hair sickeningly slicked down with pomade? With the red carnation in his lapel. What did she see in him?

What if he were to walk up to her and say, "I am the one who wrote the letters!" Would she laugh him to scorn? What had she done with the letters anyway—thrown them away? Perhaps she had shown them to the Algerian banker, and together they'd had a good laugh over them, and perhaps she had cut them into little pieces and flushed them down the toilet, cutting them with the same cuticle scissors with which she trimmed her pretty pink fingernails.

He went home and took to his bed, and slept for two days, and when he finally got up, sour, groggy, joyless, he picked up his tools and worked again on the jukeboxes, halfheartedly.

Melita didn't know what was troubling him. It was more, she realized, than she had supposed.

He mentioned, one day, tentatively, that he'd had a dream about Miss Sicily, and Melita, amused, suggested that a dream about Miss Sicily might be a dangerous dream to have. Too late, she realized it was not a dream but a reality: he was infatuated. Angelina Labbra, she remembered the name. She knew the talk about her. Miss Sicily of 1941, and why didn't she go back where she belonged? For Zammit, with the clubfoot and his dwarfish body, it was, of course, simply impossible, a dream he must abandon and forget.

"My poor Zammit," she said, mothering him even though he was so much older than she, old enough to be her father. "She's no good for you, this woman. Don't you see? You must find someone else, someone from your village." But she knew that anything she said was wrong. Because here he was, past forty, and there had been nobody, no one who responded to him, no one who would marry him, from all the women he had met. And now there was this dreadful woman from Sicily, inspiring an impossible yearning. Melita wanted to take Zammit by the hair and shake him violently until he came to his senses. But there was no remedy, only time. His dream would have to wear itself out, months and years, until he saw how silly he was being. And maybe it would never happen.

She told Rocco about it. "Can anything be done for him?"

Nothing could be done. Love was cruel, and unrequited love was crueler. In the neighborhood of the heart, there were dead-end streets and blind alleys, heaps of rubbish where you couldn't pass, and you could only hope that somehow, in the dark, with luck, you would find your way.

NON-STOP DANCE
at the Rockyvalle Sports Gardens
JUNE 27, 1942
Rhythm Swing Orchestra

———

NOTICE: SMOKE SCREEN

There is no need for alarm as to possible ill effects to the health of any person from the smoke screen, provided those who are obliged to remain in the area take the precaution of covering their noses and mouths with a wet cloth or handkerchief.

The Military Authorities of course would not use poisonous smoke. The smoke has a drying effect on the bronchial tubes, which is harmless, though irritating. It is wise to keep doors and windows shut. The smoke can be cleared from enclosed places by waving blankets.

———

On a Friday, as he walked along Archbishop Street in the early evening, Rocco ran into Beatrice, Hannibal's wife. He hadn't seen her since he'd first arrived in April, when he spent three days at the house on Strait Street, before it was bombed.

She was bedraggled, in a wrinkled, shapeless dress hanging down to her ankles, her graying hair drawn back and held by bobby pins. She was just leaving church, after a novena.

When she saw him, she rushed up to him. "I'm so glad to see you," she said, with some urgency. "It's Nardu, I'm so worried about him, I don't know what to do. My father—you remember? He's on the roof with a gun, he wants to shoot at the planes. He's going to get himself killed up there. Could you come and talk to him? He always liked you, he told me he saw you at the barbershop. Hannibal is in Rabat, and I'm alone with the children. Talk to him, talk some sense into him."

"Is he all right?"

"He doesn't know how old he is. Sometimes he thinks he's sixty, sometimes he says ninety. Last week he said he was a hundred. He isn't a hundred. He used to be a nice, pleasant man, but for a long time now he's full of cranky ideas. When you spoke with him, didn't you see how unbalanced he is? Didn't you know? All that talk about lace and Malta and getting rid of the British. He's lost his common sense, that's what happened. If the bombs don't kill him, the shrapnel will. Just last week somebody was killed in Attard. They shoot in the air, and when the pieces fall they can kill you. Will you talk to him? Will you try to put some sense into his head?"

"Where is he?"

"On the roof, waiting for the planes. Every day now this week, he's up there. I can't even get him to come down for a meal, he makes me bring the food up to him. Not that he ever eats much anyway."

Up the street, a priest carrying a large package came out of a house, head down, hurrying off in the opposite direction.

"Was that Father Hemda?"

"Yes, he lives around here."

"Why don't you have him go up and talk to Nardu?"

"Oh, he went already, but all he did was give him absolution. That's all he does, he gives everybody absolution. Poor man, he doesn't want anyone to go to hell."

Rocco went with her along Archbishop, past the University, then down St. Ursula, to a row of flats near the ruins of the Sacra Infermeria.

"My father, he talks against the Italians but he is Italian himself. His mother and father were from Catania. He hates the Italians because he never stopped hating his father. His father was just like him, always talking, talking, opinionated, big ideas, he had the answer to everything."

The tenements were heavily damaged but the debris had been pushed aside and there was a path down the middle of the street, a few feet wide. The windows were covered with sheets, rugs, planks of wood, or nothing, open to the weather. She was living on the ground floor of a building that had a huge crack in the facade, running from the roof right down to the ground. Birds with black feathers perched on the edge of the roof. When Rocco saw it, the damaged tenement, he felt a strange sense of connection, as if he'd been there, seen it, been in that house before, though he knew he never had. That big, ominous crack, as if the building were suffering a nervous breakdown, ready to split apart and come tumbling down.

She took him through the front door and showed him the stairs, pointing. "Up there," she said. "It's better I don't come. Talk to him, see what you can do."

The stairs were old, and the banister, loose and wobbly, was unreliable. Rocco took the steps two at a time, three flights up, and when he reached the top he was in a sweat. On the roof, by an empty pigeon coop, Nardu Camilleri sat on a stool, with a heavy old rifle lying across his legs. Nearby were boxes filled with soil—squash and tomatoes growing lavishly.

Despite the heat of the day, Nardu Camilleri wore a vest over his white shirt and had his brown cap on his head. He wore a tie, the same blue and red tie he always wore, with the Maltese Cross design. He seemed smaller than ever, shrunken, sinking down into himself, the gun almost as big as he was. His gray eyes pondered the sky.

"Nardu, what in the world are you doing up here?"

"I'm protecting Malta. Somebody must do it. If I don't, who will? Look at you—a soldier. You don't even have a gun. Where is your rifle?"

The high roof afforded a view of the harbor and the Three Cities on the opposite shore. Vast stretches of the Cottonera were nothing but rubble. There were still some people living out there, a few hundred, in crypts and basements. The small harbor boats, the *dgħajsas*, carried supplies across to them from Valletta, and on the return trip they carried back the dead and the injured. Minesweepers were clearing mines from the mouth of the harbor. The dockyards were twisted metal and debris.

Rocco touched the muzzle of the old rifle. "Jesus, Nardu, you're going to save Malta with that?"

"I'm not Jesus, I am Nardu Camilleri," the old man said snappily.

"I know you're not Jesus. Right now, from what I hear, you're just being a pain in the ass."

"Ass? Whose ass?"

"My ass. Beatrice's ass. Everybody's ass."

Lifting his chin, the old man stared defiantly, with all the authority of his advanced age. "Don't speak disparagingly of the human anatomy, young fellow. Your ass, as you refer to it, may be meaningless to you, but mine happens to be an important part of my earthly enterprise."

"That sounds like something Fingerly would say."

"Captain Fingerly? You know him? I offered that man the Malta lace trade, and you know what he did? He laughed."

"That gun isn't loaded, is it? They still make bullets for it?"

"I used this gun in the Great War. I killed seven Boches. I was with KOMA, the King's Own Malta Regiment, at Verdun. Now that was a war, if you want to know about war. The Marne, Ypres, Verdun. This war is nothing. These pathetic Fascists with their toy planes, they can never make their bombs fall where they are supposed to fall."

A red flag went up over St. Elmo's, and the sirens sounded an alert. Nardu Camilleri looked to the north, waiting for the planes coming from Sicily.

"Why don't you come downstairs," Rocco said. "We'll have some tea. Beatrice is worried sick over you."

"Beatrice is a fidget, all fuss and bother. What else do you expect of a woman? She worries I don't eat, she worries I don't sleep, she worries I don't change my underwear. A bomb could fall on her, she'd be worrying about the funeral arrangements."

Rocco, hands in his pockets, shook his head. "What are we going to do with you, Nardu?"

"You think I'm a child? Helpless? You think I don't know what I'm doing?"

"I think you're being very foolish."

They heard the roar and buzz of oncoming planes. Nardu Camilleri struggled to his feet, and with arthritic slowness raised the rifle, but before he was ready, two 109s swooped by, low, and were quickly past. They strafed the minesweepers in the harbor in a single run, and continued south, on their way to tear up the airfields. They had come in too low and too quickly for the heavy antiaircraft to open up on them, but the smaller guns, the Lewises, at Elmo and Fort St. Angelo, were chattering away.

They heard more 109s coming, and this time Nardu was ready, aiming at the same spot where the other two had appeared.

"Don't shoot, don't shoot," Rocco shouted.

Without lowering the rifle, the old man looked across at Rocco as if he were a roach. "Why not?"

"They'll shoot back. They're 109s, never tangle with a 109."

"Nonsense," Nardu Camilleri answered. "Let them shoot, I have better aim. Before they get me, I'll get them. Not one of them has shot back yet."

"This is not a good idea," Rocco said, aware he was getting nowhere. "Does that gun even fire?"

"I killed seven Boches with this gun," he said, and squeezed a shot off to prove the point.

The approaching planes were louder, closer but still not visible, coming in low off the Mediterranean.

"That was twenty-five years ago, Nardu. Look at it, it's rusty. Even if you do hit, you can't knock anything down. Not with that."

"Nobody wins a war with a defeatist attitude," the old man said. "When the Grand Knight, Jean de La Valette, was outnumbered by the invading Turks, five to one, do you think he threw up his hands? He fought back. And he won!"

Then the 109s were upon them, another pair, and they were already firing, strafing Valletta, shooting up the rooftops.

As Nardu Camilleri took aim, Rocco leaped and pulled him down behind the pigeon coop, out of the line of fire. He was light, feathery, tumbling like a sack of straw, and as the two of them fell, the rifle went off and Rocco felt a stinging sensation in his foot. But it was nothing he thought about because, in the next instant, bullets from one of the planes raked across the roof, shattering the boxes with the tomato plants and the squash, and ripping the upper part of the pigeon coop to shreds.

What Rocco felt was anger. A surge, a rush. He was quickly on his feet, watching as one of the planes went down to strafe the harbor while the other turned and swung back for another pass over the rooftops.

Nardu Camilleri was still down, crumpled, not moving. He seemed lifeless.

Rocco picked up the rifle, and with steady hands and a quiet, simmering rage, put the gun to his shoulder and looked down the long barrel, aiming for the cockpit of the 109. The plane came in at a shallow angle. Rocco stood and aimed, and then, as the plane hurried near, squeezed the trigger and kept firing until the gun was empty.

He didn't hit the pilot, but seemed to have hit something. As the plane soared past, the engine sputtered and there was a plume of black smoke. Rocco dropped the rifle and watched as the plane banked uncertainly and veered out to sea, looking as if it was going to have a hard time making it all the way back to Sicily.

Only then did he feel the warm, slippery wetness in his shoe, and he knew again, with a sinking forbearance, that nothing was easy, nothing simple, as the shoe on his left foot filled up with blood.

Twenty-five
"LOVE SOMEBODY, YES I DO—"

"I don't know what came over me," Rocco said, describing for Melita what happened on the roof, the way he had picked up Nardu Camilleri's rifle and started shooting at the 109. "I'd just told him not to shoot and there I was, doing what I told him not to do, shooting at a 109, out in the open."

He was in a hospital bed, in Floriana, his bandaged foot resting on a pillow.

"I don't know, I don't know," she said, taking his hand and rocking it from side to side, rhythmically. "So reckless, you had to go and get yourself shot. You had to be a hero, is that it?"

"I think I was just angry," he said. "That's all it was."

"Well, I'm angry that you were angry," she said. "Such a silly, foolish thing."

She was really bothered, he could see that, and in a way it pleased him, made him feel good, that she could be so powerfully involved over the fate of his foot.

He had got off lucky. When the British Army surgeon was done with him, all he had lost was two toes. For a while there would be crutches, and after the crutches a slight limp, but after a month or so he would walk well enough, and the absence of the two toes would be nothing that anybody would be able to guess.

For Nardu Camilleri, though, it looked like the end of the line. His body had basically stopped functioning. When Rocco pulled him down, out of the line of fire of the 109s, he stayed down and never got up. There was no damage from the fall, no broken bones, no bruised organs, just a depletion, a form of terminal fatigue. He had nothing left inside him, and had to be carried off the roof on a stretcher. In the hospital his vital signs sank, but then, strangely, he rallied, and for weeks he lived on, semicomatose, not talking, not eating, subsisting on intravenous. Father Hemda gave him absolution and the last rites, and it was a surprise to everyone that he continued to linger. Rocco wondered if he wouldn't have been better off if the 109s had got him.

"I shouldn't have pulled him down," he said to Melita. "I should have let him stand there and shoot."

At least then he would have died the way he wanted, gun in hand, instead of lying for weeks in a hospital bed, with the doctors and staff wishing he would hurry up and die because the casualties were mounting and they needed the bed.

The 109 that Rocco had fired on went down in the sea halfway along to Sicily. The shore artillery took credit for the kill, but Rocco preferred to think it was one of the bullets from the rifle that had been responsible.

"Can a rifle knock down a 109?" he asked Tony Zebra, whom he found at Hock's, eating a boiled egg with his beer. Rocco was still on crutches, but getting around. "Could a rifle do that?"

"Nothing can knock down a 109," Tony Zebra said sourly, "except a Spitfire, and that only on a good day." His last time up, a 109 had shot the tail section off his plane and he'd had to bail out into the sea.

"Gorgonzola," Rocco said.

"Gorgon who?"

"I've got this taste in my mouth, gorgonzola cheese."

There was no gorgonzola at Hock's, so they hiked over to Monico's, Rocco moving along capably on his stout wooden crutches. No gorgonzola at Monico's either, but they swilled some beer there before moving on to Captain's, the Cat and Mouse, and the Mefisto Club, and when they reached Weary's they concluded, correctly, there was no gorgonzola on the island, but the beer at Weary's was adequate, a shade better than what they'd had anywhere else, and together they sang a chorus of "Love Somebody, Yes I Do." Tony Zebra, with a few drinks in him, had a magnificent tenor, and Rocco, with a drink or not, had a moaning baritone that wobbled and was constantly off key. Melita was right, he couldn't sing.

> Love somebody, yes I do—
> Love somebody, but I won't tell who.
> Love somebody, yes I do
> And I hope somebody loves me too.

They sang it a second time, and a third, and the only problem was that Tony Zebra had nobody to love. There had been someone in New Jersey, for a while, but that was New Jersey and long ago. And now, with his nose in the shape it was in, scarred and mutilated, what hope did he have? He thought occasionally of slitting his wrists, but the prospect of blood, his own blood, great gouts of it pouring out of him, made him queasy, so for the time being at least he was doing his best to avoid anything desperate.

For the fighter pilots, June had been relatively easy, but now, in July, the Germans were back in force and the action was brisk. In the first nine days, ten Spitfire pilots were lost. One was the American, Harry Kelly, with whom Rocco had played poker on the veranda of the Point de Vue.

"Texas," Rocco said.

"Yeah, from Texas," Tony Zebra said. "A good man."

"Played a mean game of poker."

"Didn't dig Glenn Miller, though. How could anybody not like Glenn Miller?"

A few days after Harry Kelly was killed, they lost Ed Moye, from Alabama, shot down over the sea and drowned before he could be rescued. Another blitz was on, not as all-consuming as in March and April, but big enough.

The heat of midsummer was ferocious, the sun a blast furnace. Everything arid, burnt, thirsty, heat rising visibly from the roads and fields, the land warped into a feverish distortion of itself. Rocco hated it. When they taught him how to use the radio, how to send and receive, he never imagined anything like Malta, the scorching heat and the overcrowded, overbuilt towns, and the small plots of farmland baking in the sun—cactus, carob trees, and dust, dust over everything, a fog of dust every time a truck went by.

After installing a set of new records in a bar in Birkirkara, Melita saw a soldier frying an egg on the hood of a jeep.

"Where'd you get it?" she asked.

"Up the street, that cripple by the barber pole. Paid three bloody shillings for it."

The man by the barber pole had both legs but only one arm, and a black patch over his left eye. He loomed over a small suitcase loaded with eggs, his face shadowy, as if smeared with charcoal.

Melita went up to him. "You have eggs?"

"Five shillings apiece," he said, shifting his weight from one leg to the other.

Melita pointed down the street, toward the jeep. "You sold to the soldier for three shillings."

"That was before the price went up."

"The price went up in two minutes?"

A flight of dive-bombers were raiding inland. They could hear, distantly, the rumble of the bombs.

"Another minute, it goes up again," the man said.

Melita spotted several people hurrying along the street, coming for the eggs. Reluctantly, with a shrug, she opened her purse and bought four.

Carrying two eggs in each hand, she made her way to the hearse and set the eggs on the seat beside her, and drove very carefully back to Valletta. From the City Gate she walked across to Windmill, carrying the eggs, two in each hand, and when she got in the house, just as she reached the kitchen, she tripped on the cat and the eggs in her left hand were crushed, spilling across the floor, though she managed, with luck, to save the two in her other hand.

"Look at this mess," she said, despairing, as Rocco came down from upstairs. "I wanted it to be so good, eggs for supper, but look! What did I do wrong? Why is God punishing me?"

"Where'd you get them?"

"In Birkirkara, from a man with one arm. That's what it was—the cripple, he gave me the evil eye. I feel like one of these broken eggs."

He looked at her up close, as if searching for a fracture. "You're not a cracked egg."

"I'm not? Then tell me, are we good for each other?"

"Aren't we?"

"I wanted it to be so nice. I wanted it to be better."

With the remaining two eggs she made a small omelette.

"Tell me about us," she said. "Do we belong?"

He went to the cupboard, looking for bread.

"Are we meant for each other? Zammit thinks he's meant for Miss Sicily, but he's not, he's so deluded. Are we wrong too? Is it a mistake?"

"Some mistakes are better than others," he said.

Her eyes slanted away, she wanted more from him, something better. "Am I a mistake? Are you a mistake?"

"Fingerly thinks God is a mistake."

"That Fingerly, he's a mistake. And those broken eggs are a worse mistake. I'll never buy eggs again. I don't even like eggs! Is there a song about eggs? About broken eggs?"

"I don't think so," he said.

"Then I don't like that. There should be a song. Write one. What's wrong with you? Why can't you write a song about broken eggs? I don't like that at all."

Rocco was thinking about the big mistake, back there at Fort Benning, when they sent him instead of Kallitsky to Malta. If they hadn't made that mistake, he never would have found Melita—and what then? *What then?*

"You can't write a song," she said, "and you can't sing. What good are you? We should have a doctor examine you. Does it run in your family? Your father too, he doesn't sing? Not even in the shower?"

His father, him too. He should write a letter and ask why he never sang. Just a few lines, accusing, attacking. But he put it off, as he had put off other letters he intended to write, and it slipped by. The mail went out by plane to Gibraltar, but some of those planes were shot down before they arrived, and that's what he kept saying to himself: why write if they could shoot the letter down and it could disappear into the sea?

Twenty-six

AIDA'S WEDDING

On a Saturday late in July, Aida, who had worked out of Hannibal's house on Strait Street and then at a place in Rabat, gave up her career as a prostitute and married a British sailor. He served aboard a destroyer, the *Zulu*.

The reception was held in a garden behind a small restaurant on the outskirts of Rabat, an unpretentious place owned by Hannibal's brother-in-law, Bendu Tonna, who had lost his son in the first year of the bombing. The tables were surrounded by fig trees and clusters of prickly-pear cactus.

Julietta was there with the Count, and Simone arrived in a horse-drawn *karrozzin* with Vivian, who was still in mourning for Nigg. She wore black, and Aida thought it rude of her to come that way, in black, because black at a wedding was, as everyone knew, bad luck. Besides, Vivian and Nigg hadn't even been that close any more. They had quarreled, and before the suicide they hadn't talked to each other for weeks. Hannibal was going to say something to Vivian, but Aida, not eager for a scene, shushed him.

Fingerly was there, and Tony Zebra, with a few pilots from nearby Takali. And a crowd of sailors from the *Zulu*. One was taking pictures. Aboard ship he photographed attacking Stukas and Ju-88s, that was his job. He was the ship's photographer. He had never covered a wedding before.

There were whores from Strait Street and some from Rabat, decked out in lace and silk, their faces so overdone they seemed to be wearing masks. One wore white silk underwear made from the parachute of a German who had been shot down. She lifted her dress for the pilots, giving them an eyeful.

Rocco was there with Melita, and she had brought Zammit along, hoping he might meet someone who would take an interest in him—one of the women from the village, perhaps a widow, there were so many now. In any case, she thought the festivities might shake him loose and help him pull out of his hopeless infatuation.

Also there, at the wedding, was Brangle, the Wellington pilot who had flown Rocco in, back in April. Melita knew him. "He's my pilot from Liverpool, he brings the records for the jukeboxes."

Rocco squinted. "He? Him?"

"Me," Brangle said. "I'm the one."

He picked the records up in Gibraltar and flew them in to Luqa, depositing them in a tobacco shop near the airport, where Melita picked them up. That morning, he'd flown in with Dinah Shore, Helen Forrest, Peggy Lee, Kitty Kallen, and Judy Garland.

"I hope you took good care of them," Rocco said, recalling the reckless, death-flirting way Brangle had put the plane down, the day they flew in.

Hannibal footed the bill for the wedding. Through his black-market connections he had acquired several cases of table wine and champagne, but his efforts to find fresh meat met with abject failure. Even goat meat, at this point, was hard to find, and Aida was adamant about not allowing roast cat or dog to be served at her wedding.

The tables were covered with white linen, and the meal itself, served on white plates, was in keeping with the spirit of the latest rationing restrictions: on each plate one small sardine and ten peas. Fortunately, the tomato crop that summer was a bumper yield, so there was a prodigious tomato salad, spiced with garlic, pepper, and oregano. For the bride and groom, in addition to the one sardine and the ten peas, there were chicken livers that Hannibal had picked up on Gozo, served in a white sauce with a sprinkling of herbs.

The man Aida married was a career sailor, an engine-room mechanic in his late thirties, intending, after the war, to retire from the navy and go home to the Cotswolds, where he planned to grow Christmas trees. His name was Bobby Cripps and he liked whores. It had long been his ambition to marry one, and he joked openly about how he was making an honest woman of Aida by marrying her. He also joked about her wooden leg. "I got a bargain, didn't I? Top of the line. Soon as the war's over, we're bringing up a family, and just you see, every one of the girls gets born with a wooden leg. I won't say what kind of a leg the boys will be born with," he quipped, "but it won't be wood—right, Aida?" Rocco heard him give this little speech at least three times, with a leering roll of his eyes.

Vivian thought Aida had made a poor match, but Simone said at least it would get her to England and away from Malta, which was not a place to live in any more. Three dreary-looking musicians, one with a handlebar mustache, stood by the cactus: a mandolin, an accordion, and a violin. They were from Rabat, and had gone to grade school with Aida, at the St. Agatha School. They played selections from the opera *Aïda,* including a rousing version of "Celeste Aïda," and a heartfelt rendering of "Fuggiam gli ardori inospite" ("Ah, let us flee the hateful heat"). However, they tactfully avoided the doleful pieces from the end of the opera, when Aïda and Radames await their death in the gloomy tomb. They did not play "Morir! Si pura e bella," nor did they do the somber farewell, "O terra addio."

"You see," Aida said saucily, as the musicians launched into the Triumphal March, "if I had been born in Egypt, my life would have been so wonderfully different. I never would have lost my leg when that stupid horse ran into a ditch, and I would have married someone in the diplomatic corps. We would have lived on the Nile, amid the pyramids and the palm trees, and I would have smoked Egyptian cigarettes. Now, instead, I will help Bobby grow Christmas trees in the Cotswolds."

It had been her father's idea to name her Aida. For that, and for other things, she still resented him, even though he was dead. As a young man he had spent a number of years in Cairo, handling legal documents for a firm that exported dates to North America. When he returned to Malta, he often thought of going back to Cairo, but never did. He set up a legal practice in Rabat, gambled heavily, drank American whisky, invested foolishly in a firm that produced incense and Holy Communion wafers, kept a mistress, and made his wife miserable. When she died of complications arising from a gallbladder operation, Aida blamed him for driving her into an early grave. And she never stopped blaming him. She blamed him for the mistress, for the American whisky, for the incense and the communion wafers, and most of all for arranging to have her take piano lessons when she had pleaded instead for singing lessons. The piano teacher, an unpleasant man with foul breath and a scar on his lip, seduced her when she was fourteen, and her life after that was never the same.

"My father was always against me," she said, cutting into a chicken liver and lifting a piece on her fork. "Even when I was just born, he was against me. He gave me the name of a slave. He could have given me the name of a queen,

Cleopatra, but he named me for a slave who dies a horrible death in a tomb. What on earth was he ever thinking?"

"He's dead, he's dead, let him be," Simone said. "Let the dead rest." He had died of a heart attack in the first year of the bombing, during a raid, while running to get to a shelter. Simone had always been fond of him and thought Aida too harsh and judgmental, too unrelenting.

"He's dead, yes, but for me he's alive, up here," Aida said, tapping a finger against her forehead. "In here he still lives."

Hannibal blew off a string of firecrackers, then he passed out some prewar sparklers and they lit them. Everyone got up from the tables and for a few moments they walked about on the dried-out grass, waving the sparklers like magic wands.

"Where did you find them?" Aida asked, utterly delighted.

"I got them from Bendu Tonna's cousin. He had a whole box from before the war. I won't tell you what I had to pay." He lit a rocket and it hissed skyward, green and purple, and again the musicians played—slow, romantic tunes for slow dancing. Aida danced with her husband, and then with Hannibal. Simone danced with Vivian. The sailors from the *Zulu* danced with the whores from Strait Street. Rocco danced with Melita, but his foot bothered him, so he sat out the next one and Melita danced with Zammit. Rocco was surprised to see how well Zammit moved, despite the big shoe on his clubfoot. No woman had ever wanted him.

Father Hemda, who had performed the wedding, sat at a table sipping red wine, a glazed softness in his eyes as he watched the dancers. A Messerschmitt soared past, low, chased by a Spitfire, and the women were upset, watching the sky with worried frowns.

"*Xorti, xorti,*" Hannibal said. "For a wedding, if it rains it's good luck, and if they bomb, it's even luckier."

Melita danced with Fingerly, then she danced with Zammit again. Julietta danced with the Count.

"You broke her heart, you know," Simone said to Rocco, looking toward Julietta.

"No, not true," he said. "Whatever gave you that idea?"

"Oh yes, she liked you very much, but you never gave her a chance. This other girl you're with, she looks down on us. She thinks she's better than we are."

Rocco was upset to hear her say that. "If she felt that way, believe me, she wouldn't have come."

Simone pursed her lips, weighing her feelings about Melita. She didn't actively dislike her, yet she felt a distance, a vague antipathy. "Her father was killed? On the docks?"

"The first day of the bombing."

"Well, she looks like a nice girl. She is very pretty. But you broke Julietta's heart, you know. She felt something very special for you."

"She has the Count, he's a rich man."

Simone waved her hand. "He's so old—old enough to be her grandfather. All he wants is a warm body in bed with him at night. What good is that for a healthy young woman like her?"

"Are you really going to open a lace shop?"

"I am going to do that, yes. The women on Gozo think they are the only ones who can do lace, but on Malta we are better. I am going to have a shop with young girls making lace for me. The collar on Vivian's dress, I made that."

After Nigg's suicide, Vivian and Simone had drawn very much together. They came to the wedding in the same *karrozzin*, and Rocco had heard, from Tony Zebra, that they were living together in a house in Rabat, and the gossip was that they were lovers. Whatever the case, Vivian was—seemed—much changed. Rocco had seen her, his first days on Malta, flaunting herself, jaunty and brash, but now, in her new dependence on Simone, she seemed a different person, calmer, more relaxed and self-assured. Even though she wore mourning for Nigg, she didn't seem particularly grief-stricken. It was almost as if she was glad he was dead, because with him gone, she was free to pursue a different kind of life for herself. She seemed remarkably serene.

Fingerly, a glass of champagne in each hand, was outdoing himself, talking to the pilots, the ones who were new on the island, telling them exactly how the war would go. "Faster than you think, Rommel loses in North Africa. After the Afrika Korps capitulates, we invade Sicily. After Sicily, we march right up the Italian peninsula and take Rome. After that, it's a piece of cake—the cross-Channel invasion into France, across the Rhine, and on into Germany. To Berlin!"

"Piece of cake," said Smoky Joe Lowery, who had a reputation for having a hot hand at dice.

"Piece of cake," said Petro Peters, who had seen action in the Spanish Civil War.

They were all saying it, piece of cake, piece of cake. Even Nardu Camilleri who wasn't there was saying it. Even Nigg and Maroon, who were dead, and Ambrosio, who was still AWOL in Majorca, enjoying the olive groves and making love to one of his cousins. *Piece of cake. Piece of cake.* The Stukas and Ju-

88s were having another go at Valletta, and through the seven-mile distance they could hear the bombs pounding home.

"Your Captain Fingerly has fresh hands," Melita said to Rocco. "I had to slap his face."

"While you were dancing? You slapped his face?"

"He was very smooth about it, he said he was just trying to brush a mosquito off the front of my dress."

"You slapped his face and I never saw?"

"Should I do it again?"

"I'll get the photographer, I want a picture."

From the kitchen, Hannibal wheeled out the wedding cake that Bendu Tonna had made. The ration laws forbade the baking of cakes and pastries, but a wedding was a wedding, and Bendu Tonna, undeterred, had put this together out of the sugar, flour, eggs, and scraps of other things that Hannibal had paid heftily for.

"I don't know why I'm so good to her," Hannibal said, repeating it several times during the course of the afternoon. He was sweating profusely in the intense heat, and the dye from his red tie bled onto his shirt so that his chest seemed covered with blood. "In the house on Strait Street, she was nothing but trouble, always bickering and complaining. She doesn't deserve this wedding I made for her."

"If he says it again," Aida said, "I'll hit him over the head with my leg."

Hannibal had paid not just for the cake and the food but for Aida's gown as well. It was silk, with a great deal of lace, and with strings of artificial pearls sewn onto it—the silk and the lace a pale shade of pink, almost white but not white enough, because she was, after all, not a virgin, and hadn't been for a very long time.

The photographer took several pictures of her cutting the cake and feeding her husband. Then he posed them in front of the cactus and made them kiss. After the cake, Aida was dancing again. She grabbed Rocco. "Come, you must dance with the bride."

He protested, because of his foot, but gladly gave in, and for a few moments, on the grass, while the musicians played a slow song, they were a pathetic pair, she with her wooden leg and he with his bad foot, awkward and slow, like mechanical mannequins.

"Are you happy?" Rocco asked.

"Very happy," she said. "Of course, it's not the same as marrying a count, is it? Or a rich American, like Captain Fingerly, or you. But at least, after the war, he will take me away from here and we'll have our own house and we'll grow Christmas trees. The summers won't be so hot and unbearable."

"You think I'm rich? Is that what you think?"

"Isn't it true? That's what Fingerly says. He says you're a millionaire."

"He told Dominic I breed racehorses."

"It's not true? What a terrible world, no one is honest anymore. Why must you disillusion me on my wedding day?"

As they turned with the music, she lifted her head, glancing toward a cloud. "That's what I always thought about your friend Fingerly. He's a person who does not tell the truth."

When the musicians broke for a rest, the women sat around and began singing. They sang old Maltese songs, in Maltese. Simone started, and Julietta and Aida joined in, along with Vivian, and the old women from Rabat. Even the whores from Strait Street sang.

"What are they singing?" Rocco asked Melita.

"About love," she said, "old songs about love and sadness."

There seemed more of sadness in it than anything else. Slow, mournful tunes, limp with sorrow.

Then the musicians were back playing again, and Melita wanted to dance, but Rocco's foot was still giving him pain. "Then I am going to dance with Zammit," she said, and she did. Simone danced with Vivian, and Fingerly danced with Julietta.

Rocco sat with the Count, who was working steadily on a bottle of champagne and talking loosely about his associates in Berlin who were trying, in various ways, without success, to get rid of Hitler. He felt at ease with Rocco, because he was young, a good listener, *gemütlich,* with a reassuring American innocence, and like himself at that moment, slightly drunk.

"There are people who think the only way to save Germany," he said, fitting a small cigar into a holder, "is to kill him. What do you think? Should the Führer be assassinated?"

Rocco reached for the champagne and filled the Count's glass, then replenished his own. "Can it be done?"

"Last summer, an attempt was made by two junior officers, but they were unable to get near him. The Führer is well guarded."

The Count had been in touch with Field Marshal von Witzleben, who had been eager to mount a direct action against Hitler. But Hitler, suspicious, doubting Witzleben's loyalty, removed him from active service, so he was now a field marshal without an army.

Rocco spotted Zammit dancing with Simone and he wondered, fleetingly, if something might develop. They made a ludicrous couple, hopelessly mismatched, he so short and she so large she could have picked him up and carried him around.

"There are others, yes," the Count said wearily. "Stauffenberg, Schlabrendorff, Stieff. Perhaps one of them will do it. I don't have much hope for von Moltke and his crowd, the Kreisau bunch. They are too idealistic, they lack the will to actually do anything." Even worse, he thought, than getting rid of Hitler was the problem of finding the right person to replace him. "Myself, I favor a restoration of the monarchy, as many of us do. But which of the princes to put on the throne? Popitz wants the Crown Prince, but he is such a wretched, dissolute man, plainly unacceptable. Some talk about Prince Oskar of Prussia, but frankly I have my reservations. Perhaps the only thing we all agree on is that the Kaiser's fourth son, Prince August, is out of the question. The poor boy has become a fanatical Nazi, a Gruppenführer in the SS."

"So it's hopeless?"

"No, no, I would not say hopeless. There is a growing sentiment for Louis-Ferdinand, the second son of the Crown Prince. He is young and he's spent a great deal of time in America. You have heard of him?"

Rocco had not.

"But you should have," the Count said sharply. "You are in automobiles, are you not? For five years the Prince was at the Ford factory in Dearborn. He understands democracy, he knows what it is to work for a living. And he made a wonderful marriage—to the Princess Kira, of Russia. She was a Grand Duchess, you know, before the Revolution. And they are both great friends of your President, Mr. Roosevelt. For their honeymoon, he invited them to stay at the White House."

It seemed, to Rocco, a gleaming idea. You work at Dearborn, making Fords, and the next thing you know, they want to make you the king of Germany.

"Anything is possible," the Count said. "But I am less and less optimistic."

Beatrice's daughter, Marie, went running past, pursued by her brother, Joseph, in his Boy Scout uniform. Beatrice was right behind them, calling angrily to Joseph, but they were already beyond the fig trees, out of sight.

"I don't know what to do with him anymore," Beatrice complained, "he has become so difficult, so difficult."

"How is your father?" Rocco asked, rising to greet her.

"The same, the same, not very well, he has no will to live." She turned to the Count. "He saved my father's life—do you know? He did a brave thing. Very brave."

"Perhaps you will save my life someday," the Count said to Rocco drolly.

"He mentioned your name yesterday," Beatrice said, putting her hand on Rocco's arm. "He thinks of you."

"Did he really kill seven Germans, in the old war? Or was he just imagining?"

"Oh yes, they gave him a medal. He was very proud of that. He was a marksman."

The children came running back through the fig trees and disappeared through the door, into the restaurant. Beatrice went after them, shaking her head.

The Count wandered off to the men's room, and Rocco found himself by the cactus, with Julietta, demurely alluring in a blue gown, wearing a heavily jeweled necklace the Count had given her. She too, like Simone and Aida, had retired from the trade, and was now living in an apartment the Count rented for her in St. Julian's.

"You've moved up in the world," Rocco said.

"He is very kind to me."

"I'm glad for you."

She smiled wryly. "You never made love to me."

He gave a vague shrug.

"It's better this way," she said. "I've made love to so many, it's nice to think there is someone special."

She put her hands on his tie, tightening the knot. "I've made up my mind," she said. "I will go with him to Alexandria."

"When?"

"Soon, I think. The bombing is less."

"They say it's a beautiful city."

"It's for the best. Yes?"

"For the best."

The sun was slanting away toward a line of small reddish clouds. Vivian called to Aida. "The bouquet. Are you going to throw the bouquet?"

"I don't think she wants to," Julietta said. "She wants to keep it."

The bouquet was three roses set among white chrysanthemums, brought over from Gozo during the night, along with the chicken livers. Aida pulled one rose, for a keepsake, then turned her back and tossed the bouquet over her shoulder. It was Simone who caught it, and she burst into tears, because catching the bouquet meant she was the next to get married, and it was perfectly clear, to her and to everyone, that at her age it was unlikely she would ever have a husband.

Then it was not just Simone weeping but all of them, Aida, Vivian, Julietta, because everything was changing and no one quite knew any more what was happening and what lay ahead. Beatrice wept because her father was close to death, and Vivian wept for Nigg, who had stopped seeing her weeks before he shot himself and hadn't even thought to leave her a note. Aida wept because she was now a married woman and she wasn't at all sure it was a sensible thing. She knew the stories about the marriages with sailors, how they almost never worked out. Julietta wept because the others were weeping, and Simone wept because her years on Strait Street were over, and she felt old and not ready for the rest of her life, which seemed bleak and without promise. And they all wept because Malta was no longer the Malta they grew up in, too many houses and buildings had been blown up, and they all knew people who had died. It was too much to bear.

Rocco opened a fresh pack of Luckies and passed them around, then he went about with a book of matches, giving each of them a light, and they sat there at a long table, in a kind of abandonment, weeping and smoking. There were women Rocco didn't know, some of them old and gray, and even they were weeping, for reasons he couldn't imagine.

"Life is too complicated," Simone said. "I will never, never understand it."

"Don't ever leave us," Beatrice said to Aida. "After the war, don't go away and leave us alone."

"I will never leave you," Aida said. "I was born on Malta and I promise, I will die on Malta."

"What is going to happen to our little Julietta?" Simone said wanly. "Will she desert us? Will she go away forever? The world is always changing. It's so heartless, the way everything is different." While the tears streamed down her cheeks, ruining her makeup, she inhaled deeply on the cigarette. There was still some cake on her plate, but she didn't want it.

Aida inhaled, and Julietta inhaled. Julietta took out a handkerchief and wiped her eyes, then again she inhaled, and said it was all because of Malta, all of the unhappiness because of this hard, rocky, dusty, inconsiderate island. She talked about her hard childhood and the sheep she had to care for, and her miserable cousins who used to come and fool with the sheep, shamelessly, how they tormented her, but she believed in God and hoped everything, in the future, would be better than it was.

Even Melita was weeping. She wept for her parents who were dead, and for her aunt with whom she didn't get along, and for Zammit who all his life had been disappointed in love. And she wept for Rocco because any day now the war on Malta might be over and they would be sending him somewhere else, and she might never see him again. Zammit, sitting beside her, stared straight ahead, looking toward the fig trees, which were now in shadow. A tear ran down his cheek. He was the only one not smoking.

"It's the hunger," Hannibal said to Rocco. "With the rationing, they don't get enough to eat anymore. They're weak with hunger, so they get moody and they cry. That's how it happens in war—first the women fall apart, then the men go crazy, and then there is nothing left. This war has gone on too long. Either the British should win, or they should go away and leave us in peace."

Rocco thought he saw tears welling up in Hannibal's eyes. He was such a rugged man, it was disturbing to think he might break down and cry. Rocco offered him a cigarette and held the match while he lit up.

Everyone was wilted from the heat. The priest, Father Hemda, had put his head down on the table and was sound asleep.

"Where did you get the cigarettes?" Hannibal asked.

Rocco was still being supplied by Fingerly. "I play poker with the pilots," he said.

"I always favored Old Golds," Hannibal said. "You don't know where I could find some Old Golds, do you?"

Rocco looked at Hannibal's hands, big and powerful, and remembered something Fingerly had told him, that he'd seen Hannibal pick up a bottle of Black Label, wrap it in a towel, and squeeze hard with one hand until the bottle broke. He was that strong.

When they got back to Windmill Street, they were tired but it was still early in the evening, the sun just going down. Melita brewed some tea.

"You danced a lot with Zammit," Rocco said.

"He likes to dance, he's a good dancer."

Rocco noticed how solicitous she was for him, always. How she took care of him, always giving him special attention. She idolized him, because of his gift with the jukeboxes.

"Do you love him?" he asked. The question sailed out of nowhere, arriving out of the dreary fatigue at the end of a long day.

A moment passed before she answered. "Of course I love him," she said. "He's my cousin."

"I know, I know. But I mean, are you *in* love with him?"

She frowned, fiercely indignant. "What are you saying? You mean like you and me, making love? What's wrong with you, why are you saying such a thing?"

He felt shabby, foolish. "I didn't mean it that way," he said, backing off. "I don't know what I meant. It was stupid."

She went into a pout.

"Hey, it's no big deal," he said, trying to smooth it over.

"Sometimes you say strange things."

"I wasn't thinking."

"Well, you should think. Before you say such a terrible thing like that."

"Let's skip the tea and go to Monico's," he suggested, "maybe they have some biscuits."

"I don't want to go to Monico's."

"We'll take a walk."

"You're mean to me," she said. She punched him on the shoulder. "You don't like me."

"I'm not mean to you."

"Yes, you are."

"You want to hit me in the jaw? Go ahead, hit me."

She looked at him as if she might really do it. Then, after a long pause, she said, "After the war, I want to have a baby."

It was, in its suddenness, worse than a punch. She was talking again about marriage.

"Is that what you want?"

"Isn't it what every woman wants? In America, isn't that what they want? To be a mother and have a child?"

It made him uncomfortable when she talked like that.

"Don't rush me," he said.

She slanted her head off to one side, looking at him as if he were a stranger. "What does that mean?" she said.

"Nothing," he said, "it means nothing. It's just, there's a war on, isn't there?"

"I was talking about after the war."

"Right, right," he said, dim and withdrawn. Then, after a pause, "You're not pregnant, are you?"

"No, I'm not pregnant."

"Are you sure?"

She took the tea from the stove and was about to pour it, but the pot slipped from her hand and the tea splattered on the floor, and she just stood there, motionless, looking at the spilled tea all around her.

"Forget it, it's nothing," Rocco said, grabbing a rag from the sink and wiping it up.

"It's our last tea," she said. "The last of our ration."

July 23, 1942

ALLIED AIR ACTIVITY IN CHINA AND BURMA
Successful Raid on Canton

SWEDEN WARNS FOREIGN SUBMARINES

THE MALTA FRONT: THREE NIGHT RAIDERS DESTROYED

———

MINIMUM HEIGHT FOR DRAFTEES
LOWERED FROM FIVE FEET TWO INCHES TO FIVE FEET
Free Bus Tickets to National Service Headquarters in Hamrun
PENALTY FOR FAILURE TO REGISTER: ONE POUND

———

KEEP THE KIDNEYS ACTIVE
to ensure Good Health

Men and women alike lose vigour and vitality in our climate. Pains in the
small of the back set in, joints "crack" at every movement and become stiff and
swollen, sediment is left in the urine and bladder weakness causes alarm. Yet
many a kidney sufferer wastes precious time before strengthening the kidneys
with Doan's Backache Kidney Pills.

Refuse All Substitutes
ASK FOR DOAN'S

———

TEN THOUSAND PEOPLE WERE KILLED IN COLOGNE and buried in
communal graves and 140,000 officially evacuated from the city as a result of the
RAF's 1000-bomber raid on the night of May 30–31. These figures have now
been received from reliable foreign sources which report the indescribable devastation. At least 16 factories, including the railway workshops, were demolished. In the city many banks and insurance buildings were destroyed.

Part III

MUSIC IN THE NIGHT

. . . in a country that has a brilliant light but no trees, it is impossible to hide anything.

—NIGEL DENNIS, *AN ESSAY ON MALTA*

Twenty-seven

THE RHINO CARESS
TRANSATLANTIC
CONDOM DEAL

Again Fingerly was gone for a while—and this time, when he returned, he was a major. Not only that but he was living, now, not in Valletta but in a modest mansion, the Palazzo Volpe, high on a hill overlooking St. Paul's Bay. On a Friday night, soon after his return, he invited Rocco and Melita for dinner.

The palazzo had belonged to the Baroness Nessuno, a widow without heirs, now in her nineties, living out her last days as an invalid in the hospital run by the Blue Nuns.

"Nice house," Rocco said, expecting to see the Venus of Malta and Dragut's dagger, but they were still locked away in the warehouse in Paola.

"The people in these old palazzos," Melita said, "the old nobility, they were so rich." She meant disgustingly rich.

Rocco ran his finger along the leg of a marble goddess who held a horn of plenty loaded with grapes and melons. "A whole palazzo? I-3 requisitioned this?"

"Hell no, this is mine, personal. Picked it up for a song. It's a good time to invest, you might want to think of getting a parcel or two of your own."

"You got it for cigarettes?"

"Cute, Rocco. Cute. Isn't he cute?"

"I think he's very cute," Melita said protectively, touching Rocco's face. "If he weren't cute, I wouldn't sleep with him."

"You need all this?" Rocco asked. "All these rooms?"

"Style, Raven, style. You, with your interest in old cars, don't you dig style? If you must know, I paid for it not with cigarettes but with condoms."

"Whose condoms?"

"Count von Kreisen's."

"You bought a palazzo with the Count's condoms?"

"He had a whole shipload."

"A freighter full of condoms?"

"It's Catholic Malta, they don't believe in birth control, so they don't manufacture their own condoms. Any condoms on this island have to come from abroad. With the convoys getting sunk, the love life of the British serviceman has been going down the tubes. It's that simple."

The condoms in question had been made in Perth Amboy, in 1941. The brand name was Rhino Caress. They'd been shipped on a French freighter to a wholesaler in Brest, but before they were halfway across the Atlantic, the wholesaler sold the entire shipment to the Luftwaffe, and the freighter was rerouted to Bremen. Before it reached Bremen, a captain on Göring's staff, a trained accountant, seized an opportunity to turn a profit by selling the shipload to an agent in Argentina for ten percent above what the Luftwaffe had paid, and the freighter was again turned around and sent this time to Buenos Aires. As it happened, the agent in Argentina was operating on behalf of Count von Kreisen, who, because of his expertise in international trade, had been commissioned by the high command in Malta to acquire condoms for the Malta garrison, a corps of some thirty-five thousand men. The last condoms intended for Malta had been shipped with the Vian convoy in March, but the freighter carrying them, the *Clan Campbell*, was sunk twenty miles from the entrance of Grand Harbour.

In Argentina, at the Count's instruction (wireless from Malta), the shipment was transferred to a neutral Swedish vessel that sailed for Gibraltar, where the cargo was offloaded into a warehouse. The last leg—Gibraltar to Malta—was the most treacherous, because of the siege, and the Count studied a variety of options, none of which proved feasible. In the end, unable to come up with a strategy of his own, he turned to Fingerly.

"And I agreed to help out," Fingerly said, smiling coyly.

"For a commission," Rocco said.

"Of course."

"You got him the *Welshman*?"

"I did better."

"How?"

"Hey," Fingerly said, "you want all of I-3's secrets? As of the moment, a third of the original shipment has reached the island. Good enough? The rest is on the way."

Later, while a raid was on over Valletta, he took them onto the roof to watch. It was dark, the long white fingers of the searchlights swinging eagerly, probing the night. Orange flashes from the big 4.7-inch guns, and the roar, an ecstasy of flak, and wavering streams of red tracer from the heavy machine guns. Whenever Rocco saw it he was entranced, great bursts of light flaming in the night sky.

"This is one of the great wars," Fingerly said. "People in the future will wish they were us, alive in this time. It's a new heroic age, Rocco. We have a lot to thank Hitler for, he gave us this war, he made it possible. Aren't you glad to be here, on Malta?"

They had taken the bus out to the Palazzo, but the buses didn't run at night, so Fingerly drove them back in his Phantom and dropped them at the City Gate.

Some of the bombs in the last raid had fallen in Valletta and they could smell them, the stink of cordite.

"That big palazzo," Melita said. "Isn't it too much?"

"He thinks he's Lorenzo de' Medici. Maybe he is."

"I think he's just crazy. When he was a baby, somebody must have dropped him on his head."

The next day, on a flight in from Gibraltar, three Beaufighters, each with a crew of two, were shot down by a flock of 109s. The guns on all three Beaufighters failed. They crashed in the sea, and when the crews opened the wing compartments to get the inflatable dinghies, instead of the dinghies they found cartons of condoms. When they checked the ammunition wells, instead of bullets they found more condoms, which explained why the guns didn't fire. Two crew members, badly shot up, died in the water. The others floated around in their Mae Wests and were picked up by a rescue floatplane three hours later.

The condoms were part of the shipload Count von Kreisen had routed to Gibraltar. Fingerly was getting them to Malta by loading them into the wing compartments of the Beaufighters and Beauforts, which made frequent trips back and forth. He had a private arrangement with ground crews at both ends, who were paid for their efforts with figs from the Sudan and Egyptian dates. Rocco got the story from Tony Zebra, who got it from his CO, who got it from a vice admiral at the underground command center at Lascaris.

When Rocco next saw Fingerly, it was at Hock's, and Rocco confronted him. "Two were killed," he said. "Two!"

"I know, I know," Fingerly said, turning on the charm, doing his utmost to be conciliatory. "The pressure was on to get those things in, and it went too far. No ammo in the wells, that wasn't right."

"Two guys are dead," Rocco repeated. "For a few lousy condoms!"

"This matters to you," Fingerly noted. "I can see that it matters."

"Doesn't it matter to you?"

"Of course it matters," Fingerly said deliberately, with a show of concern. "It matters a great deal."

"I can't believe you did this."

"I? *I* did this? The war did this. You think I would knowingly, consciously, send two good men to their death?"

"These are your condoms, right?"

"The Count's condoms. I'm just on commission here, and the ground crews take a commission off my commission."

"Still, it's your say-so."

Fingerly shrugged evasively.

"Two guys," Rocco said. "All six of them could have been killed. More are going to get killed?"

"I know, I know," Fingerly said with feeling, "but look at it this way, if they weren't carrying the condoms, they would have been carrying lipsticks and nylons for their girlfriends, or booze and lamb chops for their poker buddies at Luqa. It's an imperfect world, Rocco."

"No dinghy, that's crazy—but no *ammo*? They never would have flown if they knew they couldn't shoot."

"Well, they do, it happens. You'd be surprised how many times these guys fly without ammo. But you're right, absolutely right. Putting condoms in the ammo wells was out of line. I gave my crew out there strict instructions: only in the dinghy compartment. I told them, if you use the ammo wells, only half of them for godsake, leave a few rounds in there for an emergency. But you know what it's like, Rocco, they get overzealous, there's a big push on, you should hear the top brass. You think they care how we get them in? It's a crisis over here, thirty-five thousand in the garrison and no condoms. Almost as bad as running out of bacon. But you're right, right as rain. I'm flying out to Gib tonight, damn it, and I'm going to give those guys hell."

Rocco hung, thinking, wondering. If life was a mistake, and if time was a mistake, and if the entire planet was a mistake, then Fingerly, wearing a new green sportshirt with his gold oak leaf pinned to the collar, was the biggest mistake of all.

"Here, have a cigar," Fingerly said, taking one from his shirt pocket.

Rocco looked at it, good Havana, and wanted it, would have grabbed it and would have enjoyed smoking it, but it seemed too obviously a bribe. He felt like punching Fingerly in the nose.

"I have to take a leak," he said, which wasn't quite true, and headed toward the back, toward the john, but walked right past it and out the rear door, into an alley full of garbage cans.

Coming down the alley, out onto Old Mint, he came upon some kids, boys, marching in step as they came down the street, a bunch, six or seven, chanting a rhyme:

> Dragut, Dragut
> In his iron suit
> Sailed the seas
> Hungry for loot.
>
> Murder and kill,
> Plunder and seize—
> Hold on to your nose
> And your shaking knees!

They broke ranks and engaged each other in imaginary swordplay, hopping about, up onto the piles of rubble, chasing each other high into the clifflike debris of a house that had been smashed by a bomb. Broken walls, sections of floor jutting out at various levels like pieces of a stage. A bathtub, a couch, huge chunks of plaster to stand on and climb among. They paused, confronting, using sticks for swords, then leaped and bounded, angling for better position. Parry and thrust, it was better than Errol Flynn.

Rocco felt like jumping in and being one of them. Dragut, Dragut, in his iron suit.

Mid-August, four merchant ships and an oil tanker arrived in Grand Harbour, badly battered after a heavy assault that had raged for several days. Fourteen supply ships had set out from England, but these five were all that survived.

The 15th was the feast of Mary's Assumption, a major holy day for the Maltese, and the convoy quickly became known as the Santa Marija convoy. Nine merchant ships had been sunk, along with two cruisers, a destroyer, and the aircraft carrier *Eagle*. Several other warships were badly damaged. For the

Royal Navy it was a disaster, with a large loss of life, but for starving Malta it was now possible to postpone the surrender date and hold out for another ten weeks.

MERCHANT NAVY DEFIES AXIS BLOCKADE OF MALTA
Ships Come Through Living Hell

WORST GAUNTLET EVER
GRIM FIGHT TO GET SHIPS THROUGH

A protective umbrella of Spitfires flew over the harbor. The Canadian ace, Screwball Beurling, aloft on the 15th when the crippled tanker *Ohio* came in, celebrated by flying upside down and low over Valletta. People knew it was Beurling—it was his signature, flying upside down. They pointed, saying his name. He'd already knocked down more of the enemy than anyone else.

"Life is upside down," Melita said. "Isn't it wonderful? If it weren't upside down, I wouldn't want to be alive. You think the ships brought any ice cream?"

She had a passion for chocolate ice cream and hadn't had any for a very long time.

"They did, they did," Rocco teased, "but it's all vanilla."

"Shoes," she said. "I hope they brought shoes."

Her few shoes all had holes in them now, and it was impossible to get new ones. The repairmen did a thriving business, making all sorts of virtuoso patches, stitching and gluing in ways never before imagined. But for a hole in the sole, the best was still a piece of cardboard inside the shoe, or a piece of linoleum.

"You think they brought honey? Sugar? Pretzels?"

"Absolutely."

"You think they brought Vaseline?"

"I'll check it out with Fingerly. Fingerly knows everything."

"Fingerly," Melita said, "he knows nothing."

"He has a plan to reorganize the government. After the war he's going to rule as the Prince of Malta, but he thinks Sultan might be better."

"What he needs is a good dose of the sandfly fever."

"You hate him that much?"

"I don't hate him, I distrust him."

"Well, he likes you. You should hear him, how he talks."

"Him? That megalomaniac?"

"He thinks you weave a spell."

"Is that what he said? I'm an enchantress?"

"He thinks you're Calypso."

"Yes, yes," she said, after thinking it over, "that's who I am. When Odysseus passed through, I kept him seven years, right here on Malta. And now I have you. You like it, under my spell?"

She started to hum, soft, haunting, the new song from America, "That Old Black Magic," dancing a slow circle around him.

"Don't do this," he said. "Voodoo gives me the creeps."

She went on humming, sultry, moving slowly around him, her long black hair falling loose and silken, weaving darkly.

Twenty-eight

THE LAST RITES OF DOMINIC MIFSUD

Early in September Rocco turned twenty-two and they celebrated with a movie.

The Trops had *The Gay Imposters,* and the Adelphi in Rabat had Basil Rathbone and Boris Karloff in *The Tower of London.* The Carlton had Marlene Dietrich and Gary Cooper in *Desire.* They settled on *The Road to Singapore,* at the Regal, from 1940: Crosby, Hope, and Dorothy Lamour.

"Then we'll eat at Dominic's."

Melita raised an eyebrow. "He's open?"

"Of course he's open."

"Nobody is open," she said. "There's no food, the restaurants are all closed."

"Dominic's is never closed."

"We'll end up in a Victory Kitchen, you'll see."

The movie was in Paola, and they cycled over, because there was no longer any fuel for the pink hearse. They kept it parked at Zammit's, with less than a gallon in it. The bikes were old and rusty. One was the spare bike belonging to Zammit—he owned two, and had lent one to Rocco months ago—and the other they'd picked up through the classifieds.

The movie was pleasant enough, some laughs, some songs. The five o'clock show. "Nice, nice," Melita said, "not bad." She'd heard *The Road to Morocco* had come out during the summer, but it would be a long time before Malta got that.

From Paola, they bicycled to St. Julian's, going through Marsa, Ħamrun, Msida, Gzira. It was a trip.

"They should make *The Road to Malta*," Melita said.

Her bike hit a rock, throwing her off balance, and she skidded on loose pebbles and went down. For a few moments she didn't move, her left wrist stinging, the pain shooting up her arm. Her dress was torn, and one of her knees was bruised.

"Look at me," she said, "I'm such a mess! This was not a good idea, coming so far. It was too much."

She was tired, and hungry. They sat a while at the edge of the road.

"Why did I fall like that?" she asked, puzzling, her face wrinkling with self-doubt. "I feel so wrong, something's not right. It was so dumb."

Rocco lit a cigarette. He lit one for her too, but she didn't want it, so he smoked them both, and they sat there, at the edge of the road, Rocco smoking the two cigarettes and Melita studying the rip in her dress, touching it, as if by handling it with her fingers it would somehow mend.

They didn't have much farther to go, they were already all the way to Gzira. They lingered a while longer, and then, when the pain in her arm subsided, they took to their bikes again. When they reached St. Julian's, they went past the church, and the bus station, and as they turned onto the street that led to Dominic's, they found it crowded with emergency vehicles, people standing about in a restless confusion.

Dominic's had been bombed.

A portion of the front wall was down, cubes of limestone scattered across the street like children's blocks. Black smoke wafted up from deep in the wreckage. A fire brigade had gone in with extinguishers, but still the smoke came, a kitchen fire, kerosene and cooking oil in the basement, where the big stove was, smoke rolling up in dark, voluptuous coils.

The survivors stood about in a daze, waiters, busboys, kitchen help, the people who had been sitting at table, dining—all stunned, unable to believe this had happened. There had always been a sense, a dreamy illusion, that Dominic's was somehow invulnerable. In fact, Dominic had shelled out plenty to his Pozzallo contact for protection against the bombers. Rocco remembered Fingerly had mentioned something about the roof, it was painted orange, as a signal to keep the bombers away. The boat was orange for the same reason, orange with some red along the gunwale. Nevertheless, somehow, in the give and take, the arrangement had broken down, and the survivors drifted about in a slowly dissolving confusion.

The Sienese chef, Lorenzo Pazzi, stood off by himself, staring at the wrecked building, in tears. "È morto," he said. "È morto."

"Who is dead?" Melita asked, approaching him.

"Dominic. Dominic is dead."

Dominic had already been taken out and carried off in an ambulance. Two waiters had also been killed, and the bartender had been injured, as had many of the diners.

"What about the Count?" Rocco asked.

"Which Count?"

"At the piano."

"Ah, the Count. I do not know where is the Count."

"Was he in yet? Was he playing?"

Lorenzo Pazzi shook his head. He didn't know. "How can it be?" he said. "How can it happen? We were talking, in the kitchen, Dominic wanted more salt in the *kawlata*. Always we had these disagreements, more salt, less salt. He worried too much. He worried about getting the food from Sicily, would it be there, every week, when he went. He worried about the boat, the bar, the waiters. He worried about that woman he brought over, that terrible woman, Angelina Labbra. He knew it was a mistake, he had a foreboding." He glanced about, baffled. "How can it be? Why did this happen?"

People from the neighborhood were rushing into the smoking ruins and coming out with whatever they could find. It was mostly women going in, but men too, and children, boys, whole families with hammers and crowbars. They came out with splintered chairs and tables, good firewood. Some of the chairs were in perfect condition, but even these would become firewood, to cook with. They came out with doors, shelves, pieces of the oak and chestnut bar, stools, molding, windowframes, parts of the white piano, strips from the flooring in the dining room. It was a frenzy, they were rushing, working against time, hurrying to get the wood out before the army salvage crew got there, because now, with the shortage of fuel, it was army policy to go into the wrecked buildings and take out the wood.

The violinist, Anton Hyzler, had been killed. Someone found his broken violin and carried it away, good for kindling. They took the gilt frames from around the paintings, leaving the canvases. They took wainscotting, drawers, the dumbwaiters, stairs, the banisters—anything that would burn in a stove. They emerged from the wreckage grimy and coughing, but again they went back in. Rocco hadn't suspected there was so much wood in there. It was as if the wood had grown overnight and now it was being harvested.

And they came out with more than just the wood. In one of the subbasements, whole cases of whisky and table wine had survived the blast, and from the kitchen there was food, a barrel of flour, bags of beans, half a horse, a barrel of fish, and two whole sheep. Even in death Dominic was the provider, and now it was all free for the taking.

It amazed Rocco how quickly they worked, swarming, like ants on a carcass. Hunger drove them. Fear of starvation and death, the knowledge that if the next convoy failed to make it in, there was nothing ahead for them, no future. There was now a deepening suspicion, more widely felt than ever before, that the British might abandon them, they might bring in their planes and their ships and make their escape, as at Dunkirk. No one said it aloud, but Rocco could see it in their faces, the knowledge that they were alone.

It had been only one plane, a Stuka. People on the street during the attack had seen it, it seemed to know exactly where it wanted to put the bomb. It was not a bomb intended for the docks or the airfields: it had been meant, deliberately, for Dominic's, the pilot identifying the building and going right for it.

The maître d' said something about Angelina Labbra. He blamed her; she was supposed to go back to Sicily but had chosen instead to remain on Malta, with the Algerian banker.

Melita caught only part of what he was saying.

"He thinks it wasn't a German in the Stuka but an Italian," Rocco told her as they moved away. "The Germans sold the Italians some of their planes, so maybe he's right. He thinks the Italians were angry at Dominic because he brought Miss Sicily over but never brought her back."

"It was revenge? That's what he thinks?"

It was a theory. The maître d' was an old man, in a daze from the bombing. Still, it seemed plausible, because why else would the plane single out that one building?

The bomb had come through the roof and plunged through the upper floor, then down through the dining room and into the kitchen below, in the basement. Not till it reached the subbasement under the kitchen did it explode. Lorenzo Pazzi, the chef, swore that not even then did it go off, but only some moments later. He remembered being thrown to the floor when the bomb crashed through, and then, later, in the explosion, he was aware of a fierce whiteness before he lost consciousness. When he came to, he saw Dominic on the floor by the stove, dead. His legs were gone.

"I hate all this," Melita said to Rocco. There was nothing good in it, the black smoke, the wreckage. "I hate Malta," she said. "Let's go home."

Strange, he thought, that she regarded the house on Windmill Street as home, feeling it was theirs, it was where they belonged. He sometimes referred to it as home, but didn't really think of it that way. It was a place, a necessary place, where they slept, where they ate and made love. But not home. He thought it must be something in women, their ability to adapt, the capacity to appropriate any mess at all and become comfortable in it: the nest, the hearth, the lair, the burrow, the den. So easy, the way they made something good out of nothing, something right out of something wrong. The air-raid sirens sounded, but it was a false alarm, and moments later the all-clear came on.

Dominic's funeral was two days later, at the Cathedral in Valletta. He'd been in business over twenty years, serving the finest meals on Malta, and nothing less than the Cathedral would do. The *Times of Malta* printed a photograph taken when he was a young man, not half as heavy as when he died, and were it not for the caption, Rocco would never have guessed it was Dominic. The picture showed him with an odd, unfocused smile, as if he'd just discovered he was the victim of a practical joke.

The Cathedral was crowded with military officers and government people. Some of the foreigners who were still on the island came to pay their respects. The Greek herpetologist, and the Countess from Poland. And the writer from Argentina, about whom very little was known. The Algerian banker was there with Miss Sicily. They were living in the same hotel in Sliema, on Ridolfo Street, the Imperial, in separate rooms, but it was widely rumored and accepted as true that they were romantically involved.

The hearse was not motorized but horse-drawn and ornate, with a flourish of glass and carved wood. Motorized hearses were now common on Malta, but the Maltese still favored the old way of burying their dead. The horse was a black mare, with loops of purple sash around its ankles and tassels hanging down its forelegs. Three black feathers rose from the headstall, and the bridle and reins were studded with brass. Rocco, who knew nothing about horses, could see at a glance that the mare was not in the best of shape, too lean, ribs overly pronounced, eyes dull and filmy.

"All these people?" he said to Melita, expressing surprise.

She nodded, scanning the crowd.

"Dominic would have been glad to see this."

"Maybe he does see it," she said uncertainly.

Rocco tried to imagine the kind of heaven Dominic would be comfortable in. It would have to be huge and sprawling, with a kitchen full of lamb and sides of beef, a wine cellar stocked with Latour and Margaux and Haut Brion, and a chorus of sopranos, every one of them with the body and eyes of Miss Sicily, singing "Panis Angelicus."

The waiters carried the coffin, each with a black carnation in his lapel. The governor wasn't there, but his deputy was, wearing a black armband. People were saying that if the old governor were still in office, instead of the new man, he would have made a point of attending personally.

When the coffin was brought in, three priests met it at the door, blessing it with holy water and incense. The organ boomed, and a baritone sang the Lord's Prayer in Maltese:

> Missierna li inti fis-Smewwiet,
> Jitqaddes Ismek,
> Tiġi saltnatek,
> Ikun li trid Int, kif fis-sema hekda fl-art . . .

The Cathedral was the Cathedral of St. John, built by the Knights in the sixteenth century. Some of the Grand Masters were buried here, in the side chapels and in the crypt below. Whatever could be removed—paintings, candlesticks, gold reliquaries—had been taken to a bomb-proof shelter, but much was unmovable and still in place, the frescoes and carved altars, and some of the statues. Too lavish, Rocco thought. Too many saints, too many angels. He felt more comfortable in churches that were simpler, less imposing.

After the mass, as the coffin was carried out, four Italian planes, Reggianes, flew over Valletta in formation, as if offering a salute. That's what people said it was, a salute to Dominic, a way of honoring him. They killed him, and now they showed respect. Rocco thought the planes were probably just doing reconnaissance.

As they were putting the coffin in the hearse, the horse let out a long, low groan, and went down. The hearse tilted sharply, about to capsize, but the pallbearers rushed to support it, keeping it from toppling, and the undertaker's assistant acted quickly to disconnect the hearse from the fallen animal. They backed the hearse clear, and for a while everyone stood about, looking at the afflicted horse, which by now lay flat on the ground, on its side. It was dying.

The undertaker was apoplectic. He stood over the horse in mute rage, and were it not for the sacredness of the occasion, would have kicked the animal until it was dead. He was in disgrace: one of the foremost undertakers on the island, to have a horse collapse at such a moment, with the admirals and colonels and the governor's deputy all looking on.

"Somebody bring me a gun," he said.

A young lieutenant produced a service pistol. The undertaker took it, went close to the horse, and then, deftly, shot it in the head.

The report of the gun was clean, sharp, definite. It was a small sound, yet it had a quality that set it apart from the din and clamor of the war: an intimacy that the bombs and the artillery did not have. With the simple clarity of that sound, the horse was dead. Not just a horse, not any horse, but the horse that had been taking Dominic Mifsud to his grave.

The widow watched. She was not more than five or six feet away when the undertaker pulled the trigger.

"You have not done well by us," she said unpleasantly. "You have not done well by us at all."

Someone called for a Red Cross van, and after some awkward moments of waiting in which everyone stood about uneasily, the van arrived, and the coffin was transferred from the hearse. They all knew what would happen next. As soon as the mourners were decently out of sight, the horse would be carted off and the carcass would be cut up and delivered to the Victory Kitchens, to supplement that night's stew.

Twenty-nine

THE PEACOCK AND
THE PEAHEN

After the funeral service at the Cathedral, Rocco and Melita walked back to Windmill Street, and they were both thinking the same thing—wondering about the jukebox, if it might still be there, pieces of it, in what was left of Dominic's bar.

"What do you suppose?" he said, half-inclined to go back and have a look. But Melita merely shrugged. It seemed ghoulish to go back now, after the funeral and the unpleasantness with the horse.

Still, in the end, she couldn't resist, and after a few cups of coffee, they made their way to St. Julian's, but only, she said, to poke around, to see how bad it was inside. Yet they both knew it was the jukebox that was drawing them. Because it was, after all, nothing ordinary, nothing common at all. It was the Wurlitzer 850, with the peacock and the peahen emblazoned on the front panel, the entire box wonderfully aglow with peacock-toned lighting. Shipped from New York to Rome only weeks before America got into the war, then to a middleman in Naples, and on to Sicily, where Dominic picked it up on one of his long night voyages to the wharf at Pozzallo, getting it from the same black-market overlord who sold wine, cheese, and slabs of pork and veal not just to him, to take back to Malta, but to the German squadrons that were doing their best to bomb Malta into oblivion.

It seemed incredible: Dominic was dead. "He was so alive," Melita said, "so full of energy."

"Life doesn't give an inch," Rocco said.

"You die when it's your time," she said impassively, "that's what happens. When it's your time, it's over."

"But who's to say when it's your time?"

"God decides."

"When your number's up, it's up?"

"Yes. God works it out, everybody has a number."

Rocco wondered about that. He'd heard Tony Zebra say much the same thing, that it's all in your number, call it God, luck, whatever. But some of the other pilots thought if you were smart, careful, watching your tail, maybe you could improve the odds and your number would come up later rather than sooner. Every day something or someone was trying to kill you: a truck, a bullet, a bomb. But if you were shrewd enough to stay out of the way, *voilà*, you were out of the way. There was no such thing as your number.

"Are we going to quarrel about this?" she said.

"We're not quarreling, we're discussing."

"I don't want to argue about death," she said. "I don't even want to think about it."

It was midafternoon when they reached St. Julian's. The street in front of Dominic's was much as it had been two days earlier, except that some of the rubble had been moved to allow traffic to pass. Where the entrance had been there was a gaping hole, and a wooden barrier blocked the way, with a sign warning against entry.

"Is it safe?"

"We'll find out," Rocco said, moving past the barrier.

They went first to the dining room, deliberately postponing the bar, where the jukebox had been. The blast had knocked most of the plaster from the walls, leaving the laths exposed. There was a large hole in the ceiling and, directly below, a hole in the floor, where the bomb had punched through. You could look up, through the ceiling, to the floor above, to the daylight coming in through the hole in the roof, and you could look down, through the hole in the floor, into the kitchen and beyond, into the subbasement, where the bomb exploded. It had whistled right through and had done considerable damage, yet it could not have been a very big bomb, not one of the blockbusters, because anything that large would have blown the entire building away.

Still, damage was done, and the people of St. Julian's had picked the place clean. Hard to believe this was the same room where the Count had played his waltzes and Miss Sicily had charmed the colonels and captains with her "Panis Angelicus." Under a chunk of plaster Rocco saw the painting of Dragut in his tent, dying. Just the crumpled canvas, not the frame, which had been taken for firewood.

He led the way to the rear, into the Green Room, where Nigg had squandered the last weeks of his life, and it too was stripped bare, the oak mantel gone, the rug gone, the paintings from the walls. Rocco wondered if anyone, in that room, had ever bet that a bomb would hit Dominic's.

They saved the bar for last, climbing over a shifting mound of rubble to get there. The stools and cocktail tables gone, the shelves, and the bar itself, thick oak, no longer there. The jukebox too, vanished from its place against the back wall.

But when they went closer, into the shadows, they found it, what was left of it. It had been thrown by the blast and crushed when the ceiling came down, smashing it to pieces.

"It's finished," Rocco said. "Gone."

Melita went close, pushing chunks of plaster aside with her feet. She bent down, digging with her hands. "Here, look," drawing out of the rubble a panel of plastic. She blew the dust away and held the panel out to him.

A waste of time, he thought, unable to understand her optimism.

"No, no," she said insistently, "there are things here. Come, help me."

He joined her, and together they lifted away a heavy piece of plaster. Underneath were some of the records, shattered.

"See?" he said, noting the futility.

But still she persisted, and then he saw what she was after. She was digging around, finding the mechanical parts—the wires, the motor that drove the turntable, the electrical packages that controlled the lighting.

"But it's broken," he said. "Even before the bomb, it didn't work. It's junk."

"Help me," she said.

He helped, and little by little, going from one spot to another, searching the rubble, they found more. They found the cellophane and the disks of polarized film that had been used to create the kaleidoscope of changing colors. And best of all, they found the translucent front panel showing the peacock and the peahen.

"Look," she said, wiping away the powdered plaster. "Isn't it wonderful? Look how beautiful they made it, the peacock with his long tail, and the peahen so close to him."

"Are there peacocks on Malta?"

"There's everything on Malta."

"Except snow."

"Only sometimes."

They found the metal racks that held the records, though they were badly bent. They found the loudspeaker, and the coin chute, and the turntable, and some of the selector buttons.

"Zammit will use it all. You will see. He works wonders."

And then, on the way out, on the far side of the room, beyond anything they might have hoped for, they found, in one piece, the curved plastic that had framed the front of the jukebox—a languid sweep of multiveined, variegated, translucent plastic, warm-toned and, when lit from within, quietly dazzling. It was buried in plaster dust, and they would never have found it if Rocco hadn't tripped over it, going down on his knees.

"Zammit will make a wonderful thing," Melita said joyously. "You'll see! You'll see!"

Not till almost a week after the funeral did Rocco learn, from Fingerly, it was not the Italians that had bombed Dominic's but the Germans. Before Angelina Labbra came over from Sicily, she'd been involved with a Luftwaffe officer, a colonel, and he blamed Dominic for taking her to Malta and not returning her. It was Teutonic vengeance in its direst form: a bomb through the roof.

"I thought only Italian opera had stuff like this," Rocco said, when Fingerly told him about it.

"It's a complicated world, Raven. A weave of interwoven webs."

"Did he drop the bomb himself?"

"Flew the Stuka and dropped the bomb," Fingerly said. "When a full colonel does that, climbs into a plane and puts his life on the line, you know he means business. Poor Dominic." He cocked his head, looking at Rocco through half-closed lids. "You don't have relatives in Sicily, do you?"

"My people were from Verona, long ago. They're all dead."

"No relatives in Sicily? Too bad. The name Vizzini mean anything to you? Carlo Vizzini? How about Salvatore Malta? Nino Cottone?"

"I should know these folks?"

"Vito Genovese?"

"Everybody knows Vito Genovese."

"Socks Lanza?"

Rocco had heard about Socks Lanza. He was a racketeer on the waterfront, in New York. "These are your new pals? Your buddies?"

"Just research, Raven, that's all, keeping the files active. It's important to know who's who in the world."

Rocco thought it strange—Genovese, Socks Lanza—but didn't pursue it because clearly, at that point, Fingerly wanted to let it go.

Vito Genovese was the one who fell in love with Anna Vernotico, but she was a married woman, so it was arranged that her husband was thrown off a roof, and three weeks later Vito Genovese married her. They honeymooned in Naples and he showed her where he'd been born. He had been the right-hand man of Lucky Luciano, and, with Joe Adonis, Albert Anastasia, and Bugsy Siegel, shot Joe the Boss Masseria while he dined at the Villa Tammaro on West Fifteenth Street, after Lucky Luciano, who arranged the hit, excused himself from the table and went to the toilet.

"No more bombs," Melita said, as if suddenly aware there hadn't been any raids for almost a week. "Isn't it wonderful? Isn't it delicious?"

No bombs and no bombers, just the pesty Messerschmitts, like insects, nasty *nemus,* buzzing and strafing, but the big bombers were gone. The weather too was improving, the September nights dipping into the sixties, bringing relief from the musty heat that built up in the hazy afternoons.

Rocco ran his finger down her spine, slowly, the bony knobs of her vertebrae, the sensuous geography of her back. Her ribs, her shoulders, intimacy of skin and bone, the way the skin was drawn taut yet slid gently over the bone, smooth and generous. "Maybe it's over," he said. "Maybe they'll never come back."

"Oh, they'll come again," she said, as if she knew. "Why should they stop now and never come back? They've been bombing so long, almost three years, it's a compulsion, even if they wanted to stop they couldn't. They're only resting, catching their breath."

On the 14th, more 109s flew against the island, and Bernie Petro Peters, who'd been at Aida's wedding, was shot down and killed. He was up over Żonqor Point, shortly after nine in the morning, cruising around, doing some aerobatics, and was bounced by two 109s coming at him out of the sun.

The same day, the destroyer *Zulu* was bombed and sunk while in the waters off Tobruk. Aida's husband, Bobby Cripps, was listed among the dead.

Rocco spoke to Beatrice about it, meeting her on a bread line in Valletta. She was living again on Strait Street, where Hannibal still had the Oasis bar. They were in a flat above the bar, while a crew worked on the house that had been bombed, rebuilding it.

"I think she knew it was not a good marriage for her," Beatrice said. "These wartime things, they never work out, especially with the sailors—it's a rootless life, always at sea. And, you know, with the kind of life Aida's had, it wasn't meant to be. She's wearing black because now she's a widow, but she doesn't cry. She has a strong attitude. She lost her leg when she was young and that hardened her, it gave her strength, and now she doesn't cry."

Rocco thought about going to see her, but he put it off. He kept telling himself he should visit, it was something he should do, but he kept finding reasons not to go. At the wedding they had danced, she with her wooden leg and he with his bad foot, and he thought then, as he thought now, that life should have been easier on her, she'd had a hard time. There was an unfairness, an imbalance. She deserved better.

Thirty

MISS SICILY

The cigarette ration was down to one pack a week and the smokers stood in long queues for a few Flags or Woodbines that would last, at most, a day or two. When they ran out, they smoked dried fig leaves, and mixtures of lemon and strawberry leaves.

Fingerly was gone for a while, to Alexandria, and when he returned the main reason why Rocco was glad to see him was because he brought in another big supply of Luckies. It was also time for his pay, which was, as usual, overdue.

"You got these in Alexandria?" Rocco asked, opening a pack and lighting up.

"Where I got them you don't need to know."

"Jerusalem? Beirut? Cyrenaica?"

"I endured Cairo. The rest we won't talk about."

He wore a fancy new silk sportshirt made in Barcelona but haggled for and bought in some murky kasbah on the coast of North Africa. He seemed leaner, taller, tougher, his quick, shadowy eyes somehow more complicated, with more darkness in them.

"Here," he said, languidly brusque, "I brought you the Purple Heart for the toes you lost. If you were expecting the Silver Star, don't hold your breath."

Rocco had never imagined that his lost toes, shot off by Nardu Camilleri in the tussle on the roof, were worth a medal, but he was glad to have it anyway.

"What do I do with it? Wear it on my lapel?"

"Wrap it in chamois, Raven. Save it for your grandchildren, they will worship you as a god."

They were in the Mefisto Club in Valletta, which, like Hock's, served flavored water when there was no beer, and it was expensive. The club, damaged by a bomb, had a slovenly, disheveled look, strips of canvas hanging on the walls to hide the holes where the plaster had been blown away.

"How do you feel about a boatride to Sicily?"

Rocco lifted his head warily.

"Pozzallo," Fingerly said.

"This is a joke, right?"

"I'm taking Angelina Labbra back to Palermo. It's an errand of mercy."

"She wants to go home? Miss Sicily?"

"She's sick of Malta."

"What about the boyfriend, the Algerian banker? I thought they were lovebirds."

"He beats her. She's a mess, Rocco, her thighs are black and blue."

"That chubby little guy? With the gold tooth?"

"He ties her to the bed and whips her with his belt. I won't tell you what he does with the gold tooth."

"What did she ever see in him?"

The waitress, a short girl with a heavy pouch of flesh under her chin, served another round of flavored water. She was all eyes for Fingerly.

"After he beats her, he's disgustingly gentle. He feeds her sherbet with a spoon, and brings flowers. He scours the black market for prosciutto and caciocavallo. Now she's tired of it all and wants to go home."

"Back to the German colonel?"

"He'll be waiting at the dock with his aide, but otherwise alone. No infantry, that's the agreement. I have a man on shore, if there's any screwing around he'll signal and we won't go in."

"I don't like it."

Fingerly toyed with his lighter. "Look at it this way—we have Angelina Labbra in the boat with us, what could go wrong? You think the German wants her damaged?"

From across the room the waitress was still staring. "You're breaking her heart," Rocco said.

"I know, I know. Maybe I can use her at the Palazzo. You think she can cook?"

That evening, at dusk, Rocco went to the wharf in St. Julian's and found Fingerly already there, in oilskins. He tossed a pair to Rocco. "Wear them, better you look like a fisherman than a GI."

"If we get caught, we get shot?"

"If we get caught, talk Maltese. We're simpleminded fishermen who lost our way."

"I don't know Maltese."

"Neither do they. Talk gibberish, I do it all the time."

They used Dominic's boat, which was still in its slot at the wharf, bright orange with red along the gunwale, one of the few fishing boats that hadn't been shot to pieces by the marauding 109s. The cabin was a wooden shed with windows and a door, built forward, toward the bow. Behind the cabin, on one side, was a low wooden locker for storage, and on the other side, a bench. At the back end was an inflated skiff, rubberized, with an outboard engine.

Miss Sicily arrived in a horse-drawn *karrozzin*, wearing a dark dress, with a shawl over her shoulders. Fingerly greeted her warmly, and they exchanged a few words in Italian. She had a large valise with her, which Rocco put aboard, and he told her how much he'd liked her singing, that first night at Dominic's. " 'Panis Angelicus,' " he remembered.

"You were there? Yes? Thank you, *grazie*," she said softly, appreciatively, then she turned away, and it was clear she did not want to talk. She sat on the slatted bench behind the cabin, keeping very much to herself.

She was beautiful, but in an odd, unsettling way. The great swirl of her hair, the cloudy dreaminess of her brow, the magnetic north of the green of her eyes—inviting, yes, Rocco thought, but it was beauty at a distance, aloof, cold, like something in a museum, roped off and protected, a stimulus for desire but somehow, despite the radiance, not real. And he wondered if that—the weirdness, the incongruity, the unreality—might have been what drove the Algerian banker alternately to beat her and shower her with kindness, because how, when you come right down to it, how, in a world of flesh and bone, do you forget about time, forget about death, and make love to a work of art? The banker, on the other hand, was a number all his own—Rocco thought he should have his teeth yanked.

As the last of the daylight faded, Fingerly steered the boat out of the bay, heading north, into the darkness. The sea was calm and the boat, gaining speed, rocked gently. Rocco sat in the rear, on the locker, across from Miss Sicily, scanning the sky for planes. The breeze tugged at his hair, and as the sky lit up with stars, he was lulled by the rocking of the boat and the beat of the engine, and forgot, for a moment, they were sailing for Sicily, which was full of Germans.

Angelina Labbra pulled the shawl around her head, shielding herself against the breeze. She glanced at Rocco, nodding, indicating she was all right, then she turned away and seemed to make a point of not looking at him again. Her gaze was fixed on Malta, a wide, dark hump of land, unlit and slipping away, vanishing in the dark.

Rocco wanted to talk with her, wanted to hear her story from her own lips. She leaves Sicily, comes to Malta, and seems content never to go back—but now, on impulse, she changes her mind. How does that happen? Did the Algerian really beat her, or did Fingerly make that up? And what led her to come over in the first place—was she fleeing the German? Afraid of him or just tired of him? And now, having run from him, how could she go back? Rocco watched as she sat there on the bench, wrapped in silence, and she seemed not a person, not a woman, but an odd, exotic flower needing attention and care, or she would wilt. And yet, again the paradox: despite the softness, she seemed strong, resilient, even willful, blossoming only for herself, in her own garden, with a kind of defiance.

Before they were halfway across, she became violently sick and leaned over the gunwale. It went on and on, a fierce, convulsive shuddering, as if she were vomiting up all of Malta, emptying herself of the weeks and months she had sojourned there, as if she had eaten an evil apple and had been under a spell, and now she was cleansing her body of the last vestiges of the poison.

When it was over, she stayed there, leaning over the gunwale, and Rocco wondered if she might be having second thoughts about going back to the German.

There was a flight of planes, a high distant droning, but when Rocco looked, he saw nothing. The sound grew louder, and then fainter. Gone.

The boat rose and fell in the water, and Rocco became fidgety, feeling they'd been out there too long. He went into the cabin.

"Are we lost?"

"No, we're not lost."

"If we're lost, I think I should know."

The only light in the cabin was the moonglow through the window.

"Don't you think I'd tell you?" Fingerly said. "Lost, that's a big item, not something I'd keep to myself. Trust me."

"Why?"

"They made me a major, didn't they? If Uncle Sam has confidence in me, why don't you? It's a cruise, Rocco, you're on the Mediterranean. Would you rather be on your secondhand lot in Brooklyn unloading a lemon on some dumb kid doesn't even know how to shift out of neutral?"

"I never sold a lemon," Rocco said indignantly. "To anybody." And then, with the same vigor: "What if they start shooting?"

"Hey, relax, you're on a boat with a beautiful woman. Miss Sicily, for god-sake."

"But what if they do?"

"We'll shoot back."

"With what?"

"Look in the locker."

Rocco stepped out of the cabin and lifted the lid on the wooden locker. There were two Thompsons inside, and a grenade launcher. It was unnerving, because it meant Fingerly had been lying, or at least seriously bending the truth. He'd been expecting a firefight all along.

He stepped back into the cabin.

"Feel better?" Fingerly asked.

"Feel worse."

The moon cast a wide swathe of silver across the water.

"What if we're off course?"

"We're not."

"But what if?"

"Sicily is so big, even if I steered south instead of north we'd run right into it. Look for a blinking green light."

The moon went behind a cloud, and for a while there was nothing but hulking darkness before them. Above, the stars spread like a glittering net. Rocco saw the two bears, the big and the small, and Orion rising off the horizon.

Then, out of the darkness, a denser darkness rose, like some mythic impenetrability, as if the night itself had coagulated and hardened into a solid mass.

"Sicily," Fingerly said. "Dead ahead."

It was Sicily without lights, in blackout, like Malta, but bigger, vaster, gargantuan. It seemed not an island but a continent.

He cut the engine to quarter speed and turned to port, running parallel to the coast, looking for the light. They went more than a mile before they saw it, a small green glow, blinking. When they turned into it, it seemed to grow brighter and more intense.

"Bring the guns in here," Fingerly said. "But when we pull in, keep them out of sight."

Angelina Labbra was on the bench, her compact open, applying lipstick, studying herself in the starchy moonlight. When Rocco opened the locker and took out the guns, she snapped the compact shut. "There were to be no guns," she said sharply.

"I hope you're right," Rocco said.

Fingerly nudged the boat slowly toward shore, and as they pulled in, the German stood forward on the wharf, his aide at a distance behind him. In the moonlight, he cut a striking figure in his Luftwaffe uniform, with the shiny black boots and the black belt holding the black holster. A tall, straight body, a relaxed arrogance in his stance. He held a bouquet of roses. If he looks that good, Rocco thought, he maybe deserves her. Miss Sicily, all to himself. But what must he feel, knowing what he knows about the Algerian banker?

Fingerly left the engine running. "Stay in here," he told Rocco, and, leaving the cabin, tossed a line to the aide. The colonel was already giving Miss Sicily a hand, helping her off the boat. Fingerly passed the suitcase up to the aide, then he stepped onto the wharf and exchanged a few words with the colonel. They shook hands, and then, suavely, Fingerly kissed Miss Sicily's hand. Quickly, he untied and was back on the boat, into the cabin, engaging the gears and moving out.

Rocco looked back and saw the German and Miss Sicily just standing there, facing each other. They didn't seem to be talking. The German still had the roses in his left hand, down at his side. Then they turned and walked back along the wharf, into the darkness. The green light had stopped blinking.

As the boat moved off, Rocco felt a sense of relief, an unburdening. The German was just another lonely man who wanted a woman, and what remained, now, was to cross the sixty miles of open sea back to Malta.

"So he gets Miss Sicily, and what do you get?"

"Me? Not me, Raven. I-3. What does I-3 get? I-3 gets safe passage tomorrow for the *Welshman*, all the way back to Alexandria."

The *Welshman* had pulled into Grand Harbour that morning, and the stevedores were still unloading, working through the night. Aviation fuel and powdered milk.

"He gave you that? He made this deal with you?"

"We negotiated."

"Miss Sicily is worth that much to him?"

"They won't touch the *Welshman*. Not tomorrow," Fingerly said, and again Rocco realized he had underestimated him. Fingerly's reach was wide, arranging and disarranging. If Miss Sicily was an exotic blossom in an unweeded garden, Fingerly was a tricky vine, snaking off in all directions, twisting through gates and fences, and you never noticed.

"But why the *Welshman*?" Rocco asked, wondering what the angle was. "I-3 has an interest in freighters?"

"I-3 has an interest in everything," Fingerly said, breezily evasive. He lit a cigarette, and in the light of the match Rocco saw his face tense and concentrated, and knew, looking at him, this would be the harder part of the trip, because without Miss Sicily aboard, they were vulnerable.

Some ten or fifteen minutes out, Fingerly slowed to quarter speed and rigged the wheel so the boat would keep moving ahead in a straight line. "Time to scram," he said, and with Rocco's help he got the rubberized skiff over the side and into the water, securing it with a line.

"Jump in and get the outboard started."

Rocco went, and Fingerly tossed the guns down, and two cans of petrol. Then he turned a light on in the cabin, making the boat brightly visible, a beacon on the water. He joined Rocco in the skiff, cut the line, and took over at the outboard, steering for Malta, and the fishing boat sailed off on its own, its wheel locked on a course that would take it east of Malta and out to sea.

"You think he'll double-cross us?"

"Not a chance," Fingerly said, seeming more himself now that they were off the boat. "But better safe than sorry."

It was a rough, lumpy ride, plenty of wind and spray. Far off, the light from the cabin of the fishing boat was a yellow blur on the water. Fingerly wore a compass on his wrist and kept checking it with a pencil flashlight. They zipped along, bouncing over the swells, and Rocco, holding fast to the grips, was thinking again about time, how it was rough, fast, relentless, it could punch you around and leave you black and blue. And he was thinking how small Malta was, how easy to miss. They could go right past it, halfway across to Tripoli, and run out of gas.

The light from the fishing boat was still faintly visible when another light hove into view, from the opposite direction, an Italian gunboat.

Fingerly cut the engine and they flattened themselves against the wet bottom. A searchbeam played across the water.

The boat moved slowly, coming close. Rocco heard the sailors talking. "Niente, niente," one was saying.

The searchbeam swung slowly. For an instant it fastened on the skiff, and Rocco tensed, ready to leap away if they opened fire. His face pressed hard against the wet, rubberized fabric, its coarse blackness rough against his cheek. Unbailed water lapped at his mouth and nose, and this too was time, the smell and taste of it, rubber and salt, the searchbeam on them like an evil paste, glued to them for a long, teasing moment, and the waiting, the waiting.

Then, with a lazy reluctance, the beam swung away. "Niente," the same voice said. The engine picked up and the boat moved on, and Fingerly waited, wanting them to be well gone before he restarted the outboard.

The gunboat headed north, toward Pozzallo, but then, picking up the receding light on the fishing boat, changed course and, switching into high speed, took up the pursuit.

They started firing long before they ever got near, the clunky chatter of the heavy-caliber gun rattling laboriously above the whine of the gunboat's high-speed engine. The firing went on for quite a while, to no effect. Then a few shells slammed home and tore things apart. The light in the cabin went out, and moments later the fuel tank went and the boat blew to pieces, pink and green spurts flaring across the water. It seemed a flower made of flame, floating, petals of fire curling voluptuously, a blazing lotus.

"He double-crossed us," Rocco said, thinking of the German.

"Maybe yes, maybe no," Fingerly answered, not ready yet to write the German off. "These Italians, some of them are cowboys, itchy fingers on the trigger." He tried to get the outboard going, but it wouldn't start. He yanked the cord several times, but nothing.

"It's flooded," Rocco said.

"You're an expert? You know boats?"

"Engines, I know engines. Give it a rest."

They waited, the swells rocking the skiff, up and down. Rocco bailed some water with his hands. Then he stopped bailing and looked at Fingerly through the dark, staring intently. "Tell me," he said, "is Major Webb really dead?"

"Why ask a foolish thing like that?"

"It crosses my mind sometimes. I get this funny feeling."

"He bothers you? He haunts?"

"Haunt is too strong a word."

"He was a good man, you would have enjoyed working with him. Smart, neat as a pin. A bony nose, bony forehead, a square bony jaw. A cragged face as rugged as bad weather in Vermont. That's where he was from, you know, the Green Mountains of Vermont. Let the good man rest."

If he was dead, yes, let him go, drift off. But if he wasn't, then Fingerly wasn't Fingerly, he was somebody else, a fiction, a fabricated self, and here they were at sea, the middle of the Mediterranean, and the old paranoia was back, twisting around in the dark. What if, and what if?

"And you," Rocco said, guessing, "—from Texas, right?"

"I never said that."

"Didn't you? I thought you did."

"Anyway," Fingerly said, "nice girl you've got there. Melita. She sings for you? Knows all the songs?"

"She knows the songs," Rocco said, aware that Fingerly had changed the subject, and still he was wondering. *What if?*

Fingerly lit a cigarette.

"Is she mellow? Smooth and easy on the draw? A rich blend of fine tobaccos?"

Rocco was bailing again. "I think we're sinking," he said. "Give that engine another try."

Fingerly yanked, and this time, first pull, the outboard snorted to life.

They moved along quickly, slapping hard against the choppy water, Rocco holding fast again, the spray washing over him. Two or three miles like that, bouncing, wet, the buzz of the engine carving through his brain like a chain saw, and Rocco, his paranoia in abeyance, concluded that Major Webb was really dead, had to be, and for better or worse, Fingerly was only Fingerly after all.

As they approached Malta, it was still night, the eastern sky touched by the barest glimmer of morning. While they were yet a goodly distance off, a jittery shore battery opened up on them, dumping shells far and near.

"Into the water," Fingerly shouted.

He left the outboard running and sent the rubber boat westward, toward Qrejten Point, and they swam hard in the opposite direction. Searchlights swept the water, and when the beams picked up the skiff, the shore battery fired a few more salvos, blowing it to tatters.

They had a long swim, and Rocco was quickly winded. A few times he stopped and paddled around, catching his breath. Fingerly was up ahead, swimming vigorously, and Rocco struggled to keep up. Then, for Fingerly, something went wrong. Rocco saw him splashing around wildly, and moments later, one arm raised, he went under. Rocco hurried on, and when he reached the spot, Fingerly surfaced, choking and spouting water.

"Cramp," he said. "Can't move my goddamn leg."

He went down again, and Rocco, taking a good gulp of air, went down after him, but when he hooked an arm onto Fingerly and tried to pull him up, Fingerly put a stranglehold on him and together they sank, Rocco feeling his chest would burst for lack of air.

They moved downward in the black water, Fingerly clinging firmly and Rocco struggling to break free, the two of them locked together, turning and wheeling in the struggle. Then Rocco got his hand under Fingerly's chin, pushing his head far back, and managed to break loose, moving quickly back up and crashing through the surface.

Fingerly didn't come up.

Rocco was coughing, spitting salt water, thinking Fingerly was going to die down there, but as he took a deep breath, preparing to go down again, Fingerly broke through, gasping, sucking for air. He was about ten feet off, and Rocco kept his distance, watching warily.

Slowly, Fingerly got his breathing back. He coughed and wheezed, but his arms were in motion and he was afloat.

"I'm all right," he said.

"You sure? How's the leg?"

"Just a lousy cramp."

"You can make it?"

"I think so. Yeah."

They were swimming again, slow exhausted strokes, Rocco trailing slightly behind. There wasn't much farther to go.

They came ashore near the Madliena Tower, and as they washed in they were cut up by the rocks. Fingerly gashed his left arm, and Rocco got his shins badly scraped. It was the early hours of the morning, the sky beginning to brighten, and nowhere to get a cup of coffee, nothing to do but get on the road and hike to Valletta. In the long swim, they had shed their shoes, and made their way, now, in stocking feet.

After some ten or fifteen minutes, they met a jeep that picked them up and took them along to Valletta. From the City Gate, they hurried over to the Barracca Gardens for a look at the harbor, to check on the *Welshman*.

It had already sailed. They could see it in the distance, smoke from its stack coiling black in the sky. Fingerly, confident, gave a thumbs-up sign. "You know who's aboard, don't you?"

"Not King George," Rocco said.

"The Count, Rocco. Your old pal, Count von Kreisen."

It took Rocco by surprise.

"He finally screwed up his courage and sailed. Things have been so quiet this month, he figured it was worth the risk."

"Julietta?"

"Of course. She too. They're inseparable. You used to have an eye for her, didn't you."

Rocco gazed at the ship, watching as it faded into the mist. It stung, to think they were gone. He was glad for them, glad they'd finally escaped Malta, but still, it smarted, because he'd liked them and now they were gone, and no good-bye. He hadn't seen them since Dominic's funeral, and it was unlikely he'd ever see either of them again. That was how it was on Malta. You met people and got to know them fast, and then, just as quickly, they were out of your life forever.

"It was arranged in a hurry," Fingerly said, "they didn't know for sure they were going till the ship came in yesterday. The Count took my Malta collection with him. He bought all of it, the Venus of Malta, Dragut's dagger, the armor, the paintings, the Roman tablets. I got to be fond of the old guy, he had a quaint sense of humor. Said if I ever find the real Maltese Falcon, he'll buy that too, even if it's fake."

"You really think the Luftwaffe won't go after it?"

"They're home free, Rocco. All the way to Alexandria."

Thirty-one

BEAN CODE, BEAN CODE

The *Welshman* did make it into Alexandria, but almost not. It had to dodge torpedoes from a submarine, shells from a destroyer, and heavy-caliber fire from two gunboats. But no planes attacked it, so the German colonel may in fact have kept his word—though Rocco had his doubts.

"It stinks," he said to Melita, cracking his knuckles. They were in the kitchen, on Windmill Street, sharing a peach. "Doesn't it stink? Life stinks. Fingerly stinks."

"That's what I've been telling you all along about your Fingerly," she said. "He's no good. You should have let him drown. Where is he now?"

"Cairo, I think, but maybe Sicily—I think he has friends there."

"A bomb should fall on him."

Rocco smiled. "He's too smart for that."

"He's not so smart."

"He reads Egyptian hieroglyphics."

"That makes him smart? There was a man in Valletta could read fourteen languages, but his wife was cheating, and when he found out, he took a rope and hanged himself. Was that smart?"

"Fingerly doesn't have a wife."

"I know, I know. He doesn't like women. He pretends, but he's really not interested."

Rocco was surprised. "Fingerly? That's what you think?"

"That's what I think."

"You should hear him talk about the whores in St. Julian's."

"That's what I mean, he's all talk. His sexuality, it's all in his mind. Or it's somewhere else, but not with women."

Rocco thought she was wrong.

"So then I'm wrong," she said, reaching for the cat.

"Do you like being wrong?"

"I love being wrong. But about Fingerly, I'm right."

Later that afternoon, she visited Christina at her place in Floriana, and found her horribly upset. Warby had gone off on a reconnaissance flight and was overdue. He was flying across North Africa, taking more pictures of the Via Balbia. It had happened before—he would fly off and disappear, and not be heard from till a day or two later. Once, he was shot down, and a few times he'd had mechanical problems and had to put down in the desert, but one way or another he'd always managed to get home all right. This time it was four days, and no word, no word at all.

Melita tried to comfort her, telling her not to worry. "He always comes back, doesn't he?"

"But four days."

"I know, I know, it's long."

"Too long."

"But he'll be all right."

"No, he won't. Don't you see?"

"I do see. He'll be fine, I know it."

The next day, the late October rains began to fall. Stubborn, drenching rain, all day, a downpour. The following day too. Sweet-smelling rain, whole sheets of it, forming rivulets and swift streams that gushed through the streets, rushing downhill into the sea. The blistering heat of summer was gone.

The third day of rain, Rocco and Melita went walking, and were soon soaked. They went to the square in front of the Cathedral, and the rain poured down, splashing wildly.

"What if I melted?" she said. "What if the rain took me and washed me away? What then?"

"Yes—what then?"

"Then you wouldn't have me!"

"Would that be good or bad?"

"You might be better off." She laughed. Her head was tilted back, eyes closed, face to the sky, the rain spilling over her, wet clothes clinging to her body.

The good news that day was that Christina's Warby was all right. He wasn't dead, hadn't been shot down, hadn't vanished into the sea. He was in Gibraltar. He'd had engine trouble and had put down in the desert, in North Africa, and when the British found him they arrested him, thinking he was a spy. He carried a German Luger (he never flew without it), an Italian hunting knife, and the clothes he was wearing bore no resemblance to anything that was regulation RAF. They sent him all the way to Gibraltar as a prisoner, before it was confirmed he was really British, as he said he was.

"Crazy Warby," Melita said, in the rain.

"Lucky Christina," Rocco said.

"Maybe not so lucky," Melita said. Warby had a wife in England, it was a bad marriage, and his main reason for volunteering for Malta was to get away from the mess back there. And there were signs now, already, that his thing with Christina was also falling apart, though she was still mad about him.

"So—not lucky," Rocco said. "But the rain is lucky. No?"

"Yes, the rain is very lucky," as it pelted her face. "But I want so much for her to be happy. She deserves good luck. And Zammit too. And everyone. And you."

"And you," he said.

"Happy rain," she said.

The rain soaked the parched, chalky soil and brought back a feathery greenness, small bursts of flowers, a second spring that lasted for a while, temperatures running in the seventies.

Melita went off to Santa Venera, and Rocco, wandering, went to a parapet overlooking the harbor. In his wallet he found the picture of Theresa Flum. He'd forgotten it. It was bittersweet, the memory swimming back to him, that day at Coney Island. They took the picture in a photo booth in a penny arcade. Bittersweet, and gone, he didn't need it any more, it was over. Time to let it go. He tore the picture, slowly, and watched the small pieces fluttering off, down to the water.

A few days after the rain, the farmer, at Maqluba, was out working on his terraced plot. Where there had been tomatoes during the summer, he now had rows of beans, the plants spreading out on a network of strings that were mounted on sticks. When he saw Rocco, he lifted his hat, and Rocco waved. Rocco wanted to ask if he ever planted strawberries, but the farmer spoke no English and Rocco had only the vaguest Maltese.

In the shed, Rocco switched on the wireless and the tubes glowed, warming up. As he turned the dials, he picked up some jazz, and then a lot of Morse Code. The dots and dashes were rattling away, grinding out messages, some of it in low-level jargon code:

> THE SHOE BELONGS TO THE FOOT
>
> THE HAND DOES NOT KNOW THE APPLE
>
> CAESAR NEEDS A BATH
>
> THE WIND BOTHERS THE LEAVES

It was camouflage, smokescreen, masquerade, the codes racing on, each with its own resonance, snarling and winking, like life itself: codes nested inside other codes, an infinite regress. And the only code Rocco could read was simpleminded Morse, the dots and dashes. Chica boom, he thought. Babalu.

He was tired and went back to a frequency that was transmitting jazz. It was fragmented by static. He leaned on the table, resting his head on his forearm, and almost dozed off, or maybe did, a dreamy limbo between waking and sleeping, and what he knew was that Fingerly was right: everything was a code. Fingerly was the Fingerly Code, as ENIGMA was the ENIGMA Code, and time was the Time Code. Life was the Life Code, and Tony Zebra was the Zebra Code, but to be the Zebra Code was bad news, because Tony Zebra was never going to escape from Malta and would never fulfill his dream of seeing India.

He was up, by the door, calling to the farmer in his beans. "Hey you, old man, are you a code, too? What kind of a code are you? A bean code?" Beans, magic beans, Jack in the beanstalk, the beantree rising to the castle in the sky, up and up, the golden goose. The farmer didn't understand a word he said, merely lifted his arms and shrugged, helpless.

But Rocco wasn't at the door calling to the farmer, *bean code, bean code,* it was a dream, and now it was gone, and as he sat there by the radio, eyes closed, head resting on his forearm, he heard a plane, far off, the lulling hum of the engine. It hung lazily, a sound like the buzzing of a fly. Then, suddenly, it was louder, and much closer, and he was yanked from his drowsiness. It was a 109. He didn't have to look, he knew the sound, the tone of the Daimler Benz engine, like a low, sad, flatted note from somebody humming the blues.

He was quickly up and outside, and there it was, a 109 with a yellow nose, circling above the farm. The radio mast had caught its attention. The pilot was inspecting the storage shed, trying to decide if it was a military installation or just a dummy target not worth his ammunition.

It was low, very close, and there was a terrifying intimacy: himself, the plane, and the farmer. The whole nose section, in front of the cockpit, was yellow. The rudder was yellow too. On the fuselage, just behind the cockpit, was a large white number: 711.

As the plane turned, Rocco saw the pilot, head covered by the leather helmet, the face long and narrow, a large nose protruding over wide, thin lips. He would remember the face if he saw it again. Keeping his eye on the plane, he moved cautiously away from the shed, toward the sinkhole, not running but moving steadily. On the terraced hill, the farmer stood among his beans, watching as the plane swept back and forth.

The plane angled off, then it turned and, in a rush, it swept back, guns blazing. Rocco raced for the sinkhole, hunkering down at the edge, and when he looked back he saw the shed exploding, blown to pieces by cannon shells, all the kerosene stored there going up in a rage of flame. The plane circled, inspecting the damage, then it was gone, and the farm was quiet again, a dense silence, only the flames of the burning kerosene and the sifting column of smoke.

Rocco looked for the farmer, and found him among the bean plants on the terraced slope, on the ground, in the thick foliage. He was on his back, and dead. Rocco checked for a wound but couldn't find one, no blood, no visible mark, and suspected a stroke or a heart attack. He looked toward the stone shed, the small flames still burning there, then he leaned down and picked the farmer up, one arm under the old man's knees, the other under his shoulders, and carried him to the house.

Rocco brought him into the bedroom and put him on the bed. The farmer lived alone, no sign of anyone else in the house. He straightened the old man's limbs, putting his arms down at his sides, and removed a spray of vine that had caught onto his shirt. With a corner of the bedspread, he wiped away a smear of dirt on the old man's forehead, then he went out of the house and made his way to Żurrieq. He stopped at the police station, and, after reporting the incident, he hitched a ride to Valletta.

Thirty-two

PINPOINTS OF LIGHT DANCING ALL AROUND HIM

At Hock's, he found Tony Zebra at a back table having a beer, good Munich Löwenbräu, black-market stuff flown in on a bomber from North Africa. It had been captured from the Germans, who captured it from the British, who had purchased huge quantities of it in neutral Lisbon from an agent who'd had it shipped from Bremen, and now it was in British hands again, and somebody with the right connections had slipped some into Malta. Hock grabbed a dozen cases, richer than gold and dreamier, stubby brown bottles with a blue label, and Tony Zebra was soaking up his share.

The table was set against a stucco wall, a cloud of flies buzzing about. One settled on the back of Tony Zebra's hand, and another on his nose. He didn't brush them away. Rocco told him about the dead farmer in the farmhouse back at Maqluba, and the 109.

Tony Zebra lifted his glass. "To the dead farmer."

They drank to the dead farmer, and to all the dead pilots—Harry Kelly, and Moye, and Petro Peters, and all the others.

"Good men," Tony Zebra said.

"Good men."

"The best. Better than the best."

"I want to fly," Rocco said.

"It's a lousy, thankless business."

"So I hear. I don't want to do it for a living."

"Then you don't want to fly."

"But I do."

"No you don't."

"How about right now?"

"Yeah? Tell me about it."

"We'll go to Takali and you can put me in a Spitfire."

It was a joke, a fantasy. Tony Zebra laughed, lifting his glass to toast the idea. "Maybe, while you're up, you'll bash a few 109s."

"You never know," Rocco said.

"You can't fly," Zebra said.

"I flew, I flew. Didn't I tell you? The summer before I joined up, at a field in the Catskills."

Zebra's face spread in a rubbery smile. "Hey, Rocco, a Piper Cub is not a Spitfire."

"Who said a Piper Cub? I checked out on a Grumman Wildcat."

"You're pulling my leg."

"Right, I'm pulling your leg."

"You know about magnetos and superchargers and fuel mix? Flaps and rudder? You know about oil pressure and propeller pitch?"

"Sure," Rocco said, with no great show of confidence.

"You know about air-screw revolutions? Radiator shutters? Glycol temp?"

Rocco looked him straight in the eye. "Would I risk my neck just for the hell of it?"

Tony Zebra didn't blink. "I think you would. Yes. For the hell of it."

"To each his own," Rocco said.

"Are you shit-faced?"

"No. But you are."

"He wants to fly," Tony Zebra said, talking to the picture of King George on the wall.

"You think he cares?" Rocco said.

"What about Melita? Where is she on this?"

"She's fixing a jukebox in Paola."

Tony Zebra tossed off the rest of his beer, and gave Rocco a long, complicitous stare. "This is lunatic, you know."

"Let's go to Takali," Rocco said.

"You think so?"

"Why not?"

The flies were thick, busy with Tony Zebra's hair, into his ears. "Let's shuck these black pests," he said, and, unsteadily, he was up, on his feet, heading for the door, slightly looped and ready for anything.

They hitched a ride on the back of a supply truck that would be passing through Takali on its way out to a gun position on the Wardija Ridge. It was loaded with ammunition for the Bofors guns.

"I think you must be pretty drunk," Tony Zebra said.

"I had two beers. How many did you put down?"

Tony Zebra extended a hand, steady as a rock. "You should have seen me when I trashed that Savoia Marchetti last week. It's the best way to fly, relaxed and cool."

Rocco knew there were two kinds of pilots, the ones who drank and the ones who didn't. Tony Zebra drank, and it amazed everyone that he was still alive.

At Takali, the planes were parked in protective pens a considerable distance from the runway. In the dispersal hut, a few of the pilots were playing poker. Zulu Swales, now a major, was poring over a flight schedule. Tony Zebra kibitzed with the poker players, then he brought Rocco up the line a bit, to a supply hut, where they picked up Mae Wests and leather flying helmets.

They walked a long distance, out among the airplane pens.

"I've got just the thing for you," Tony Zebra said. "You're going to like this, it's your lucky day."

Rocco had the feeling that if they kept on walking, they would march themselves right off the end of the island, into the sea.

"Over there," Tony Zebra said, pointing to a pen made of limestone blocks and sandbags.

What Rocco saw, in the pen, was not a Spitfire but an old biplane that looked as if it might have flown in World War I. It was, in fact, of more recent vintage, but definitely obsolete.

Tony Zebra smiled. "The last of the Gloster Gladiators."

It was bruised and dented, and Rocco liked it. He had a thing about biplanes. They had a charm that no single-wing airplane could ever have. Biplanes inspired in him the same feelings that he had when he looked at a Model T, or a Cord, or a Duesenberg.

"Before the Hurricanes and Spits, this was all they had on the island, a few of these. They sent them up three at a time to fight the Italians. It was a morale boost for the villagers. They saw the Gladiators up there and called them *Faith, Hope,* and *Charity.* This is the last one still flying."

It wasn't the first time Rocco heard the story, though he couldn't remember when, or where. Maybe in one of the shelters. The famous Gloster Gladiators.

The number on the side of this one was N5520. Up front, by the nose, in a clumsily painted script, was the name: FAITH. It was going to be easier, yes, than a Spitfire. What had he been thinking anyway? A Spitfire?

"It flies?"

"They use it for met flights, checking the weather. It does two-fifty and has a good rate of climb. You can go six miles up, if you don't forget your oxygen. Never flew it myself, but they say it handles like a sexy broad."

A mechanic, a Maltese sergeant, came by.

"This ready to go, Joe?"

"Full tank of fuel, sure. But Captain Oslo is taking it back to Hal Far at 1500. You spoke to him?"

"Change in plans, Joe. Officer Raven, here, will be taking it up, but we'll be back before 1500, if the Captain should ask. You get that hole fixed on the last Spit I flew?"

"On BR528? The boys are still working on that."

"What about this one right here?" Tony asked, pointing to a Spitfire in a nearby pen.

"That? Major Swales flew it this morning. It's set to go, all checked out."

They wheeled the Spitfire out, pushing it by the wings, then the Gladiator, and Tony Zebra helped Rocco into the cockpit. The parachute was in place, on the seat, and Tony got him harnessed in. "You sure you want to do this?"

Rocco adjusted the straps. "Why not?"

"If you spot a Messerschmitt, run like hell."

"Are the guns loaded?"

Tony Zebra called to the mechanic. "Joe? The guns?"

The guns were ready, two Browning machine guns mounted in the fuselage, and two more under the lower wings. No cannon.

Tony Zebra pointed out the altimeter, the air-speed gauge, the oil, the flaps, the throttle. The dials and handles. How to move the stick. He didn't seem so drunk any more.

"If Fighter Control talks to you, don't answer, don't give your name. Use my name all you want, I'm hoping this will be my ticket out of here."

They were both thinking of Leo Nomis, of the 229th, who took off without permission for a strafing raid over Sicily, and was grounded, back in August. He was an American. They wrote him up for unauthorized consumption of fuel, and as a punishment, transferred him to the Middle East. But it was a joke, because a transfer out of the hell of Malta to anywhere else in the world could only be a move up.

"You want to join Leo Nomis in Egypt?"

"Why not," Tony Zebra said. "It's desert, but at least they eat. They have food, Rocco. Lamb chops, sirloin, potato chips. Sure beats Maconochie's."

"I hate the desert."

"You they won't touch. You don't belong to them. They'll just put you in handcuffs and ship you back to your unit. Or they'll shoot you as a spy. Nothing to worry about."

He showed Rocco how to jettison the canopy and bail out, if it should come to that.

"I never bailed. What do I pull?"

"You pull hard on your dick. This is crazy, you know? Don't try a nosedive, and don't try an outside loop, and when you land, remember to keep the freaking nose up. Maybe they won't shoot you, they'll shoot me."

"They can't shoot either of us."

"You don't think so?"

"We're Americans. It would mean the end of Lend Lease, no more easy American aid."

"The United States Congress would go to bat for us? I like it, I like it. I'll taxi out first. You sure you flew before?"

"Plenty of times."

"Solo?"

"Right, solo. What's this thing?"

"Hell, that fires the guns."

"What about this?"

"That starts your engine." He jumped off the wing and went over to the Spitfire, and in short order, after getting their engines turning over, they taxied out in the direction of the runway. Rocco liked it, the roar of the propeller and the vibrations in the frame. It was like driving a car, but bumpier, and noisier.

When they reached the strip, Tony Zebra gunned his engine and was quickly away, racing down the field and lifting, swiftly up. Then Rocco moved into position and set himself to go. There was chatter from the control tower, which he ignored. He gave it full throttle, and the plane shot down the field, veering sharply to the left. He overcorrected, swinging too far to the right, but straightened it out and got off the ground, lifting away just in time to clear a cluster of stone huts. The chatter from the tower continued, barely controlled hysteria. He was up, climbing, looking around for Tony Zebra, and turned in a wide arc, leveling off. When he looked back, he saw the field drawing away from him.

Then he heard Tony Zebra on the R/T. "Talk to me, Rocco. Do you hear me?"

"Where the hell are you?"

"Behind and above. Keep it steady and I'll follow along."

Rocco looked down and the whole of Malta lay below him, the small, irregularly shaped fields fenced off by stone walls, and the honey-colored stone houses huddled together in the villages, with their narrow, winding streets. It was like April, when he first came in, the small fields green with crops, the island living again, not dry and bare as in the long hot summer. The sea was darkly blue, but in the shallows, where the water hugged the shore, it was fiercely green.

"You got the feel of it yet?"

"I think so. Sort of."

Tony Zebra talked him through some turns, left and right. "More rudder," he said. "More rudder."

They went up, then down, then up again.

"Feeling better?"

"It drives like a Cadillac."

"Hell, it's got a Bristol Mercury engine in it, over eight hundred horses. You up to trying an inside loop?"

"Why not."

"Pull your stick back."

Rocco did, and up he went.

"Keep it back, keep it back. That's right."

In a moment, he was at the top of the loop, hanging upside down, the world above him, on top of his head. Blood rushed to his brain, and then, as he slid down the far side of the loop and pulled out level, he felt lightheaded, strange.

"How was that?" he said over the R/T.

"Sloppy. Let's gain some angels."

Tony Zebra was in front now and led Rocco on a great soaring arc, off to the left, low over the water, then up, up, climbing. They flew into a cloud, a tall fluffy thing shaped like a tower—a great white density, and Rocco was in it.

Then, still climbing, he broke upward out of the cloud and flew into a burst of color, a shattered rainbow of refracted light washing across the wings and fuselage, streams of red, green, blue. The engine still ran but the sound was gone, the propeller spinning silently, pulling him aloft, ever higher, into the spectral maze, the plane alive with pinpoints of color dancing all around him. I'm dead, he thought, thinking he'd crashed, and this was how it was after you went down. Up ahead, he saw a face, and only after a moment did he realize it was Melita. He wondered if she was dead too.

The plane soared soundlessly, and he thought how wonderful death was, to have a body that flew, a body clear as glass, flashing with sparks of color, and no sound. There was no sound to death at all.

Then he heard Tony Zebra shouting on the R/T. "Level off, Rocco. You hear? Level off. You got your oxygen on? Switch on your oxygen."

The oxygen, yes. With his left hand he fumbled about and found the lever. But it was on. He was getting oxygen.

"Where are you, Tony?"

"Behind you. Level off, before you stall."

"Do you see those lights?"

"What lights?"

"The blinking beacons."

He leveled off and, looking about, noticed that the colored lights were fading. And then, looking forward, as his vision cleared, what he saw in front of him was a whole squadron of Ju-88s, coming head-on.

"Holy shit."

"Keep it steady, keep it steady," Tony Zebra said, intensely earnest, sounding like a stone-sober low-talent actor in a low-budget black-and-white B movie.

In a moment, they were into the 88s, bombers all around them, above and below, and still more ahead. Rocco looked left, into the cockpit of a passing bomber, the pilot staring right back at him, incredibly close, his oxygen mask making him look weirdly alien. At the speed they were at, they could not have been opposite each other for more than an instant, yet the moment seemed drawn out, elastic, wingtips almost touching, barely a few feet apart.

When Rocco looked forward again, he was heading straight into an oncoming bomber. He jerked the stick hard, pulling up, and the bomber passed a few feet below him. Then, climbing, he had to level off sharply to avoid a bomber directly above. The Gladiator wobbled violently, left and right.

"Steady, steady," Tony Zebra again, flat and firm.

And then—that quick—the bombers were gone, behind them. It was over, they had passed through.

"Probably just been unloading on a convoy," Tony Zebra said, sounding more like himself. "They're low on fuel and rushing home to Sicily. Out of ammo too, or those tailgunners would have tattooed us as we came through."

Rocco glanced back, and the bombers vanished in the direction of a wide strip of land stretching darkly across the sea. Clusters of mountains loomed under a few white patches of cumulus. One of the mountains, to the east, was a great swollen thing, twice as tall as any of the others, a plume of steam rising from the peak.

"That's Etna out there, isn't it?"

"That's Etna."

"If that's Etna, then it must be Sicily."

"You get smarter every day."

Rocco executed a 180-degree turn and headed for Sicily.

"Don't even think of it," Tony Zebra said.

But Rocco kept on course.

"Rocco? Rocco? You hearing me? You don't want to go to Sicily. You don't want to do this."

Rocco didn't respond.

Tony Zebra turned and flew along behind him.

"You can't take that crate into combat. You hear? What are you trying to prove?"

From Rocco there was nothing but silence, the slow power of the Gladiator's engine drawing him inexorably along.

"You'll get yourself killed. Don't you know that? You'll get both of us killed."

"Go home," Rocco said.

"Hell, turn that crate around. Come on, now."

"I don't want you along," Rocco said. "Go back."

"You think Melita wants this?"

"We didn't discuss it."

"You can't bring that dead farmer back to life, you know."

"I know that."

"So why are you being so dumb? Don't you know there's no such thing as evening the score? All you can do is end up dead."

Rocco flew on in silence, and for a while it was silence talking to silence, Tony Zebra's silence speaking to Rocco's silence, and Rocco's silence not answering.

"All right, all right," Tony Zebra said, acquiescing. "What the hell. Let's gain some angels, we don't want the 109s diving down on us. By now they already know we're coming."

He pulled in front of Rocco and led the way, climbing.

"And when we get there, it's quick in and out. *Capisce?* No hanging around. If we're not away fast, they'll have twenty 109s chasing us."

They crossed the coast near Pozzallo, flew over Ragusa, and then, straight ahead, lay the airfield at Comiso.

A puff of flak burst beneath the Gladiator and it rocked, side to side. Flak erupted ahead of them, and all around them. Tony Zebra led the way down, diving on the airfield for a strafing run, and as Rocco maneuvered to begin his own dive, he lost sight of the Spitfire and he was on his own.

What he saw first, as he raced down, were the shadows. Then, closer, he saw the planes on the ground, casting the shadows, and could even see the markings, black crosses on their wings and swastikas on the rudders. He was upon them very fast, seven of them sitting in a row, each with a yellow nose, on the grass, at a distance from the tarmac. One of them moved away, heading for the tarmac, taking off.

Descending, Rocco kept his eye on the remaining six, lined up like loaves of bread. As he swept in, coming in low, he opened fire, using the two guns under his wings.

A matter of seconds, that's all it was. When he looked back, he saw that nothing had changed, the six planes sitting where they were, nothing broken, nothing burning. He wondered if his rounds had even touched them.

Small tracer fire came at him from a gun emplacement at the edge of the field. It seemed harmless and irrelevant. He knew it was aimed at him, yet somehow he felt insulated, safe. It couldn't touch him, it was something in a different world.

He turned and went back for another run, firing this time with all four guns and saw two of the planes burst into flames.

He was about to bank and go back for a third run, but Tony Zebra was screaming over the R/T: "Out of here now, damn it, head for home! Head for home!"

Then he saw Tony Zebra racing low across the field, barely thirty feet off the ground, chased by a 109. Rocco stayed low, heading for the coast, and when he was far enough out over the water, away from the guns on the ground, he pulled back on the stick and gained altitude. Looking back, he saw a pile of black smoke going up over Comiso, and no sign of Tony Zebra.

"Tony? Tony? You okay?"

"Barely, you sonofabitch. Didn't I say to hit and clear out? What were you hanging around for?"

"What's the smoke back there—you bash something?"

"The 109 flew into a fuel dump."

"Where the hell are you?"

"On top of you."

Then he came down to Rocco's right and they flew side by side, and he radioed Fighter Control to let them know they were coming in. He didn't want the shore guns opening up on them, thinking they were the enemy.

"You did all right for a guy who never flew."

"I told you, I checked out in a P-38."

"I thought it was a Grumman Wildcat."

"That too," Rocco said.

They were halfway back to Malta.

"It's always a good feeling to kill a few planes on the ground. How many'd you get?"

"Two, I think. It was hard to tell."

A 109 came out of the sun and raked past them, tracers like blue vines sprouting from its wings. Rocco saw some pieces flying off Tony Zebra's plane, and an instant later his own was hit, bullets ripping through the top wing.

"You okay, Rocco?"

"I'm here, I'm here. Something flew off your tail."

"Don't I know it. Get down and hug the water till I take care of this clown."

As Rocco dove, Tony Zebra peeled off sharply, to starboard, but not soon enough. The 109 was back, and he got on Zebra's tail. Rocco watched as, above him, they turned and turned, with agonizing indecision. Then Tony Zebra broke away, climbed and looped back, and they went at each other head-on, firing. They flew right past each other, close, a near collision, and then, for a few moments, they were far apart, as if uncertain about reengaging.

Rocco saw what they were doing: they were climbing, angling for position. The German, in a high arc, came looping back, firing, but Tony Zebra slipped off at an angle, and with a turn to the right he was suddenly on the German's tail, holding through an interminable sequence of loops and rolls, and closing for the kill.

But then it went bad for Tony Zebra. His plane slowed and wobbled, and by the time he got it under control, the German had swung around behind him and blasted him with his cannon.

Rocco heard him over the radio shouting a mayday position to ground control. Then he rolled the plane over, and gravity dumped him out of the cockpit.

The 109 was still up there, circling. When the chute opened, he made a pass and gave a burst with his machine guns, and Tony Zebra dropped his arms to his side and went limp. Rocco couldn't tell if he was hit or just playing dead.

He gunned the Gladiator's engine and pulled back on the stick, putting the ship into a steep climb, heading for the 109. Didn't think about it, just did it—a kind of reflex, from the rage and panic inside him. The 109 was still circling, greedily focused on the slowly descending parachute.

From several hundred yards, coming up from behind and underneath,

Rocco fired a heavy burst, but he was too far away. He squeezed off another burst that missed, and then, as he closed, he fired a third time—but this time, nothing. He was out of ammunition.

He flew past the 109, overshooting it, and it picked up on him, following on his tail. He wove left, then right, evading, trying to keep out of the line of fire. A cannon shot flashed past him, inches above the cockpit canopy. He changed direction, and tracers from the 109's machine guns sprayed past, a few rounds tearing into the rudder.

Then he stopped weaving and went into a tight turn. It was something he'd heard the pilots talking about, and it came back to him as if he'd known it all his life: maintain a tight turn, inside your pursuer's radius, and he'll never be able to line you up. And it was working, the old Gladiator agile and maneuverable, enabling him to narrow the circle, and the 109 couldn't touch him.

At one point, in the turning, they were opposite each other, still circling, and Rocco saw the pilot plainly. They looked across at each other, cold and hard, as if in a game, competing, sizing each other up. Intimate, personal. It was not the same pilot who had attacked the farm, but it was the same plane, the same number on the fuselage, 711, and the same emblem, a red heart, on the yellow nose. Around and around, Rocco narrowing the circle, keeping it as tight as possible, giving the 109 a hard time.

They'd been far up, but now they were descending, corkscrewing down, Rocco unaware of it, unconscious of the downward slide. Machine-gun tracers went scattering past, a short burst, and then another. A few rounds pierced the upper wing. The German was toying with him, not even using the cannon now, merely rat-tat-tatting with the machine guns. He was that confident.

Then Rocco saw, with alarm, the water rising up, drawing near. He hit the pedals hard, trying to correct the downward drift, but did it wrong, and the Gladiator, still banking, plunged sharply, and it seemed hopeless. He kicked again, in desperation, and when the craft finally stabilized, it was only a few feet off the surface.

The 109 followed him right down, pursuing in the tight turn, and Rocco, craning his neck, trying to see where it was, spotted it just at the moment when the German, concentrating on the pursuit, miscalculated his position, and his left wing dipped into the sea. The sudden drag ripped the wing off at the root, pulling it clean away, and somehow, in the splitting apart, in the rending of metal and cable and electrical wire, the fuel tank sparked and the plane exploded, pieces flying off in all directions. What was left of the fuselage settled into the water, burning, giving off black smoke. It sat there a slow moment, and then it slipped under.

Rocco gained some altitude, up off the water, looking for Tony Zebra. He turned and wheeled, searching, but found nothing. He went higher, extending his angle of vision, but still nothing, and then he came lower, crisscrossing, back and forth, thinking his skirmish with the 109 might have taken him miles from where Tony Zebra went down. Back and forth, sweeping over the water, unsure of his position, and running out of gas.

Then, banking, he looked down, and there he was, on his back, in the water. He'd managed to get free of the parachute, but his dinghy wasn't inflated, and he was down there in his Mae West, face-up and floating. Rocco circled, looking for a sign, some movement, some indication that he was all right, but nothing, nothing at all.

Thirty-three
MELITA HUMMING

"Why," Melita said, "why did you ever do that?" She was upset with him, and worried. There was something withdrawn and desolate in her tone, as if she would vanish if she could. Yet she was also secretly pleased, because he was, after all, a hero, having risked his life the way he had. "What was it? Whatever got into you?"

"I don't know," he said quietly.

"How crazy, flying an airplane—you!"

Yes, it was crazy.

"You could have been killed."

He could have been killed.

"Did you want to die? Is that it?"

"No," he said, "that really wasn't it."

They were in the house on Windmill Street, in the room they used as a bedroom. He was in his underwear, changing into fresh clothes. She sat on a chair, studying him as if he were a stranger, someone she hardly knew.

"Then what?" she said. "What were you thinking?"

"The farmer was dead. I guess I must have felt I had to do something. Didn't you ever feel that way? That you had to react? We never talked, he couldn't speak English, but I felt something for him. He was out there every day, pruning and weeding. There was no reason for him to be dead."

"And when you came down, you crashed and nearly killed yourself. Was that smart? And Tony Zebra, he's a pilot, and he nearly got killed. I'll never forgive him for putting you in a plane and sending you up to shoot."

"The shooting was my idea."

"Then I'll never forgive you," she said steamily. "You don't love me."

"Why do you say that?"

"You do dangerous things."

"Do I?"

"Yes, you do."

He slipped into his shirt and started buttoning it. "Let's go shopping," he said.

"The stores are empty."

"But there are all these classifieds," he said, picking up the newspaper.

"Do you love me?"

"I do, I do."

"No you don't."

"I love you so much I'm going to buy you a piano."

"I don't want a piano."

"Sure you do. There's a secondhand upright for thirty-five pounds."

Thirty-five pounds wasn't cheap. An office clerk would have to work four months to earn that much.

"Tell me about the future," she said. "Tell me how wonderful everything is going to be after the war."

"Life is pretty wonderful right now," he said. "Look at all these fabulous ads."

There was a camera, a stove, a Remington portable typewriter, a gramophone, and a Singer sewing machine. The Singer came with a ruffler, a tucker, and all the home-stitching accessories.

"Talk to my aunt," she said, "she's the one who sews."

"Somebody here wants an accordion. Do we have an accordion to sell?"

She put her hands over her ears. "I'm not listening to you. Do you hear, Rocco Raven? I can't hear a word you're saying."

"Hey, here's one. 'Six airmen require dancing lessons in the evenings, Rabat area. BOX 777.' It could be a whole new career for you. Some fox-trot, some jitterbug, maybe some of the old classics—the Charleston and the shimmy-shake."

She was off the chair now and on the floor, on her back, twirling her rosary beads, letting them wrap around her forefinger. "What do you know about it?" she said in a flat, drab, lemon-sour tone.

"What do I know about what?"

"About anything," she said. "About anything at all."

Not only was she on the floor, twirling her rosary, but—when he looked at her now—she was shrinking. Her legs, her arms, all of her, becoming smaller and smaller.

"Why are you doing that?" he asked.

"Doing what?"

"What you're doing."

"Get on the floor with me," she said.

"Not if you're going to be like that."

"Like what," she said, knowing perfectly well what he meant.

Smaller and smaller, even her feet, her face. Her hair was smaller.

"You may never see me again," she said.

"Is that what you'd like? Is that what you think about?"

"I think about a lot of things."

She was the size of a small doll. If she kept shrinking, soon she would vanish.

"I'll never fly again," he said. "Is that what you want me to say? You want me never to fly a plane again?"

"Oh no, no, no," she said. "I love it that you flew. My ace, my hero. My darling!"

Rocco wasn't sure, was it sarcasm or was it true love?

"What do you want?" he asked. "Why are you doing this? I can hardly see you anymore."

"Come down on the floor with me. Then we'll be together."

A large rat came into the room, whiskers twitching. Rocco saw it and clapped his hands to frighten it away. It didn't scare easily. It moved about, sniffing, then went slowly across the room, toward Melita. It was much larger than she was. Rocco took off a shoe and hurled it, but missed. He took off the other shoe and went closer, aiming carefully, and this time hit the rat squarely, leaving it momentarily stunned. Rocco picked up the first shoe he'd thrown, held it by the toe, and slammed the heel, hard, on the rat's head. Did it again and again.

He looked around for Melita.

"You didn't have to do that," she said.

"I didn't?"

"It was too much. It wasn't necessary."

He couldn't see her.

"Where are you?" he asked.

"Over here."

"Where?"

"Right here."

He saw where the voice was coming from, but there was nothing there, just a stain on the bare wooden floor, a dark black stain the color of her hair, the size of a penny.

She was humming again, he could hear her humming. They could be a thousand miles apart and he would always hear her, the low, moody sound, softly fading.

After he'd been fished out of the water by a rescue seaplane, Tony Zebra spent three days at the Mtarfa Hospital. It was thought he might have suffered a concussion, or a skull fracture, but his skull and brain proved to be in no worse shape than before he'd been shot down, and even he would have acknowledged that wasn't saying much. One of the bullets from the 109 had grazed his left thigh, giving him a flesh wound high up, barely missing his groin, and everyone who looked at it—the doctors, the nurses, his CO, the priest who lived in the hospital, and the three old ladies who washed the floors—kept telling him how lucky he was.

He was in a room with a German pilot who spoke poor English and no Italian, and an Italian from Foggia who spoke fragmentary German and no English at all. Tony Zebra, who had poor Italian and worse German, was the intermediary, helping them converse, the German blaming Mussolini and the Italians for messing up the war, and the Italian blaming Hitler for having started the war in the first place. Clearly they would have come to blows, but the German had his left leg in traction and the Italian's arms, both of them, were in plaster.

The German made paper airplanes with swastikas on them and sent them sailing in the direction of the Italian, some of them right on target into his face. The Italian, both arms in plaster, couldn't throw them back and had to bear the insult patiently. His patience was rewarded, though, because one of the nurses, a short girl with sullen eyes, saw how afflicted he was and took pity on him, coming to him in the night and making love to him in his bed. It was a comeuppance for the German, who, as an oberleutnant, outranked the Italian, who was only a sottotenente, and while the Italian and the nurse were busy with each other in the dark, the German spent a lot of time muttering and blowing his nose. Nor was it easy for Tony Zebra, who listened to the moans of pleasure and the heavy breathing and cursed his luck, wishing that he too might have been a sottotenente from Foggia, with both of his arms in plaster.

Rocco brought Tony Zebra a tube of toothpaste, for which he'd paid plenty, and a bag of apples for which he'd shelled out even more. He was still on subsistence wages from Fingerly, barely enough to get by on and usually overdue. Melita had to sell a few more Jack Teagarden records so Rocco could pay for the apples.

Fingerly brought a box of chocolates, from Switzerland via Portugal and Port Said. Tony Zebra opened the box and Fingerly passed it around. The Italian had to be helped, he wanted a caramel. Fingerly picked one out for him and put it in his mouth, and as he did that, Rocco thought he looked strangely like a priest passing out holy communion.

The big news all that week was the thrashing that Montgomery was giving Rommel. The details were just beginning to filter through. During the spring and early summer, the Panzer Army had fought hard, pushing the British out of Libya and driving a wedge into western Egypt—but now, at Alamein, it was all unraveling. After a week of heavy fighting, the German and Italian divisions, below strength, took devastating losses, and by the first days of November they were in full retreat. The Afrika Korps, down to its last twenty-two tanks, was heading to Fulka, and beyond. The Italian Tenth Corps was abandoned at the Alamein line, with no fuel, no trucks, no water. On the second day of the battle, half of the Trento Division had been overrun, and before the battle was over, the entire Ariete armored division was lost, as well as the Littorio armored and the Trieste mechanized. It was the beginning of the end for Rommel in North Africa.

"Didn't I say so?" Fingerly said with quiet delight, his grin lighting up the gloomy, dimly lit room, the window boarded over because all of the glass had been knocked out by the bombing. "Rommel is getting his ass kicked. Tell me, Raven, did I call this or did I not?"

The German was again making paper airplanes, with swastikas penciled all over them. He had smoky blue eyes.

"It's the turning point," Fingerly said with relaxed confidence. He put the chocolates down on Tony Zebra's bed and lit a cigarette. He no longer smoked Camels but was using now a South African brand, which he had learned about from Zulu Swales, who, now that he was a major, had a steady supply coming in from Capetown. "After this, for the Axis," he said, exhaling silkily, "it's down the toilet. The Italians surrender, the Luftwaffe folds, the Reich collapses, and it's bluebirds in the trees again."

It was the 8th of November. American forces, the U.S. Second Corps, had just landed at Oran and Casablanca, and a combined American and British force went into Algiers. Rommel had Montgomery chasing him from the east and now the Americans were advancing from the west. And Rocco was missing the action. If they hadn't sent him to Malta—if they had sent Kallitsky, as they were supposed to—then he would be out there where he belonged, with the 9th Infantry, in Casablanca, with the task force under George Patton.

"Bye-bye Rommel," Fingerly repeated, "it's merely a matter of time. Nevertheless, you have to hand it to the old fox, he's the smartest tactician in the war. Monty will beat him, but only because he has twice the men and supplies. He'll win with the sheer weight of his barrage. If he can find him."

Rommel was on the run, but on Malta people were still hungry, and this week, again, it was flavored water instead of beer, and the 109s were still making their antipersonnel raids, dropping thermos bombs, butterfly bombs, pencil bombs.

The Italian's girlfriend, the nurse with fleshy lips, came in, and, spotting the chocolates, grabbed the box and made herself comfortable on the edge of the Italian's bed. She fed him a chocolate, and then fed herself, couldn't stop, taking one after another. The German was still making paper airplanes. He flew one that hit Fingerly in the ear, and one that hit Rocco on the nose.

"No more candy for him," Tony Zebra said. "He gets nothing. *Niente. Nichts.*"

"Not even a bedpan," Rocco said.

"Not even me," said the nurse, holding on her lap the box of chocolates, which was now empty, her round, sullen eyes roving lustily, and Tony Zebra hated it that she was sitting on the Italian's bed rather than on his.

After three days in the hospital, Tony Zebra was signed out and he made his way back to Takali, bruised but ready to fly again. For the unauthorized attack on Comiso, he received an unofficial reprimand from his CO, and for blowing up the fuel depot he was given a handshake and a slap on the back. The fuel depot had blown up because the 109 crashed into it; but if Tony Zebra hadn't been tangling with the 109, it wouldn't have crashed and the depot would still be there, so it was, in effect, the same as if Tony Zebra had personally dropped a bomb on it. Or so, at least, it was considered, and he was awarded a bar to his DFC.

The only reward he wanted, however, was to be sent home. Or at least to India, which was still in his thoughts. The Ganges, the Taj Mahal, and the pretty girls wearing the red dot on their forehead, who he liked to imagine would be kinder to him and more sensible than some of the girls he'd met in Jersey City.

So when they handed him the bar to his DFC, he tried to give it back in exchange for a ticket out of Malta, because he deserved it: he was long overdue to be rotated out. In July, the Malta tour for the fighter pilots had been capped at three months—recognition, finally, that anything more than three months was tantamount to a death sentence. But Tony Zebra had been there since March and now it was November, and still they kept him on. Pilots he'd never even had a chance to meet had come and gone, and here he was, still at Takali, still flying, still unable to shoot straight, and still lucky, not just because he was alive, but because whenever he went up, one way or another, crazily, enemy planes fell out of the sky, and Command was only too eager to give him credit for the kills.

In his darkest moments, he theorized that he was still on Malta because somebody in Command must have placed a high-stakes bet that his string of knockdowns would outdistance Screwball Beurling's, and the only way that was going to happen, if it happened at all, was if they kept him on Malta for the duration of the siege, and then some. The thought gripped him, it became an obsession. Somebody was betting on him, as if he were a horse, and it sparked his rage. Sooner or later he would find the madman who had placed the bet, and even if it was the Air Vice Marshal himself, he would strangle him with his bare hands and smoke a cigar at his funeral.

Then another thought replaced the first, even more unpleasant. If he was still on Malta because somebody in Command was betting on him, then somebody else, not in Command, had to be covering the bet—betting, in effect, that he would get killed. And that was worse. Somebody wishing him ill, actually putting money on the line, hoping that he'd go down.

Tony Zebra resolved that if he ever found the sadist who was betting against him, he would not only smoke a cigar at the funeral, but he would dig the grave and volunteer to be a pallbearer.

The day after he emerged from the hospital, he was up in the air again, flying, on his way home after a strafing raid against Sicily. As he came in over Malta, approaching Takali, when he looked down, he spotted, beneath him, on the road from Mosta to Rabat, the silver and maroon of Fingerly's two-toned Phantom convertible, the top up, hurrying along, raising a swirl of white dust on the unpaved road.

Fingerly?

Yes, Fingerly. If anybody was taking bets against him, who else? Even as he thought it, he knew it was irrational, without foundation—but, as a guess, it was irresistible. Fingerly at the hub, taking bets not just from the Air Vice Marshal and dozens of others at Lascaris, but from abroad, all over the Mediterranean, because Fingerly would know how to milk a thing like this, he would get the last bitter ounce out of it.

Tony Zebra screamed, the cockpit filling with his desolate rage, and he banked the plane, came full around, and, still screaming, dipped the nose and came at the Phantom from behind, closing fast and firing a long burst, using up the last of his ammunition. With his usual bad aim, he missed, his cannon shells hitting, instead, a storage shed at the edge of the road by a farm, blowing it to pieces.

The shed was a black-market storehouse, loaded with underwear that raised good prices from those who could afford to pay. When Tony Zebra's cannon shells trashed the shed and blasted it apart, billowing undergarments blew away in the wind, slips and undershirts, brassières, bloomers, and boxer shorts, fluttering across the countryside, coming to rest on the cactus, on the olive trees, on the potato fields, on the stone walls. The following day, the archbishop, who had been waging an ardent but unsuccessful campaign against the black-marketeers, was on the radio, offering a prayer of thanksgiving for the destruction of the shed, which he described as a warehouse mortgaged to sin. He praised the unknown RAF pilot who had destroyed it, declared him a hero, and though he didn't know his name, conferred upon him a plenary indulgence, which would enable him, after death, to bypass the pains and agony of purgatory and go directly to his eternal reward in heaven. Tony Zebra, who spent the day with a bottle of bourbon, never heard the broadcast, and was condemned to spend his remaining days on Malta without ever learning of his wonderful good luck.

DECISIVE MOMENT IN STRUGGLE FOR STALINGRAD
SEA OF FIRE SEPARATES OPPOSING ARMIES

HITLER SPEAKS AT SPORTZ PALAST

8TH ARMY TROOPS FIGHTING SOUTH OF BENGHAZI

OVER 550 GERMAN AND ITALIAN AIRCRAFT CAPTURED IN CYRENAICA

ROMMEL ADMITS HEAVY LOSSES IN EGYPT
"Battle of El Alamein Indescribable"

GENERAL GEORG VON BISMARCK KILLED IN DESERT FIGHTING
Egypt—According to German prisoners of war, General von Bismarck, in command of the 21st Panzer Division, was killed in the recent desert fighting.

BOXING AT THE ODEON
Hamrun—6 p.m.
Three 4-Round Contests

SPECTACULAR U-BOAT KILL
CHASED U-BOAT FOR FIVE HOURS THEN RAMMED IT FOUR TIMES

———

COLISEUM THEATRE
Leslie Howard
IT'S LOVE I'M AFTER
Rock Shelter on Premises

———

Thirty-four

ROMMEL ON THE RUN

In North Africa, in the desert, on a day when drenching rain fell, turning the sand into a muddy paste, Field Marshal Erwin Rommel sat in his car, a Volkswagen Kübel, holding a sandwich that his aide, Günther, had prepared for him.

He'd been racing about in the rain, inspecting the positions, doing his best to pull things together. But it was hopeless. The full weight of Montgomery's army was bearing down on him, and here he was, with what was left of the battered Panzer Army, and no gasoline.

He needed four hundred tons a day if the tanks and trucks were to move, and there were whole days when they had nothing. The supply ships heading for Benghazi were, with dreadful regularity, torpedoed and sunk, one after the other. The *Panuco* went down, then the *Proserpina*. The *Tergestea*, and the *Hans Arp*. Kesselring airlifted eighty tons of fuel, enabling them to move on, evading Montgomery, but when they reached Agedabia they were out of gas again, and beyond the range of any more airlifts.

In the Kübel car he was already thinking it out, sifting the details: how and where to surrender his army.

After the big battle at Alamein, it was fall back, fall back, fall back, the rear guard mining the roads and booby-trapping deserted buildings. He was not well, still the bothersome problem with his blood pressure. He was dizzy, there were fainting spells. And he was gripped by depression. "I wish I were selling newspapers on a streetcorner in Berlin," he told an aide. "Then I could sleep nights, without this awful burden." On his birthday, a cake arrived from Kesselring, and, from Lucie, a box of macaroons. He was fifty-one. No officer over forty had survived in the desert as long as he had.

Almost every day he wrote to Lucie, sometimes twice a day. They'd been married twenty-five years, skiing together, climbing mountains, swimming, riding horses. Women offered themselves to him, but he turned them away, joking with Lucie about the chances he let slip through his fingers.

Even at Alamein, at the height of the battle, even then he wrote, when most of his tanks were being destroyed. "*Meine liebste Lu*—We're just being crushed by the enemy's weight. I've tried to salvage a part of my army, but I wonder if I'll succeed. At night I lie awake, racking my brains for a way out of this for my poor troops. The dead are lucky, for them it's over. I think of you constantly, with love and feeling. Perhaps fate will be merciful and we may see each other again?"

That was at Alamein. Now he was eight hundred miles away, at Agedabia, and still he wrote, scribbling in his tent, or in the car, one letter merging into another, hope into despair, despair into dream, dream into doubt that twisted into boyish optimism. "I dare not hope for a favorable turn in our fortunes. I dare not. But miracles do happen!"

Do they? Do they?

Miracles?

He sat in the Volkswagen, depressed, still holding the sandwich Günther had made for him. There had been better days, when they raced across the desert, from victory to victory. They had hunted gazelle, in cars, firing at them with machine guns, and then enjoyed a feast of fresh meat roasted on a spit. Sometimes he led forays into British territory, raiding the storage depots. They came back with Argentine corned beef, butter from Canada, canned milk from America, English bacon. They came back with British uniforms, which they wore, after tearing off the insignia.

As he sat in the car, the sandwich in his hand, General Seidemann came running over. He was shouting, excited. Waving his arms. The entire coast was littered with drums. He had seen it himself, flying in his Storch. From El Agheila to Mersa Brega, the shore was strewn with drums of fuel. It was a fantasy. Who would believe! Thousands of drums of petrol, from the *Hans Arp*, which had been sunk.

Rommel leaped from the car and tossed the half-eaten sandwich in the sand. "Show me," he shouted. "Show me! I must see for myself!"

Already the troops were at the shore, wading in, retrieving the floating drums. They had fuel. They would make it, yes, to the Mersa Brega line, and once again Montgomery would be cheated, denied yet another chance to deliver the knockout blow.

"Thousands," Seidemann cried. "Just look at them! Look!"

Rommel was thinking ahead again, thinking beyond Mersa Brega and beyond Tripolatania, thinking of leading his army all the way to Tunisia, where the land was fertile and the rolling hills were alive with flowers and orchards and horses, and there was plenty of fresh water. Water to drink, and to wash in. Water to pour over your head and forget the murderous time in the desert.

Thirty-five

NARDU CAMILLERI SPEAKS OF LOVE WORLD NEWS ROUNDUP/GENERAL PATTON IN MOROCCO CHRISTINA'S SEETHING SIMMERING MALTA CONGA LINE

All through July, Nardu Camilleri had been close to death, but in August his condition stabilized, and though he never became well enough to leave the hospital, it seemed, for a while, that he might recover. In September he sank again, his vital signs deteriorated, and as the days wore on, it was a surprise to everyone that he was still alive. He lingered on into October, and by the end of the month he had entered a strange limbo in which, though it was clear that death was certain, there were times—whole hours, or entire afternoons—when he was alert and even talkative, giving the impression that at any moment he might get out of bed, walk out of the hospital, and resume his spirited advocacy of a Free Malta and the expansion of the lace trade.

Rocco had visited him two or three times over the summer, and now he went again and found him in one of his rare moments of lucidity, awake and fully conscious of his surroundings. He was in a ward, a long, crowded room, the beds lined up on either side of a narrow aisle.

He wore a white hospital gown and was propped up on two pillows, with the sheet folded back, down at his waist. He was pale, shriveled, his lips dry and cracked. His eyes, filmy, were faded brown smudges in his wrinkled face.

There was a time when Rocco had thought of him as an old gnarled tree with crusty bark all over him and roots growing into the floor. But when he looked at him now, the neatly tucked hospital sheet covering his skinny legs, he saw that he was not a tree but a bed of withered flowers, old and faded, long past their season, waiting to be turned over and plowed under.

"I remember you," Nardu Camilleri said after studying Rocco's face for a long time, as if examining a foreign postage stamp whose worth he was trying to determine. His voice was surprisingly strong, and seemed to have gained in vigor as his body withered, stealing for itself whatever last energy was left in his dying bones. "You're the one whose foot I shot off. You came to say good-bye to me before I die."

"They tell me you're going to get well," Rocco said, for lack of anything better to say.

"Who told you that? I am ninety years old, it isn't right for me to live any longer."

"I thought you wanted to live to a hundred."

"I did, but not anymore. There has been too much bombing."

"The bombing is just about over," Rocco said. "Soon the war will move on to Sicily, and Italy."

The thought that the war in Malta might come to an end did not seem important to the old man.

"The earth," he said, "this earth we live on, has been around for millions of years. Against all of that, the vastness of time, what is a human life? We are nothing, not even a whisper." There was an untroubled sureness in the way he said it, a sense of satisfaction, as if it had taken him a lifetime to figure it out, and he was sure, now, that he had the answer.

He reached out, feebly, and put his hand on Rocco's arm. "But the lace trade," he said, "there is a future in it, it's worth investing. We talked about that before, did we not? Buy cheap, sell dear. That's the whole secret to existence."

A nurse came by to take his temperature. She was making the rounds with a glassful of thermometers, one into each patient's mouth. As soon as she was past him and moving down the line, he took the thermometer out of his mouth and turned to Rocco with a special earnestness.

"You found your woman? Did you?"

"I found my woman," Rocco said.

"Good. You took my advice. Is she beautiful?"

Rocco nodded.

"You married her? The priest blessed your union?"

Rocco smiled, thinking it an odd question from a man who had spent the better part of his life as the doorman for a brothel.

Nardu Camilleri looked at him through narrowed lids. "Malta, you know, is very fussy about these things."

"Yes, I know."

The nurse passed by, on her way back to her station, and seeing the thermometer in Nardu's hand, took it and replaced it under his tongue. "He has to keep it in for three minutes," she said to Rocco, nastily, as if blaming him. She seemed in need of sleep, but who on Malta could get a night's sleep, with the sirens and the alerts?

As soon as she was gone, the old man had the thermometer out of his mouth again. "Love is an abandonment," he said, his eyes lit by an energy that seemed to rise from the last flicker of life inside him. "When you are in love, you lose yourself in the beloved. You may think you are still yourself, but you are not, because you exist totally for her. When you eat, it's not for yourself you eat, but for her. When you wash, when you shave, when you clip your nails, it's for her you do these things and no one else. Your existence is her existence. When you read a newspaper or take a drink, it's not you doing these things— it's her. She is your new self: you are her and she is you. When you cough, when you piss, it is no longer you, it is this woman who obsesses you and possesses your soul. Love is an immolation. That is why, in all the stories, the lovers die. The physical death is a symbol of the spiritual death that takes place as soon as the lovers fall in love and merge their identities. Knowing this, anyone who allows himself to fall in love must be, of course, a fool. And yet, who can resist? Who, knowing the joy of the experience, would refuse? We are the fools of love, clowns of the universe, and if I believed in God, I would say, with Dante, that the joke is divine. But Dante was an Italian and I am sick to death of the Italians, and I am, at this moment, falling asleep. God I will discuss with you at some other time, if I live."

He slipped the thermometer back into his mouth just as the nurse started down the line again, with clipboard and pencil, recording the temperatures, and by the time she reached him, he was already dozing, the thermometer slanting from the corner of his mouth like a glass cigarette. She took it, read it, jotted a number, and moved briskly along.

Rocco lingered, watching the old man as he slept, and didn't understand why it was that he liked him. Even so old, so close to death, he was still filled up with himself, his wild opinions and queer imaginings. Beatrice, his daughter, was right: his mind was no longer sound. Yet there was something genuine about him, a kind of honesty, a probing for some kind of truth about life, as if his brain were a drill, carving into the hard granite of existence, and every day, despite all his effort, he came up with nothing but dust.

Rocco thought about what he had said, about life being nothing, a meaningless whisper—but he didn't want to believe that. Nardu himself, lying there, dying, was not nothing—how could he be?—even though he preferred to think of himself that way, as vanishing, passing into namelessness, as if he'd never been born. It bothered Rocco. How could the old man find comfort in such hopelessness? How could hopelessness create solace and give him a sense of peace?

Then he thought of Melita, and she especially, she was not nothing. No, not at all, it was not possible for him to think of her that way. When they first met, in the April bombing, it was lust that brought them together, sheer physical urgency, but now it was more than that, it was a need, a dependency, deeper than sex and stronger than desire. He knew it, felt it, the time she went away and he didn't know where she was, and he scoured the island, imagining the worst. And he knew it even more strongly when they were swimming at Ghallis Point, when the 109 went after her, shooting, and he thought she dead. What he knew, and now understood, was that he couldn't live without her. The lust was still there, but it had grown into something else, it had become a bond, a terrible belonging. This was love, he thought, and it frightened him, because in some ways it was more than he'd bargained for—or ever imagined. If he survived the war, he would come back for her, because he had to, because she was the one, and that's how it was. It was no longer a passing thought, an idea he toyed with, but a settled fact, something he felt very sure about.

It was going to be hell when orders came through for him to leave. He was beginning to think—hope—the orders might never arrive, that maybe, possibly, they had forgotten all about him, back there at Second Corps. Maybe he was one of the lost, one of the unknowns. And who, in the end, really and truly cared?

On his way out of the hospital, he passed through another large ward, where a priest was going from bed to bed, pausing briefly and making the sign of the cross. It was Father Hemda, who had performed the wedding ceremony for Aida and her sailor. He wore a black cassock, with a purple stole around his neck, and was passing out absolution. Not hearing confessions, simply going from bed to bed and absolving the sinners, whether they wanted to be absolved or not. He was disheveled, with a few days' growth of beard, looking as if he'd been sleeping in his cassock, which was badly wrinkled. Rocco recalled what Julietta had said, how Father Hemda would visit the house on Strait Street and pray with them, giving everyone absolution. He wanted no one to go to hell and was bent on saving everyone, even the ones who couldn't care less.

Rocco paused to greet him, and the priest, without recognizing him, made the sign of the cross, mumbling some words in Latin. *Ego te absolvo a peccatis tuis, in nomine patris, et filii, et . . .* It was the formula for absolution. Rocco had never heard these words except in the confessional—and now, in the strangeness of the moment, hearing them in the crowded ward, being forgiven without having confessed, he felt a buoyancy, a lightness, an odd sense of relief and exhilaration.

"Thank you," he said to the priest, feeling genuinely grateful, "thank you," and went rushing out, down the long flight of stairs, out the door, and back to Valletta.

November 13, 1942

DISSENSION IN GERMANY
Generals Want Military Dictatorship

SPREADING REVOLT IN BALKANS

SERIOUS DAMAGE IN ROMANIAN OILFIELDS

Twenty-four thousand Jews living in Belgium have been deported to work for Germany in Northern France or the Ukraine, according to the Independent Belgian news agency.

FRANCO REFUSES HITLER NAVAL AND AIR BASES

PATTON IN NORTH AFRICA

"It is my mission to cross Morocco and strike at the Axis forces wherever they might be found," said General Patton, United States C-in-C, Morocco, in an official proclamation to Morocco over the radio on Wednesday. "It is my wish that the country's normal life, political as well as economic, should proceed as far as possible. I am sure that all the inhabitants of Morocco realize that the American army is here with the sole purpose of fighting against the Axis forces and of contributing to the elimination all over the world of all Nazi activities in all spheres as soon as possible."

They went to eat that night, as they now usually did, to a Victory Kitchen, the one on Kingsway. With food harder to find than ever the kitchens had become a necessary evil, the meals undercooked or overdone, rarely appetizing, not particularly nourishing, and never enough. But still it was something to eat.

At the end of the queue, they found Christina. She wasn't dancing any more, except on rare occasions, because she had taken on more responsibilities in her job with the RAF. She was no longer just a plotter, tracking the incoming planes, but was now working as an assistant to the flight controller. Still at Lascaris, down in the Hole.

She was reading a newspaper.

"Isn't it sickening what they're doing to the Jews?"

"Which Jews?"

"In Belgium. They're sending them to work camps in Germany."

Rocco glanced at the story.

"The Germans hate the Jews," Melita said.

"They deported twenty-four thousand," Rocco read from the paper.

"They ship them in boxcars," Christina said. "Those crazy Nazis, they want to be the only ones left."

In Paris, Genoa, Barcelona, many of the dancers and musicians she'd worked with were Jews. It was hard for her to believe what was happening.

"Where's Warby?" Rocco asked.

"I don't think even God knows," she said.

In August, Warby Warburton had come back to Malta for a third tour on the island, and now, in a few days, his tour would be over. He had the DSO and the DFC, but still he wore gray flannel trousers, sometimes a cravat, and on some days he drove around in pajamas and slippers. It had been up and down between him and Christina, the last few months. He seemed to be drifting away from her, detaching himself in not too subtle ways, and she was beginning to accept that it was not going to end happily.

The smell in the Victory Kitchen was less than appetizing. A middle-aged Maltese woman, with a kerchief around her hair, ladled a watery stew from an iron cauldron. Each serving had a small piece of meat and a few peas, the meat not easy to identify and of a distinctly greenish cast.

"Are we really going to eat this stuff?" Christina asked, sickened. She lifted the meat on her spoon, studied it, and dropped it back on the dish. "To hell with this," she said.

Melita agreed emphatically. "Yes, yes. To hell with this."

Rocco, starved, was ready to eat anything, but was drawn along by the momentum. "Right, right. Who needs green meat?"

People were grumbling, muttering, sniffing the meat suspiciously—old men, women with children, a few nuns, a paunchy man with half his teeth missing, a man with one ear, a man with one hand, a blind man, a girl with languid eyes, a priest with a beard.

"To hell with this," the priest said.

"To hell with it all," Christina said, grabbing hold of the blind man, "come, come, let's conga," grabbing Rocco and Melita, and the man with no teeth, "let's do it, make a conga line," and they formed up and, with Christina in the lead, congaed right out of the Victory Kitchen and onto the street, one-two-three-*kick*, one-two-three-*kick*, others linking up with them, women and children, and as they moved down Kingsway, a crowd of soldiers joined in, and a few policemen, even some priests in black cassocks and old ladies in faldettas, and quite a few nuns. Somebody with a trumpet appeared, and someone with a drum. A man with a tuba. Everyone had had enough—too much war, too much siege, too much Victory Kitchen food, too much too much.

Down the long straight length of Kingsway they went, a winding, snaking line, weaving and kicking. By the time they reached St. John's Street, they were more than a hundred. By the time they reached Palace Square, they were over two hundred. By the time they reached St. Elmo's, the line stretched the whole long length of Kingsway, and they swung around and came up on Merchants, counting and kicking. They turned onto the side streets, crisscrossing through all of Valletta, on Bull and Bounty and Archbishop and Old Theatre, the tuba oomping and the drum thumping, keeping the rhythm, and the trumpet blowing fancy riffs, with Christina up front, leading the way, and the blind man behind her holding onto her hips, and Melita behind the blind man, and Rocco behind her, everyone counting and kicking, kicking away the war, kicking away the misery, kicking away the hunger, the death, the rats, the dust, the bad smells, the noise of the guns.

As Christina led them onto St. Christopher, the sirens sounded, but why should they care? They kicked and counted, and when four 109s flew over, chased by a gaggle of Spitfires, it meant nothing. The tuba blew, the drum thumped, and Rocco, with his hands on Melita's hips, whose hands were on the blind man's hips, thought this was better than anything, better than ENIGMA, better than Miss Sicily going home to Sicily, better than the 109 that had tried to kill him but crashed in the sea instead.

People were still emerging from their bombed-out houses and joining in. Rocco glanced back, and behind him now was a nun, her hands on his hips. He looked back again, and instead of the nun it was the barber from the shop on Kingsway, the one that Nardu Camilleri used to go to for a trim. It seemed the whole world was back there, everyone, swinging and kicking. Was Rommel back there? Was Kesselring? Hermann Göring? Not Julietta, though, no, not her, because she was in Alexandria, away from it all, among the palm trees and the sun-bleached pastel villas, with the Count.

He turned again, looking back, and this time, behind him, it was Adolf Hitler, the Führer himself. The nose larger than he'd imagined, face puffy, eyes weary, the stubby mustache exactly what it was: a stubby mustache. He looked worn out. One-two-three-*kick*. Rocco suffered a paroxysm of self-doubt, wondering if he was losing his sanity. Adolf Hitler? He turned again, another glimpse, and still he was there, Hitler, his hands on Rocco's hips, looking weary, too tired for words, yet he was counting and kicking, and seemed, despite his fatigue, to be having a good time. He was getting his ass kicked at Stalingrad—so what better, to get away from it all, than a conga line in Malta?

Hitler's nose was running. Rocco saw it, the viscous flow, running down into the mustache. The Führer snorted, sucking it in, collecting it in his throat, and spat. His spit was fire, a great glob of flame, hitting the street with a flash and a puff of smoke. One-two-three-*spit*, hawking it up, thick globs of fire, to the left and the right. This is no good, no good at all, Rocco thought, it has to stop.

He looked back over his shoulder, and saw with relief that this time it was not Adolf Hitler behind him but Melita. Strange, though. She had been in front of him, his hands on her hips, and suddenly, somehow, she was behind him. In front of him now was Christina, still going strong, leading the way.

"Are we in love?" Melita said, in his ear, over the din of the counting and kicking.

"We are in love," Rocco said.

"Is it forever?"

"It's forever."

"You will never leave me?"

"I will never leave you."

"We will always be together?"

"Always."

It was all lies, he knew and she knew, but lies, fictions, were better than truth if the only truth was bombs and green meat in your soup. Yes, he would never leave her, because that's how it was now, because Nardu Camilleri was right: love was an immolation. One way or another he would come back for her and they would marry, that's how it would be. It was already a marriage. He belonged and she belonged. This was the answer, he thought. Yes, this was the key.

Christina was indefatigable, taking them uphill and downhill, onto streets so steep they were built entirely of stairs, and other streets as straight and level as a kitchen floor. It was a bad time for her, as bad as it gets, because any day now her Warby would be gone, his third tour on Malta finished, and he'd be off again to Egypt, or wherever. She might never see him again. They went past the Greek church that had been bombed, and the Palace that had been bombed, and the Law Courts that had been bombed, and the Sacra Infermeria that had been bombed. They passed the Manoel Theatre, which was still standing, and the Auberge de Provence, which, magically, had never been touched. Some, beyond their strength, dropped out. The tuba. The nun with the harelip. The man with one ear. Adolf Hitler dropped out. But most kept going, kicking along, because alive and kicking was better than not.

After they'd been through most of Valletta, she led them through the City Gate, into Floriana. They followed her to Vilhena Terrace, where her flat was, and there, in the gathering dark, she left them, and with weary exhilaration the line fell apart, people wandering off, some still linked together in smaller lines, counting and kicking, home to their own neighborhoods. Rocco and Melita stood a moment, gazing at the moon, and Rocco, at that moment, not knowing why, was thinking of his father, thinking it was time to write a letter, he'd sent so few. But his father hardly wrote either, never had much to say, and what did the moon have to do with it anyway?

When Melita saw Christina the next day, Christina told her how she had gone to bed exhausted, and cried all night. She wept for Warby, who had brought her brandy from Greece, earrings from Algiers, perfume from Casablanca. He'd brought dates from the Nile and oranges from Jaffa. She would see him again in a day or two, she expected, but then, by the end of the week, he'd be gone, and this time it was unlikely he'd be back, his tour on Malta being officially over. She wasn't even sure she loved him any more, things had been so rocky and confused the last several weeks and months. When they went out together, she saw he was giving long glances to other women, and she wondered if, on his lengthy stopovers in Cairo, he might have been seeing someone else.

She had wept and sobbed right through the night, and she told Melita how terrible it was, and Melita told Rocco. He was polishing his shoes. "Sobbing is good for the soul," he said, meaning it sympathetically, but as it came out he realized, too late, it sounded crass. Melita threw a cigarette at him. It was lit, the burning tip stinging the back of his hand and leaving a black smudge on the skin. She lit another and threw that as well.

"Don't do that," he said, "they're valuable. Don't you know how precious they are?"

She lit another, and another, and threw them, lighting and throwing in an orgy of waste—deliberate, angry waste, until the pack was empty, and Rocco was on his hands and knees, picking them up, reaching under the chairs, under the bed, extinguishing the pink burning tips and salvaging what he could.

Thirty-six

ZED MIR MIN

Fingerly was gone again, for several days, and when he came back this time, he was in uniform, wearing the silver oak leaves of a lieutenant colonel. He caught up with Rocco outside of Hock's, and Rocco, seeing the oak leaves—not the gold of a major but the bright silver of a lieutenant colonel—taunted him for not yet being a general. "Not good enough? Not good enough yet for the gold stars?"

"Don't rush me, Raven, everything in its season."

What he brought back with him, for Rocco, was not only a supply of Luckies but orders, from the Second Corps, to rejoin his outfit, the 9th Infantry, which had landed a week ago at Casablanca.

"When?" Rocco asked.

"You fly out next Saturday."

"That soon?"

"You want to stay forever? I thought you hated Malta."

"I do, I do."

"But you can't bear to give up that sweet piece of Maltese dessert you've been nibbling on. Didn't I warn you about these Maltese sirens?"

"A plane?" Rocco said. "A Wellington?"

"An old Blenheim. Out of Luqa."

"Then I guess this time it's for real."

"Realer than you think."

Rocco noticed Fingerly's uniform was a shade off color, like the uniform the tailor in Tarxien had made for him.

"What about you?" he asked.

"Me? I'm gone, out of here. Malta, good-bye." He put his fingers to his lips and blew a kiss. "Three hours from now, Raven, I dance into the blue, at 1600 hours."

"Where to?" Rocco asked, imagining that it had to be the Holy Land, which Fingerly had talked about so much and so often. He figured Fingerly had his agents on the prowl for a piece of Veronica's veil, or one of the nails from the Crucifixion, or a footprint of Mohammed. Or the Holy Grail, which people, serious people, were actually looking for.

"Is that it?" Rocco asked. "Palestine?"

Fingerly grinned, slyly, and yet again Rocco understood that Fingerly was beyond him, in a space all his own, a shadow world of hidden doors and secret compartments. It wasn't Palestine that interested him. He was on his way, undercover, to Romania.

"What's in Romania?"

"Dirty work for I-3. Unpleasantness. But then, the juicy part. There's a barber in Bucharest has the original score of a string quartet by Benjamin Franklin. Can you believe? He wrote it in Paris and left it with a lady friend."

"Benjamin Franklin never wrote a string quartet," Rocco said dubiously.

"Benjamin Franklin did everything," Fingerly said, running his fingers through his thick, dark hair.

"In Paris?"

"In Paris. The lady's daughter sold it in Vienna, when she needed cash flow. From Vienna it bounced to Warsaw, Prague, St. Petersburg. The barber in Bucharest got it from his uncle, who stole it from a private collection in Albania."

"Is it any good?"

"The quartet?"

"It's good music?"

"Rocco, it's Benjamin Franklin." And then, warmly, something conspiratorial in his tone, "Look, there's something I want you to do for me," taking a key from his pocket. "This is for that warehouse I brought you to in Paola." He held the key between thumb and forefinger, gesturing with it, tapping Rocco on the chest with it. "Remember the mummy I showed you? Zed Mir Min?"

"I thought you sold him to the Count, with the other junk."

"Not Zed Mir Min, I'd never part with him. We're old friends. I'm shipping him to Gibraltar and I'll pick him up when I'm finished in the Balkans. There's a submarine coming in tonight and sailing tomorrow, but I won't be here. The crate is in the warehouse—can you put it aboard? Will you do this for me?"

"Tomorrow?"

"Noon, at Kalafrana."

"Kalafrana? The subs are in Lazaretto Creek. Kalafrana is where they keep the Sunderlands."

"Right, right. But this one ties up at Kalafrana. Be early, they wait for nobody."

"They know who I am? They'll let me through the gate with a mummy under my arm?"

"They know me, there won't be a problem."

"You won't be there."

"Use my name. Tell them you're I-3, flash your ID."

"I don't have ID."

"Didn't I pin something on you when I took you into Lascaris?"

"The blue tag? I threw it away. I gave it to the kid, Joseph."

"You'll be in the pink hearse. Anybody in a pink hearse they'll be glad to see."

"No pink hearse," Rocco said. "No gas, no gas for months. Didn't you know?"

"Go to Eddie Fenech on Fleur-de-Lys Street, he likes Americans. He'll sell you all the gas you need. His brother-in-law steals from the central depot. Tell him I sent you."

Fingerly still held the key, offering it, but Rocco, thumbs hooked onto his belt, was unresponsive.

"Do this for me," Fingerly said again. "Will you?"

Rocco knew what he was saying. He was reminding him that he had saved his life, that first day, at the airfield, when the 109 was strafing and he pulled Rocco down into a trench. He held out the key, shiny yellow brass. "Do it," he repeated.

Rocco tilted his head uncertainly, his tongue pushing around against the inside of his cheek. Then, with a lazy shrug, took it.

"Chica boom," Fingerly said.

"Fleur-de-Lys? In Valletta?"

"In Birkirkara. Talk to Eddie." He pulled a wad of rolled-up paper money, British sterling, out of his pocket. "Here's your last from I-3," he said, "we're all square. Plus a bonus for not getting killed. Inflation is eroding the currency, spend it fast. Buy your girlfriend a fur coat. If I ever do anything with used cars, I'll look you up." Then, with a wave of his hand, and already on the move, "Nice working with you, Raven. Enjoy the war, it's the only war you have. See you again some time, in Oklahoma."

He hurried off, and Rocco, holding the key and the wad of money, called after him. "Oklahoma?"

"It's as good a place as any," Fingerly said, not bothering to look back. He went past a shoe store, a barber's, and a radio shop, then around the corner and out of sight, gone, that quickly, and Rocco was left standing there, staring at the vacant air. He felt a strange, buoyant emptiness, something he could almost hear, a hollow sound, like a sour note from an untuned piano, because he knew that was the end of it, it was done and finished. Settled, over. *Finito. Spicca. Ganz und gar.* He would never see Fingerly again.

Malta was emptying out. The Greek herpetologist had left in October, as had the countess from Poland, who had sailed for Brazil, hoping eventually to make her way to Pittsburgh, where she had relatives. Julietta and Count von Kreisen were in Alexandria. Most of the pilots Rocco knew had already been rotated out—Daddy Longlegs, Johnny Plagis, Smoky Joe Lowery. Bull Turner was back and forth to Gibraltar and Alexandria, doing liaison work with the navy. Not Tony Zebra, though. He was still on Malta, where he didn't want to be.

A few days after he had fired on Fingerly's Phantom but hit the black-market shed instead, he was flying again, engaging the 109s, and crashed his plane into a radio mast that rose above a police station in Mosta. He walked away from the wreckage, shaken but unhurt, and was made the leader of a newly formed squadron, a mix of Americans and Australians. "Before it's over," he told Rocco, "they're going to make me wing commander of Takali, even though it sticks in their craw that I'm from New Jersey and never went to Oxford. That's what they have in mind. I know it, I feel it coming. I think I'll swallow cyanide."

They had him flying sorties over Sicily, a bomb under each wing, hitting the airfields, going for Comiso, Gela, Fontanarossa. He liked to fly over Etna and look down into the surly mouth of the volcano, because for him it symbolized life itself, hot mud boiling and rumbling in a steamy miasma, nothing but trouble. He would open his canopy so he could smell the sulfurous stink.

On a Monday, less than a week after he crashed into the radio mast, he was up again, cruising over Malta, flying patrol with Giddings, Gass, and Stoop. In a foggy state of depression, he broke away from the group and flew solo into a whole cloud of 109s. He was so sick of Malta, so demoralized and dejected, that he didn't care if the 109s blew him to pieces. He was tired of it all: the dust, the cactus, and the tins of bully beef, sick of the occasional Ovaltine and the dwindling cigarette supply. In desperation he had joined the poker games, hoping to win a few extra smokes, but he lost, lost, lost, and by a warehouse one night, under a full moon, he held up a black-market salesman at gunpoint and absconded with seven cartons of Philip Morris, but in his room at the Point de Vue the mice broke into them and tore them apart and he never got to smoke any of them. He was sick of the pubs that were out of beer, and the re-run movies, and the glare of the sun, and dismal bouts of the Malta dog that sent him racing for the toilet.

So, with suicidal abandon, he flew into the oncoming Messerschmitts. But again, despite the odds, he was untouchable, and had, this time, luck that he wasn't looking for and didn't want. Flying into the formation and crossing at an angle, he caused such confusion that two of the planes, veering sharply to avoid him, collided with two other planes, and the four dropped like rocks into the sea. The other members of his flight, Stoop, Gass, and Giddings, watching from a distance, reported back that he had knocked down another four.

"I think I want to die," Tony Zebra confided to Rocco. "I'd rather pass out of existence—vanish from the earth—than spend another miserable month on Malta. Why don't they understand that? Can't they see that Malta is tearing me apart and where I really belong is in India? Don't they understand it's a war crime to keep me here any longer?"

This time they gave him the DSO.

After Fingerly left Rocco with the key to the warehouse in Paola, Rocco picked up a newspaper and made his way back to Windmill Street still amazed that Fingerly was departing the island, never to return. He went to the upstairs room, the one without a roof, and after chasing the pigeons, he sat on the floor and wrote to his father. From Malta, he'd written only a few times, and from his father there had been only one letter, in which he wrote about the tomatoes he'd grown that came up fat as melons, though the carrots and radishes had been a disappointment. Rocco in one of his letters had mentioned Melita, but it was a letter that received no response. He shrugged it off. Wartime mail was an iffy thing anyway.

He wrote about the way things had been with them the last few years, the way they were drifting apart. Even before he joined the army, they'd been seeing each other less and less. His father had sold the house in Flatbush and moved in with the widow in Bensonhurst, and Rocco was out there on his own, living at a Y. When they saw each other, there was always a shadow of bad feeling, about one thing or another. But now, as he sat alone in the room without a roof, the bad feelings faded, or at least they seemed less relevant, and he thought it was important to write this letter, to say in words the things that he felt.

"What I want you to know," he wrote, "is that as far as I'm concerned, everything between us is all right. I hope that's how you feel too. Is it? It used to be I was confused about a lot of things, but not, I think, anymore. Or not as much, anyway. The way I see it, life is like an old car that gets fussy and finicky. You have to treat it just right or it will stall."

The words, he realized, didn't exactly say what he wanted them to say, yet it was, in any case, an attempt to close the gap, an effort to move closer than they'd been.

"Anyway," he added, "I've been in this war almost eight months now, and still it amazes me. Sometimes you get cocky and think nothing can hurt you, but then there are times you feel any minute there will be a bomb, a big one, with your name on it, and it makes you think. You get philosophical, living on Malta. You also see things, sometimes, that aren't there. It's the sun, it does things with your eyes. But Melita thinks it isn't the sun, she thinks the island is haunted, and she loves it, she never wants to leave."

He was going to stop there, but then he was remembering again, thinking about when he was young, when things between them were better than they were now. He remembered the backhoe, his father sitting high up there on the big machine and plowing up the streets, making holes for the sewers. One day his father let him sit at the controls and fool around. He was ten, or eleven, and it was the best time ever. His father showed him how to move the big scooper, left and right, up and down. He did that—moved the scooper. But then he yanked at something, when his father wasn't looking, and the scooper swung around and knocked over a fire hydrant, and water gushed like crazy. They were soaked. "Wasn't it the best?" he wrote. "Wasn't it, for both of us, the damn best that ever happened?"

He was inclined to write more, there were other things he wanted to say, but he left the rest of the page blank and folded it, and put it in an envelope. His father was in Bensonhurst, but he addressed the letter, unthinkingly, to the house he'd grown up in, in Flatbush, with the small garden in the backyard and the purple hydrangea bush, which gave, in some years, big beautiful flowers, but some years not.

* * *

Thursday morning, with Melita, he picked up the hearse at Zammit's, and with the little bit of gas that was left, got it over to Eddie Fenech's autoshop in Birkirkara, where Eddie's wife, a simian-browed woman with pretty eyes and a gravy-stained apron, filled the tank with all the petrol it could take. There was no pump. The petrol was in gallon-sized tins, each marked as the property of the Royal Malta Artillery, and it wasn't cheap. With what he paid, Rocco could have bought a secondhand piano, or a whole coop of egg-laying hens, but the hens would have been hard to find because most of the hens on the island had already been cooked and eaten.

They drove to Paola, to the warehouse where Fingerly had kept his stash. It started as a cloudy day, rain falling, welcome wetness damping down the dust, though by the time they got to Paola, the rain had stopped and the sky began to clear.

Rocco still found it hard to believe Fingerly was off the island and wouldn't be back. Since April, they'd been stitched into each other's lives. The mood, the manner, the sliding baritone voice, the banter, the tongue-in-cheek irony, the cash flow, chica boom. Eight months of Fingerly, and now he was gone, and it was good riddance, but also a void. They had been through so much together, life and death, and yet what Rocco felt was that they were strangers. He didn't know any more about Fingerly the person, the sensing self that felt and suffered—if he did feel and suffer—than on that first frantic day in April, when Fingerly picked him up at Luqa airfield.

In Paola, carrying a flashlight, he led Melita down the long flight of stone stairs into the underground warehouse.

"How old, do you figure?"

"This place?" She studied the stonework. "Three or four hundred years. Always these dark, underground holes, for slaves and prisoners. From the Knights, and before the Knights." She found it depressing.

He led her along the stone corridor, past the padlocked doors, across cobblestones and heavy iron drainage grates, and at the last door he took out Fingerly's key and fumbled at the lock. It was like revisiting a haunted house. Fingerly gone, his stuff gone, the stone storage room swept clean, nothing there but the packing case containing the mummy, and an old wooden table with some tools on it: a screwdriver, hammer, crowbar, a few candles.

"You want to see it?"

"No."

"Not even a peek?"

He picked up the crowbar and pried the lid open. Inside, there was an abundance of wood shavings and crumpled paper, which he cleared away, getting at the coffin.

"Look," he said, shining the flash on the coffin's lid, at the painted birds and snakes, the hieroglyphics.

She looked, bending close, touched the wood, then drew away.

He opened the lid, and the mummy was as he remembered it, the brownish-gray wrappings drawn away at the mouth, some teeth showing, part of the cheek, the upper lip, the revealed skin dark and leathery, embalmed in silence.

"It's ugly," Melita said. "I don't want to look." She did though, briefly. "What in the world does he want with a thing like that?"

"What does he want with anything?" Rocco wondered, noticing, as he spoke, a brown envelope taped to the inside of the lid, the envelope bearing the name of the Seven Seas Stamp Den, on Old Mint, where Rocco had stopped when he was looking for Nigg.

He detached the envelope, and found inside a glassine wrapper containing a block of four stamps. American stamps. He removed them from the glassine, looked closely, and saw it was the Curtiss Jenny stamp, four of them, in mint condition, each with a picture of the Curtiss Jenny bi-wing airplane—but at the center, inside the frame, the plane had been printed upside down, by mistake, making each stamp worth a small fortune, and with four of them in a block like this, a big small fortune.

"He found this in Malta?" he said with some surprise.

"What?"

"This, these," showing her, explaining about the way the plane had been printed upside down. The pretty colors, rose and blue. U.S. POSTAGE: 24 cents.

"That makes it valuable? Upside down? It looks like that plane you flew and nearly got killed in, with the double wings."

He studied the stamps, pored over them. He had dreamed of finding one of these when he was a kid.

"Pretty colors," he said.

She shrugged. Stamps were stamps, even big small-fortune stamps.

He put them back in the envelope, reattached the envelope to the lid, then closed the coffin and hammered the packing case shut. The case didn't have Fingerly's name on it, just a few rows of numbers.

"We have to carry this all the way upstairs?"

"Light as a feather," he said.

But when he lifted one end, it was heavier than he'd imagined, and he quickly realized there was something else in there besides the mummy and the stamps, something under the mummy's coffin, in a false bottom. More of Fingerly's mysterious booty, gold, platinum, maybe the Maltese Falcon itself, the genuine article, right there in the crate. With Fingerly, anything was possible.

"What do you think?" he asked Melita.

"I think it's a lot of hot air," she said.

He picked up the crowbar, half inclined to tear the false bottom open.

"Let it be," she said.

"Yes?"

"I think so."

That's what he thought too, reluctantly. Whatever it was, better to leave it untouched. It was Malta, full of strangeness and mystery, codes and counter-codes, layers and levels, sublevels, and, as Fingerly had said, trap doors through which you could fall and disappear, and this was one he really didn't want to go through.

They went back up and found an off-duty soldier willing to lend a hand. He had a bushy head of black hair. He'd been boozing, and had a mild buzz on.

"What you got in 'ere, mate? A bloody corpse?"

"How'd you guess?"

They made it through the long stone corridor easily enough, but it was hard up the stairs. They stopped often, adjusting their grip. When they reached the top, Melita opened the back of the hearse and they slid the crate in.

Rocco gave him a pack of Luckies.

"Glad to oblige, mate. Any time. I specialize in dead bodies myself, y' know. Back home I was a undertaker's assistant. Used to drive a hearse just like this one, 'cept it weren't pink, of course. It was a decent day's pay and no bloody bombs to worry about."

Rocco drove off, turning onto the road to Kalafrana, with Melita beside him and the mummy in the back, in the crate. The traffic was heavy and slow, clogged with military vans and supply trucks, and horse-drawn wagons. Wagons were much in use now because of the severe fuel shortage. Even the military were using them for some of their transport.

Below Santa Lucija, the traffic ground to a standstill, nothing moving on the long, narrow road. Rocco stepped out and walked up the line, to see what the problem was. "Has to be a bomb," a corporal in one truck said, but a deliveryman on a wagon thought it was probably a flat tire on a staff car, or an overheated engine. Further along, Rocco came upon a sergeant sitting on the bumper of a truck loaded with rifle ammunition. He was eating fish out of a can, and had a bottle of beer.

"It'll be a while," he said, offering Rocco a swig of beer, but Rocco declined.

"How long do you think?"

"Long enough."

Rocco peered down the road, seeing nothing but stopped trucks and wagons. "Somebody break an axle?"

"Hell, no, it's more than that."

An army truck had collided with a wagon carrying a crop of melons from Gozo, and the wagon tipped over, dumping melons all over the road, hundreds of them. The truck that hit the wagon swerved off and hit another truck, knocking it over on its side, and they were waiting now for a wrecker crew to clear the road. One of the wagon's two horses suffered a broken leg and had to be shot, and there were some soldiers out there, helping the farmer to pick up the melons, which were too precious to be abandoned. The farmer had come all the way from Gozo, crossing on the ferry, and now he had a broken wagon, a dead horse, and a load of bruised melons that he didn't dare walk away from.

"Melons?" Rocco said. "In November?"

"It's a late crop, sure, that's what makes them so valuable. These Gozo farmers, they're raking it in."

"Cantaloupes?"

"Watermelons. He's selling right there at the roadside to anyone who wants, four shillings apiece. That's as much as I get in wages for a day. How about you, Yank? You get better'n that?"

"They'll be a while, you think?"

"Well, you know how it is. A dead horse, an overturned wagon, two trucks smashed, watermelons everywhere. The driver of the truck that did the damage bashed his head through the windshield."

Rocco went back to the hearse. "Melons," he said to Melita, through the rolled-down window.

"Whose melons?"

"Some farmer from Gozo. All over the road."

He drummed his fingers on the roof.

"This is no good," she said, glancing at her watch.

He stood on the running board, trying to see ahead, as if seeing might hurry it along. But all that he saw was the long line of trucks and wagons, extending into an indefinite haze. At the edge of the road it was farmland, a sloping hill, plowed and messy after a harvest of late vegetables. Halfway up the hill was a gun emplacement, an antiaircraft gun surrounded by sandbags.

He slid into the hearse and sat motionless, staring straight ahead.

"What do you think?" he said.

"I don't know," she said.

He continued to sit, staring at the truck in front of him—then turned the ignition, and after a moment's hesitation, drove the hearse off the road and onto the plowed field, bouncing over the rugged, uneven terrain. They went a far distance that way, shaking and rattling, and slipping about. At one point the hearse sank in a depression of soft soil, coming to a dead stop, but Rocco floored the accelerator, spinning the wheels, and the tires finally caught.

When they reached the point where the accident had occurred, they saw that one of the trucks had been removed and a crew was working on the other one, hooking it to a tow. The farmer from Gozo was at the edge of the road with his two horses, one of them dead, the other swinging its head from side to side. A few soldiers were gathering the remaining melons, but most of them were already stacked on the wagon, which was off the road and quite a wreck, having lost all of its wheels. The farmer, a middle-aged man with graying hair, was smoking a pipe, sitting on a rock, looking on as the army crew struggled with the second truck.

Then they were past it and back on the road, moving quickly, raising a cloud of dust. On a sharp turn Rocco narrowly missed an oncoming truck, and on another turn he barely avoided a small animal, a little lumpish thing making its way across the road.

"A hedgehog," Melita said.

"A hedgehog? What's a hedgehog? Malta has hedgehogs?"

"Oh, Malta has hedgehogs and even weasels. What we don't have is wild horses. And no giraffes."

As they moved down past Żejtun, they were caught behind a slow-moving convoy of trucks and there was nothing to do but inch along. Eventually the convoy turned off, and Rocco picked up speed, coming into Birżebbuġa, where they met more traffic and it was agonizingly slow, going through town. Then, swinging left, they were quickly down into Kalafrana, and they reached the bay.

At the gate, they were stopped, but when Rocco mentioned Fingerly's name, they were waved on. They drove through a complex of maintenance sheds, and came out on an area facing the bay, where the Sunderland flying boats were lined up. Tied up at the pier was the submarine, ready to cast off.

"Didn't think you'd make it," a petty officer said.

Two sailors heaved the packing crate from the hearse and took it aboard. It was all very quick.

Rocco had never been that close to a submarine. It had an odd, simple elegance, plain and powerful, like a great black whale that knew every nook and cranny of the neighborhood: primordial, and deadly serious. It had a sullen beauty to it, yet he couldn't imagine why anyone would want to sail that way, submerged, closed in by H_2O. The mere thought of it made him claustrophobic.

At exactly noon, the sub slipped away, low in the water, moving out toward the mouth of the bay. A lone seaman stood watch in the conning tower.

It was impressive, a solemn slowness in the way it moved, cutting through the water, its long wake swirling like bridal lace behind it. The mummy was on its way, and Rocco felt lightened, free of Fingerly at last, the debt paid, canceled, all square and even.

"He saved my life. Did I tell you?"

"You told me."

"The first day, when I flew in to Luqa, he pulled me into a trench seconds before the bullets ripped past. I hate the 109s."

They watched as the sub turned and passed through the mouth of the harbor, and it was Melita who noticed first that the seaman had disappeared from the conning tower. The sub was slipping under, submerging as it passed into the open sea. There was a moment when it was still slimly visible, riding calmly, and then, swiftly, it was out of sight as if it had never been there, the wake gone.

Still they lingered, watching. After the morning rain, the day was clear, and in the mild coolness of November, the sun was a comfort. There was a vibrancy in the air, a quiet brilliance. The war in Malta was winding down. There were still bombings and strafings, but nothing like what there had been, nothing like the ferocious blitz of April, when Rocco first arrived.

"I love the sea," Melita said, "it's so strong, it means so much."

The blue of the sky and the blue of the sea formed a moody counterpoint, as if they were in dialogue.

"How peaceful," she said. "How wonderful!"

They tarried, enjoying the sun. But then, as they were about to head back for the car, there was an explosion at sea, ripping through the surface, sending up a wide, white geyser. It lifted and surged, tons of churning water, rising in a kind of slow motion, then hovering, in seeming defiance of gravity. When the water fell back, rings of waves rippled away from the center.

A stunned silence took hold. For a while, there was nothing—no motion, no sound, only the bright, hard glare of the sun. Then a heavy-throated siren went off, and within moments two Sunderlands took to the air, rising from the water and heading for the spot out there where the day had broken and all of the good feeling went horribly wrong. The submarine had struck a mine.

There was a rush of sailors, running onto the pier, and a rescue boat pulled out, moving out of the bay at high speed, followed by two large launches.

Melita broke down, weeping, shaking with heavy sobs. "All those poor boys," she said. "All of them, all of them!"

The ones they had just talked to, the petty officer and the sailors who carried the crate aboard. It was unlikely there would be any survivors. She sobbed uncontrollably, all of the anguish and fear of the months and years coming to focus for her now, pouring out of her, an internal upheaval and collapse. She leaned against Rocco, sobbing into his chest, and with both arms he held her up. There was no strength in her, and he thought she would fall.

Then the tears slowed and she caught her breath. She stepped back from him, and, along with the grief, there was anger and bitterness. "That thing," she said, "that stupid, horrid, horrible thing," still weeping, "that mummy, I told you it was bad luck, I knew it, knew it." And then, full of guilt and blame, blaming Fingerly, blaming Rocco, blaming herself, with both fists she pounded on Rocco's arms and chest as if, lashing out, she could change it all, undo what had happened, not just this moment but all of the past, the whole long horror of the war. Rocco grabbed hold of her wrists and held her to himself, and slowly, then, she came back, breathing more evenly, still weeping.

"Let's go," she said, exhausted, her face wet and ragged, "I don't want to be here anymore."

On the drive back to Valletta, they went through Birżebbuġa and then north, along the main road, passing the long stretch where the traffic had been at a standstill. The farmer was still there, with his broken wagon loaded with melons. He was still smoking his pipe. The dead horse was gone, and the other one, the white one, was halfway up the hill, nosing about by the sandbags surrounding the antiaircraft gun.

In Tarxien, Rocco pulled up in front of a pub, thinking Melita might want something to eat.

"No, nothing for me," she said.

"You're hungry, you need something."

"In there? They don't have anything."

She stayed in the hearse.

When he came out of the pub, he had a hard-boiled egg and a slice of bread wrapped in newspaper, and two bottles of beer.

"A cooked egg," he said, showing it to her.

"I don't want it," she said.

He drove on, through Paola, and when they reached Marsa, he parked at a spot where there was a view of Grand Harbour, the whole long length of it, with the bulwarked flank of Valletta to the left, and at the right, the huge stone fortresses of the Three Cities area jutting into the harbor. Some of the sunken ships had been removed, though quite a few remained, rusted prows and smokestacks jutting up out of the water.

He peeled the egg for her.

"No," she said, "you take it."

"I got it for you."

"Take half, then."

"All I want is a beer. I don't feel like eating."

She took the egg and broke off half, leaving the other half for him, on the newspaper.

"Go ahead," he said.

He opened a beer and drank some off, and she ate, a few quick bites.

"Have it all," he said. "Finish it."

"I can't," she said guiltily.

"I bought it for you."

She hesitated, then took the rest and chewed slowly.

Seagulls wheeled high over the harbor. A few squatted among the rocks at the edge of the water, on the far side of a rusty fence. A brackish smell came off the water, mingling with odors of oil and tar.

"Let's go to Gozo," Rocco said.

She seemed not to understand.

"You said we should go to Gozo and live there," he said. "So let's go."

"You can't," she said, "you have orders."

"I know I can't, but I will. Fingerly is gone."

"You always said if you got orders, you would go."

"We'll live on Gozo till the war is over, then we'll work it out from there."

"I don't want you to do that."

"It was your idea."

"It was a bad idea."

"I don't want to leave you," he said.

"But you have to. This is how it is."

"We'll go to Gozo and I'll find work on a farm. We'll be out of all this."

"But we would not be happy."

"Of course we will."

She said nothing for a while, as if thinking it over, trying to visualize what it would be like. Then she said, "It's what fate gave us. Malta is where I belong. It was a foolish thought, to run away to Gozo. And you, you have to do what you have to do."

He stared ahead, through the windshield, studying the rocks, the gulls, the water. "Do you want your beer?"

"Half, only half."

"You're sure?"

"I'm sure."

Carefully, he poured half of her bottle into his empty bottle, not losing a drop.

"Such a genius," she said.

She put the bottle to her lips, taking a small swallow. She had never had a great taste for beer.

"We'll think about it," he said, wanting to keep Gozo, or at least the idea of Gozo, afloat. "We'll think it over."

"No," she said firmly. "I don't want to think it over. I don't want to talk about it again."

The piece of bread was still on the newspaper, on the seat between them.

"Half?" he said.

"Yes," she said. "Half."

He broke it apart and gave her the larger piece, and she took it, and they ate slowly, sitting there, looking at the prows and funnels of the sunken ships, and the gulls wheeling lazily.

When Rocco had thought Fingerly was in Heliopolis, he wasn't in Heliopolis but in Palermo. When he thought he was in Cairo, he was in Catania, and when he thought he was in Casablanca, he was in Messina, or Marsala, or Agrigento, moving about undercover, in warehouses, farmhouses, in the back rooms of bars and cantinas, meeting with the leaders of the Sicilian Mafia. Rocco learned about it from Tony Zebra, who got it from Warby Warburton, the reconnaissance pilot, who on three occasions flew Fingerly to Sicily in a twin-engine Maryland, from which he bailed out at five hundred feet and later made his way back to Malta by boat.

"Fingerly? In a parachute?" Rocco was thinking of the slacks, the flowery sportshirt, the dark sunglasses.

"In a parachute," Tony Zebra said.

He was consulting with the Mafia because the Mafia and the Fascists hated each other, and in the wisdom of the ages, the enemy of your enemy could, at the right moment, be considered your friend. If and when Sicily was invaded—and it seemed more, now, a question of *when* rather than *if*—it was thought the Mafia could ease the way and help things along. There were pre-invasion details to be gleaned, maps, pictures of port areas, information on minefields and gun emplacements, and during the invasion itself the Mafia might be relied upon to persuade the Italian troops—at least the Sicilians among them—to take off their uniforms and go home.

In Villalba, Fingerly met with Don Calogero Vizzini, the boss of bosses of the Sicilian Mafia. In Mussomeli, he met with Genco Russo, known in his territory as Zu Peppi, the Ras of Mussomeli. In Villabate he met with Nino Cottone, the close friend of the Brooklyn racketeer, Joe Profaci.

"The Sicilian Mafia?" Rocco said, laughing. "Forget it, it doesn't exist. Didn't Mussolini wipe them out twenty years ago? Most of them are still in jail. First he made the trains run on time, then he got rid of the Mafia."

"He did, he did," Tony Zebra said, "but they're like roaches, always there in the woodwork."

"And now Uncle Sam is rehabilitating them? After the invasion, we put them in charge? We make them mayors and aldermen? And it's Fingerly who is doing this?"

"Hey—you're angry with me?"

"I'm angry with you."

"What did I do?"

"You're giving me this cock-and-bull."

"Cock-and-bull? That's what you think? Talk to the OSS. Talk to Naval Intelligence, they're using the New York Mafia to button up the waterfront and stop the sabotage. Didn't you know? The Bundists are getting the piss kicked out of them by the mob, and they haven't realized yet it's the mob that's doing it."

"That's New York. We're talking Sicily."

Tony Zebra rolled his shoulders, like a boxer loosening up. "Hey, look, Naval Intelligence in Manhattan, B-1, B-7, they have people who talk Sicilian better than the Sicilians. You think they're not going to use these guys in Sicily when the time comes, when the troops hit the beaches? They'll be waving gold handkerchiefs with Lucky Luciano's initial, the big black L. You know what invasion is like, Rocco. It brings looting, muddy roads, black market, typhoid, dysentery, orphans, unwanted pregnancies, chaos. The Mafia will restore order in Sicily. That's the theory. Talk to the navy guys, Thayer and McFall, and Haffenden. Talk to Section F and the Ferret Squad. Talk to the OSS and the SI. Talk to Lucky Luciano."

"Luciano is in deep freeze. In Dannemora."

"They moved him to a country club near Albany, a place called Great Meadow. He's royalty, his reach is infinite."

"Him? Not him. Only Fingerly is infinite."

"You think Fingerly is God?"

"I think he's the devil, but he saved my ass, my first day on Malta, so I won't say a word against him." He paused to light a cigarette. "You think Fingerly talks to Luciano? That's what you think? Luciano is the arranger and the fixer?"

As he said it, it flashed home to him that the messages he'd been receiving and sending, Ostrich, X, Daddy, a dozen others, must have been, half of them at least, to and from the Mafia. Luciano probably had his own ham operator in his prison cell at Great Meadow, paid for by the OSS.

"The Fulton Fish Market," Tony Zebra said. "Socks Lanza, you heard of him? And all those other jokers cozy with Luciano—suddenly they're all patriots. You think they want America to lose this war? If America goes down, how in the world will they ever earn a living?"

Rocco was so upset, he lit another cigarette, forgetting he had just lit one. He lit a third and had them all going at once.

"But these are murderers," he said. "Aren't they?"

"They're murderers."

"They're extortionists. White slavers. They beat people up."

"Yes, they beat people up."

"They deal drugs. They run prostitution rings and spread syphilis and disease."

"Luciano had syphilis but he was cured," Tony Zebra said. "He had gonorrhea seven times."

"You're his doctor?"

"I wrote a term paper on him in Criminology 101. Flunked the course."

"These are not good people."

Tony Zebra agreed, shaking his head slowly.

"They hang people from meat hooks."

"True, true. Luciano himself was hung up, by his wrists, in Staten Island. That's one of the things that made him so mean."

"Fingerly talks to these people?"

"Somebody is talking to them."

"But Fingerly? And Luciano?"

"I think they talk to each other in whispers, long distance, in Luciano's Sicilian dialect."

"It's a strange world," Rocco said. "It gets stranger and stranger." And only then, as a flight of Spitfires roared by, did he notice that Tony Zebra had done something to his nose. He had applied makeup, concealing the scars.

"Would you like to fly again?" Tony Zebra said.

"When?"

"Right now."

"Melita would kill me."

"She was pretty sore?"

"She thinks I have a death wish. She still hasn't forgiven me for getting my toes blown off."

"Meyer Lansky," Tony Zebra said.

"I know the name."

"If you ever bring Melita's jukeboxes to America, have Fingerly put you in touch with Meyer Lansky. He controls the jukeboxes in New York. The Emby Corporation. That's his cover. The M in EMBY is Meyer Lansky. Distribution, it's a racket. He controls New York, New Jersey, Connecticut, and Pennsylvania."

"You think Meyer Lansky would go for the Bethlehem Jukebox, and the Lourdes Jukebox, and the St. Agatha Jukebox?"

"He's Jewish, sure, but Rocco, he's a businessman, he doesn't let ethnic hangups interfere with business. It's very American, right? Equality, diversity. Difference. Luciano thinks the same way, he's very big on difference. He works with the Jews and the Irish—if they get the job done, they get the job done. That's why he had to eliminate Maranzaro, he was stuck in the old thinking, wanted to go to war against the Jewish gangs and the German gangs. But Luciano saw the time for that was over. The new way, he has a word for it, somebody told me, he calls it *multiculturalismo*. He and Lansky are really thick, they see eye to eye on just about everything. They won't let ethnic pride and prejudice poison their operation. If Luciano has a hit to make, he'd just as soon give the contract to Bugsy Siegel as to one of his own. It's a new world, Rocco. Isn't it inspiring?"

One of Rocco's three cigarettes burned down, and he lit another, still keeping three going, smoking them all, as if the three were only one. He knew what Fingerly was doing in Sicily. He wasn't preparing the way for the invasion; he was trying to get his hands on one of the old temples the Greeks had built there. He would pay for it with condoms, then take it apart, piece by piece, ship it stateside, and sell it to some millionaire with a big backyard.

"You've been on Malta too long," Tony Zebra said, borrowing one of Rocco's lit cigarettes for a puff, then handing it back.

"Is that my trouble?"

"That's your trouble."

"What do you know?"

"I know it all."

"Only Fingerly knows it all."

"You think so?"

"Well, some of it."

The day after Tony Zebra told Rocco about Fingerly's undercover activities in Sicily, there was a letter from Julietta.

It was long, written on several pages of scented pink paper, in a broad, open handwriting that hid nothing. She loved Alexandria—the shops, the palm trees, the mosques, the bazaars, the nightclubs, the wonderful beaches along the Corniche, and the view of the sea from the Count's villa.

She also mentioned that she was pregnant.

Not, of course, by the Count, who is simply too old, though he is fatuous enough to believe he is the father. German men, you understand, even the gentlest, like my Freddie, are completely delusional when it comes to masculinity and their virile powers. But I won't bore you with the details, except to say, sadly, I have no idea who the father is. It might be that pilot you played poker with, the one with the moustache, who got killed in July, or the British admiral who was so upset when he lost in the bidding for Miss Sicily—you can't imagine how crushed he was, the poor man, he whimpered like a child when he told me about it. Or the bartender who works in Hock's—I did like him, he had such wonderful teeth, and a sweet, generous smile. The one thing I am sure of, my dearest Rocco, is that the father is not you, as we were never so lucky as to find ourselves in bed together. Nevertheless, if my Freddie suspected the child I am carrying might not be his, he would have no use for me and my life would not be worth a slice of bread. He knows, of course, that I was with other men when I was on Strait Street, and he rather likes that. It delights him that, at his age, he is still vigorous enough to command the affections of a woman of experience, as he prefers to call me. But if he had any idea that I am carrying another man's child, he would be beside himself. What am I to do? I am telling you all this, dear Rocco, because I have to tell someone, and you are a person I can trust. If it's a boy, I will name him after you. Would you like that? His saint will be your saint, St. Rocco. Such a good, strong name, and I have always liked St. Rocco and prayed to him, even though I know very little about him.

The letter came in on a BOAC Lodestar that flew regularly now, at night, three times a week, between Egypt and Malta. The pilot was someone Tony

Zebra had played golf with when they were in training together in Scotland, at Montrose.

There was a postscript:

The Count has found an out-of-the-way bistro with a piano, where he plays his waltzes, as he did at Dominic's, and it makes me sad to remember those happy times. I've written to Simone and Aida but receive nothing in reply and I wonder if my letters reach them. If this reaches you, please tell them I wait to hear from them. I miss my dear friends from Malta so very, very much. But it's better here, especially now that Rommel has been beaten off and the Germans are no longer a threat. The food is good, and there are none of the shortages you have in Malta. And I do enjoy sleeping late in the morning!

Rocco showed the letter to Melita, who sniffed the perfume, and didn't like it at all that Julietta was thinking of naming the baby after him.

"I'm hungry," she said. "Are you hungry?"

He was hungry. The food situation was worse than ever, even more desperate than in August, when they were saved by the Santa Marija convoy. Rocco had lost twenty pounds, Tony Zebra more than thirty. Rocco remembered how gaunt Screwball Beurling was when they sent him home, after he'd shot down his twenty-ninth plane—in a couple of months he'd lost fifty pounds. Weight loss improved his deadliness, it made his eyes keener. He boasted that he could hit a teacup at three hundred yards.

Even Melita, she too was losing weight, but still there was flesh on her bones, and it was still magical, stirring him, the sweet fervor of slow arousal. Flesh soft and lissom, he could feel the bone underneath, the silken way her skin moved when he touched her, a soft, forlorn sensuousness.

"Look at me, I'm losing my breasts," worrying over the way her body was shrinking. "Soon there will be nothing, nothing."

Her breasts were smaller, but still ripe and ample, tender in their fullness, supple in the palms of his hands.

"Right now, this moment," she said, "what I most want is an orange, a cold orange that's been in the icebox for days. I can taste it, I can feel my teeth biting into it."

A government decision had already been announced about what would be done with the oranges when they ripened in December. They would be given to pregnant women and children under seven. If the crop was a good one, the children and pregnant women might each get a dozen oranges over the course of the season.

November 20, 1942

TURIN ROCKED BY TWO-TON BOMBS
RAID ON ITALIAN ARSENAL
ALL BRITISH BOMBERS RETURN

JAPANESE NAVAL DEFEAT IN SOLOMONS
LOSSES GREATER THAN FIRST CLAIMED

NEW DIVISIONS THROWN IN AT STALINGRAD
1000 Enemy Killed in Day's Fighting

DEATH SENTENCE FOR ESPIONAGE

Valletta, November 19. Yesterday, the death sentence was pronounced for Carmelo Borg Pisani, who was found guilty on three charges: espionage, taking up arms against the Government, and forming part of a conspiracy to overthrow the Government. The proceedings were held in camera and the sentence was read in public. It is understood that Borg Pisani was one of Carlo Mallia's Irredentist Group with headquarters in Rome.

"They're going to execute him? Actually going to do it?"

"Who?"

"That nut. Borg Pisani. The one that went to Italy and came back in a rowboat to do espionage, but they caught him when he landed. Don't you remember? The Italians dropped him a mile from shore and he rowed in, with a radio and a gun."

"He deserves to die," Melita said.

"Why?"

"He deserves."

"But he never hurt a fly, they caught him before he could do anything. He's a fool, a clown."

"He's a traitor."

"So put him in jail, make him wash latrines. They have to hang him?"

"Yes, they should hang him."

She was firm, no softness, and Rocco saw now how deeply the war had affected her, there were levels of anger he could only glimpse. He remembered what Tony Zebra had said about the women on the farms who went after the downed German pilots with pitchforks.

"Let's not spoil the day," she said.

He looked at her, a long gaze, the slope of her jaw, the turn of her lips, and it filtered through to him that it wasn't Borg Pisani she was angry with, but him, because he was leaving.

The letter from Julietta had reached Rocco on the 19th, a Thursday. That night, a convoy with four merchant ships sailed into Grand Harbour, carrying thirty-five thousand tons of food and supplies, from Alexandria.

Even more important than its arrival was the fact that it came in unharmed. It had been attacked by a few torpedo bombers, but the merchant ships were never touched and the only damage was to one of the cruisers. There had been no major effort to stop the ships, nothing like the all-out assaults on the convoys that sailed in March and June, and the August convoy that lost nine merchant ships and an aircraft carrier. It was clear to everyone: the siege had been lifted.

Friday morning, news of the convoy spread and people rushed to see the ships, huge crowds gathering at the wharves and docks, cheering the crews. On both sides of the harbor, in Valletta and in the Three Cities, people climbed onto rooftops, looking toward the harbor in a kind of delirium. A balmy breeze ruffled the water. Not since before the war had there been so many big ships in the harbor—in French Creek and Dockyard Creek and Kalkara Creek, and Rinella Creek by Fort Ricasoli. By noon, two brass bands were in place, playing patriotic tunes, one in the Lower Barracca Gardens, in Valletta, and the other across the harbor, at Fort St. Angelo.

Rocco and Melita went down to the Barriera Wharf, below the St. Barbara bastion. People were singing, waving rosaries and handkerchiefs. Mothers with babies, and soldiers, clerks, secretaries, farmers from the outlying villages. A nun carried a brown puppy in her arms. A woman sold black-market apples out of a suitcase. A man with one arm, a veteran, had a barrel of water and a ladle, you could drink from the ladle for half a shilling.

Rocco nudged Melita. "Want an apple?"

He bought three and gave one to the nun with the puppy.

He thought he saw Aida, in a black dress, but it was someone else. He saw Father Hemda, but he vanished in the crowd, and though Rocco kept his eye out for him, he never saw him again.

A squadron of Spitfires flew overhead, forming a protective umbrella. A few 109s made an approach, but they were driven off before they reached the coast. Bombers from Malta had been pounding the Sicilian airfields through the night and early morning, making it hard for the 109s to get off the ground. The war, at last, had turned around.

Hanging from the windows of the tenements were signs painted on sheets:

SAVE MALTA

KILL THE HUN

PRAISE GOD

MOTHER OF GOD SAVE US

The brass bands competed with each other across the harbor. First one, then the other, back and forth. Not far from where Melita and Rocco stood, an old couple were arguing, the man insisting the convoy was a failure, only four freighters, hardly enough when all of Malta was starving. After the Santa Marija convoy, in August, instead of more food in the ration they received less. "It's the same now, never enough," he said, hollow-cheeked and gaunt. "What good are four when we need eight? What good are eight when we need sixteen?" But the woman, short, thick-boned, her forehead sprinkled with black moles, mocked him, chiding him for his pessimism. "Look at all the ships," she cried, "the ships, the ships—the war is over! Don't you see? There are no more bombs, it's over!"

A Spitfire, swooping low over the harbor, came within inches of hitting a smokestack on a destroyer. The near miss drew a loud, long groan from the crowd. "It's Tony Zebra," Rocco said. "He crashed eight planes and he's looking for number nine." Rocco had the numbers wrong. He didn't know about the two Tony Zebra had crashed in training, at Montrose, and the two he'd crashed over the English Channel before he was assigned to Malta. He was working on number thirteen, and even on Malta, thirteen was bad luck.

Suddenly, halfway down the wharf, Rocco saw—thought he saw—Fingerly, off in the crowd, towering among the shorter Maltese. He was in uniform, with two British officers, one dark, with a mustache, the other sandy-haired, the three with their heads together about something. Rocco forged through the crowd, half the length of the wharf, but when he reached the two British officers, Fingerly wasn't there.

"Where is he?" he asked, glancing about anxiously.

"Where's who?"

"Fingerly."

"What's a Fingerly," asked the one with the mustache, with a brash smile. "Too much celebrating, old chap? Found yourself a tub of gin?"

"That wasn't Fingerly? You were talking with him."

The one with sandy hair shrugged, and the one with the mustache, still smiling, looked at Rocco as if he were in need of medical attention.

Rocco found his way back to Melita, fumbling through the crowd. The sun was like black fire in her hair.

"I saw him," he said, "I know I saw him."

"He's gone," she said.

"But I saw him. I thought I saw Aida too, but it was somebody else. I saw Father Hemda, and I know it was him, but now I'm not so sure."

"Are you all right?"

"I'm going through déjà vu, but it isn't déjà vu. It *was* Fingerly, I really saw him."

"He's going crazy," she said idly, gazing into his confused brown eyes. "His last day on Malta and he's falling apart. Do you want some water?"

"No, not at that price. Half a shilling? He should be shot."

A ship's horn moaned in the harbor, and the Spitfires, circling above, stroked the air with the mellow groan of their Merlin engines. The brass bands still played, back and forth, the brass notes flattening out across the water, stark and lonesome.

"Enough," Melita said wearily. "Let's go."

They negotiated their way off the wharf and back to the Victoria Gate, and wandered around on the streets of Valletta, which were crowded, though not as packed as the wharf had been.

"It was him," Rocco said, still thinking of Fingerly. "Exactly him."

"Does it matter? You're through with him, he's gone. Why are you bothering yourself?"

He was bothering himself because he understood now that Fingerly was never gone, he was always there. Even absent he was present, part of the atmosphere, in the air you breathed, the smell in your nostrils.

"If that was Fingerly, it means Benjamin Franklin is not in Bucharest but right here, in Malta. Why did he say he was headed for Romania? Why did he lie to me? All those times he was in Sicily, he said he was somewhere else. You think he's going back to Palermo?"

"He lies because he doesn't know how not to lie. You told me so yourself. A priest is a priest, a plumber is a plumber, and Fingerly is a liar. But that wasn't Fingerly you saw, it was somebody else. Don't be silly over this."

"You're right, you're right. But why did he have to lie to me?"

"You saw somebody who wasn't there and you're making a big thing. Why are you being so strange?"

"First I'm silly and now I'm strange? Which way do you like me better?"

"I like you better when I have you home with me, under the sheets."

"That sounds serious."

"It is serious. Tomorrow, when you're gone, it's going to be terrible. Maybe I'll make lace, like my aunt. Or I'll become a nun and sell rosary beads."

His last day with her. It was hard to believe. Tomorrow he'd be on a plane, on his way to another country, and at night they'd be in different beds. Her eyes, nose, teeth, the way her lips widened when she smiled, and tomorrow he wouldn't see that smile.

For how long?

They turned a corner, onto St. Ursula, and in front of them, as solid as truth, was Marie, Beatrice's girl, with a boy Rocco mistook for Joseph, but it was her cousin. Marie was prettily made up, hair in a long braid, a hint of rouge on her cheeks.

"What a lovely dress," Melita said, admiring the neatly sewn taffeta, gray and pink, with piping and pleats. "Did your mother make it?"

"My mother started it, but Simone finished it. She made the lace. It's my wedding dress. This is my cousin Emmanuel, we're getting married."

"Oh?" Melita said. "When is that?"

"Today, I think. But maybe not till next year. Are you married?"

"No, we're not married," Melita said.

"Are you getting married?"

"I have to go away," Rocco said.

"Why? Don't you like us?"

"Of course I like you. It's the war."

"The war is over," she said.

"Here in Malta it's over, nearly over, but they're still fighting in other places."

"Will it be a long time, the war?"

"I think so. Yes."

"I wanted to marry Joseph, but he wasn't interested. I talked to him but he didn't want to listen."

"Joseph is your brother," Rocco said. "You can't marry your own brother."

"I know, I know. That's what Joseph says. So now I'll marry Emmanuel instead. I wanted to have a white gown, but my mother didn't make it yet. Father Hemda is going to do the wedding."

The boy Emmanuel didn't say a word. He stood by, silent and shy, hands in his pockets, large dark eyes roving from Rocco to Melita, back and forth.

"How old are you?" Melita asked Marie.

"Seven."

"I thought you were fourteen," Rocco said, intending it as a compliment.

"Were you married when you were seven?" she asked Melita.

"I don't think so, no," Melita said. "But I wish."

Marie looked up at her shyly. "You have some lipstick for me?"

"Your mother lets you use lipstick?"

"It's her wedding day," Rocco said.

"Ah yes, her wedding day. In that case," Melita said, taking the lipstick from her purse, "she shall have anything she wants. But promise, Marie, you'll wipe it off before your mother sees."

Bending, she applied the lipstick, then opened her compact so Marie could look at herself.

"What about Joseph?" Rocco said. "Is Joseph getting married?"

"Joseph wants to be a priest," Marie said, admiring herself in the mirror.

"I thought he wanted to be a soldier. He's always in his Boy Scout uniform, playing war."

"Yes, yes, he wants to be a soldier, and a pilot too. He's going to be everything. But he doesn't like girls."

"Maybe he'll change his mind," Rocco said.

"Joseph never changes his mind."

A Spitfire passed low over the street, just above the rooftops.

"How's your mother?" Rocco asked.

"She doesn't talk to my father anymore. She liked it better in Rabat and wants to go back there to live, but my father wants to stay on Strait Street."

"What about you?" Rocco asked. "Would you rather be on Strait Street or in Rabat?"

Before she could answer, the air was punctured by sharp, popping sounds, a rapid pattering, like small-arms fire. A blast went off close to Rocco's head, leaving him briefly stunned, his right ear ringing.

It was firecrackers, dozens of them, falling through the air, exploding before they hit the ground, and when Rocco looked up he saw, on the roof across the street, Joseph in his Boy Scout uniform, lighting them and throwing them down into the crowd, whole long strings of firecrackers. He ran back and forth along the rooftops, tenement to tenement, pausing only to light another string and toss them into the street.

"He's always in trouble," Marie said, sounding like her mother.

"Where'd he get them?" Rocco asked.

"He stole them from a warehouse. They're from one of the ships that came in last August, the Santa Marija ships."

Rocco glanced at Melita. "Malta is starving and they send firecrackers?"

"Oh, they sent candles too," Marie said, "and scissors and witch hazel for the barbers. Joseph stole a lot of witch hazel."

"What else did he get?"

"Chocolate bars."

"Did he give you any?"

"No, but I stole some from him."

"You're going to have a good life, Marie."

"I want to be very rich. Do you think it will happen?"

Up on the roof, Joseph lit rockets and Roman candles. He raced about, back and forth, a wild, pyrotechnic dance, igniting flares, pinwheels, whizzbangs, fizgigs, girandoles. Clouds of smoke rose all around him and he could hardly be seen, darting with his box of matches from one cluster of noisemakers to the next. A rocket, a big one, went up with a resounding *boom*—a long snaky thing twisting and winding, shedding yellow and red scallops in the dark blue afternoon sky.

Rocco and Melita moved on, heading back to Windmill. As they went past the Auberge de Castille, which was now nothing but a shell, an American officer on a bicycle came riding along too fast, and, swerving to avoid a group of nuns, crunched into Rocco, sending him to the ground.

The officer helped him up. He was a major, with a bony nose, bony forehead, a square bony jaw, a cragged face that seemed, somehow, full of bad weather. But he was apologetic, helping Rocco to his feet, and tipped his hat to Melita.

"Are you all right, soldier? You in one piece?" His pale gray eyes showed genuine concern.

"Fine, fine," Rocco said, dusting himself off, his knee stinging where it hit the ground. When he looked at the major, there seemed something familiar about him, something from long ago, as if, at one time or another, somewhere, they might have met. For a moment he felt he was on the edge of remembering, but it remained a blur. "Are you from Oklahoma?" he asked, not entirely sure why.

"Me? Hell no, I'm from Vermont."

He was on the bike again, pedaling fast, rushing to get somewhere. A dog barked. A ship in the harbor sounded its horn. A bunch of boys ran by, playing war, shooting at each other with imaginary rifles, making gun noises with their mouths, and again Rocco had a sense of layer upon layer, fold upon fold. Dragut, Dragut, in his iron suit. Malta dog, Malta fungus. A flock of pigeons descended all around them, pecking for whatever it is that pigeons peck for, a great swarm of them, with tiny eyes and shimmering feathers, green and purple, and Rocco knew that what Tony Zebra had said was true, he had been on Malta too long.

Thirty-eight

ZAMMIT'S
MOTHER-OF-GOD
MADONNA JUKEBOX

At the bombed-out house on Windmill Street, Melita made an early supper. She made widow's soup, *soppa ta' l-armla,* in a copper kettle. It was called widow's soup because, in ordinary times, even the poorest of widows could afford the ingredients. But now food was in such short supply that a good widow's soup was considered a delicacy. You threw in whatever you could find, vegetables, garlic, an egg if you could get one, and *rikotta.* But *rikotta* was scarcer than eggs, and even if you found some it would cost a small fortune.

She had found *rikotta.*

"Where? Where'd you get it? It cost?"

"It sure did."

"How much?"

She wouldn't tell.

"You traded Benny Goodman? Woody Herman? Jack Teagarden?"

She shook her head.

"A whole jukebox?"

She was mum.

"You didn't trade the pink hearse?"

"Now you're getting silly again. Just enjoy."

"You must have traded Zammit. Right? You gave him up in exchange for the *rikotta.*"

They brought the soup upstairs, to the roofless room on the top floor where they'd first made love. She had set up a small table and lit a few candles.

"This is better than Dominic's ever was," she said.

They ate, and still he had Fingerly on his mind.

"It was him, I know it was."

"Does it matter?" she said wearily.

"It matters, it matters."

"Time matters," she said. "Love matters, hate matters. But not Fingerly, Fingerly doesn't matter."

"This is good soup," he said.

"It better be good."

"Good widow's soup."

"But I'm not a widow," she said, "and I don't want to be. Do you understand? I do not want to be a widow."

There was a firmness, a quiet urgency, and he understood. She was telling him not to get killed. And more, so much more. She was telling him not to forget her, not to let her slip from his thoughts. She was telling him to come back for her after the war, because what they'd had together, the eight months, good and bad, was too precious to throw away. April to November, enduring the bombs, and it seemed, already, a whole long lifetime.

The cat, Byron, came drowsily from another room and rubbed his flank against Rocco's leg, emitting a low grumble. Rocco reached down and scratched behind his ears, then picked him up and put him on the table, letting him lap some soup from his bowl.

In the dark, with very little gas left in the hearse, they drove to Zammit's, in Santa Venera.

"I came to say good-bye," Rocco said.

Zammit was in his carpenter's apron, burdened with small tools, a small saw in his hand. "You are leaving?"

"Yes, it's time to go."

"The war," Zammit said, "it's so unpleasant, nothing is easy anymore."

The brandy was long gone, as were the vermouth and the sherry. The empty bottles had candles stuck in them, but they were well burned down and, with the shortages, candles were almost as hard to find as something to drink.

What Zammit had was a bottle of anisette, which a pub owner had given him in exchange for a jukebox, in July. Zammit thought the jukebox worth three bottles at least, but the pub owner held firm, arguing that since there wasn't any electricity, the jukebox wasn't even something he could use, so it was one bottle or nothing, take it or leave it.

Electricity was still a problem. Through most of the summer, service to households had been cut off. It was back now, but in Santa Venera and the other small villages it was unreliable. Zammit had been without power for the last three weeks. He had a generator, but to run it he needed petrol. He had one tin, five gallons, which he'd been saving for a special occasion, securely locked in the basement.

"If this is his last night on Malta," he said, "then we are going to have music."

He went down into the cellar and brought up his last tin of petrol.

Rocco didn't want him to use it. It seemed extravagant. Even with the convoy in, petrol would continue to be scarce until a few more tankers arrived. But Zammit insisted. He went behind the house to the generator, poured the petrol and started the engine, and inside the house the lights came on. Melita hurried about, making sure the blackout curtains were in place.

"Electric light, it's a miracle," Zammit said. "And music is even better!"

He turned on the jukebox in the living room, punched all the buttons, and the music came on. It was Sinatra, then Crosby, then Kitty Kallen, then Judy Garland. He got the glasses, cordial glasses with silver rims, and poured the anisette.

"The last night?" he said.

"The last night," Rocco said.

"To life," Zammit said, lifting his glass.

"To the jukeboxes," Rocco said.

Sinatra sang "I'll Never Smile Again." The Crosby song was "White Christmas." Kitty Kallen did a forlorn "Love for Sale," and Judy Garland wove her way through "That Old Black Magic."

The records moved one after another from the stack to the spinning turntable, moody, sullen, bittersweet, full of love and hope and despair. "Street of Dreams," "Last Call for Love." The speaker tone was rich and dark, heavy on the bass, a lonely feeling. The languid torment of the heart.

The jukebox in the living room wasn't the only one in the house. Again, as in April, when Rocco was there for the first time, the house was full, jukeboxes everywhere, some nearly finished, others just starting. Seven, at the moment, were playable. Tools and scraps of wood were scattered haphazardly, on the floor, on chairs and tables. But it was a disciplined chaos, Zammit knew where everything was. After a fallow period, a time in which his work had come to a standstill, he was active again and surging ahead.

Melita was delighted. "You've been busy, busy, busy," she said brightly. She hadn't been there for a while, not for a few weeks, and it was gratifying to see that he had emerged from his impasse and was again generating new ideas.

"Come, come upstairs," he said, "both of you, let me show you what I made with the pieces you brought me. I've been working, yes. God in heaven, have I been working!" And as the music played, he led the way upstairs to the room in the back, with a window facing on the garden.

"I thought you were just brooding," Melita said.

"Oh, I'm over that," he said. "It's all behind me. I am working again."

With the scraps and pieces they had salvaged from the wreckage at Dominic's, Zammit had created his masterpiece. It was an evolutionary leap beyond anything he'd done before. There were echoes and resonances from his earlier work, yet an unmistakable freshness, a wonderful strangeness and originality.

In September, when Melita brought him the plastic and the twisted metal from the Wurlitzer 850, he'd been unable to do anything with them. He explored, pondered, worried. He made sketches and scribbled idly, and at length he simply set the fragments aside.

But then, out of nowhere, it had all come together for him, and in a great rush over the course of seven days, with almost no sleep at all, he assembled random pieces of wood, metal, glass, and plastic, cutting and gluing, sawing and hammering, soldering and screwing together. When he was done, he was aware that he'd been beside himself, in a creative frenzy, reaching far out and touching something magical, something he hardly understood, and he had brought back with him a piece of the magic and put it into this odd, eccentric box that glowed and came alive with wonderful music.

The box was big, so big it would be impossible to fit it through the doorway. If it should ever have to be moved, it would have to be taken apart and reassembled. Zammit had used the warm-toned translucent segments from the Wurlitzer, linking them with sections of walnut and rosewood, bits of stained glass, and some of the car parts Rocco had picked up—a taillight, a hubcap, a spark plug that sparked. On his bicycle, one day, Zammit rode out and found the wreckage of a 109, from which he took a small portion of the fuselage bearing the plane's group emblem, a red heart set against a yellow background—this too he incorporated into the jukebox.

But by far the most unusual part of the box was a panel of frosted glass in the front, set directly below the records and framed by the luminous plastic from the Wurlitzer. When a record played, the frosted glass lit up with images that moved in slow motion, projected from within by a miniature device rigged on the other side of the glass.

All of the images, in color, were images of the Blessed Mother. A whole litany of images, showing the Virgin in her multiple manifestations.

"Our Lady of Liesse," Zammit said, as the first image appeared. "Do you know Our Lady of Liesse?" he asked Rocco.

Rocco did not.

"Our Lady of Liesse merged into Our Lady of Guadalupe, then Our Lady of Lourdes, Our Lady of Fatima, Our Lady of Damascus, Our Lady of Pompeii."

"So many?" Melita said. "Do you really need so many?"

"There should be fewer?"

She shrugged uncertainly, not wanting him to imagine she didn't appreciate the brilliance of his accomplishment, because an accomplishment it certainly was, this jukebox that embodied the Mother in all of her various guises and modalities, Queen of the Angels, Mother of Mercy, Refuge of Sinners, Star of the Sea—they were all there, a flowing iconography, one image after another, the Virgin revealed in her multiple apparitions.

At one moment, she took on the appearance of the Venus of Malta, which Zammit had seen at the National Museum before it was closed because of the bombing, the only difference being that the Virgin had her clothes on, and the Venus of Malta did not. Later, she looked a shade like Queen Victoria, and in her final apparition she bore a remarkable resemblance to Miss Sicily—and when Melita saw that, she realized Zammit had been less than candid when he'd told her that his infatuation was a thing of the past. She was saddened, because she understood now, more fully than ever before, that he would never be happy. Love was cruel, full of snares, risks, pitfalls, wrenching agonies. And unrequited love was the worst of all.

The jukebox glowed. In the darkened room it shimmered with warm color tones that shifted subtly in waves and jabs of light, coy glimmerings, a muted version of the aurora borealis. The box seemed to float, as if lifted from the ground, hovering in space.

Zammit called it the Mother-of-God Madonna Jukebox, and, insofar as the Madonna was a woman, he thought it appropriate that the only voices heard from this jukebox should be the voices of women—Kitty Kallen, Dinah Shore, Kate Smith, the Andrews Sisters, Helen O'Connell, Judy Garland, Peggy Lee . . . It had been his desire to include only virgins in the jukebox, in honor of Mary, who was both mother and virgin, but it was, alas, an imperfect world, and a good song, sung by anyone, regardless of the condition of the maidenhead, was, as he put it, nothing to sneeze at.

The box was an achievement, though Melita couldn't help but feel that this time Zammit had gone too far, beyond all reason and plausibility. In a single stroke, he had abandoned whatever sense of order, harmony, or symmetry that may have been present in his earlier work. Even in his surreal phase there had been a lingering hint of classical balance, but Zammit had invented, now, a post-futurist nostalgic anti-world that harkened back to the baroque yet at the same time denied it, a bold and fearless neo-baroque that out-baroqued the baroque in its dreamy lopsidedness. It drew from too many sources, was a thing too grand. It was greedy, gluttonous in its desire to be all things, a compendium of time remembered and forgotten. Looking at the jukebox, seeing how lusciously lopsided it was, top-heavy, full of slanting angles and off-centered curves, Melita knew that Zammit's frustration over Miss Sicily had been simply too much for him, he was losing his mind.

Zammit stood by the jukebox, smiling, like a proud father. Or an enraptured groom, showing off his bride. "Yes?" he asked, wanting approval.

"Yes," Melita said, nodding.

"Is it the best?"

"The very best," she said, and meant it, because despite the reservations that she had, she saw—knew—that this jukebox was the finest he'd ever made, a work of art like no other. Top-heavy, yes. Lopsided, yes. Yet paradoxically light, floating, rising up off the floor. In its oddness, it almost seemed to dance. "Without question," she said, "the best. The most magnificent."

"It's better than a Duesenberg," Rocco said.

"What's a Duesenberg?" Zammit asked.

"It's just some stupid old car," Melita said.

They went downstairs, and for a while they sat around and had more anisette. They talked about Tony Zebra, who had been promoted to wing commander of Takali, and Nardu Camilleri, who seemed to have made up his mind to live forever.

Zammit took to puttering on the jukebox in the dining room, a lavish piece that was to have live goldfish swimming around in it, but there were some technical details yet to be worked out. While Zammit tinkered, drilling holes and turning screws, Rocco and Melita stepped outside, behind the house, where the tomatoes and the squash grew during the summer, and where Zammit had dumped the jukeboxes that were his failures. His failures outnumbered his successes. In the chalky light cast by the moon, the rejected jukeboxes resembled old weatherworn megaliths, relics of an ancient time, waiting to be discovered. They were boxes for which he'd had high hopes, but things had gone wrong. Boxes in which he sought a technical or aesthetic breakthrough of one sort or another, but something was lacking, or something simply didn't work, and the result was the jukebox graveyard behind the house.

Rocco lit a cigarette and passed it to Melita, then lit one for himself. He pulled the smoke deep to the bottom of his lungs, then let it go, a steady stream through his nostrils, and for a while they just stood there, in the garden, under a hazy moon, the smoke from their cigarettes hanging all around them, between them.

"It's already November," Melita said. "You came in April, and now it's November."

"I'll come back," he said.

"Yes, yes," she said lightly, in a tone mildly flavored with skepticism. "Like Douglas MacArthur, right? 'I shall return.'"

"Don't make a joke," he said. "I really will come back."

"No you won't. You will forget all about me."

"I'll come back," he repeated.

"Why should there be a happy ending? Is that what you believe? There are happy endings?"

"You don't like happy endings?"

"I like them, yes, but in life, tell me, where are they?"

He understood, then, when she said that, that lurking inside her, deep in her feelings, was a latent fatalism. It was the fatalism of the Maltese, which ran even deeper than their religion. And why not, after so many centuries of domination—from the Phoenicians, Carthaginians, Romans, all the way to the Arabs, the Knights, and now the British. A quiet hopelessness had settled in. Rocco had sensed this about them, talking with them. In Melita too there was this feeling of abandonment, hidden under her smile, under her tenderness. All along, while they had been making love, living together, she had been preparing, every day, for the worst, knowing that sometime, sooner or later, he would go, one way or another. And now it was happening.

They heard music from the house. Zammit had punched a button on one of the jukeboxes. It was Tommy Dorsey, "I'll Never Smile Again," with the skinny kid, Sinatra, singing, and Rocco wished he hadn't chosen that one.

Afterward, the new Benny Goodman came on, "Jersey Bounce," and that was better. Melita threw her cigarette away, but Rocco held his between his lips, and they danced. A fast, lively jitterbug, bending and twisting.

"Again," Rocco called to Zammit, when the record ran down. "Play it again."

Zammit played it again and again, and that's how they spent the night, jitterbugging, hurling their bodies around, feeling the bounce, the syncopation.

In the brisk, chilly night air, their warm breath made long sleeves of white vapor, but they were hot, warm, sweating.

Then Zammit did a strange thing. He played all of the jukeboxes at once. First Glenn Miller came on—then, on top of that, Woody Herman, and someone else, then the voice of Martha Tilton, and more, and more. He went from room to room, turning the jukeboxes on, all seven of them going simultaneously, a weird jumble, and yet, strangely, it was more than mere noise: it was, in a way, a great rainbow of sound, if sound could be thought of as a form of color, a wandering stream of refracted light.

"He lost his heart to Miss Sicily," Melita said. "He will never be the same."

"Not his heart. He lost his soul."

"Yes, everything."

It was good that Angelina Labbra was back in Sicily, gone. Otherwise Zammit would still be waiting outside her window at the Imperial Hotel, with another bouquet of wildflowers, hoping to catch a glimpse of her.

As the music played—all seven songs together—Rocco and Melita just stood there in the garden, smoking, not dancing, but it was as if they were dancing, because that whole long moment, as they listened, under the moon, it seemed that they were drifting, in slow motion.

Then, with bittersweet finality, one by one the records came to an end. For a few lingering moments, Glenn Miller played on, "That Old Black Magic," and then that too was gone, and it was just the silence of the night, the hazy moon, the bright orange tips of the cigarettes.

"Where will they send you?"

"After Morocco? Sicily, I guess, when they invade, then up through Italy."

"Take care," she said. "Will you take care?"

"I'm only a radioman."

"But you do crazy things."

"Do I?"

"You should pray more. You should have faith. I wish you had more faith."

"That sounds like something Fingerly used to say. But I think he meant it as a joke."

"Wait," she said, slipping off her shoes, "I want you to take them."

"Your shoes?"

"I wore these when we met. Don't you remember? You were so passionate."

The shoes were blue pumps with holes in the soles. She had slipped pieces of linoleum inside to protect her feet.

"Blue shoes," he said.

She had blue shoes, red shoes, and white shoes, and they all had holes. New shoes were still impossible, everybody was wondering if a supply had come in on the latest convoy.

Rocco had his cigarette in his left hand. He was going to put it to his lips and inhale again, but didn't, just stood there, looking at Melita, at the shoes she held in her hand. He stood quietly, veiled in cigarette smoke, trying to imprint the moment on his memory, because this moment, more than any of the others, was the one he wanted never to forget.

EPILOGUE: 1945

When Rocco was in North Africa, back with his unit, only one of Melita's letters reached him. And later, when he was in Sicily, and then on the Italian mainland, there was nothing at all. He wrote often, but suspected that his letters, like hers, had little chance of finding their way.

As the war dragged on, he was for the most part behind the lines, at one headquarters or another, working a radio, away from the worst of the fighting, though there were times when shells fell all around him. Once, a fuel truck blew up close by and his legs were burned, and a few weeks later, during a mortar attack, he took some shrapnel in his shoulder.

In Agrigento and Randazzo, and then at Salerno, and in the Liri Valley, he thought of Melita constantly, cursing himself for having been so dutiful about leaving Malta and reconnecting with his unit. In Rome, when they finally got there, he negotiated a three-day pass and tried to make it down to Malta, but could only manage as far as Naples. Many times he tried to phone, but in the general mess of things, the phone, any phone, was little more than wishful thinking. The war had made a hash of everything.

He carried three pictures of her. In one, she sat on a rock by the sea, in a long skirt, and in another she stood in front of a trellis of roses. Neither photo offered any clue that an air war had been raging at the time and thousands of homes were being bombed to pieces. In the third picture, she was with Rocco and he had his arm around her. There was a playful irony on her lips, and a hint of loneliness in her gaze. This one, and the one by the trellis, had both been taken at Aida's wedding.

He was in Rome for two months, then he was pulled out of his division and sent up into the Netherlands, to Amsterdam, and then, toward the end, he was in Rotterdam, far from the front, processing radio transmissions for a lieutenant general who had lost one eye in the Battle of the Bulge.

He was thinking he'd get back into used cars after the war, and make a living that way, until something better came along. He liked cars, he was comfortable when he was near them. He thought he might go back, too, for more college work, take some courses, he could finish the degree at night while he worked the cars by day. All sorts of things seemed possible.

When the Germans surrendered in May, he tried again to travel down to Malta, but the army kept him on a short leash in the Netherlands. Then, in August, on only a few hours' notice, they shipped him home.

Home was the Y on Eastern Parkway, where he'd been living for a while before he joined up. They'd held his mail for him while he was away, and in the great pile of stuff that was waiting for him, there was a letter from Zammit. It had followed him through half of Europe, from base camp to base camp, always missing him, and then, somehow, it made its way to Brooklyn, getting there before he did. When he read it, he was so overcome he had to put it down and walk away, needing to distance himself from it physically. What the letter said, in the first lines, with numbing directness, was that Melita was dead. She'd been killed by a bomb.

Zammit, distraught, had written on the day of the funeral, in a barely legible script, and when Rocco returned to the letter, he still couldn't believe what it said, couldn't absorb it. Melita dead? It was incomprehensible. As if he'd opened a door onto a room where there was no floor, just a hole, darkness, an emptiness he wasn't ready for.

And the other thing in the letter, toward the end, in the final lines, almost hidden there, was something which, in his grief, he had only barely noted. What Zammit mentioned, toward the end, in his crabbed script, was that there was a child—a boy, born about seven months after Rocco had left. Zammit was raising him. It was, he wrote, the least he could do, given the circumstances. All over Malta, he wrote, there were orphans.

Rocco reread the letter many times, and it sent a coldness through him, which he couldn't shake off. It was August and warm, but even when he stood in the sun, he was comfortless, carrying the cold inside him. Then, one day, he was not merely cold but shivering, feverish, and he was sick for a week, in bed, turning and tossing, with vivid, wide-awake dreams in which he saw Melita, close, nearby. But when he reached to touch her, she was never there. He spoke aloud, hallucinating, talking to the walls.

When the fever was gone, his mind cleared, and what came into focus for him, more sharply than before, was that he had a son. His grief for Melita had pushed that into the background, but now it surfaced, tugging at his thoughts. A boy, already two years old. He was a link, a connection, and as Rocco regained his strength, recovering after the fever, he understood that one way or another, and soon, he had to go back to Malta. The boy was there, drawing him. And it wasn't just the boy, it was Melita, because he still couldn't accept that she was dead. He had to see Zammit and hear him tell it, had to confirm with his own senses that she really was gone, because still there was the incomprehension, the disbelief. *Why,* and *why? And how could it be?*

He talked to the owner of the used-car lot, who had been good to him before, taking him on when he was just out of high school, and now he was good to him again, especially now, because Rocco had been in the war and had come back with a Purple Heart. He advanced Rocco some money, and with that, along with what he'd saved from his combat pay, Rocco set out for Malta. He bought a berth aboard a freighter that took him to Gibraltar, and then, with luck, he met up with an RAF captain who shoehorned him onto a Lodestar bound for Luqa. Sooner than he expected, he was on Malta, seeing it again after three years.

It was much changed. There was rebuilding to be done, but the streets were clear and the wreckage mostly gone. Some of the bars he'd frequented were still in business, but many were no longer around. Hock's was gone, and Hock himself, Rocco learned, had left for America and was running a bar and grill in Philadelphia. The Big Peter had been replaced by a shoe store, and the Pink Garter was now a flower shop. But the streets were the same, Kingsway and South and Old Bakery and Merchants, all of them drawing him, pulling him back to the days and nights when he strolled there with Melita.

At Zammit's, everything was different. Zammit was no longer making jukeboxes. There wasn't a jukebox in the house, and the failed jukeboxes that had stood in the garden behind the house had been carted off to a dump. With the war over, the big companies were gearing up again, producing glimmering hyperglow dreamboxes molded from phenol resins and complicated thermoplastics, and all Zammit knew was wood and stained glass. He had no regrets, no regrets at all. He understood that his time had come and gone, and he made his living now doing again what he knew best: making repairs, working on radios and phonographs, on anything that needed fixing, sewing machines, the big fans in the movie houses.

Jukeboxes were better, Rocco thought. He liked it better when Zammit was working on the jukeboxes.

Zammit had aged. He was gray, and some of his front teeth were missing. He was still in his forties, yet he seemed an old man, tired and worn out. Melita used to joke about his being old before his time, and now he was even older, and slower. He walked with a shuffle, and what he drank was Coca-Cola, a great deal of it. "My doctor told me not to touch whisky anymore," he said, "but I think it's a mistake. I felt better when I had a little anisette now and then."

They were in the parlor, once cluttered with tools and jukeboxes, but now, like the rest of the house, it was a model of neatness, none of the old mess and jumble. The boy was upstairs, sleeping. Rocco hadn't seen him yet. They sat on easy chairs that Zammit had made from car seats, from a Bugatti that had been wrecked in the bombing, and as they sat there, in the drowsy hum of early afternoon, Zammit told Rocco, as well as he could, about Melita.

It had happened on a Tuesday, in the afternoon, in the small garden by Zammit's house. She was hoeing weeds away from a patch of vegetables, rows of chicory and artichokes. The big bombing raids were over, but food was still scarce, and if you had a patch of land you grew what you could. Even up on the flat roofs of the houses you grew things, in clay pots and wooden boxes. Nevertheless, the worst was over. There were no more Stukas and Ju-88s, no more Messerschmitt 109s strafing the towns and the aerodromes.

But on that Tuesday afternoon, while Melita was hoeing the garden, a single plane appeared over the island, coming in low under the radar, black against the bright purple sky. Everyone who saw it agreed it had to be a Stuka, because of the angled, seagull shape of the wings. The droning of its engine cut through the balmy afternoon like a buzz saw.

It was, obviously, a plane that didn't belong where it was. The war had moved north, into Italy, into France and Belgium, and on into Germany. But this one plane, that afternoon, came low off the horizon, moving south, and as it crossed the island it dropped one bomb, for no reason that anyone could understand. It may simply have been a gesture, an expression of despair, because it was only a matter of time, now, before Berlin would be overrun. The shore batteries, caught by surprise, never opened fire. The men at the guns watched in a kind of astonishment as it passed over and then disappeared in the far haze over the Mediterranean.

The bomb fell not in the garden where Melita was working but in a neighboring plot, yet the blast was so strong she was hurled from the garden all the way out to the other side of the road. When they picked her up, nobody wanted to look at her. Her face was gone.

"It happened," Zammit said fatalistically.

Rocco sat motionless.

"Such craziness. Even God must be confused."

"And the boy?" Rocco asked.

"He looks like his mother. June, he was born in June, after you left. You left in November."

"Why didn't she tell me? Why didn't she say anything before I went?"

Zammit moved in his chair, uncomfortably. "She did what she thought best. It was the war, you remember how it was. I think, before you left, she didn't know for certain she was pregnant."

"She was sick a few times," Rocco remembered. "She was tired, she seemed upset."

"Come, he's upstairs. He's taking a nap."

Rocco followed him up, to a room once filled with wood for the jukeboxes, but now there was only a bed, a bureau, a rug, and light coming through a small window. And on the floor, a black-haired boy playing with a toy car.

"I thought you were asleep," Zammit said to him.

The boy was drowsy-eyed. Looking at him, Rocco never doubted he was his son. There was a pulse, an invisible instinct. He had made love to Melita so many times, all over Malta, in towns whose names he couldn't even remember, and at times they'd been careless, unthinking, not bothering about protection. So yes, of course. Why not? This boy, this stranger, this dark-haired Maltese half-breed, playing with his toy car, a maroon Rolls-Royce, rolling it back and forth on the rug: his son, his very own, deposited there like a rock, changing everything.

Rocco got down on the floor and touched the boy's face, ran his fingers through his hair. The boy did not shy away. His eyes were Melita's, darkly blue and quietly lonesome.

"Does he talk?"

"Not yet."

"No words?"

"Boys, some boys, are like that. The doctor said he'll be a late talker."

He could walk, he slept in a bed, he drank from a cup. But he didn't talk and he was still in diapers.

Rocco put his finger in the boy's hand, and the boy held onto it, a firm grip.

Then he let go, and Rocco felt, suddenly, a strange detachment, a need to move off and get away. It was all somehow too much for him. The room, the boy, and Zammit, even Zammit—it was too much to take in, and he needed to get away.

"I'll be back," he said, and as he moved out of the room and down the stairs, he was conscious of a barely restrained sense of panic, as if he were out on the road and suddenly aware he was lost, with no map, no direction, no signs anywhere to tell him where he was or where he was heading.

He caught a bus to Valletta, and when he got there he walked, up and down the streets. On Zachary, Kingsway, Old Theatre, crossing back and forth, wearing himself out. He was on West and Old Mint and St. Lucy's, thinking of Melita, expecting, crazily, at any turn, to see her. He was on Kingsway again, then on Strait and Christopher—and then, amazingly, there she was, walking ahead of him, the long skirt down to her ankles, black hair clasped at the back of her head by a barrette. His heart raced. She went around a corner, onto Merchants, and he ran to catch up, but when he reached the corner she was gone. He searched frantically, from shop to shop, and then, in a camera store, found her. She was at the counter, buying a roll of film. But when she turned, it was wrong, all wrong, the wrong face, wrong eyes, a stranger, and what had he been thinking anyway? He sensed, vaguely, in an uncaring way, that he was losing his grip.

He crossed over to Windmill, where he had lived with her all those months in the bombed-out house with the big hole in the roof. The house had been rebuilt, and the downstairs floor had been made over into a shop. It was a lace shop, and he saw someone moving about inside, a woman. He thought he might go in and see how the place was changed. He could tell the woman who he was, could tell her he'd lived there with Melita when there was a hole in the roof and they had listened to the radio, the propaganda from Rome, and they had played cards while the bombs fell on the Cottonera. But would the woman care? Would it have any importance for her that Melita had stood before a broken mirror, in that house, brushing her hair and fixing her lipstick?

He lingered, looking through the window, watching as the woman adjusted things on the shelves. Then he moved on, walking again with a quick stride. He was on Bounty, and Bull, and Fountain, down by St. Elmo's, then across on Old Hospital, and ended in the Lower Barracca Gardens, looking out at the water. It was a dreary sky, overcast, a vast stretch of cloud like gray laundry, and as he stood there gazing, what he felt was that somehow she was out there, on the water, dead, yes, but somehow still alive. Because how could she be dead? *How?*

He looked and looked, and saw a flash of light, something burning, as if someone were standing out there on the water, wrapped in flames, and he remembered the first time he'd seen her, that day on Old Bakery, she was walking along, during the air raid, and he followed, and she seemed, for a moment, to burst into flame. It was the strangeness of Malta, the obliqueness, slanting light, things weird and impossible. And now again, out on the water, not far from where he stood, there it was, a cone of flame.

But he saw, then, it was only the sun, a flare of light reflecting off the water as the sun, struggling, broke briefly through the clouds, and he knew again there was no magic here, nothing mysterious or out of the ordinary. The sky was the sky, and the water merely water. Melita was dead. And what bothered him, what wouldn't go away, was that if he hadn't left the island when he did, she might still be alive.

It was simple mathematics: if he hadn't left and rejoined his unit, he would have been with her, and if he had been with her that Tuesday when the plane flew over, she wouldn't have been there in the garden, hoeing weeds. She would have been somewhere else—at a movie, or on a beach, or maybe, God knows, on the other island, over on Gozo. She would still be alive, at this moment. But that wasn't how it went, the numbers were wrong. And what he felt now was guilt, because what he sensed, vaguely, was that there must have been in him a desire to go, a desire to be away from her for a time, only too glad to have the war as an excuse. Was that it? Was that what happened? Without consciously thinking it, he'd wanted to be away from her? And was, therefore, in the strange mix of things, responsible for her death? Could it be?

He thought he might go back to the house on Windmill Street and go inside, talk to the woman there and tell her what it had been like, living there. But instead he caught a bus and went out to Santa Venera, back to Zammit's, and told him he would take the boy home with him.

Zammit said nothing, merely looked at him, doubtfully, as if wondering if he knew what he was doing.

"He's mine," Rocco said, "isn't he?"

Zammit nodded wearily.

"I'll take him back with me. We'll be all right, we'll manage."

"It's not your fault," Zammit said, reading Rocco's mind. "Even if you had stayed, something would have happened."

"Maybe not," Rocco said.

Zammit shrugged. "God lets these things happen, we don't know why. God wanted her. That's how it is."

"God is to blame?"

"No," Zammit said. "No one is to blame."

The boy was in the living room, on the couch, napping. When Rocco went in, he woke, opening his eyes dreamily. He had the car with him, the maroon Rolls-Royce, had fallen asleep holding it. Rocco knew it was not going to be easy, taking care of him and teaching him things. It would come, he supposed, he would somehow figure it out.

He sat on the edge of the couch and picked up the car. It was metal and well made, with precise detail. The bumpers, the hood ornament, the door handles, the fenders. He took the boy's fingers and touched them to the parts of the car. "Headlight," he said. "Bumper. Tire. Running board." The boy liked it, touching the car, the separate parts. It was all in the details, that was the whole thing. The details, and the words. Rocco thought if the boy could grow to understand that, that the words mattered, then he would be all right. Because without the words, how would there be anything to remember?

Zammit hovered nearby. "Anisette," he said wistfully. "Let me go look, maybe I have a bottle in the cellar."

Rocco looked at the boy, and again he saw Melita. She was there inside him, in the eyes, the face.

He grabbed hold of him and lifted him, high up, heavier than he'd expected. The boy liked it up there, near the ceiling, it brought a smile. Rocco lowered him, then hoisted him up again, and Rocco too was smiling, feeling a feathery strangeness in the thought that the boy was his son.

"You like that, do you? Way up there? You like it? Yes? Yes?"